EX LIBRIS

VINTAGE CLASSICS

WHAT MAISIE KNEW

Henry James was born on 15 April 1843 in New York to a wealthy and intellectual family and as a youth travelled widely and studied in Europe. He briefly studied law at Harvard before he took up writing full-time. His first novel, *Watch and Ward*, was published in 1871 and many followed including *Roderick Hudson* (1875), *Washington Square* (1880), *The Portrait of a Lady* (1881), *The Awkward Age* (1899), *The Wings of the Dove* (1902), *The Ambassadors* (1903) and *The Golden Bowl* (1904). He also wrote short stories, reviews, biographies, plays and travel books. After a brief period in Paris, James moved to London. He later settled in Rye in Sussex and became a British citizen in 1915. Henry James died on 28 February 1916.

OTHER NOVELS BY HENRY JAMES

Watch and Ward
Roderick Hudson
The American
The Europeans
Confidence
Washington Square
The Portrait of a Lady
The Bostonians
The Princess Casamassima
The Reverberator
The Tragic Muse
The Other House
The Spoils of Poynton
The Awkward Age
The Sacred Fount
The Wings of the Dove
The Ambassadors
The Golden Bowl
The Outcry
The Ivory Tower
The Sense of the Past

HENRY JAMES

What Maisie Knew

AND

The Pupil

VINTAGE BOOKS
London

Published by Vintage 2007

2 4 6 8 10 9 7 5 3

What Maisie Knew was first published in 1897
This revised edition was first published in 1907–9
'The Pupil' was first published in 1891
This revised edition was first published in 1907–9

Vintage
Random House, 20 Vauxhall Bridge Road,
London SW1V 2SA

www.vintage-classics.info

Addresses for companies within The Random House Group Limited
can be found at: www.randomhouse.co.uk/offices.htm

The Random House Group Limited Reg. No. 954009

A CIP catalogue record for this book
is available from the British Library

ISBN 9780099511946
Twin Edition ISBN 9780099503774

The Random House Group Limited makes every effort to ensure that
the papers used in its books are made from trees that have been
legally sourced from well-managed and credibly certified forests. Our
paper procurement policy can be found at:
www.randomhouse.co.uk/paper.htm

Mixed Sources
Product group from well-managed
forests and other controlled sources
www.fsc.org Cert no. TT-COC-2139
© 1996 Forest Stewardship Council
FSC

Typeset by SX Composing DTP, Rayleigh, Essex
Printed in the UK by CPI Bookmarque, Croydon, CR0 4TD

Contents

PREFACE

I RECOGNISE again, for the first of these three Tales⋆, another instance of the growth of the 'great oak' from the little acorn; since 'What Maisie Knew' is at least a tree that spreads beyond any provision its small germ might on a first handling have appeared likely to make for it. The accidental mention had been made to me of the manner in which the situation of some luckless child of a divorced couple was affected, under my informant's eyes, by the re-marriage of one of its parents – I forget which; so that, thanks to the limited desire for its company expressed by the step-parent, the law of its little life, its being entertained in rotation by its father and its mother, wouldn't easily prevail. Whereas each of these persons had at first vindictively desired to keep it from the other, so at present the re-married relative sought now rather to be rid of it – that is to leave it as much as possible, and beyond the appointed times and seasons, on the hands of the adversary; which malpractice, resented by the latter as bad faith, would of course be repaid and avenged by an equal treachery. The wretched infant was thus to find itself practically disowned, rebounding from racquet to racquet like a tennisball or a shuttlecock. This figure could but touch the fancy to the quick and strike one as the beginning of a story – a story commanding a great choice of developments. I recollect, however, promptly thinking that for a proper symmetry the second parent should marry too – which in the case named to

⋆This preface is taken from a piece that Henry James wrote to introduce an edition of *What Maisie Knew* which included both 'The Pupil' and another story called 'In the Cage'.

me indeed would probably soon occur, and was in any case what the ideal of the situation required. The second step-parent would have but to be correspondingly incommoded by obligations to the offspring of a hated predecessor for the misfortune of the little victim to become altogether exemplary. The business would accordingly be sad enough, yet I am not sure its possibility of interest would so much have appealed to me had I not soon felt that the ugly facts, so stated or conceived, by no means constituted the whole appeal.

The light of an imagination touched by them couldn't help therefore projecting a further ray, thanks to which it became rather quaintly clear that, not less than the chance of misery and of a degraded state, the chance of happiness and of an improved state might be here involved for the child, round about whom the complexity of life would thus turn to fineness, to richness – and indeed would have but so to turn for the small creature to be steeped in security and ease. Sketchily clustered even, these elements gave out that vague pictorial glow which forms the first appeal of a living 'subject' to the painter's consciousness; but the glimmer became intense as I proceeded to a further analysis. The further analysis is for that matter almost always the torch of rapture and victory, as the artist's firm hand grasps and plays it – I mean, naturally, of the smothered rapture and the obscure victory, enjoyed and celebrated not in the street but before some innermost shrine; the odds being a hundred to one, in almost any connection, that it doesn't arrive by any easy first process at the *best* residuum of truth. That was the charm, sensibly, of the picture thus at first confusedly showing; the elements so couldn't but flush, to their very surface, with some deeper depth of irony than the mere obvious. It lurked in the crude postulate like a buried scent; the more the attention hovered the more aware it became of the fragrance. To which I may add that the more I scratched the surface and penetrated, the more potent, to the intellectual nostril, became this virtue. At last, accordingly, the residuum, as I have called it, reached, I was in presence of the red dramatic spark that glowed at the core of my vision and that, as I gently blew upon it, burned higher and clearer. This precious particle was the *full* ironic truth – the most interesting item to be read into the child's situation. For satisfaction of the mind, in other words, the small expanding consciousness would have to be saved, have to become presentable as a register of impressions; and saved by the experience of certain advantages, by some enjoyed profit and some achieved confidence, rather than coarsened, blurred, sterilised, by ignorance and pain. This better state, in the young life, would reside in the exercise of a function other than that of disconcerting the selfishness of its parents – which was all that had on the face of the matter seemed reserved to it in the way of criticism applied to their rupture. The early relation would be exchanged for a later; instead of simply submitting to the inherited tie and the imposed complication, of suffering from them, our little wonder-working agent would create, without design, quite fresh elements of this order – contribute, that is, to the formation of a fresh tie, from which it would then (and for all the world as if through a small demonic foresight) proceed to derive great profit.

This is but to say that the light in which the vision so readily grew to a wholeness was that of a second marriage on both sides; the father having, in the freedom of divorce, but to take another wife, as well as the mother, under a like licence, another husband, for the case to begin, at least, to stand beautifully on its feet. There would be thus a perfect logic for what might come – come even with the mere attribution of a certain sensibility (if but a mere relative fineness) to either of the new parties. Say the prime cause making for the ultimate attempt to shirk on one side or the other, and better still if on both, a due share of the decreed burden should have been, after all, in each progenitor, a constitutional inaptitude for *any* burden, and a base intolerance of it: we should thus get a motive not requiring, but happily dispensing with, too particular a perversity in the step-parents. The child seen as creating by the fact of its forlornness a relation between its step-parents, the more intimate the better, dramatically speaking; the child, by the mere appeal of neglectedness and the mere consciousness of relief, weaving about, with the best faith in the world, the close web of sophistication; the child becoming a centre and pretext for a fresh system of misbehaviour, a system moreover of a nature to spread and ramify: *there* would be the 'full' irony, there the promising theme into which the hint I had originally picked up would logically flower. No themes are so human as those that reflect for us, out of the confusion of life, the close connection of bliss and bale, of the things that help with the things that hurt, so dangling before us for ever that bright hard medal, of so strange an alloy, one face of which is somebody's right and ease and the other somebody's pain and wrong. To live with all intensity and perplexity and felicity in its terribly mixed little world would thus be the part of my interesting small mortal; bringing people together who would be at least more correctly separate; keeping people separate who would be at least more correctly together; flourishing, to a degree, at the cost of many conventions and proprieties, even decencies; really keeping the torch of virtue alive in an air tending infinitely to smother it; really in short making confusion worse confounded by drawing some stray fragrance of an ideal across the scent of selfishness, by sowing on barren strands, through the mere fact of presence, the seed of the moral life.

All this would be to say, I at once recognised, that my light vessel of consciousness, swaying in such a draught, couldn't be with verisimilitude a rude little boy; since, beyond the fact that little boys are never so 'present', the sensibility of the female young is indubitably, for early youth, the greater, and my plan would call, on the part of my protagonist, for 'no end' of sensibility. I might impute that amount of it without extravagance to a slip of a girl whose faculties should have been well shaken up; but I should have so to depend on its action to keep my story clear that I must be able to show it in all assurance as naturally intense. To this end I should have of course to suppose for my heroine dispositions originally promising, but above all I should have to invest her with perceptions easily and almost infinitely quickened. So handsomely fitted out, yet not in a manner too grossly to affront probability, she might well see me through the whole course of my design; which design, more and more attractive as I turned it over, and dignified by the most delightful difficulty, would be to make and to keep her so limited consciousness the very field of my picture while at the same time guarding with care the integrity of the objects represented. With the charm of this possibility, therefore, the project for 'Maisie' rounded itself and loomed large – any subject looming large, for that matter, I am bound to add, from the moment one is ridden by the law of entire expression. I have already elsewhere noted, I think, that the memory of my own work preserves for me no theme that, at some moment or other of its development, and always only waiting for the right connection or chance, hasn't signally refused to remain humble, even (or perhaps all the more resentfully) when fondly selected for its conscious and hopeless humility. Once 'out', like a house-dog of a temper above confinement, it defies the mere whistle, it roams, it hunts, it seeks out and 'sees' life; it can be brought back but by hand and then only to take its futile thrashing. It wasn't at any rate for an idea seen in the light I here glance at not to have due warrant of its value – how could the value of a scheme so finely workable *not* be great? The one presented register of the whole complexity would be the play of the child's confused and obscure notation of it, and yet the whole, as I say, should be unmistakeably, should be honourably there, seen through the faint intelligence, or at the least attested by the imponderable presence, and still advertising its sense.

I recall that my first view of this neat possibility was as the attaching problem of the picture restricted (while yet achieving, as I say, completeness and coherency) to what the child might be conceived to have *understood* – to have been able to interpret and appreciate. Further reflection and experiment showed me my subject strangled in that extreme of rigour. The infant mind would at the best leave great gaps and voids; so that with a systematic surface possibly beyond reproach we should nevertheless fail of clearness of sense. I should have to stretch the matter to what my wondering witness materially and inevitably *saw*; a great deal of which quantity she either wouldn't understand at all or would quite misunderstand – and on those lines, only on those, my task would be prettily cut out. To that then I settled – to the question of giving it *all*, the whole situation surrounding her, but of giving it only through the occasions and connections of her proximity and her attention; only as it might pass before her and appeal to her, as it might touch her and affect her, for better or worse, for perceptive gain or perceptive loss: so that we fellow witnesses, we not more invited but only more expert critics, should feel in strong possession of it. This would be, to begin with, a plan of absolutely definite and measurable application – that in itself always a mark of beauty; and I have been interested to find on re-perusal of the work that some such controlling grace successfully rules it. Nothing could be more 'done', I think, in the light of its happiest intention; and this in spite of an appearance that at moments obscures my consistency. Small children have many more perceptions than they have terms to translate them; their vision is at any moment much richer, their apprehension even constantly stronger, than their prompt, their at all producible, vocabulary. Amusing therefore as it might at the first blush have seemed to restrict myself in this case to the terms as well as to the experience, it became at once plain that such an attempt would fail. Maisie's terms accordingly play their part – since her simpler conclusions quite depend on them; but our own commentary constantly attends and amplifies. This it is that on occasion, doubtless, seems to represent us as going so 'behind' the facts of her spectacle as to exaggerate the activity of her relation to them. The difference here is but of a shade: it is her relation, her activity of spirit, that determines all our own concern – we simply take advantage of these things better than she herself. Only, even though it is her interest that mainly makes matters interesting for us, we inevitably note this in figures that are not yet at her command and that are nevertheless required whenever those aspects about her and those parts of her experience that she understands darken off into others that she rather tormentedly misses. All of which gave me a high firm logic to observe; supplied the force for which the straightener of almost any tangle is grateful while he labours, the sense of pulling at threads intrinsically worth it – strong enough and fine enough and entire enough.

Of course, beyond this, was another and well-nigh equal charm – equal in spite of its being almost independent of the acute constructional, the endless expressional question. This was the quite different question of the particular kind of truth of resistance I might be able to impute to my central figure – *some* intensity, some continuity of resistance being naturally of the essence of the subject. Successfully to resist (to resist, that is, the strain of observation and the assault of experience) what would that be, on the part of so young a person, but to remain fresh, and still fresh, and to have even a freshness to communicate? – the case being with Maisie to the end that she treats her friends to the rich little spectacle of objects embalmed in her wonder. She wonders, in other words, to the end, to the death – the death of her childhood, properly speaking; after which (with the inevitable shift, sooner or later, of her point of view) her situation will change and become another affair, subject to other measurements and with a new centre altogether. The particular reaction that will have led her to that point, and that it has been of an exquisite interest to study in her, will have spent itself; there will be another scale, another perspective, another horizon. Our business meanwhile therefore is to extract from her current reaction whatever it may be worth; and for that matter we recognise in it the highest exhibitional virtue. Truly, I reflect, if the theme had had no other beauty it would still have had this rare and distinguished one of its so expressing the variety of the child's values. She is not only the extraordinary 'ironic centre' I have already noted; she has the wonderful importance of shedding a light far beyond any reach of her comprehension; of lending to poorer persons and things, by the mere fact of their being involved with her and by the special scale she creates for them, a precious element of dignity. I lose myself, truly, in appreciation of my theme on noting what she does by her 'freshness' for appearances in themselves vulgar and empty enough. They become, as she deals with them, the stuff of poetry and tragedy and art; she has simply to wonder, as I say, about them, and they begin to have meanings, aspects, solidities, connections – connections with the 'universal!' – that they could scarce have hoped for. Ida Farange alone, so to speak, or Beale alone, that is either of them otherwise connected – what intensity, what 'objectivity' (the most developed degree of *being* anyhow thinkable for them) would they have? How would they repay at all the favour of our attention?

Maisie makes them portentous all by the play of her good faith, makes her mother above all, to my vision – unless I have wholly failed to render it – concrete, immense and awful; so that we get, for our profit, and get by an economy of process interesting in itself, the thoroughly pictured creature, the striking figured symbol. At two points in particular, I seem to recognise, we enjoy at its maximum this effect of associational magic. The passage in which her father's terms of intercourse with the insinuating but so strange and unattractive lady whom he has had the detestable levity to whisk her off to see late at night, is a signal example of the all but incalculable way in which interest may be constituted. The facts involved are that Beale Farange is ignoble, that the friend to whom he introduces his daughter is deplorable, and that from the commerce of the two, *as* the two merely, we would fain avert our heads. Yet the thing has but to become a part of the child's bewilderment for these small sterilities to drop from it and for the *scene* to emerge and prevail – vivid, special, wrought hard, to the hardness of the unforgettable; the scene that is exactly what Beale and Ida and Mrs Cuddon, and even Sir Claude and Mrs Beale, would never for a moment have succeeded in making their scant unredeemed importances – namely *appreciable*. I find another instance in the episode of Maisie's unprepared encounter, while walking in the Park with Sir Claude, of her mother and that beguiled attendant of her mother, the encouraging, the appealing 'Captain', to whom this lady contrives to commit her for twenty minutes while she herself deals with the second husband. The human substance here would have seemed in advance well-nigh too poor for conversion, the three 'mature' figures of too short a radiation, too stupid (*so* stupid it was for Sir Claude to have married Ida!), too vain, too thin, for any clear application; but promptly, immediately, the child's own importance, spreading and contagiously acting, has determined the *total* value otherwise. Nothing of course, meanwhile, is an older story to the observer of manners and the painter of life than the grotesque finality with which such terms as 'painful', 'unpleasant' and 'disgusting' are often applied to his results; to that degree, in truth, that the free use of them as weightily conclusive again and again re-enforces his estimate of the critical sense of circles in which they artlessly flourish. Of course under that superstition I was punctually to have had read to me the lesson that the 'mixing-up' of a child with anything unpleasant confessed itself an aggravation of the unpleasantness, and that nothing could well be more disgusting than to attribute to Maisie so intimate an 'acquaintance' with the gross immoralities surrounding her.

The only thing to say of such lucidities is that, however one may have 'discounted' in advance, and as once for all, their general radiance, one is disappointed if the hour for them, in the particular connection, doesn't strike – they so keep before us elements with which even the most sedate philosopher must always reckon. The painter of life has indeed work cut out for him when a considerable part of life offers itself in the guise of that sapience. The effort really to see and really to represent is no idle business in face of the *constant* force that makes for muddlement. The great thing is indeed that the muddled state too is one of the very sharpest of the realities, that it also has colour and form and character, has often in fact a broad and rich comicality, many of the signs and values of the appreciable. Thus it was to be, for example, I might gather, that the very principle of Maisie's appeal, her undestroyed freshness, in other words that vivacity of intelligence by which she indeed does vibrate in the infected air, indeed does flourish in her immoral world, may pass for a barren and senseless thing, or at best a negligible one. For nobody to whom life at large is *easily* interesting do the finer, the shyer, the more anxious small vibrations, fine and shy and anxious with the passion that precedes knowledge, succeed in being negligible: which is doubtless one of many reasons why the passage between the child and the kindly, friendly, ugly gentleman who, seated with her in Kensington Gardens under a spreading tree, positively answers to her for her mother as no one has ever answered, and so stirs her, filially and morally, as she has never been stirred, throws into highest relief, to my sense at least, the side on which the subject is strong, and becomes the type-passage – other advantages certainly aiding, as I may say – for the expression of its beauty. The active, contributive close-circling wonder, as I have called it, in which the child's identity is guarded and preserved, and which makes her case remarkable exactly by the weight of the tax on it, provides distinction for her, provides vitality and variety, through the operation of the tax – which would have done comparatively little for us hadn't it been monstrous. A pity for us surely to have been deprived of this just reflection. 'Maisie' is of 1907.

WHAT MAISIE KNEW

THE litigation had seemed interminable and had in fact been complicated; but by the decision on the appeal the judgement of the divorce-court was confirmed as to the assignment of the child. The father, who, though bespattered from head to foot, had made good his case, was, in pursuance of this triumph, appointed to keep her: it was not so much that the mother's character had been more absolutely damaged as that the brilliancy of a lady's complexion (and this lady's, in court, was immensely remarked) might be more regarded as showing the spots. Attached, however, to the second pronouncement was a condition that detracted, for Beale Farange, from its sweetness – an order that he should refund to his late wife the twenty-six hundred pounds put down by her, as it was called, some three years before, in the interest of the child's maintenance and precisely on a proved understanding that he would take no proceedings: a sum of which he had had the administration and of which he could render not the least account. The obligation thus attributed to her adversary was no small balm to Ida's resentment; it drew a part of the sting from her defeat and compelled Mr Farange perceptibly to lower his crest. He was unable to produce the money or to raise it in any way; so that after a squabble scarcely less public and scarcely more decent than the original shock of battle his only issue from his predicament was a compromise proposed by his legal advisers and finally accepted by hers.

His debt was by this arrangement remitted to him and the little girl disposed of in a manner worthy of the judgement-seat of Solomon. She was divided in two and the portions tossed impartially to the disputants. They would take her, in rotation, for six months at a time; she would spend half the year with each. This was odd justice in the eyes of those who still blinked in the fierce light projected from the tribunal – a light in which neither parent figured in the least as a happy example to youth and innocence. What was to have been expected on the evidence was the nomination, *in loco parentis*, of some proper third person, some respectable or at least some presentable friend. Apparently, however, the circle of the Faranges had been scanned in vain for any such ornament; so that the only solution finally meeting all the difficulties was, save that of sending Maisie to a Home, the partition of the tutelary office in the manner I have mentioned. There were more reasons for her parents to agree to it than there had ever been for them to agree to anything; and they now prepared with her help to enjoy the distinction that waits upon vulgarity sufficiently attested. Their rupture had resounded, and after being perfectly insignificant together they would be decidedly striking apart. Had they not produced an impression that warranted people in looking for appeals in the newspapers for the rescue of the little one – reverberation, amid a vociferous public, of the idea that some movement should be started or some benevolent person should come forward? A good lady came indeed a step or two: she was distantly related to Mrs Farange, to whom she proposed that, having children and nurseries wound up and going, she should be allowed to take home the bone of contention and, by working it into her system, relieve at least one of the parents. This would make every time, for Maisie, after her inevitable six months with Beale, much more of a change.

'More of a change?' Ida cried. 'Won't it be enough of a change for her to come from that low brute to the person in the world who detests him most?'

'No, because you detest him so much that you'll always talk to her about him. You'll keep him before her by perpetually abusing him.'

Mrs Farange stared. 'Pray, then, am I to do nothing to counteract his villainous abuse of *me*?'

The good lady, for a moment, made no reply: her silence was a grim judgement of the whole point of view. 'Poor little monkey!' she at last exclaimed; and the words were an epitaph for the tomb of Maisie's childhood. She was abandoned to her fate. What was clear to any spectator was that the only link binding her to either parent was this lamentable fact of her being a ready vessel for bitterness, a deep little porcelain cup in which biting acids could be mixed. They had wanted her not for any good they could do her, but for the harm they could, with her unconscious aid, do each other. She should serve their anger and seal their revenge, for husband and wife had been alike crippled by the heavy hand of justice, which in the last resort met on neither side their indignant claim to get, as they called it, everything. If each was only to get half this seemed to concede that neither was so base as the other pretended, or, to put it differently, offered them both as bad indeed, since they were only as good as each other. The mother had wished to prevent the father from, as she said, 'so much as looking' at the child; the father's plea was that the mother's lightest touch was 'simply contamination'. These were the opposed principles in which Maisie was to be educated – she was to fit them together as she might. Nothing could have been more touching at first than her failure to suspect the ordeal that awaited her little unspotted soul. There were persons horrified to think what those in charge of it would combine to try to make of it: no one could conceive in advance that they would be able to make nothing ill.

This was a society in which for the most part people were occupied only with chatter, but the disunited couple had at last grounds for expecting a time of high activity. They girded their loins, they felt as if the quarrel had only begun. They felt indeed more married than ever, inasmuch as what marriage had mainly suggested to them was the unbroken opportunity to quarrel. There had been 'sides' before, and there were sides as much as ever; for the sider too the prospect opened out, taking the pleasant form of a superabundance of matter for desultory conversation. The many

friends of the Faranges drew together to differ about them; contradiction grew young again over teacups and cigars. Everybody
was always assuring everybody of something very shocking, and
nobody would have been jolly if nobody had been outrageous. The
pair appeared to have a social attraction which failed merely as
regards each other: it was indeed a great deal to be able to say for
Ida that no one but Beale desired her blood, and for Beale that if
he should ever have his eyes scratched out it would be only by his
wife. It was generally felt, to begin with, that they were awfully
good-looking – they had really not been analysed to a deeper
residuum. They made up together for instance some twelve feet
three of stature, and nothing was more discussed than the
apportionment of this quantity. The sole flaw in Ida's beauty was a
length and reach of arm conducive perhaps to her having so often
beaten her ex-husband at billiards, a game in which she showed a
superiority largely accountable, as she maintained, for the resentment finding expression in his physical violence. Billiards was her
great accomplishment and the distinction her name always first
produced the mention of. Notwithstanding some very long lines
everything about her that might have been large and that in many
women profited by the licence was, with a single exception,
admired and cited for its smallness. The exception was her eyes,
which might have been of mere regulation size, but which overstepped the modesty of nature; her mouth, on the other hand, was
barely perceptible, and odds were freely taken as to the measure-
ment of her waist. She was a person who, when she was out – and
she was always out – produced everywhere a sense of having been
seen often, the sense indeed of a kind of abuse of visibility, so that
it would have been, in the usual places, rather vulgar to wonder at
her. Strangers only did that; but they, to the amusement of the
familiar, did it very much: it was an inevitable way of betraying an
alien habit. Like her husband she carried clothes, carried them as a
train carries passengers: people had been known to compare their
taste and dispute about the accommodation they gave these articles,

though inclining on the whole to the commendation of Ida as less overcrowded, especially with jewellery and flowers. Beale Farange had natural decorations, a kind of costume in his vast fair beard, burnished like a gold breastplate, and in the eternal glitter of the teeth that his long moustache had been trained not to hide and that gave him, in every possible situation, the look of the joy of life. He had been destined in his youth for diplomacy and momentarily attached, without a salary, to a legation which enabled him often to say 'In *my* time in the East': but contemporary history had somehow had no use for him, had hurried past him and left him in perpetual Piccadilly. Every one knew what he had – only twenty-five hundred. Poor Ida, who had run through everything, had now nothing but her carriage and her paralysed uncle. This old brute, as he was called, was supposed to have a lot put away. The child was provided for, thanks to a crafty godmother, a defunct aunt of Beale's, who had left her something in such a manner that the parents could appropriate only the income.

I

THE child was provided for, but the new arrangement was inevitably confounding to a young intelligence intensely aware that something had happened which must matter a good deal and looking anxiously out for the effects of so great a cause. It was to be the fate of this patient little girl to see much more than she at first understood, but also even at first to understand much more than any little girl, however patient, had perhaps ever understood before. Only a drummer-boy in a ballad or a story could have been so in the thick of the fight. She was taken into the confidence of passions on which she fixed just the stare she might have had for images bounding across the wall in the slide of a magic-lantern. Her little world was phantasmagoric – strange shadows dancing on a sheet. It was as if the whole performance had been given for her – a mite of a half-scared infant in a great dim theatre. She was in short introduced to life with a liberality in which the selfishness of others found its account, and there was nothing to avert the sacrifice but the modesty of her youth.

Her first term was with her father, who spared her only in not letting her have the wild letters addressed to her by her mother: he confined himself to holding them up at her and shaking them, while he showed his teeth, and then amusing her by the way he chucked them, across the room, bang into the fire. Even at that moment, however, she had a scared anticipation of fatigue, a guilty sense of not rising to the occasion, feeling the charm of the violence with which the stiff unopened envelopes, whose big monograms – Ida bristled with monograms – she would have liked to see, were made to whizz, like dangerous missiles, through the air. The greatest effect of the great cause was her own greater importance, chiefly revealed to her in the larger freedom with which she was handled, pulled hither and thither and kissed, and the proportionately greater niceness she was obliged to show. Her features had somehow become prominent; they were so perpetually nipped by the gentlemen who came to see her father and the smoke of whose cigarettes went into her face. Some of these gentlemen made her strike matches and light their cigarettes; others, holding her on knees violently jolted, pinched the calves of her legs till she shrieked – her shriek was much admired – and reproached them with being toothpicks. The word stuck in her mind and contributed to her feeling from this time that she was deficient in something that would meet the general desire. She found out what it was: it was a congenital tendency to the production of a substance to which Moddle, her nurse, gave a short ugly name, a name painfully associated at dinner with the part of the joint that she didn't like. She had left behind her the time when she had no desires to meet, none at least save Moddle's, who, in Kensington Gardens, was always on the bench when she came back to see if she had been playing too far. Moddle's desire was merely that she shouldn't do that, and she met it so easily that the only spots in that long brightness were the moments of her wondering what would become of her if, on her rushing back, there should be no Moddle on the bench. They still went to the Gardens, but there was a difference even there; she was impelled perpetually to look at the legs of other children and ask her nurse if *they* were toothpicks. Moddle was terribly truthful; she always said: 'Oh my dear, you'll not find such another pair as your own.' It seemed to have to do with something else that Moddle often said: 'You feel the strain – that's where it is; and you'll feel it still worse, you know.'

Thus from the first Maisie not only felt it, but knew she felt it. A part of it was the consequence of her father's telling her he felt it too, and telling Moddle, in her presence, that she must make a

point of driving that home. She was familiar, at the age of six, with
the fact that everything had been changed on her account, everything ordered to enable him to give himself up to her. She was to
remember always the words in which Moddle impressed upon her
that he did so give himself: 'Your papa wishes you never to forget,
you know, that he has been dreadfully put about.' If the skin on
Moddle's face had to Maisie the air of being unduly, almost
painfully, stretched, it never presented that appearance so much as
when she uttered, as she often had occasion to utter, such words.
The child wondered if they didn't make it hurt more than usual;
but it was only after some time that she was able to attach to the
picture of her father's sufferings, and more particularly to her
nurse's manner about them, the meaning for which these things
had waited. By the time she had grown sharper, as the gentlemen
who had criticised her calves used to say, she found in her mind a
collection of images and echoes to which meanings were attachable
– images and echoes kept for her in the childish dusk, the dim
closet, the high drawers, like games she wasn't yet big enough to
play. The great strain meanwhile was that of carrying by the right
end the things her father said about her mother – things mostly
indeed that Moddle, on a glimpse of them, as if they had been
complicated toys or difficult books, took out of her hands and put
away in the closet. A wonderful assortment of objects of this kind
she was to discover there later, all tumbled up too with the things,
shuffled into the same receptacle, that her mother had said about
her father.

   She had the knowledge that on a certain occasion which every
day brought nearer her mother would be at the door to take her
away, and this would have darkened all the days if the ingenious
Moddle hadn't written on a paper in very big easy words ever so
many pleasures that she would enjoy at the other house. These
promises ranged from 'a mother's fond love' to 'a nice poached egg
to your tea', and took by the way the prospect of sitting up ever so
late to see the lady in question dressed, in silks and velvets and

diamonds and pearls, to go out: so that it was a real support to
Maisie, at the supreme hour, to feel how, by Moddle's direction,
the paper was thrust away in her pocket and there clenched in her
fist. The supreme hour was to furnish her with a vivid
reminiscence, that of a strange outbreak in the drawing-room on
the part of Moddle, who, in reply to something her father had just
said, cried aloud: 'You ought to be perfectly ashamed of yourself –
you ought to blush, sir, for the way you go on!' The carriage, with
her mother in it, was at the door; a gentleman who was there, who
was always there, laughed out very loud; her father, who had her
in his arms, said to Moddle: 'My dear woman, I'll settle *you*
presently!' – after which he repeated, showing his teeth more than
ever at Maisie while he hugged her, the words for which her nurse
had taken him up. Maisie was not at the moment so fully conscious
of them as of the wonder of Moddle's sudden disrespect and
crimson face; but she was able to produce them in the course of five
minutes when, in the carriage, her mother, all kisses, ribbons, eyes,
arms, strange sounds and sweet smells, said to her: 'And did your
beastly papa, my precious angel, send any message to your own
loving mamma?' Then it was that she found the words spoken by
her beastly papa to be, after all, in her little bewildered ears, from
which, at her mother's appeal, they passed, in her clear shrill voice,
straight to her little innocent lips. 'He said I was to tell you, from
him,' she faithfully reported, 'that you're a nasty horrid pig!'

II

IN that lively sense of the immediate which is the very air of a child's mind the past, on each occasion, became for her as indistinct as the future: she surrendered herself to the actual with a good faith that might have been touching to either parent. Crudely as they had calculated they were at first justified by the event: she was the little feathered shuttlecock they could fiercely keep flying between them. The evil they had the gift of thinking or pretending to think of each other they poured into her little gravely-gazing soul as into a boundless receptacle, and each of them had doubtless the best conscience in the world as to the duty of teaching her the stern truth that should be her safeguard against the other. She was at the age for which all stories are true and all conceptions are stories. The actual was the absolute, the present alone was vivid. The objurgation for instance launched in the carriage by her mother after she had at her father's bidding punctually performed was a missive that dropped into her memory with the dry rattle of a letter falling into a pillar-box. Like the letter it was, as part of the contents of a well-stuffed post-bag, delivered in due course at the right address. In the presence of these overflowings, after they had continued for a couple of years, the associates of either party sometimes felt that something should be done for what they called 'the real good, don't you know?' of the child. The only thing done, however, in general, took place when it was sighingly remarked that she fortunately wasn't all the year round where she happened to be at the awkward moment, and that, furthermore, either from extreme cunning or from extreme stupidity, she appeared not to take things in.

The theory of her stupidity, eventually embraced by her parents, corresponded with a great date in her small still life: the complete vision, private but final, of the strange office she filled. It was literally a moral revolution and accomplished in the depths of her nature. The stiff dolls on the dusky shelves began to move their arms and legs; old forms and phrases began to have a sense that frightened her. She had a new feeling, the feeling of danger; on which a new remedy rose to meet it, the idea of an inner self or, in other words, of concealment. She puzzled out with imperfect signs, but with a prodigious spirit, that she had been a centre of hatred and a messenger of insult, and that everything was bad because she had been employed to make it so. Her parted lips locked themselves with the determination to be employed no longer. She would forget everything, she would repeat nothing, and when, as a tribute to the successful application of her system, she began to be called a little idiot, she tasted a pleasure new and keen. When therefore, as she grew older, her parents in turn announced before her that she had grown shockingly dull, it was not from any real contraction of her little stream of life. She spoiled their fun, but she practically added to her own. She saw more and more; she saw too much. It was Miss Overmore, her first governess, who on a momentous occasion had sown the seeds of secrecy; sown them not by anything she said, but by a mere roll of those fine eyes which Maisie already admired. Moddle had become at this time, after alternations of residence of which the child had no clear record, an image faintly embalmed in the remembrance of hungry disappearances from the nursery and distressful lapses in the alphabet, sad embarrassments, in particular, when invited to recognise something her nurse described as 'the important letter haitch'. Miss Overmore, however hungry, never disappeared: this marked her somehow as of higher rank, and the character was confirmed by a prettiness that Maisie supposed to be extraordinary. Mrs Farange had described her as almost too pretty, and some one had asked what that mattered so long as Beale wasn't there. 'Beale or no

Beale,' Maisie had heard her mother reply, 'I take her because she's a lady and yet awfully poor. Rather nice people, but there are seven sisters at home. What do people mean?'

Maisie didn't know what people meant, but she knew very soon all the names of all the sisters; she could say them off better than she could say the multiplication-table. She privately wondered more-over, though she never asked, about the awful poverty, of which her companion also never spoke. Food at any rate came up by mysterious laws; Miss Overmore never, like Moddle, had on an apron, and when she ate she held her fork with her little finger curled out. The child, who watched her at many moments, watched her particularly at that one. 'I think you're lovely,' she often said to her; even mamma, who was lovely too, had not such a pretty way with the fork. Maisie associated this showier presence with her now being 'big', knowing of course that nursery-governesses were only for little girls who were not, as she said, 'really' little. She vaguely knew, further, somehow, that the future was still bigger than she, and that a part of what made it so was the number of governesses lurking in it and ready to dart out. Everything that had happened when she was really little was dormant, everything but the positive certitude, bequeathed from afar by Moddle, that the natural way for a child to have her parents was separate and successive, like her mutton and her pudding or her bath and her nap.

'*Does* he know he lies?' – that was what she had vivaciously asked Miss Overmore on the occasion which was so suddenly to lead to a change in her life.

'Does he know –?' Miss Overmore stared; she had a stocking pulled over her hand and was pricking at it with a needle which she poised in the act. Her task was homely, but her movement, like all her movements, graceful.

'Why papa.'

'That he "lies"?'

'That's what mamma says I'm to tell him – "that he lies and he knows he lies".' Miss Overmore turned very red, though she laughed out till her head fell back; then she pricked again at her muffled hand so hard that Maisie wondered how she could bear it. '*Am* I to tell him?' the child went on. It was then that her companion addressed her in the unmistakeable language of a pair of eyes of deep dark grey. 'I can't say No,' they replied as distinctly as possible; 'I can't say No, because I'm afraid of your mamma, don't you see? Yet how can I say Yes after your papa has been so kind to me, talking to me so long the other day, smiling and flashing his beautiful teeth at me the time we met him in the Park, the time when, rejoicing at the sight of us, he left the gentlemen he was with and turned and walked with us, stayed with us for half an hour?' Somehow in the light of Miss Overmore's lovely eyes that incident came back to Maisie with a charm it hadn't had at the time, and this in spite of the fact that after it was over her governess had never but once alluded to it. On their way home, when papa had quitted them, she had expressed the hope that the child wouldn't mention it to mamma. Maisie liked her so, and had so the charmed sense of being liked by her, that she accepted this remark as settling the matter and wonderingly conformed to it. The wonder now lived again, lived in the recollection of what papa had said to Miss Overmore: 'I've only to look at you to see you're a person I can appeal to for help to save my daughter.' Maisie's ignorance of what she was to be saved from didn't diminish the pleasure of the thought that Miss Overmore was saving her. It seemed to make them cling together as in some wild game of 'going round'.

III

SHE was therefore all the more startled when her mother said to her in connection with something to be done before her next migration: 'You understand of course that she's not going with you.'

Maisie turned quite faint. 'Oh I thought she was.'

'It doesn't in the least matter, you know, what you think,' Mrs Farange loudly replied; 'and you had better indeed for the future, miss, learn to keep your thoughts to yourself.' This was exactly what Maisie had already learned, and the accomplishment was just the source of her mother's irritation. It was of a horrid little critical system, a tendency, in her silence, to judge her elders, that this lady suspected her, liking as she did, for her own part, a child to be simple and confiding. She liked also to hear the report of the whacks she administered to Mr Farange's character, to his pretensions to peace of mind: the satisfaction of dealing them diminished when nothing came back. The day was at hand, and she saw it, when she should feel more delight in hurling Maisie at him than in snatching her away; so much so that her conscience winced under the acuteness of a candid friend who had remarked that the real end of all their tugging would be that each parent would try to make the little girl a burden to the other – a sort of game in which a fond mother clearly wouldn't show to advantage. The prospect of not showing to advantage, a distinction in which she held she had never failed, begot in Ida Farange an ill humour of which several persons felt the effect. She determined that Beale at any rate should feel it; she reflected afresh that in the study of how to be odious to him she must never give way. Nothing could incommode him more than not to get the good, for the child, of a nice female appendage who had clearly taken a fancy to her. One of the things Ida said to the appendage was that Beale's was a house in which no decent woman could consent to be seen. It was Miss Overmore herself who explained to Maisie that she had had a hope of being allowed to accompany her to her father's, and that this hope had been dashed by the way her mother took it. 'She says that if I ever do such a thing as enter his service I must never expect to show my face in this house again. So I've promised not to attempt to go with you. If I wait patiently till you come back here we shall certainly be together once more.'

Waiting patiently, and above all waiting till she should come back there, seemed to Maisie a long way round – it reminded her of all the things she had been told, first and last, that she should have if she'd be good and that in spite of her goodness she had never had at all. 'Then who'll take care of me at papa's?'

'Heaven only knows, my own precious!' Miss Overmore replied, tenderly embracing her. There was indeed no doubt that she was dear to this beautiful friend. What could have proved it better than the fact that before a week was out, in spite of their distressing separation and her mother's prohibition and Miss Overmore's scruples and Miss Overmore's promise, the beautiful friend had turned up at her father's? The little lady already engaged there to come by the hour, a fat dark little lady with a foreign name and dirty fingers, who wore, throughout, a bonnet that had at first given her a deceptive air, too soon dispelled, of not staying long, besides asking her pupil questions that had nothing to do with lessons, questions that Beale Farange himself, when two or three were repeated to him, admitted to be awfully low – this strange apparition faded before the bright creature who had braved everything for Maisie's sake. The bright creature told her little charge frankly what had happened – that she had really been unable to hold out. She had broken her vow to Mrs Farange; she had struggled for three days and then had come straight to Maisie's papa and told him the simple truth. She adored his daughter; she couldn't give her up; she'd make for her any sacrifice. On this basis it had been arranged that she should stay; her courage had been rewarded; she left Maisie in no doubt as to the amount of courage she had required. Some of the things she said made a particular impression on the child – her declaration for instance that when her pupil should get older she'd understand better just how 'dreadfully bold' a young lady, to do exactly what she had done, had to be.

'Fortunately your papa appreciates it; he appreciates it *immensely*' – that was one of the things Miss Overmore also said, with a striking insistence on the adverb. Maisie herself was no less impressed with what this martyr had gone through, especially after hearing of the terrible letter that had come from Mrs Farange. Mamma had been so angry that, in Miss Overmore's own words, she had loaded her with insult – proof enough indeed that they must never look forward to being together again under mamma's roof. Mamma's roof, however, had its turn, this time, for the child, of appearing but remotely contingent, so that, to reassure her, there was scarce a need of her companion's secret, solemnly confided – the probability there would be no going back to mamma at all. It was Miss Overmore's private conviction, and a part of the same communication, that if Mr Farange's daughter would only show a really marked preference she would be backed up by 'public opinion' in holding on to him. Poor Maisie could scarcely grasp that incentive, but she could surrender herself to the day. She had conceived her first passion, and the object of it was her governess. It hadn't been put to her, and she couldn't, or at any rate she didn't, put it to herself, that she liked Miss Overmore better than she liked papa; but it would have sustained her under such an imputation to feel herself able to reply that papa too liked Miss Overmore exactly as much. He had particularly told her so. Besides she could easily see it.

IV

ALL this led her on, but it brought on her fate as well, the day when her mother would be at the door in the carriage in which Maisie now rode on no occasions but these. There was no question at present of Miss Overmore's going back with her: it was universally recognised that her quarrel with Mrs Farange was much too acute. The child felt it from the first; there was no hugging nor exclaiming as that lady drove her away – there was only a frightening silence, unenlivened even by the invidious enquiries of former years, which culminated, according to its stern nature, in a still more frightening old woman, a figure awaiting her on the very doorstep. 'You're to be under this lady's care,' said her mother. 'Take her, Mrs Wix,' she added, addressing the figure impatiently and giving the child a push from which Maisie gathered that she wished to set Mrs Wix an example of energy. Mrs Wix took her and, Maisie felt the next day, would never let her go. She had struck her at first, just after Miss Overmore, as terrible; but something in her voice at the end of an hour touched the little girl in a spot that had never even yet been reached. Maisie knew later what it was, though doubtless she couldn't have made a statement of it: these were things that a few days' talk with Mrs Wix quite lighted up. The principal one was a matter Mrs Wix herself always immediately mentioned: she had had a little girl quite of her own, and the little girl had been killed on the spot. She had had absolutely nothing else in all the world, and her affliction had broken her heart. It was comfortably established between them that Mrs Wix's heart was broken. What Maisie felt was that she had been, with passion and anguish, a mother, and that this was something Miss Overmore was not, something (strangely, confusingly) that mamma was even less.

So it was that in the course of an extraordinarily short time she found herself as deeply absorbed in the image of the little dead Clara Matilda, who, on a crossing in the Harrow Road, had been knocked down and crushed by the cruellest of hansoms, as she had ever found herself in the family group made vivid by one of seven. 'She's your little dead sister,' Mrs Wix ended by saying, and Maisie, all in a tremor of curiosity and compassion, addressed from that moment a particular piety to the small accepted acquisition. Somehow she wasn't a real sister, but that only made her the more romantic. It contributed to this view of her that she was never to be spoken of in that character to any one else – least of all to Mrs Farange, who wouldn't care for her nor recognise the relationship: it was to be just an unutterable and inexhaustible little secret with Mrs Wix. Maisie knew everything about her that could be known, everything she had said or done in her little mutilated life, exactly how lovely she was, exactly how her hair was curled and her frocks were trimmed. Her hair came down far below her waist – it was of the most wonderful golden brightness, just as Mrs Wix's own had been a long time before. Mrs Wix's own was indeed very remarkable still, and Maisie had felt at first that she should never get on with it. It played a large part in the sad and strange appearance, the appearance as of a kind of greasy greyness, which Mrs Wix had presented on the child's arrival. It had originally been yellow, but time had turned that elegance to ashes, to a turbid sallow unvenerable white. Still excessively abundant, it was dressed in a manner of which the poor lady appeared not yet to have recognised the supersession, with a glossy braid, like a large diadem, on the top of the head, and behind, at the nape of the neck, a dingy rosette like a large button. She wore glasses which, in humble reference to a divergent obliquity of vision, she called her straighteners, and a little ugly snuff-coloured dress trimmed with satin bands in the form of scallops and glazed with antiquity. The straighteners, she explained to Maisie, were put on for the sake of others, whom, as

she believed, they helped to recognise the bearing, otherwise
doubtful, of her regard; the rest of the melancholy garb could only
have been put on for herself. With the added suggestion of her
goggles it reminded her pupil of the polished shell or corslet of a
horrid beetle. At first she had looked cross and almost cruel; but this
impression passed away with the child's increased perception of her
being in the eyes of the world a figure mainly to laugh at. She was
as droll as a charade or an animal toward the end of the 'natural
history' – a person whom people, to make talk lively, described to
each other and imitated. Every one knew the straighteners; every
one knew the diadem and the button, the scallops and satin bands;
every one, though Maisie had never betrayed her, knew even Clara
Matilda.

It was on account of these things that mamma got her for such
low pay, really for nothing: so much, one day when Mrs Wix had
accompanied her into the drawing-room and left her, the child
heard one of the ladies she found there – a lady with eyebrows
arched like skipping-ropes and thick black stitching, like ruled lines
for musical notes on beautiful white gloves – announce to another.
She knew governesses were poor; Miss Overmore was unmention-
ably and Mrs Wix ever so publicly so. Neither this, however, nor
the old brown frock nor the diadem nor the button, made a
difference for Maisie in the charm put forth through everything,
the charm of Mrs Wix's conveying that somehow, in her ugliness
and her poverty, she was peculiarly and soothingly safe; safer than
any one in the world, than papa, than mamma, than the lady with
the arched eyebrows; safer even, though so much less beautiful,
than Miss Overmore, on whose loveliness, as she supposed it, the
little girl was faintly conscious that one couldn't rest with quite the
same tucked-in and kissed-for-good-night feeling. Mrs Wix was as
safe as Clara Matilda, who was in heaven and yet, embarrassingly,
also in Kensal Green, where they had been together to see her little
huddled grave. It was from something in Mrs Wix's tone, which in
spite of caricature remained indescribable and inimitable, that

Maisie, before her term with her mother was over, drew this sense of a support, like a breast-high banister in a place of 'drops', that would never give way. If she knew her instructress was poor and queer she also knew she was not nearly so 'qualified' as Miss Overmore, who could say lots of dates straight off (letting you hold the book yourself), state the position of Malabar, play six pieces without notes and, in a sketch, put in beautifully the trees and houses and difficult parts. Maisie herself could play more pieces than Mrs Wix, who was moreover visibly ashamed of her houses and trees and could only, with the help of a smutty forefinger, of doubtful legitimacy in the field of art, do the smoke coming out of the chimneys.

They dealt, the governess and her pupil, in 'subjects', but there were many the governess put off from week to week and that they never got to at all: she only used to say 'We'll take that in its proper order.' Her order was a circle as vast as the untravelled globe. She had not the spirit of adventure – the child could perfectly see how many subjects she was afraid of. She took refuge on the firm ground of fiction, through which indeed there curled the blue river of truth. She knew swarms of stories, mostly those of the novels she had read; relating them with a memory that never faltered and a wealth of detail that was Maisie's delight. They were all about love and beauty and countesses and wickedness. Her conversation was practically an endless narrative, a great garden of romance, with sudden vistas into her own life and gushing fountains of home-liness. These were the parts where they most lingered; she made the child take with her again every step of her long, lame course and think it beyond magic or monsters. Her pupil acquired a vivid vision of every one who had ever, in her phrase, knocked against her – some of them oh so hard! – every one literally but Mr Wix, her husband, as to whom nothing was mentioned save that he had been dead for ages. He had been rather remarkably absent from his wife's career, and Maisie was never taken to see his grave.

V

THE second parting from Miss Overmore had been bad enough, but this first parting from Mrs Wix was much worse. The child had lately been to the dentist's and had a term of comparison for the screwed-up intensity of the scene. It was dreadfully silent, as it had been when her tooth was taken out; Mrs Wix had on that occasion grabbed her hand and they had clung to each other with the frenzy of their determination not to scream. Maisie, at the dentist's, had been heroically still, but just when she felt most anguish had become aware of an audible shriek on the part of her companion, a spasm of stifled sympathy. This was reproduced by the only sound that broke their supreme embrace when, a month later, the 'arrangement', as her periodical uprootings were called, played the part of the horrible forceps. Embedded in Mrs Wix's nature as her tooth had been socketed in her gum, the operation of extracting her would really have been a case for chloroform. It was a hug that fortunately left nothing to say, for the poor woman's want of words at such an hour seemed to fall in with her want of everything. Maisie's alternate parent, in the outermost vestibule – he liked the impertinence of crossing as much as that of his late wife's threshold – stood over them with his open watch and his still more open grin, while from the only corner of an eye on which something of Mrs Wix's didn't impinge the child saw at the door a brougham in which Miss Overmore also waited. She remembered the difference when, six months before, she had been torn from the breast of that more spirited protectress. Miss Overmore, then also in the vestibule, but of course in the other one, had been thoroughly audible and voluble; her protest had rung out bravely and she had declared that something – her pupil didn't know exactly what – was a regular wicked shame. That had at the time dimly recalled to Maisie the far-away moment of Moddle's great outbreak: there seemed always to be 'shames' connected in one way or another with her migrations. At present, while Mrs Wix's arms tightened and the smell of her hair was strong, she further remembered how, in pacifying Miss Overmore, papa had made use of the words 'you dear old duck!' – an expression which, by its oddity, had stuck fast in her young mind, having moreover a place well prepared for it there by what she knew of the governess whom she now always mentally characterised as the pretty one. She wondered whether this affection would be as great as before: that would at all events be the case with the prettiness Maisie could see in the face which showed brightly at the window of the brougham.

The brougham was a token of harmony, of the fine conditions papa would this time offer: he had usually come for her in a hansom, with a four-wheeler behind for the boxes. The four-wheeler with the boxes on it was actually there, but mamma was the only lady with whom she had ever been in a conveyance of the kind always of old spoken of by Moddle as a private carriage. Papa's carriage was, now that he had one, still more private, somehow, than mamma's; and when at last she found herself quite on top, as she felt, of its inmates and gloriously rolling away, she put to Miss Overmore, after another immense and talkative squeeze, a question of which the motive was a desire for information as to the continuity of a certain sentiment. 'Did papa like you just the same while I was gone?' she enquired – full of the sense of how markedly his favour had been established in her presence. She had bethought herself that this favour might, like her presence and as if depending on it, be only intermittent and for the season. Papa, on whose knee she sat, burst into one of those loud laughs of his that, however prepared she was, seemed always, like some trick in a frightening game, to leap forth and make her jump. Before Miss Overmore could speak he replied: 'Why, you little donkey, when you're away what have I left to do but just to love her?' Miss Overmore hereupon immediately took her from him, and they had a merry little scrimmage over her of which Maisie caught the surprised perception in the white stare of an old lady who passed in a victoria. Then her beautiful friend remarked to her very gravely: 'I shall make him understand that if he ever again says anything as horrid as that to you I shall carry you straight off and we'll go and live somewhere together and be good quiet little girls.' The child couldn't quite make out why her father's speech had been horrid, since it only expressed that appreciation which their companion herself had of old described as 'immense'. To enter more into the truth of the matter she appealed to him again directly, asked if in all those months Miss Overmore hadn't been with him just as she had been before and just as she would be now. 'Of course she has, old girl – where else could the poor dear be?' cried Beale Farange, to the still greater scandal of their companion, who protested that unless he straightway 'took back' his nasty wicked fib it would be, this time, not only him she would leave, but his child too and his house and his tiresome troubles – all the impossible things he had succeeded in putting on her. Beale, under this frolic menace, took nothing back at all; he was indeed apparently on the point of repeating his extravagance, but Miss Overmore instructed her little charge that she was not to listen to his bad jokes: she was to understand that a lady couldn't stay with a gentleman that way without some awfully proper reason.

Maisie looked from one of her companions to the other; this was the freshest gayest start she had yet enjoyed, but she had a shy fear of not exactly believing them. 'Well, what reason *is* proper?' she thoughtfully demanded.

'Oh a long-legged stick of a tomboy: there's none so good as that.' Her father enjoyed both her drollery and his own and tried again to get possession of her – an effort deprecated by their comrade and leading again to something of a public scuffle. Miss Overmore declared to the child that she had been all the while with good friends; on which Beale Farange went on: 'She means good friends of mine, you know – tremendous friends of mine. There has been no end of *them* about – that I *will* say for her!' Maisie felt bewildered and was afterwards for some time conscious of a vagueness, just slightly embarrassing, as to the subject of so much amusement and as to where her governess had really been. She didn't feel at all as if she had been seriously told, and no such feeling was supplied by anything that occurred later. Her embarrassment, of a precocious instinctive order, attached itself to the idea that this was another of the matters it was not for her, as her mother used to say, to go into. Therefore, under her father's roof during the time that followed, she made no attempt to clear up her ambiguity by an ingratiating way with housemaids; and it was an odd truth that the ambiguity itself took nothing from the fresh pleasure promised her by renewed contact with Miss Overmore. The confidence looked for by that young lady was of the fine sort that explanation can't improve, and she herself at any rate was a person superior to any confusion. For Maisie moreover concealment had never necessarily seemed deception; she had grown up among things as to which her foremost knowledge was that she was never to ask about them. It was far from new to her that the questions of the small are the peculiar diversion of the great: except the affairs of her doll Lisette there had scarcely ever been anything at her mother's that was explicable with a grave face. Nothing was so easy to her as to send the ladies who gathered there off into shrieks, and she might have practised upon them largely if she had been of a more calculating turn. Everything had something behind it: life was like a long, long corridor with rows of closed doors. She had learned that at these doors it was wise not to knock – this seemed to produce from within such sounds of derision. Little by little, however, she understood more, for it befell that she was enlightened by Lisette's questions, which reproduced the effect of her own upon those for whom she sat in the very darkness of Lisette. Was she not herself convulsed by such innocence? In the presence of it she often imitated the shrieking ladies. There were at any rate things she really couldn't tell even a French doll. She could only pass on her lessons and study to produce on Lisette the impression of having mysteries in her life, wondering the while whether she succeeded in the air of shading off, like her mother, into the unknowable. When the reign of Miss Overmore followed that of Mrs Wix she took a fresh cue, emulating her governess and bridging over the interval with the simple expectation of trust. Yes, there were matters one couldn't 'go into' with a pupil. There were for instance days when, after prolonged absence, Lisette, watching her take off her things, tried hard to discover where she had been. Well, she discovered a little, but never discovered all. There was an occasion when, on her being particularly indiscreet, Maisie replied to her – and precisely about the motive of a disappearance – as she, Maisie, had once been replied to by Mrs Farange: 'Find out for yourself!' She mimicked her mother's sharpness, but she was rather ashamed afterwards, though as to whether of the sharpness or of the mimicry was not quite clear.

VI

SHE became aware in time that this phase wouldn't have shone by lessons, the care of her education being now only one of the many duties devolving on Miss Overmore; a devolution as to which she was present at various passages between that lady and her father – passages significant, on either side, of dissent and even of displeasure. It was gathered by the child on these occasions that there was something in the situation for which her mother might 'come down' on them all, though indeed the remark, always dropped by her father, was greeted on his companion's part with direct contradiction. Such scenes were usually brought to a climax by Miss Overmore's demanding, with more asperity than she applied to any other subject, in what position under the sun such a person as Mrs Farange would find herself for coming down. As the months went on the little girl's interpretations thickened, and the more effectually that this stretch was the longest she had known without a break. She got used to the idea that her mother, for some reason, was in no hurry to reinstate her: that idea was forcibly expressed by her father whenever Miss Overmore, differing and decided, took him up on the question, which he was always putting forward, of the urgency of sending her to school. For a governess Miss Overmore differed surprisingly; far more for instance than would have entered into the bowed head of Mrs Wix. She observed to Maisie many times that she was quite conscious of not doing her justice, and that Mr Farange equally measured and equally lamented this deficiency. The reason of it was that she had mysterious responsibilities that interfered – responsibilities, Miss Overmore intimated, to Mr Farange himself and to the friendly noisy little house and those who came there. Mr Farange's remedy for every inconvenience was that the child should be put at school – there were such lots of splendid schools, as everybody knew, at Brighton and all over the place. That, however, Maisie learned, was just what would bring her mother down: from the moment he should delegate to others the housing of his little charge he hadn't a leg to stand on before the law. Didn't he keep her away from her mother precisely because Mrs Farange was one of these others?

There was also the solution of a second governess, a young person to come in by the day and really do the work; but to this Miss Overmore wouldn't for a moment listen, arguing against it with great public relish and wanting to know from all comers – she put it even to Maisie herself – if they didn't see how frightfully it would give her away. 'What am I supposed to be at all, don't you see, if I'm not here to look after her?' She was in a false position and so freely and loudly called attention to it that it seemed to become almost a source of glory. The way out of it of course was just to do her plain duty; but that was unfortunately what, with his excessive, his exorbitant demands on her, which every one indeed appeared quite to understand, he practically, he selfishly prevented. Beale Farange, for Miss Overmore, was now never anything but 'he', and the house was as full as ever of lively gentlemen with whom, under that designation, she charmingly talked about him. Maisie meanwhile, as a subject of familiar gossip on what was to be done with her, was left so much to herself that she had hours of wistful thought of the large loose discipline of Mrs Wix; yet she none the less held it under her father's roof a point of superiority that none of his visitors were ladies. It added to this odd security that she had once heard a gentleman say to him as if it were a great joke and in obvious reference to Miss Overmore: 'Hanged if she'll let another woman come near you – hanged if she ever will. She'd let fly a stick at her as they do at a strange cat!' Maisie greatly preferred gentlemen as inmates in spite of their also having their way – louder but sooner over – of laughing out at her. They pulled and pinched, they teased and tickled her; some of them even, as they termed it, shied things at her, and all of them thought it funny to call her by names having no resemblance to her own. The ladies on the other hand addressed her as 'You poor pet' and scarcely touched her even to kiss her. But it was of the ladies she was most afraid.

She was now old enough to understand how disproportionate a stay she had already made with her father; and also old enough to enter a little into the ambiguity attending this excess, which oppressed her particularly whenever the question had been touched upon in talk with her governess. 'Oh you needn't worry: she doesn't care!' Miss Overmore had often said to her in reference to any fear that her mother might resent her prolonged detention. 'She has other people than poor little *you* to think about, and has gone abroad with them; so you needn't be in the least afraid she'll stickle this time for her rights.' Maisie knew Mrs Farange had gone abroad, for she had had weeks and weeks before a letter from her beginning 'My precious pet' and taking leave of her for an indeterminate time; but she had not seen in it a renunciation of hatred or of the writer's policy of asserting herself, for the sharpest of all her impressions had been that there was nothing her mother would ever care so much about as to torment Mr Farange. What at last, however, was in this connection bewildering and a little frightening was the dawn of a suspicion that a better way had been found to torment Mr Farange than to deprive him of his periodical burden. This was the question that worried our young lady and that Miss Overmore's confidences and the frequent observations of her employer only rendered more mystifying. It was a contradiction that if Ida had now a fancy for waiving the rights she had originally been so hot about her late husband shouldn't jump at the monopoly for which he had also in the first instance so fiercely fought; but when Maisie, with a subtlety beyond her years, sounded this new ground her main success was in hearing her mother more freshly abused. Miss Overmore had up to now rarely deviated from a decent reserve, but the day came when she expressed herself with a vividness not inferior to Beale's own on the subject of the lady who had fled to the Continent to wriggle out of her job. It would serve this lady right, Maisie gathered, if that contract, in the shape of an overgrown and underdressed daughter, should be shipped straight out to her and landed at her feet in the midst of scandalous excesses.

The picture of these pursuits was what Miss Overmore took refuge in when the child tried timidly to ascertain if her father were disposed to feel he had too much of her. She evaded the point and only kicked up all round it the dust of Ida's heartlessness and folly, of which the supreme proof, it appeared, was the fact that she was accompanied on her journey by a gentleman whom, to be painfully plain on it, she had – well, 'picked up'. The only terms on which, unless they were married, ladies and gentlemen might, as Miss Overmore expressed it, knock about together, were the terms on which she and Mr Farange had exposed themselves to possible misconception. She had indeed, as has been noted, often explained this before, often said to Maisie: 'I don't know what in the world, darling, your father and I should do without you, for you just make the difference, as I've told you, of keeping us perfectly proper.' The child took in the office it was so endearingly presented to her that she performed a comfort that helped her to a sense of security even in the event of her mother's giving her up. Familiar as she had grown with the fact of the great alternative to the proper, she felt in her governess and her father a strong reason for not emulating that detachment. At the same time she had heard somehow of little girls – of exalted rank, it was true – whose education was carried on by instructors of the other sex, and she knew that if she were at school at Brighton it would be thought an advantage to her to be more or less in the hands of masters. She turned these things over and remarked to Miss Overmore that if she should go to her mother perhaps the gentleman might become her tutor.

'The gentleman?' The proposition was complicated enough to make Miss Overmore stare.

'The one who's with mamma. Mightn't that make it right – as right as your being my governess makes it for you to be with papa?'

Miss Overmore considered; she coloured a little; then she embraced her ingenious friend. 'You're too sweet! I'm a *real* governess.'

'And couldn't he be a real tutor?'

'Of course not. He's ignorant and bad.'

'Bad –?' Maisie echoed with wonder.

Her companion gave a queer little laugh at her tone. 'He's ever so much younger –' But that was all.

'Younger than you?'

Miss Overmore laughed again; it was the first time Maisie had seen her approach so nearly to a giggle. 'Younger than – no matter whom. I don't know anything about him and don't want to,' she rather inconsequently added. 'He's not my sort, and I'm sure, my own darling, he's not yours.' And she repeated the free caress into which her colloquies with Maisie almost always broke and which made the child feel that *her* affection at least was a gage of safety. Parents had come to seem vague, but governesses were evidently to be trusted. Maisie's faith in Mrs Wix for instance had suffered no lapse from the fact that all communication with her had temporarily dropped. During the first weeks of their separation Clara Matilda's mamma had repeatedly and dolefully written to her, and Maisie had answered with an enthusiasm controlled only by orthographical doubts; but the correspondence had been duly submitted to Miss Overmore, with the final effect of its not suiting her. It was this lady's view that Mr Farange wouldn't care for it at all, and she ended by confessing – since her pupil pushed her – that she didn't care for it herself. She was furiously jealous, she said; and that weakness was but a new proof of her disinterested affection. She pronounced Mrs Wix's effusions moreover illiterate and unprofitable; she made no scruple of declaring it monstrous that a

woman in her senses should have placed the formation of her
daughter's mind in such ridiculous hands. Maisie was well aware
that the proprietress of the old brown dress and the old odd
headgear was lower in the scale of 'form' than Miss Overmore; but
it was now brought home to her with pain that she was
educationally quite out of the question. She was buried for the time
beneath a conclusive remark of her critic's: 'She's really beyond a
joke!' This remark was made as that charming woman held in her
hand the last letter that Maisie was to receive from Mrs Wix; it was
fortified by a decree proscribing the preposterous tie. 'Must I then
write and tell her?' the child bewilderedly asked: she grew pale at
the dreadful things it appeared involved for her to say. 'Don't
dream of it, my dear – *I'll* write: you may trust me!' cried Miss
Overmore; who indeed wrote to such purpose that a hush in which
you could have heard a pin drop descended upon poor Mrs Wix.
She gave for weeks and weeks no sign whatever of life: it was as if
she had been as effectually disposed of by Miss Overmore's
communication as her little girl, in the Harrow Road, had been
disposed of by the terrible hansom. Her very silence became after
this one of the largest elements of Maisie's consciousness; it proved
a warm and habitable air, into which the child penetrated further
than she dared ever to mention to her companions. Somewhere in
the depths of it the dim straighteners were fixed upon her;
somewhere out of the troubled little current Mrs Wix intensely
waited.

VII

IT quite fell in with this intensity that one day, on returning from a walk with the housemaid, Maisie should have found her in the hall, seated on the stool usually occupied by the telegraph-boys who haunted Beale Farange's door and kicked their heels while, in his room, answers to their missives took form with the aid of smoke-puffs and growls. It had seemed to her on their parting that Mrs Wix had reached the last limits of the squeeze, but she now felt those limits to be transcended and that the duration of her visitor's hug was a direct reply to Miss Overmore's veto. She understood in a flash how the visit had come to be possible – that Mrs Wix, watching her chance, must have slipped in under protection of the fact that papa, always tormented in spite of arguments with the idea of a school, had, for a three days' excursion to Brighton, absolutely insisted on the attendance of her adversary. It was true that when Maisie explained their absence and their important motive Mrs Wix wore an expression so peculiar that it could only have had its origin in surprise. This contradiction indeed peeped out only to vanish, for at the very moment that, in the spirit of it, she threw herself afresh upon her young friend a hansom crested with neat luggage rattled up to the door and Miss Overmore bounded out. The shock of her encounter with Mrs Wix was less violent than Maisie had feared on seeing her and didn't at all interfere with the sociable tone in which, under her rival's eyes, she explained to her little charge that she had returned, for a particular reason, a day sooner than she first intended. She had left papa – in such nice lodgings – at Brighton; but he would come back to his dear little home on the morrow. As for Mrs Wix, papa's companion supplied

Maisie in later converse with the right word for the attitude of this personage: Mrs Wix 'stood up' to her in a manner that the child herself felt at the time to be astonishing. This occurred indeed after Miss Overmore had so far raised her interdict as to make a move to the dining-room, where, in the absence of any suggestion of sitting down, it was scarcely more than natural that even poor Mrs Wix should stand up. Maisie at once enquired if at Brighton, this time, anything had come of the possibility of a school; to which, much to her surprise, Miss Overmore, who had always grandly repudiated it, replied after an instant, but quite as if Mrs Wix were not there:

'It may be, darling, that something *will* come. The objection, I must tell you, has been quite removed.'

At this it was still more startling to hear Mrs Wix speak out with great firmness. 'I don't think, if you'll allow me to say so, that there's any arrangement by which the objection *can* be "removed". What has brought me here today is that I've a message for Maisie from dear Mrs Farange.'

The child's heart gave a great thump. 'Oh mamma's come back?'

'Not yet, sweet love, but she's coming,' said Mrs Wix, 'and she has – most thoughtfully, you know – sent me on to prepare you.'

'To prepare her for what, pray?' asked Miss Overmore, whose first smoothness began, with this news, to be ruffled.

Mrs Wix quietly applied her straighteners to Miss Overmore's flushed beauty. 'Well, miss, for a very important communication.'

'Can't dear Mrs Farange, as you so oddly call her, make her communications directly? Can't she take the trouble to write to her only daughter?' the younger lady demanded. 'Maisie herself will tell you that it's months and months since she has had so much as a word from her.'

'Oh but I've written to mamma!' cried the child as if this would do quite as well.

'That makes her treatment of you all the greater scandal,' the governess in possession promptly declared.

'Mrs Farange is too well aware,' said Mrs Wix with sustained spirit, 'of what becomes of her letters in this house.'

Maisie's sense of fairness hereupon interposed for her visitor. 'You know, Miss Overmore, that papa doesn't like everything of mamma's.'

'No one likes, my dear, to be made the subject of such language as your mother's letters contain. They were not fit for the innocent child to see,' Miss Overmore observed to Mrs Wix.

'Then I don't know what you complain of, and she's better without them. It serves every purpose that I'm in Mrs Farange's confidence.'

Miss Overmore gave a scornful laugh. 'Then you must be mixed up with some extraordinary proceedings!'

'None so extraordinary,' cried Mrs Wix, turning very pale, 'as to say horrible things about the mother to the face of the helpless daughter!'

'Things not a bit more horrible, I think,' Miss Overmore returned, 'than those you, madam, appear to have come here to say about the father!'

Mrs Wix looked for a moment hard at Maisie, and then, turning again to this witness, spoke with a trembling voice. 'I came to say nothing about him, and you must excuse Mrs Farange and me if we're not so above all reproach as the companion of his travels.'

The young woman thus described stared at the apparent breadth of the description – she needed a moment to take it in. Maisie, however, gazing solemnly from one of the disputants to the other, noted that her answer, when it came, perched upon smiling lips. 'It will do quite as well, no doubt, if you come up to the requirements of the companion of Mrs Farange's!'

Mrs Wix broke into a queer laugh; it sounded to Maisie an unsuccessful imitation of a neigh. 'That's just what I'm here to make known – how perfectly the poor lady comes up to them herself.' She held up her head at the child. 'You must take your mamma's message, Maisie, and you must feel that her wishing me to come to you with it this way is a great proof of interest and affection. She sends you her particular love and announces to you that she's engaged to be married to Sir Claude.'

'Sir Claude?' Maisie wonderingly echoed. But while Mrs Wix explained that this gentleman was a dear friend of Mrs Farange's, who had been of great assistance to her in getting to Florence and in making herself comfortable there for the winter, she was not too violently shaken to perceive her old friend's enjoyment of the effect of this news on Miss Overmore. That young lady opened her eyes very wide; she immediately remarked that Mrs Farange's marriage would of course put an end to any further pretension to take her daughter back. Mrs Wix enquired with astonishment why it should do anything of the sort, and Miss Overmore gave as an instant reason that it was clearly but another dodge in a system of dodges. She wanted to get out of the bargain: why else had she now left Maisie on her father's hands weeks and weeks beyond the time about which she had originally made such a fuss? It was vain for Mrs Wix to represent – as she speciously proceeded to do – that all this time would be made up as soon as Mrs Farange returned: she, Miss Overmore, knew nothing, thank heaven, about her confederate, but was very sure any person capable of forming that sort of relation with the lady in Florence would easily agree to object to the presence in his house of the fruit of a union that his dignity must ignore. It was a game like another, and Mrs Wix's visit was clearly the first move in it. Maisie found in this exchange of asperities a fresh incitement to the unformulated fatalism in which her sense of her own career had long since taken refuge; and it was the beginning for her of a deeper prevision that, in spite of Miss Overmore's brilliancy and Mrs Wix's passion, she should live to see a change in the nature of the struggle she appeared to have come into the world to produce. It would still be essentially a struggle, but its object would now be *not* to receive her.

Mrs Wix, after Miss Overmore's last demonstration, addressed herself wholly to the little girl, and, drawing from the pocket of her

dingy old pelisse a small flat parcel, removed its envelope and
wished to know if *that* looked like a gentleman who wouldn't be
nice to everybody – let alone to a person he would be so sure to
find so nice. Mrs Farange, in the candour of new-found happiness,
had enclosed a 'cabinet' photograph of Sir Claude, and Maisie lost
herself in admiration of the fair smooth face, the regular features,
the kind eyes, the amiable air, the general glossiness and smartness
of her prospective stepfather – only vaguely puzzled to suppose
herself now with two fathers at once. Her researches had hitherto
indicated that to incur a second parent of the same sex you had
usually to lose the first. '*Isn't* he sympathetic?' asked Mrs Wix, who
had clearly, on the strength of his charming portrait, made up her
mind that Sir Claude promised her a future. 'You can see, I hope,'
she added with much expression, 'that *he's* a perfect gentleman!'
Maisie had never before heard the word 'sympathetic' applied to
anybody's face; she heard it with pleasure and from that moment it
agreeably remained with her. She testified moreover to the force of
her own perception in a small soft sigh of response to the pleasant
eyes that seemed to seek her acquaintance, to speak to her directly.
'He's quite lovely!' she declared to Mrs Wix. Then eagerly, irre-
pressibly, as she still held the photograph and Sir Claude continued
to fraternise, 'Oh can't I keep it?' she broke out. No sooner had she
done so than she looked up from it at Miss Overmore: this was
with the sudden instinct of appealing to the authority that had long
ago impressed on her that she mustn't ask for things. Miss
Overmore, to her surprise, looked distant and rather odd, hesitating
and giving her time to turn again to Mrs Wix. Then Maisie saw
that lady's long face lengthen; it was stricken and almost scared, as
if her young friend really expected more of her than she had to
give. The photograph was a possession that, direly denuded, she
clung to, and there was a momentary struggle between her fond
clutch of it and her capability of every sacrifice for her precarious
pupil. With the acuteness of her years, however, Maisie saw that
her own avidity would triumph, and she held out the picture to

Miss Overmore as if she were quite proud of her mother. 'Isn't he just lovely?' she demanded while poor Mrs Wix hungrily wavered, her straighteners largely covering it and her pelisse gathered about her with an intensity that strained its ancient seams.

'It was to *me*, darling,' the visitor said, 'that your mamma so generously sent it; but of course if it would give you particular pleasure –' She faltered, only gasping her surrender.

Miss Overmore continued extremely remote. 'If the photograph's your property, my dear, I shall be happy to oblige you by looking at it on some future occasion. But you must excuse me if I decline to touch an object belonging to Mrs Wix.'

That lady had by this time grown very red. 'You might as well see him this way, miss,' she retorted, 'as you certainly never will, I believe, in any other! Keep the pretty picture, by all means, my precious,' she went on: 'Sir Claude will be happy himself, I dare say, to give me one with a kind inscription.' The pathetic quaver of this brave boast was not lost on Maisie, who threw herself so gratefully on the speaker's neck that, when they had concluded their embrace, the public tenderness of which, she felt, made up for the sacrifice she imposed, their companion had had time to lay a quick hand on Sir Claude and, with a glance at him or not, whisk him effectually out of sight. Released from the child's arms Mrs Wix looked about for the picture; then she fixed Miss Overmore with a hard dumb stare; and finally, with her eyes on the little girl again, achieved the grimmest of smiles. 'Well, nothing matters, Maisie, because there's another thing your mamma wrote about. She has made sure of me.' Even after her loyal hug Maisie felt a bit of a sneak as she glanced at Miss Overmore for permission to understand this. But Mrs Wix left them in no doubt of what it meant. 'She has definitely engaged me – for her return and for yours. Then you'll see for yourself.' Maisie, on the spot, quite believed she should; but the prospect was suddenly thrown into confusion by an extraordinary demonstration from Miss Overmore.

'Mrs Wix,' said that young lady, 'has some undiscoverable reason for regarding your mother's hold on you as strengthened by the fact that she's about to marry. I wonder then – on that system – what our visitor will say to your father's.'

Miss Overmore's words were directed to her pupil, but her face, lighted with an irony that made it prettier even than ever before, was presented to the dingy figure that had stiffened itself for departure. The child's discipline had been bewildering – it had ranged freely between the prescription that she was to answer when spoken to and the experience of lively penalties on obeying that prescription. This time, nevertheless, she felt emboldened for risks; above all as something portentous seemed to have leaped into her sense of the relations of things. She looked at Miss Overmore much as she had a way of looking at persons who treated her to 'grown up' jokes. 'Do you mean papa's hold on me – do you mean *he's* about to marry?'

'Papa's not about to marry – papa *is* married, my dear. Papa was married the day before yesterday at Brighton.' Miss Overmore glittered more gaily; meanwhile it came over Maisie, and quite dazzlingly, that her 'smart' governess was a bride. 'He's my husband, if you please, and I'm his little wife. So *now* we'll see who's your little mother!' She caught her pupil to her bosom in a manner that was not to be outdone by the emissary of her predecessor, and a few moments later, when things had lurched back into their places, that poor lady, quite defeated of the last word, had soundlessly taken flight.

VIII

AFTER Mrs Wix's retreat Miss Overmore appeared to recognise that she was not exactly in a position to denounce Ida Farange's second union; but she drew from a table-drawer the photograph of Sir Claude and, standing there before Maisie, studied it at some length.

'Isn't he beautiful?' the child ingenuously asked.

Her companion hesitated. 'No – he's horrid,' she, to Maisie's surprise, sharply returned. But she debated another minute, after which she handed back the picture. It appeared to Maisie herself to exhibit a fresh attraction, and she was troubled, having never before had occasion to differ from her lovely friend. So she only could ask what, such being the case, she should do with it: should she put it quite away – where it wouldn't be there to offend? On this Miss Overmore again cast about; after which she said unexpectedly: 'Put it on the schoolroom mantelpiece.'

Maisie felt a fear. 'Won't papa dislike to see it there?'

'Very much indeed; but that won't matter *now*.' Miss Overmore spoke with peculiar significance and to her pupil's mystification.

'On account of the marriage?' Maisie risked.

Miss Overmore laughed, and Maisie could see that in spite of the irritation produced by Mrs Wix she was in high spirits. 'Which marriage do you mean?'

With the question put to her it suddenly struck the child she didn't know, so that she felt she looked foolish. So she took refuge in saying: 'Shall *you* be different –?' This was a full implication that the bride of Sir Claude would be.

'As your father's wedded wife? Utterly!' Miss Overmore replied. And the difference began of course in her being addressed, even by

Maisie, from that day and by her particular request, as Mrs Beale. It was there indeed principally that it ended, for except that the child could reflect that she should presently have four parents in all, and also that at the end of three months the staircase, for a little girl hanging over banisters, sent up the deepening rustle of more elaborate advances, everything made the same impression as before. Mrs Beale had very pretty frocks, but Miss Overmore's had been quite as good, and if papa was much fonder of his second wife than he had been of his first Maisie had foreseen that fondness, had followed its development almost as closely as the person more directly involved. There was little indeed in the commerce of her companions that her precocious experience couldn't explain, for if they struck her as after all rather deficient in that air of the honeymoon of which she had so often heard – in much detail, for instance, from Mrs Wix – it was natural to judge the circumstance in the light of papa's proved disposition to contest the empire of the matrimonial tie. His honeymoon, when he came back from Brighton – not on the morrow of Mrs Wix's visit, and not, oddly, till several days later – his honeymoon was perhaps perceptibly tinged with the dawn of a later stage of wedlock. There were things dislike of which, as the child knew it, wouldn't matter to Mrs Beale now, and their number increased so that such a trifle as his hostility to the photograph of Sir Claude quite dropped out of view. This pleasing object found a conspicuous place in the schoolroom, which in truth Mr Farange seldom entered and in which silent admiration formed, during the time I speak of, almost the sole scholastic exercise of Mrs Beale's pupil.

Maisie was not long in seeing just what her stepmother had meant by the difference she should show in her new character. If she was her father's wife she was not her own governess, and if her presence had had formerly to be made regular by the theory of a humble function she was now on a footing that dispensed with all theories and was inconsistent with all servitude. That was what she had meant by the drop of the objection to a school; her small companion was no longer required at home as – it was Mrs Beale's own amusing word – a little duenna. The argument against a successor to Miss Overmore remained: it was composed frankly of the fact, of which Mrs Beale granted the full absurdity, that she was too awfully fond of her stepdaughter to bring herself to see her in vulgar and mercenary hands. The note of this particular danger emboldened Maisie to put in a word for Mrs Wix, the modest measure of whose avidity she had taken from the first; but Mrs Beale disposed afresh and effectually of a candidate who would be sure to act in some horrible and insidious way for Ida's interest and who moreover was personally loathsome and as ignorant as a fish. She made also no more of a secret of the awkward fact that a good school would be hideously expensive, and of the further circumstance, which seemed to put an end to everything, that when it came to the point papa, in spite of his previous clamour, was really most nasty about paying. 'Would you believe,' Mrs Beale confidentially asked of her little charge, 'that he says I'm a worse expense than ever, and that a daughter and a wife together are really more than he can afford?' It was thus that the splendid school at Brighton lost itself in the haze of larger questions, though the fear that it would provoke Ida to leap into the breach subsided with her prolonged, her quite shameless non-appearance. Her daughter and her successor were therefore left to gaze in united but helpless blankness at all Maisie was not learning.

This quantity was so great as to fill the child's days with a sense of intermission to which even French Lisette gave no accent – with finished games and unanswered questions and dreaded tests; with the habit, above all, in her watch for a change, of hanging over banisters when the door-bell sounded. This was the great refuge of her impatience, but what she heard at such times was a clatter of gaiety downstairs; the impression of which, from her earliest childhood, had built up in her the belief that the grown-up time was the time of real amusement and above all of real intimacy. Even Lisette, even Mrs Wix had never, she felt, in spite of hugs and tears, been so intimate with her as so many persons at present were with Mrs Beale and as so many others of old had been with Mrs Farange. The note of hilarity brought people together still more than the note of melancholy, which was the one exclusively sounded, for instance, by poor Mrs Wix. Maisie in these days preferred none the less that domestic revels should be wafted to her from a distance: she felt sadly unsupported for facing the inquisition of the drawing-room. That was a reason the more for making the most of Susan Ash, who in her quality of under-housemaid moved at a very different level and who, none the less, was much depended upon out of doors. She was a guide to peregrinations that had little in common with those intensely definite airings that had left with the child a vivid memory of the regulated mind of Moddle. There had been under Moddle's system no dawdles at shop-windows and no nudges, in Oxford Street, of 'I *say*, look at *'er*!' There had been an inexorable treatment of crossings and a serene exemption from the fear that – especially at corners, of which she was yet weakly fond – haunted the housemaid, the fear of being, as she ominously said, 'spoken to'. The dangers of the town equally with its diversions added to Maisie's sense of being untutored and unclaimed.

The situation, however, had taken a twist when, on another of her returns, at Susan's side, extremely tired, from the pursuit of exercise qualified by much hovering, she encountered another emotion. She on this occasion learnt at the door that her instant attendance was requested in the drawing-room. Crossing the threshold in a cloud of shame she discerned through the blur Mrs Beale seated there with a gentleman who immediately drew the pain from her predicament by rising before her as the original of the photograph of Sir Claude. She felt the moment she looked at him that he was by far the most shining presence that had ever made her gape, and her pleasure in seeing him, in knowing that he took hold of her and kissed her, as quickly throbbed into a strange shy pride in him, a perception of his making up for her fallen state, for Susan's public nudges, which quite bruised her, and for all the lessons that, in the dead schoolroom, where at times she was almost afraid to stay alone, she was bored with not having. It was as if he had told her on the spot that he belonged to her, so that she could already show him off and see the effect he produced. No, nothing else that was most beautiful ever belonging to her could kindle that particular joy – not Mrs Beale at that very moment, not papa when he was gay, nor mamma when she was dressed, nor Lisette when she was new. The joy almost overflowed in tears when he laid his hand on her and drew her to him, telling her, with a smile of which the promise was as bright as that of a Christmas-tree, that he knew her ever so well by her mother, but had come to see her now so that he might know her for himself. She could see that his view of this kind of knowledge was to make her come away with him, and, further, that it was just what he was there for and had already been some time: arranging it with Mrs Beale and getting on with that lady in a manner evidently not at all affected by her having on the arrival of his portrait thought of him so ill. They had grown almost intimate – or had the air of it – over their discussion; and it was still further conveyed to Maisie that Mrs Beale had made no secret, and would make yet less of one, of all that it cost to let her go. 'You seem so tremendously eager,' she said to the child, 'that I hope you're at least clear about Sir Claude's relation to you. It doesn't appear to occur to him to give you the necessary reassurance.'

Maisie, a trifle mystified, turned quickly to her new friend. 'Why it's of course that you're *married* to her, isn't it?'

Her anxious emphasis started them off, as she had learned to call it; this was the echo she infallibly and now quite resignedly produced; moreover Sir Claude's laughter was an indistinguishable part of the sweetness of his being there. 'We've been married, my dear child, three months, and my interest in you is a consequence, don't you know? of my great affection for your mother. In coming here it's of course for your mother I'm acting.'

'Oh I know,' Maisie said with all the candour of her

competence. 'She can't come herself – except just to the door.'
Then as she thought afresh: 'Can't she come even to the door
now?'

'There you are!' Mrs Beale exclaimed to Sir Claude. She spoke
as if his dilemma were ludicrous.

His kind face, in an hesitation, seemed to recognise it; but he
answered the child with a frank smile. 'No – not very well.'

'Because she has married you?'

He promptly accepted this reason. 'Well, that has a good deal to
do with it.'

He was so delightful to talk to that Maisie pursued the subject.
'But papa – *he* has married Miss Overmore.'

'Ah you'll see that he won't come for you at your mother's,' that
lady interposed.

'Yes, but that won't be for a long time,' Maisie hastened to
respond.

'We won't talk about it now – you've months and months to put
in first.' And Sir Claude drew her closer.

'Oh that's what makes it so hard to give her up!' Mrs Beale made
this point with her arms out to her stepdaughter. Maisie, quitting
Sir Claude, went over to them and, clasped in a still tenderer
embrace, felt entrancingly the extension of the field of happiness.
'*I'll* come for you,' said her stepmother, 'if Sir Claude keeps you
too long: we must make him quite understand that! Don't talk to
me about her ladyship!' she went on to their visitor so familiarly
that it was almost as if they must have met before. 'I know her
ladyship as if I had made her. They're a pretty pair of parents!' cried
Mrs Beale.

Maisie had so often heard them called so that the remark
diverted her but an instant from the agreeable wonder of this grand
new form of allusion to her mother; and that, in its turn, presently
left her free to catch at the pleasant possibility, in connection with
herself, of a relation much happier as between Mrs Beale and Sir
Claude than as between mamma and papa. Still the next thing that

happened was that her interest in such a relation brought to her lips a fresh question. 'Have you seen papa?' she asked of Sir Claude.

It was the signal for their going off again, as her small stoicism had perfectly taken for granted that it would be. All that Mrs Beale had nevertheless to add was the vague apparent sarcasm: 'Oh papa!'

'I'm assured he's not at home,' Sir Claude replied to the child; 'but if he had been I should have hoped for the pleasure of seeing him.'

'Won't he mind your coming?' Maisie asked as with need of the knowledge.

'Oh you bad little girl!' Mrs Beale humorously protested.

The child could see that at this Sir Claude, though still moved to mirth, coloured a little; but he spoke to her very kindly. 'That's just what I came to see, you know – whether your father *would* mind. But Mrs Beale appears strongly of the opinion that he won't.'

This lady promptly justified that view to her stepdaughter. 'It will be very interesting, my dear, you know, to find out what it is today that your father does mind. I'm sure *I* don't know!' – and she seemed to repeat, though with perceptible resignation, her plaint of a moment before. 'Your father, darling, is a very odd person indeed.' She turned with this, smiling, to Sir Claude. 'But perhaps it's hardly civil for me to say that of his not objecting to have *you* in the house. If you knew some of the people he does have!'

Maisie knew them all, and none indeed were to be compared to Sir Claude. He laughed back at Mrs Beale; he looked at such moments quite as Mrs Wix, in the long stories she told her pupil, always described the lovers of her distressed beauties – 'the perfect gentleman and strikingly handsome'. He got up, to the child's regret, as if he were going. 'Oh I dare say we should be all right!'

Mrs Beale once more gathered in her little charge, holding her close and looking thoughtfully over her head at their visitor. 'It's so charming – for a man of your type – to have wanted her so much!'

'What do you know about my type?' Sir Claude laughed. 'Whatever it may be I dare say it deceives you. The truth about me is simply that I'm the most unappreciated of – what do you call the fellows? – "family-men". Yes, I'm a family-man; upon my honour I am!'

'Then why on earth,' cried Mrs Beale, 'didn't you marry a family-woman?'

Sir Claude looked at her hard. '*You* know who one marries, I think. Besides, there *are* no family-women – hanged if there are! None of them want any children – hanged if they do!'

His account of the matter was most interesting, and Maisie, as if it were of bad omen for her, stared at the picture in some dismay. At the same time she felt, through encircling arms, her protectress hesitate. 'You do come out with things! But you mean her ladyship doesn't want any – really?'

'Won't hear of them – simply. But she can't help the one she *has* got.' And with this Sir Claude's eyes rested on the little girl in a way that seemed to her to mask her mother's attitude with the consciousness of his own. 'She must make the best of her, don't you see? If only for the look of the thing, don't you know? one wants one's wife to take the proper line about her child.'

'Oh I know what one wants!' Mrs Beale cried with a competence that evidently impressed her interlocutor.

'Well, if you keep *him* up – and I dare say you've had worry enough – why shouldn't I keep Ida? What's sauce for the goose is sauce for the gander – or the other way round, don't you know? I mean to see the thing through.'

Mrs Beale, for a minute, still with her eyes on him as he leaned upon the chimneypiece, appeared to turn this over. 'You're just a wonder of kindness – that's what you are!' she said at last. 'A lady's expected to have natural feelings. But *your* horrible sex –! Isn't it a horrible sex, little love?' she demanded with her cheek upon her stepdaughter's.

'Oh I like gentlemen best,' Maisie lucidly replied.

The words were taken up merrily. 'That's a good one for *you*!' Sir Claude exclaimed to Mrs Beale.

'No,' said that lady: 'I've only to remember the women she sees at her mother's.'

'Ah they're very nice now,' Sir Claude returned.

'What do you call "nice"?'

'Well, they're all right.'

'That doesn't answer me,' said Mrs Beale; 'but I dare say you do take care of them. That makes you more of an angel to want this job too.' And she playfully whacked her smaller companion.

'I'm not an angel – I'm an old grandmother,' Sir Claude declared. 'I like babies – I always did. If we go to smash I shall look for a place as responsible nurse.'

Maisie, in her charmed mood, drank in an imputation on her years which at another moment might have been bitter; but the charm was sensibly interrupted by Mrs Beale's screwing her round and gazing fondly into her eyes, 'You're willing to leave me, you wretch?'

The little girl deliberated; even this consecrated tie had become as a cord she must suddenly snap. But she snapped it very gently. 'Isn't it my turn for mamma?'

'You're a horrible little hypocrite! The less, I think, now said about "turns" the better,' Mrs Beale made answer. '*I* know whose turn it is. You've not such a passion for your mother!'

'I say, I say: *do* look out!' Sir Claude quite amiably protested.

'There's nothing she hasn't heard. But it doesn't matter – it hasn't spoiled her. If you knew what it costs me to part with you!' she pursued to Maisie.

Sir Claude watched her as she charmingly clung to the child. 'I'm so glad you really care for her. That's so much to the good.'

Mrs Beale slowly got up, still with her hands on Maisie, but emitting a soft exhalation. 'Well, if you're glad, that may help us; for I assure you that I shall never give up any rights in her that I may consider I've acquired by my own sacrifices. I shall hold very fast to my interest in her. What seems to have happened is that she has brought you and me together.'

'She has brought you and me together,' said Sir Claude.

His cheerful echo prolonged the happy truth, and Maisie broke out almost with enthusiasm: 'I've brought you and her together!'

Her companions of course laughed anew and Mrs Beale gave her an affectionate shake. 'You little monster – take care what you do! But that's what she does do,' she continued to Sir Claude. 'She did it to me and Beale.'

'Well then,' he said to Maisie, 'you must try the trick at *our* place.' He held out his hand to her again. 'Will you come now?'

'Now – just as I am?' She turned with an immense appeal to her stepmother, taking a leap over the mountain of 'mending', the abyss of packing that had loomed and yawned before her. 'Oh *may* I?'

Mrs Beale addressed her assent to Sir Claude. 'As well so as any other way. I'll send on her things tomorrow.' Then she gave a tug to the child's coat, glancing at her up and down with some ruefulness. 'She's not turned out as I should like – her mother will pull her to pieces. But what's one to do – with nothing to do it on? And she's better than when she came – you can tell her mother that. I'm sorry to have to say it to you – but the poor child was a sight.'

'Oh I'll turn her out myself!' the visitor cordially said.

'I shall like to see how!' – Mrs Beale appeared much amused. 'You must bring her to show me – we can manage that. Good-bye, little fright!' And her last word to Sir Claude was that she would keep him up to the mark.

IX

THE idea of what she was to make up and the prodigious total it came to were kept well before Maisie at her mother's. These things were the constant occupation of Mrs Wix, who arrived there by the back stairs, but in tears of joy, the day after her own arrival. The process of making up, as to which the good lady had an immense deal to say, took, through its successive phases, so long that it heralded a term at least equal to the child's last stretch with her father. This, however, was a fuller and richer time: it bounded along to the tune of Mrs Wix's constant insistence on the energy they must both put forth. There was a fine intensity in the way the child agreed with her that under Mrs Beale and Susan Ash she had learned nothing whatever; the wildness of the rescued castaway was one of the forces that would henceforth make for a career of conquest. The year therefore rounded itself as a receptacle of retarded knowledge – a cup brimming over with the sense that now at least she was learning. Mrs Wix fed this sense from the stores of her conversation and with the immense bustle of her reminder that they must cull the fleeting hour. They were surrounded with subjects they must take at a rush and perpetually getting into the attitude of triumphant attack. They had certainly no idle hours, and the child went to bed each night as tired as from a long day's play. This had begun from the moment of their reunion, begun with all Mrs Wix had to tell her young friend of the reasons of her ladyship's extraordinary behaviour at the very first.

It took the form of her ladyship's refusal for three days to see her little girl – three days during which Sir Claude made hasty merry

dashes into the schoolroom to smooth down the odd situation, to
say 'She'll come round, you know; I assure you she'll come
round', and a little even to compensate Maisie for the indignity he
had caused her to suffer. There has never in the child's life been,
in all ways, such a delightful amount of reparation. It came out by
his sociable admission that her ladyship had not known of his visit
to her late husband's house and of his having made that person's
daughter a pretext for striking up an acquaintance with the
dreadful creature installed there. Heaven knew she wanted her
child back and had made every plan of her own for removing her;
what she couldn't for the present at least forgive any one
concerned was such an officious underhand way of bringing about
the transfer. Maisie carried more of the weight of this resentment
than even Mrs Wix's confidential ingenuity could lighten for her,
especially as Sir Claude himself was not at all ingenious, though
indeed on the other hand he was not at all crushed. He was
amused and intermittent and at moments most startling; he
impressed on his young companion, with a frankness that agitated
her much more than he seemed to guess, that he depended on her
not letting her mother, when she should see her, get anything out
of her about anything Mrs Beale might have said to him. He came
in and out; he professed, in joke, to take tremendous precautions;
he showed a positive disposition to romp. He chaffed Mrs Wix till
she was purple with the pleasure of it, and reminded Maisie of the
reticence he expected of her till she set her teeth like an Indian
captive. Her lessons these first days and indeed for long after
seemed to be all about Sir Claude, and yet she never really
mentioned to Mrs Wix that she was prepared, under his inspiring
injunction, to be vainly tortured. This lady, however, had
formulated the position of things with an acuteness that showed
how little she needed to be coached. Her explanation of
everything that seemed not quite pleasant – and if her own footing
was perilous it met that danger as well – was that her ladyship was
passionately in love. Maisie accepted this hint with infinite awe

and pressed upon it much when she was at last summoned into the presence of her mother.

There she encountered matters amid which it seemed really to help to give her a clue – an almost terrifying strangeness, full, none the less, after a little, of reverberations of Ida's old fierce and demonstrative recoveries of possession. They had been some time in the house together, and this demonstration came late. Pre-occupied, however, as Maisie was with the idea of the sentiment Sir Claude had inspired, and familiar, in addition, by Mrs Wix's anecdotes, with the ravages that in general such a sentiment could produce, she was able to make allowances for her ladyship's remarkable appearance, her violent splendour, the wonderful colour of her lips and even the hard stare, the stare of some gorgeous idol described in a story-book, that had come into her eyes in consequence of a curious thickening of their already rich circumference. Her professions and explanations were mixed with eager challenges and sudden drops, in the midst of which Maisie recognised as a memory of other years the rattle of her trinkets and the scratch of her endearments, the odour of her clothes and the jumps of her conversation. She had all her old clever way – Mrs Wix said it was 'aristocratic' – of changing the subject as she might have slammed the door in your face. The principal thing that was different was the tint of her golden hair, which had changed to a coppery red and, with the head it profusely covered, struck the child as now lifted still further aloft. This picturesque parent showed literally a grander stature and a nobler presence, things which, with some others that might have been bewildering, were handsomely accounted for by the romantic state of her affections. It was her affections, Maisie could easily see, that led Ida to break out into questions as to what had passed at the other house between that horrible woman and Sir Claude; but it was also just here that the little girl was able to recall the effect with which in earlier days she had practised the pacific art of stupidity. This art again came to her aid: her mother, in getting rid of her after an interview in which she had achieved a hollowness beyond her years, allowed her fully to understand she had not grown a bit more amusing.

She could bear that; she could bear anything that helped her to feel she had done something for Sir Claude. If she hadn't told Mrs Wix how Mrs Beale seemed to like him she certainly couldn't tell her ladyship. In the way the past revived for her there was a queer confusion. It was because mamma hated papa that she used to want to know bad things of him; but if at present she wanted to know the same of Sir Claude it was quite from the opposite motive. She was awestruck at the manner in which a lady might be affected through the passion mentioned by Mrs Wix; she held her breath with the sense of picking her steps among the tremendous things of life. What she did, however, now, after the interview with her mother, impart to Mrs Wix was that, in spite of her having had her 'good' effect, as she called it − the effect she studied, the effect of harmless vacancy − her ladyship's last words had been that her ladyship's duty by her would be thoroughly done. Over this announcement governess and pupil looked at each other in silent profundity; but as the weeks went by it had no consequences that interfered gravely with the breezy gallop of making up. Her ladyship's duty took at times the form of not seeing her child for days together, and Maisie led her life in great prosperity between Mrs Wix and kind Sir Claude. Mrs Wix had a new dress and, as she was the first to proclaim, a better position; so it all struck Maisie as a crowded brilliant life, with, for the time, Mrs Beale and Susan Ash simply 'left out' like children not invited to a Christmas party. Mrs Wix had a secret terror which, like most of her secret feelings, she discussed with her little companion, in great solemnity, by the hour: the possibility of her ladyship's coming down on them, in her sudden highbred way, with a school. But she had also a balm to this fear in a conviction of the strength of Sir Claude's grasp of the situation. He was too pleased − didn't he constantly say as much? − with the good impression made, in a wide circle, by Ida's sacrifices; and he came into the schoolroom repeatedly to let them know how beautifully he felt everything had gone off and everything would go on.

He disappeared at times for days, when his patient friends understood that her ladyship would naturally absorb him; but he always came back with the drollest stories of where he had been, a wonderful picture of society, and even with pretty presents that showed how in absence he thought of his home. Besides giving Mrs Wix by his conversation a sense that they almost themselves 'went out', he gave her a five-pound note and the history of France and an umbrella with a malachite knob, and to Maisie both chocolate-creams and story-books, besides a lovely greatcoat (which he took her out all alone to buy) and ever so many games in boxes, with printed directions, and a bright red frame for the protection of his famous photograph. The games were, as he said, to while away the evening hour; and the evening hour indeed often passed in futile attempts on Mrs Wix's part to master what 'it said' on the papers. When he asked the pair how they liked the games they always replied 'Oh immensely!' but they had earnest discussions as to whether they hadn't better appeal to him frankly for aid to understand them. This was a course their delicacy shrank from; they couldn't have told exactly why, but it was a part of their tenderness for him not to let him think they had trouble. What dazzled most was his kindness to Mrs Wix, not only the five-pound note and the 'not forgetting' her, but the perfect consideration, as she called it with an air to which her sounding of the words gave the only grandeur Maisie was to have seen her wear save on a certain occasion hereafter to be described, an occasion when the poor lady was grander than all of them put together. He shook hands with her, he recognised her, as she said, and above all, more than once, he took her, with his stepdaughter, to the pantomime and, in the crowd, coming out, publicly gave her his arm. When he met them in sunny Piccadilly he made merry and turned and walked with them, heroically suppressing his consciousness of the stamp of his company, a heroism that – needless for Mrs Wix to sound *those* words – her ladyship, though a blood-relation, was little enough the woman to be capable of. Even to the hard heart of childhood there was something tragic in such elation at such humanities: it brought home to Maisie the way her humble companion had sidled and ducked through life. But it settled the question of the degree to which Sir Claude was a gentleman: he was more of one than anybody else in the world – 'I don't care,' Mrs Wix repeatedly remarked, 'whom you may meet in grand society, nor even to whom you may be contracted in marriage.' There were questions that Maisie never asked; so her governess was spared the embarrassment of telling her if he were more of a gentleman than papa. This was not moreover from the want of opportunity, for there were no moments between them at which the topic could be irrelevant, no subject they were going into, not even the principal dates or the auxiliary verbs, in which it was further off than the turn of the page. The answer on the winter nights to the puzzle of cards and counters and little bewildering pamphlets was just to draw up to the fire and talk about him; and if the truth must be told this edifying interchange constituted for the time the little girl's chief education.

It must also be admitted that he took them far, further perhaps than was always warranted by the old-fashioned conscience, the dingy decencies, of Maisie's simple instructress. There were hours when Mrs Wix sighingly testified to the scruples she surmounted, seemed to ask what other line one *could* take with a young person whose experience had been, as it were, so peculiar. 'It isn't as if you didn't already know everything, is it, love?' and 'I can't make you any worse than you *are*, can I, darling?' – these were the terms in which the good lady justified to herself and her pupil her pleasant conversational ease. What the pupil already knew was indeed rather taken for granted than expressed, but it performed the useful function of transcending all textbooks and supplanting all studies. If the child couldn't be worse it was a comfort even to herself that she was bad – a comfort offering a broad firm support to the fundamental fact of the present crisis: the fact that mamma was fearfully jealous. This was another side of the circumstance of mamma's passion, and the deep couple in the schoolroom were not long in working round to it. It brought them face to face with the idea of the inconvenience suffered by any lady who marries a gentleman producing on other ladies the charming effect of Sir Claude. That such ladies wouldn't be able to help falling in love with him was a reflection naturally irritating to his wife. One day when some accident, some crash of a banged door or some scurry of a scared maid, had rendered this truth particularly vivid, Maisie, receptive and profound, suddenly said to her companion: 'And you, my dear, are you in love with him too?'

Even her profundity had left a margin for a laugh; so she was a trifle startled by the solemn promptitude with which Mrs Wix plumped out: 'Over head and ears. I've *never*, since you ask me, been so far gone.'

This boldness had none the less no effect of deterrence for her when, a few days later – it was because several had elapsed without a visit from Sir Claude – her governess turned the tables. 'May I ask you, miss, if *you* are?' Mrs Wix brought it out, she could see, with hesitation, but clearly intending a joke. 'Why *rather*!' the child made answer, as if in surprise at not having long ago seemed sufficiently to commit herself; on which her friend gave a sigh of apparent satisfaction. It might in fact have expressed positive relief. Everything was as it should be.

Yet it was not with them, they were very sure, that her ladyship was furious, nor because she had forbidden it that there befell at last a period – six months brought it round – when for days together he scarcely came near them. He was 'off', and Ida was 'off', and they were sometimes off together and sometimes apart; there were seasons when the simple students had the house to themselves, when the very servants seemed also to be 'off' and dinner became a reckless forage in pantries and sideboards. Mrs Wix reminded her disciple on such occasions – hungry moments often, when all the support, of the reminder was required – that the 'real life' of their companions, the brilliant society in which it was inevitable they should move and the complicated pleasures in which it was almost presumptuous of the mind to follow them, must offer features literally not to be imagined without being seen. At one of these times Maisie found her opening it out that, though the difficulties were many, it was Mrs Beale who had now become the chief. Then somehow it was brought fully to the child's knowledge that her stepmother had been making attempts to see her, that her mother had deeply resented it, that her stepfather had backed her stepmother up, that the latter had pretended to be acting as the representative of her father, and that her mother took the whole thing, in plain terms, very hard. The situation was, as Mrs Wix declared, an extraordinary muddle to be sure. Her account of it brought back to Maisie the happy vision of the way Sir Claude and Mrs Beale had made acquaintance – an incident to which, with her stepfather, though she had had little to say about it to Mrs Wix, she had during the first weeks of her stay at her mother's found more than one opportunity to revert. As to what had taken place the day Sir Claude came for her, she had been vaguely grateful to Mrs Wix for not attempting, as her mother had attempted, to put her through. That was what Sir Claude had called the process when he warned her of it, and again afterwards when he told her she was an awfully good 'chap' for having foiled it. Then it was that, well aware Mrs Beale hadn't in the least really given her up, she had asked him if he remained in communication with her and if for the time everything must really be held to be at an end between her stepmother and herself. This conversation had occurred in consequence of his one day popping into the schoolroom and finding Maisie alone.

X

HE was smoking a cigarette and he stood before the fire and looked at the meagre appointments of the room in a way that made her rather ashamed of them. Then before (on the subject of Mrs Beale) he let her 'draw' him – that was another of his words; it was astonishing how many she gathered in – he remarked that really mamma kept them rather low on the question of decorations. Mrs Wix had put up a Japanese fan and two rather grim texts; she had wished they were gayer, but they were all she happened to have. Without Sir Claude's photograph, however, the place would have been, as he said, as dull as a cold dinner. He had said as well that there were all sorts of things they ought to have; yet governess and pupil, it had to be admitted, were still divided between discussing the places where any sort of thing would look best if any sort of thing should ever come and acknowledging that mutability in the child's career which was naturally unfavourable to accumulation. She stayed long enough only to miss things, not half long enough to deserve them. The way Sir Claude looked about the schoolroom had made her feel with humility as if it were not very different from the shabby attic in which she had visited Susan Ash. Then he had said in abrupt reference to Mrs Beale: 'Do you think she really cares for you?'

'Oh awfully!' Maisie had replied.

'But, I mean, does she love you for yourself, as they call it, don't you know? Is she as fond of you, now, as Mrs Wix?'

The child turned it over. 'Oh I'm not every bit Mrs Beale has!'

Sir Claude seemed much amused at this. 'No; you're not every bit she has!'

He laughed for some moments, but that was an old story to Maisie, who was not too much disconcerted to go on: 'But she'll never give me up.'

'Well, I won't either, old boy: so that's not so wonderful, and she's not the only one. But if she's so fond of you, why doesn't she write to you?'

'Oh on account of mamma.' This was rudimentary, and she was almost surprised at the simplicity of Sir Claude's question.

'I see – that's quite right,' he answered. 'She might get at you – there are all sorts of ways. But of course there's Mrs Wix.'

'There's Mrs Wix,' Maisie lucidly concurred. 'Mrs Wix can't abide her.'

Sir Claude seemed interested. 'Oh she can't abide her? Then what does she say about her?'

'Nothing at all – because she knows I shouldn't like it. Isn't it sweet of her?' the child asked.

'Certainly; rather nice. Mrs Beale wouldn't hold her tongue for any such thing as that, would she?'

Maisie remembered how little she had done so; but she desired to protect Mrs Beale too. The only protection she could think of, however, was the plea: 'Oh at papa's, you know, they don't mind!'

At this Sir Claude only smiled. 'No, I dare say not. But here we mind, don't we? – we take care what we say. I don't suppose it's a matter on which I ought to prejudice you,' he went on; 'but I think we must on the whole be rather nicer here than at your father's. However, I don't press that; for it's the sort of question on which it's awfully awkward for you to speak. Don't worry, at any rate: I assure you I'll back you up.' Then after a moment and while he smoked he reverted to Mrs Beale and the child's first enquiry. 'I'm afraid we can't do much for her just now. I haven't seen her since that day – upon my word I haven't seen her.' The next instant, with a laugh the least bit foolish, the young man slightly coloured: he must have felt this profession of innocence to be excessive as addressed to Maisie. It was inevitable to say to her, however, that of course her mother loathed the lady of the other house. He couldn't go there again with his wife's consent, and he wasn't the man – he begged her to believe, falling once more, in spite of himself, into the scruple of showing the child he didn't trip – to go there without it. He was liable in talking with her to take the tone of her being also a man of the world. He had gone to Mrs Beale's to fetch away Maisie, but that was altogether different. Now that she was in her mother's house what pretext had he to give her mother for paying calls on her father's wife? And of course Mrs Beale couldn't come to Ida's – Ida would tear her limb from limb. Maisie, with this talk of pretexts, remembered how much Mrs Beale had made of her being a good one, and how, for such a function, it was her fate to be either much depended on or much missed. Sir Claude moreover recognised on this occasion that perhaps things would take a turn later on; and he wound up by saying: 'I'm sure she does sincerely care for you – how can she possibly help it? She's very young and very pretty and very clever: I think she's charming. But we must walk very straight. If you'll help me, you know, I'll help *you*,' he concluded in the pleasant fraternising, equalising, not a bit patronising way which made the child ready to go through anything for him and the beauty of which, as she dimly felt, was that it was so much less a deceitful descent to her years than a real indifference to them.

It gave her moments of secret rapture – moments of believing she might help him indeed. The only mystification in this was the imposing time of life that her elders spoke of as youth. For Sir Claude then Mrs Beale was 'young', just as for Mrs Wix Sir Claude was: that was one of the merits for which Mrs Wix most commended him. What therefore was Maisie herself, and, in another relation to the matter, what therefore was mamma? It took her some time to puzzle out with the aid of an experiment or two that it wouldn't do to talk about mamma's youth. She even went so far one day, in the presence of that lady's thick colour and marked lines, as to wonder if it would occur to any one but herself to do so. Yet if she wasn't young then she was old; and this threw an odd light on her having a husband of a different generation. Mr Farange was still older – that Maisie perfectly knew; and it brought her in due course to the perception of how much more, since Mrs Beale was younger than Sir Claude, papa must be older than Mrs Beale. Such discoveries were disconcerting and even a trifle confounding: these persons, it appeared, were not of the age they ought to be. This was somehow particularly the case with mamma, and the fact made her reflect with some relief on her not having gone with Mrs Wix into the question of Sir Claude's attachment to his wife. She was conscious that in confining their attention to the state of her ladyship's own affections they had been controlled – Mrs Wix perhaps in especial – by delicacy and even by embarrassment. The end of her colloquy with her stepfather in the schoolroom was her saying: 'Then if we're not to see Mrs Beale at all it isn't what she seemed to think when you came for me.'

He looked rather blank. 'What did she seem to think?'

'Why that I've brought you together.'

'She thought that?' Sir Claude asked.

Maisie was surprised at his already forgetting it. 'Just as I had brought papa and her. Don't you remember she said so?'

It came back to Sir Claude in a peal of laughter. 'Oh yes – she said so!'

'And *you* said so,' Maisie lucidly pursued.

He recovered, with increasing mirth, the whole occasion. 'And *you* said so!' he retorted as if they were playing a game.

'Then were we all mistaken?'

He considered a little. 'No, on the whole not. I dare say it's just what you *have* done. We *are* together – it's really most odd. She's thinking of us – of you and me – though we don't meet. And I've no doubt you'll find it will be all right when you go back to her.'

'Am I going back to her?' Maisie brought out with a little gasp which was like a sudden clutch of the happy present.

It appeared to make Sir Claude grave a moment; it might have made him feel the weight of the pledge his action had given. 'Oh some day, I suppose! We've plenty of time.'

'I've such a tremendous lot to make up,' Maisie said with a sense of great boldness.

'Certainly, and you must make up every hour of it. Oh I'll *see* that you do!'

This was encouraging; and to show cheerfully that she was reassured she replied: 'That's what Mrs Wix sees too.'

'Oh yes,' said Sir Claude; 'Mrs Wix and I are shoulder to shoulder.'

Maisie took in a little this strong image; after which she exclaimed: 'Then I've done it also to you and her – I've brought *you* together!'

'Blest if you haven't!' Sir Claude laughed. 'And more, upon my word, than any of the lot. Oh you've done for *us*! Now if you could – as I suggested, you know, that day – only manage me and your mother!'

The child wondered. 'Bring you and *her* together?'

'You see we're not together – not a bit. But I oughtn't to tell you such things; all the more that you won't really do it – not you. No, old chap,' the young man continued; 'there you'll break down. But it won't matter – we'll rub along. The great thing is that you and I are all right.'

'*We're* all right!' Maisie echoed devoutly. But the next moment, in the light of what he had just said, she asked: 'How shall I ever leave you?' It was as if she must somehow take care of him.

His smile did justice to her anxiety. 'Oh well, you needn't! It won't come to that.'

'Do you mean that when I do go you'll go with me?'

Sir Claude cast about. 'Not exactly "with" you perhaps; but I shall never be far off.'

'But how do you know where mamma may take you?'

He laughed again. 'I don't, I confess!' Then he had an idea, though something too jocose. 'That will be for you to see – that she shan't take me too far.'

'How can I help it?' Maisie enquired in surprise. 'Mamma doesn't care for me,' she said very simply. 'Not really.' Child as she was, her little long history was in the words; and it was as impossible to contradict her as if she had been venerable.

Sir Claude's silence was an admission of this, and still more the tone in which he presently replied: 'That won't prevent her from – some time or other – leaving me with you.'

'Then we'll live together?' she eagerly demanded.

'I'm afraid,' said Sir Claude, smiling, 'that that will be Mrs Beale's real chance.'

Her eagerness just slightly dropped at this; she remembered Mrs Wix's pronouncement that it was all an extraordinary muddle. 'To take me again? Well, can't you come to see me there?'

'Oh I dare say!'

Though there were parts of childhood Maisie had lost she had all childhood's preference for the particular promise. 'Then you *will* come – you'll come often, won't you?' she insisted; while at the moment she spoke the door opened for the return of Mrs Wix. Sir Claude hereupon, instead of replying, gave her a look which left her silent and embarrassed.

When he again found privacy convenient, however – which happened to be long in coming – he took up their conversation very much where it had dropped. 'You see, my dear, if I shall be able to go to you at your father's it yet isn't at all the same thing for Mrs Beale to come to you here.' Maisie gave a thoughtful assent to this proposition, though conscious she could scarcely herself say just where the difference would lie. She felt how much her stepfather saved her, as he said with his habitual amusement, the trouble of that. 'I shall probably be able to go to Mrs Beale's without your mother's knowing it.'

Maisie stared with a certain thrill at the dramatic element in this.

'And she couldn't come here without mamma's –?' She was unable to articulate the word for what mamma would do.

'My dear child, Mrs Wix would tell of it.'

'But I thought,' Maisie objected, 'that Mrs Wix and you –'

'Are such brothers-in-arms?' – Sir Claude caught her up. 'Oh yes, about everything but Mrs Beale. And if you should suggest,' he went on, 'that we might somehow or other hide her peeping in from Mrs Wix –'

'Oh I don't suggest *that*!' Maisie in turn cut him short.

Sir Claude looked as if he could indeed quite see why. 'No; it would really be impossible.' There came to her from this glance at what they might hide the first small glimpse of something in him that she wouldn't have expected. There had been times when she had had to make the best of the impression that she was herself deceitful; yet she had never concealed anything bigger than a thought. Of course she now concealed this thought of how strange it would be to see *him* hide; and while she was so actively engaged he continued: 'Besides, you know, I'm not afraid of your father.'

'And you are of my mother?'

'Rather, old man!' Sir Claude returned.

XI

IT must not be supposed that her ladyship's intermissions were not qualified by demonstrations of another order – triumphal entries and breathless pauses during which she seemed to take of everything in the room, from the state of the ceiling to that of her daughter's boot-toes, a survey that was rich in intentions. Sometimes she sat down and sometimes she surged about, but her attitude wore equally in either case the grand air of the practical. She found so much to deplore that she left a great deal to expect, and bristled so with calculation that she seemed to scatter remedies and pledges. Her visits were as good as an outfit; her manner, as Mrs Wix once said, as good as a pair of curtains; but she was a person addicted to extremes – sometimes barely speaking to her child and sometimes pressing this tender shoot to a bosom cut, as Mrs Wix had also observed, remarkably low. She was always in a fearful hurry, and the lower the bosom was cut the more it was to be gathered she was wanted elsewhere. She usually broke in alone, but sometimes Sir Claude was with her, and during all the earlier period there was nothing on which these appearances had had so delightful a bearing as on the way her ladyship was, as Mrs Wix expressed it, under the spell. 'But *isn't* she under it!' Maisie used in thoughtful but familiar reference to exclaim after Sir Claude had swept mamma away in peals of natural laughter. Not even in the old days of the convulsed ladies had she heard mamma laugh so freely as in these moments of conjugal surrender, to the gaiety of which even a little girl could see she had at last a right – a little girl whose thoughtfulness was now all happy selfish meditation on good omens and future fun.

Unaccompanied, in subsequent hours, and with an effect of changing to meet a change, Ida took a tone superficially disconcerting and abrupt – the tone of having, at an immense cost, made over everything to Sir Claude and wishing others to know that if everything wasn't right it was because Sir Claude was so dreadfully vague. 'He has made from the first such a row about you,' she said on one occasion to Maisie, 'that I've told him to do for you himself and try how he likes it – see? I've washed my hands of you; I've made you over to him; and if you're discontented it's on him, please, you'll come down. So don't haul poor *me* up – I assure you I've worries enough.' One of these, visibly, was that the spell rejoiced in by the schoolroom fire was already in danger of breaking; another was that she was finally forced to make no secret of her husband's unfitness for real responsibilities. The day came indeed when her breathless auditors learnt from her in bewilderment that what ailed him was that he was, alas, simply not serious. Maisie wept on Mrs Wix's bosom after hearing that Sir Claude was a butterfly; considering moreover that her governess but half-patched it up in coming out at various moments the next few days with the opinion that it was proper to his 'station' to be careless and free. That had been proper to every one's station that she had yet encountered save poor Mrs Wix's own, and the particular merit of Sir Claude had seemed precisely that he was different from every one. She talked with him, however, as time went on, very freely about her mother; being with him, in this relation, wholly without the fear that had kept her silent before her father – the fear of bearing tales and making bad things worse. He appeared to accept the idea that he had taken her over and made her, as he said, his particular lark; he quite agreed also that he was an awful fraud and an idle beast and a sorry dunce. And he never said a word to her against her mother – he only remained dumb and discouraged in the face of her ladyship's own overtopping earnestness. There were occasions when he even spoke as if he had wrenched his little charge from the arms of a parent who had fought for her tooth and nail.

This was the very moral of a scene that flashed into vividness one day when the four happened to meet without company in the drawing-room and Maisie found herself clutched to her mother's breast and passionately sobbed and shrieked over, made the subject of a demonstration evidently sequent to some sharp passage just enacted. The connection required that while she almost cradled the child in her arms Ida should speak of her as hideously, as fatally estranged, and should rail at Sir Claude as the cruel author of the outrage. 'He has taken you *from* me,' she cried; 'he has set you *against* me, and you've been won away and your horrid little mind has been poisoned! You've gone over to him, you've given yourself up to side against me and hate me. You never open your mouth to me – you know you don't; and you chatter to him like a dozen magpies. Don't lie about it – I hear you all over the place. You hang about him in a way that's barely decent – he can do what he likes with you. Well then, let him, to his heart's content: he has been in such a hurry to take you that we'll see if it suits him to keep you. I'm very good to break my heart about it when you've no more feeling for me than a clammy little fish!' She suddenly thrust the child away and, as a disgusted admission of failure, sent her flying across the room into the arms of Mrs Wix, whom at this moment and even in the whirl of her transit Maisie saw, very red, exchange a quick queer look with Sir Claude.

The impression of the look remained with her, confronting her with such a critical little view of her mother's explosion that she felt the less ashamed of herself for incurring the reproach with which she had been cast off. Her father had once called her a heartless little beast, and now, though decidedly scared, she was as stiff and cold as if the description had been just. She was not even frightened enough to cry, which would have been a tribute to her mother's wrongs: she was only, more than anything else, curious about the opinion mutely expressed by their companions. Taking the earliest opportunity to question Mrs Wix on this subject she elicited the remarkable reply: 'Well, my dear, it's her ladyship's game, and we must just hold on like grim death.' Maisie could interpret at her leisure these ominous words. Her reflections indeed at this moment thickened apace, and one of them made her sure that her governess had conversations, private, earnest and not infrequent, with her denounced stepfather. She perceived in the light of a second episode that something beyond her knowledge had taken place in the house. The things beyond her knowledge – numerous enough in truth – had not hitherto, she believed, been the things that had been nearest to her: she had even had in the past a small smug conviction that in the domestic labyrinth she always kept the clue. This time too, however, she at last found out – with the discreet aid, it had to be confessed, of Mrs Wix. Sir Claude's own assistance was abruptly taken from her, for his comment on her ladyship's game was to start on the spot, quite alone, for Paris, evidently because he wished to show a spirit when accused of bad behaviour. He might be fond of his stepdaughter, Maisie felt, without wishing her to be after all thrust on him in such a way; his absence therefore, it was clear, was a protest against the thrusting. It was while this absence lasted that our young lady finally discovered what had happened in the house to be that her mother was no longer in love.

The limit of a passion for Sir Claude had certainly been reached, she judged, some time before the day on which her ladyship burst suddenly into the schoolroom to introduce Mr Perriam, who, as she announced from the doorway to Maisie, wouldn't believe his ears that one had a great hoyden of a daughter. Mr Perriam was short and massive – Mrs Wix remarked afterwards that he was 'too fat for the pace'; and it would have been difficult to say of him whether his head were more bald or his black moustache more bushy. He seemed also to have moustaches over his eyes, which, however, by no means prevented these polished little globes from rolling round the room as if they had been billiard-balls impelled by Ida's celebrated stroke. Mr Perriam wore on the hand that pulled his moustache a diamond of dazzling lustre, in consequence

of which and of his general weight and mystery our young lady
observed on his departure that if he had only had a turban he would
have been quite her idea of a heathen Turk.

'He's quite my idea,' Mrs Wix replied, 'of a heathen Jew.'

'Well, I mean,' said Maisie, 'of a person who comes from the
East.'

'That's where he *must* come from,' her governess opined – 'he
comes from the City.' In a moment she added as if she knew all
about him. 'He's one of those people who have lately broken out.
He'll be immensely rich.'

'On the death of his papa?' the child interestedly enquired.

'Dear no – nothing hereditary. I mean he has made a mass of
money.'

'How much, do you think?' Maisie demanded.

Mrs Wix reflected and sketched it. 'Oh many millions.'

'A hundred?'

Mrs Wix was not sure of the number, but there were enough of
them to have seemed to warm up for the time the penury of the
schoolroom – to linger there as an afterglow of the hot heavy light
Mr Perriam sensibly shed. This was also, no doubt, on his part, an
effect of that enjoyment of life with which, among her elders,
Maisie had been in contact from her earliest years – the sign of
happy maturity, the old familiar note of overflowing cheer. 'How
d'ye do, ma'am? How d'ye do, little miss?' – he laughed and
nodded at the gaping figures. 'She has brought me up for a peep –
it's true I wouldn't take you on trust. She's always talking about
you, but she'd never produce you; so today I challenged her on the
spot. Well, you ain't a myth, my dear – I back down on that,' the
visitor went on to Maisie; 'nor you either, miss, though you might
be, to be sure!'

'I bored him with you, darling – I bore every one,' Ida said, 'and
to prove that you *are* a sweet thing, as well as a fearfully old one, I
told him he could judge for himself. So now he sees that you're a
dreadful bouncing business and that your poor old Mummy's at

least sixty!' – and her ladyship smiled at Mr Perriam with the charm that her daughter had heard imputed to her at papa's by the merry gentlemen who had so often wished to get from him what they called a 'rise'. Her manner at that instant gave the child a glimpse more vivid than any yet enjoyed of the attraction that papa, in remarkable language, always denied she could put forth.

Mr Perriam, however, clearly recognised it in the humour with which he met her. 'I never said you ain't wonderful – did I ever say it, hey?' and he appealed with pleasant confidence to the testimony of the schoolroom, about which itself also he evidently felt something might be expected of him. 'So this is their little place, hey? Charming, charming, charming!' he repeated as he vaguely looked round. The interrupted students clung together as if they had been personally exposed; but Ida relieved their embarrassment by a hunch of her high shoulders. This time the smile she addressed to Mr Perriam had a beauty of sudden sadness. 'What on earth is a poor woman to do?'

The visitor's grimace grew more marked as he continued to look, and the conscious little schoolroom felt still more like a cage at a menagerie. 'Charming, charming, charming!' Mr Perriam insisted; but the parenthesis closed with a prompt click. 'There you are!' said her ladyship. 'By-bye!' she sharply added. The next minute they were on the stairs, and Mrs Wix and her companion, at the open door and looking mutely at each other, were reached by the sound of the large social current that carried them back to their life.

It was singular perhaps after this that Maisie never put a question about Mr Perriam, and it was still more singular that by the end of a week she knew all she didn't ask. What she most particularly knew – and the information came to her, unsought, straight from Mrs Wix – was that Sir Claude wouldn't at all care for the visits of a millionaire who was in and out of the upper rooms. How little he would care was proved by the fact that under the sense of them Mrs Wix's discretion broke down altogether; she was capable of a

transfer of allegiance, capable, at the altar of propriety, of a
desperate sacrifice of her ladyship. As against Mrs Beale, she more
than once intimated, she had been willing to do the best for her,
but as against Sir Claude she could do nothing for her at all. It was
extraordinary the number of things that, still without a question,
Maisie knew by the time her stepfather came back from Paris –
came bringing her a splendid apparatus for painting in water-
colours and bringing Mrs Wix, by a lapse of memory that would
have been droll if it had not been a trifle disconcerting, a second
and even a more elegant umbrella. He had forgotten all about the
first, with which, buried in as many wrappers as a mummy of the
Pharaohs, she wouldn't for the world have done anything so
profane as use it. Maisie knew above all that though she was now,
by what she called an informal understanding, on Sir Claude's
'side', she had yet not uttered a word to him about Mr Perriam.
That gentleman became therefore a kind of flourishing public
secret, out of the depths of which governess and pupil looked at
each other portentously from the time their friend was restored to
them. He was restored in great abundance, and it was marked that,
though he appeared to have felt the need to take a stand against the
risk of being too roughly saddled with the offspring of others, he at
this period exposed himself more than ever before to the presumption of having created expectations.

If it had become now, for that matter, a question of sides, there
was at least a certain amount of evidence as to where they all were.
Maisie of course, in such a delicate position, was on nobody's; but
Sir Claude had all the air of being on hers. If therefore Mrs Wix
was on Sir Claude's, her ladyship on Mr Perriam's and Mr Perriam
presumably on her ladyship's, this left only Mrs Beale and Mr
Farange to account for. Mrs Beale clearly was, like Sir Claude, on
Maisie's, and papa, it was to be supposed, on Mrs Beale's. Here
indeed was a slight ambiguity, as papa's being on Mrs Beale's didn't
somehow seem to place him quite on his daughter's. It sounded, as
this young lady thought it over, very much like puss-in-the-corner,

and she could only wonder if the distribution of parties would lead to a rushing to and fro and a changing of places. She was in the presence, she felt, of restless change: wasn't it restless enough that her mother and her stepfather should already be on different sides? That was the great thing that had domestically happened. Mrs Wix, besides, had turned another face: she had never been exactly gay, but her gravity was now an attitude as public as a posted placard. She seemed to sit in her new dress and brood over her lost delicacy, which had become almost as doleful a memory as that of poor Clara Matilda. 'It *is* hard for him,' she often said to her companion; and it was surprising how competent on this point Maisie was conscious of being to agree with her. Hard as it was, however, Sir Claude had never shown to greater advantage than in the gallant generous sociable way he carried it off: a way that drew from Mrs Wix a hundred expressions of relief at his not having suffered it to embitter him. It threw him more and more at last into the schoolroom, where he had plainly begun to recognise that if he was to have the credit of perverting the innocent child he might also at least have the amusement. He never came into the place without telling its occupants that they were the nicest people in the house – a remark which always led them to say to each other 'Mr Perriam!' as loud as ever compressed lips and enlarged eyes could make them articulate. He caused Maisie to remember what she had said to Mrs Beale about his having the nature of a good nurse, and, rather more than she intended before Mrs Wix, to bring the whole thing out by once remarking to him that none of her good nurses had smoked quite so much in the nursery. This had no more effect than it was meant to on his cigarettes: he was always smoking, but always declaring that it was death to him not to lead a domestic life.

He led one after all in the schoolroom, and there were hours of late evening, when she had gone to bed, that Maisie knew he sat there talking with Mrs Wix of how to meet his difficulties. His consideration for this unfortunate woman even in the midst of them continued to show him as the perfect gentleman and lifted the subject of his courtesy into an upper air of beatitude in which her very pride had the hush of anxiety. 'He leans on me – he leans on me!' she only announced from time to time; and she was more surprised than amused when, later on, she accidentally found she had given her pupil the impression of a support literally supplied by her person. This glimpse of a misconception led her to be explicit – to put before the child, with an air of mourning indeed for such a stoop to the common, that what they talked about in the small hours, as they said, was the question of his taking right hold of life. The life she wanted him to take right hold of was the public: 'she' being, I hasten to add, in this connection, not the mistress of his fate, but only Mrs Wix herself. She had phrases about him that were full of easy understanding, yet full of morality. 'He's a wonderful nature, but he can't live like the lilies. He's all right, you know, but he must have a high interest.' She had more than once remarked that his affairs were sadly involved, but that they must get him – Maisie and she together apparently – into Parliament. The child took it from her with a flutter of importance that Parliament was his natural sphere, and she was the less prepared to recognise a hindrance as she had never heard of any affairs whatever that were not involved. She had in the old days once been told by Mrs Beale that her very own were, and with the refreshment of knowing that she *had* affairs the information hadn't in the least overwhelmed her. It was true and perhaps a little alarming that she had never heard of any such matters since then. Full of charm at any rate was the prospect of some day getting Sir Claude in; especially after Mrs Wix, as the fruit of more midnight colloquies, once went so far as to observe that she really believed it was all that was wanted to save him. This critic, with these words, struck her disciple as cropping up, after the manner of mamma when mamma talked, quite in a new place. The child stared as at the jump of kangaroo.

'Save him from what?'

Mrs Wix debated, then covered a still greater distance. 'Why just from awful misery.'

XII

SHE had not at the moment explained her ominous speech, but the light of remarkable events soon enabled her companion to read it. It may indeed be said that these days brought on a high quickening of Maisie's direct perceptions, of her sense of freedom to make out things for herself. This was helped by an emotion intrinsically far from sweet – the increase of the alarm that had most haunted her meditations. She had no need to be told, as on the morrow of the revelation of Sir Claude's danger she was told by Mrs Wix, that her mother wanted more and more to know why the devil her father didn't send for her: she had too long expected mamma's curiosity on this point to express itself sharply. Maisie could meet such pressure so far as meeting it was to be in a position to reply, in words directly inspired, that papa would be hanged before he'd again be saddled with her. She therefore recognised the hour that in troubled glimpses she had long foreseen, the hour when – the phrase for it came back to her from Mrs Beale – with two fathers, two mothers and two homes, six protections in all, she shouldn't know 'wherever' to go. Such apprehension as she felt on this score was not diminished by the fact that Mrs Wix herself was suddenly white with terror: a circumstance leading Maisie to the further knowledge that this lady was still more scared on her own behalf than on that of her pupil. A governess who had only one frock was not likely to have either two fathers or two mothers: accordingly if even with these resources Maisie was to be in the streets, where in the name of all that was dreadful was poor Mrs Wix to be? She had had, it appeared, a tremendous brush with Ida, which had begun and ended with the request that she would be pleased on the spot

to 'bundle'. It had come suddenly but completely, this signal of
which she had gone in fear. The companions confessed to each
other the dread each had hidden the worst of, but Mrs Wix was
better off than Maisie in having a plan of defence. She declined
indeed to communicate it till it was quite mature; but meanwhile,
she hastened to declare, her feet were firm in the schoolroom.
They could only be loosened by force: she would 'leave' for the
police perhaps, but she wouldn't leave for mere outrage. That
would be to play her ladyship's game, and it would take another
turn of the screw to make her desert her darling. Her ladyship had
come down with extraordinary violence: it had been one of many
symptoms of a situation strained – 'between them all', as Mrs Wix
said, 'but especially between the two' – to the point of God only
knew what.

Her description of the crisis made the child balance. 'Between
which two? – papa and mamma?'

'Dear no. I mean between your mother and *him*.'

Maisie, in this, recognised an opportunity to be really deep.
'"Him"? – Mr Perriam?'

She fairly brought a blush to the scared face. 'Well, my dear, I
must say what you *don't* know ain't worth mentioning. That it
won't go on for ever with Mr Perriam – since I *must* meet you –
who can suppose? But I meant dear Sir Claude.'

Maisie stood corrected rather than abashed. 'I see. But it's about
Mr Perriam he's angry?'

Mrs Wix waited. 'He says he's not.'

'Not angry? He has told you so?'

Mrs Wix looked at her hard. 'Not about *him*.'

'Then about some one else?'

Mrs Wix looked at her harder. 'About some one else.'

'Lord Eric?' the child promptly brought forth.

At this, of a sudden, her governess was more agitated. 'Oh why,
little unfortunate, should we discuss their dreadful names?' – and
she threw herself for the millionth time on Maisie's neck. It took

her pupil but a moment to feel that she quivered with insecurity, and, the contact of her terror aiding, the pair in another instant were sobbing in each other's arms. Then it was that, completely relaxed, demoralised as she had never been, Mrs Wix suffered her wound to bleed and her resentment to gush. Her great bitterness was that Ida had called her false, denounced her hypocrisy and duplicity, reviled her spying and tattling, her lying and grovelling to Sir Claude. 'Me, *me*,' the poor woman wailed, 'who've seen what I've seen and gone through everything only to cover her up and ease her off and smooth her down? If I've been an 'ipocrite it's the other way round: I've pretended, to him and to her, to myself and to you and to every one, *not* to see! It serves me right to have held my tongue before such horrors!' What horrors they were her companion forbore too closely to enquire, showing even signs not a few of an ability to take them for granted. That put the couple more than ever, in this troubled sea, in the same boat, so that with the consciousness of ideas on the part of her fellow mariner Maisie could sit close and wait. Sir Claude on the morrow came in to tea, and then the ideas were produced. It was extraordinary how the child's presence drew out their full strength. The principal one was startling, but Maisie appreciated the courage with which her governess handled it. It simply consisted of the proposal that whenever and wherever they should seek refuge Sir Claude should consent to share their asylum. On his protesting with all the warmth in nature against this note of secession she asked what else in the world was left to them if her ladyship should stop supplies.

'Supplies be hanged, my dear woman!' said their delightful friend. 'Leave supplies to me – I'll take care of supplies.'

Mrs Wix rose to it. 'Well, it's exactly because I knew you'd be so glad to do so that I put the question before you. There's a way to look after us better than any other. The way's just to come along with us.'

It hung before Maisie, Mrs Wix's way, like a glittering picture, and she clasped her hands in ecstasy. 'Come along, come along, come along!'

Sir Claude looked from his stepdaughter back to her governess. 'Do you mean leave this house and take up my abode with you?'

'It will be the right thing – if you feel as you've told me you feel.' Mrs Wix, sustained and uplifted, was now as clear as a bell.

Sir Claude had the air of trying to recall what he had told her; then the light broke that was always breaking to make his face more pleasant. 'It's your happy thought that I shall take a house for you?'

'For the wretched homeless child. Any roof – over *our* heads – will do for us; but of course for you it will have to be something really nice.'

Sir Claude's eyes reverted to Maisie, rather hard, as she thought; and there was a shade in his very smile that seemed to show her – though she also felt it didn't show Mrs Wix – that the accommodation prescribed must loom to him pretty large. The next moment, however, he laughed gaily enough. 'My dear lady, you exaggerate tremendously *my* poor little needs.' Mrs Wix had once mentioned to her young friend that when Sir Claude called her his dear lady he could do anything with her; and Maisie felt a certain anxiety to see what he would do now. Well, he only addressed her a remark of which the child herself was aware of feeling the force. 'Your plan appeals to me immensely; but of course – don't you see? – I shall have to consider the position I put myself in by leaving my wife.'

'You'll also have to remember,' Mrs Wix replied, 'that if you don't look out your wife won't give you time to consider. Her ladyship will leave *you*.'

'Ah my good friend, I do look out!' the young man returned while Maisie helped herself afresh to bread and butter. 'Of course if that happens I shall have somehow to turn round; but I hope with all my heart it won't. I beg your pardon,' he continued to his stepdaughter, 'for appearing to discuss that sort of possibility under your sharp little nose. But the fact is I *forget* half the time that Ida's your sainted mother.'

'So do I!' said Maisie, her mouth full of bread and butter and to put him the more in the right.

Her protectress, at this, was upon her again. 'The little desolate precious pet!' For the rest of the conversation she was enclosed in Mrs Wix's arms, and as they sat there interlocked Sir Claude, before them with his teacup, looked down at them in deepening thought. Shrink together as they might they couldn't help, Maisie felt, being a very large lumpish image of what Mrs Wix required of his slim fineness. She knew moreover that this lady didn't make it better by adding in a moment: 'Of course *we* shouldn't dream of a whole house. Any sort of little lodging, however humble, would be only too blest.'

'But it would have to be something that would hold us all,' said Sir Claude.

'Oh yes,' Mrs Wix concurred; 'the whole point's our being together. While you're waiting, before you act, for her ladyship to take some step, our position here will come to an impossible pass. You don't know what I went through with her for you yesterday – and for our poor darling; but it's not a thing I can promise you often to face again. She cast me out in horrible language – she has instructed the servants not to wait on me.'

'Oh the poor servants are all right!' Sir Claude eagerly cried.

'They're certainly better than their mistress. It's too dreadful that I should sit here and say of your wife, Sir Claude, and of Maisie's own mother, that she's lower than a domestic; but my being betrayed into such remarks is just a reason the more for our getting away. I shall stay till I'm taken by the shoulders, but that may happen any day. What also may perfectly happen, you must permit me to repeat, is that she'll go off to get rid of us.'

'Oh if she'll only do that!' Sir Claude laughed. 'That would be the very making of us!'

'Don't say it – don't say it!' Mrs Wix pleaded. 'Don't speak of anything so fatal. You know what I mean. We must all cling to the right. You mustn't be bad.'

Sir Claude set down his tea-cup; he had become more grave and he pensively wiped his moustache. 'Won't all the world say I'm awful if I leave the house before – before she has bolted? They'll say it was my doing so that made her bolt.'

Maisie could grasp the force of this reasoning, but it offered no check to Mrs Wix. 'Why need you mind that – if you've done it for so high a motive? Think of the beauty of it,' the good lady pressed.

'Of bolting with *you*?' Sir Claude ejaculated.

She faintly smiled – she even faintly coloured. 'So far from doing you harm it will do you the highest good. Sir Claude, if you'll listen to me, it will save you.'

'Save me from what?'

Maisie, at this question, waited with renewed suspense for an answer that would bring the thing to some finer point than their companion had brought it to before. But there was on the contrary only more mystification in Mrs Wix's reply. 'Ah from you know what!'

'Do you mean from some other woman!'

'Yes – from a real bad one.'

Sir Claude at least, the child could see, was not mystified; so little indeed that a smile of intelligence broke afresh in his eyes. He turned them in vague discomfort to Maisie, and then something in the way she met them caused him to chuck her playfully under the chin. It was not till after this that he good-naturedly met Mrs Wix. 'You think me much worse than I am.'

'If that were true,' she returned, 'I wouldn't appeal to you. I do, Sir Claude, in the name of all that's good in you – and oh so earnestly! We can help each other. What you'll do for our young friend here I needn't say. That isn't even what I want to speak of now. What I want to speak of is what you'll *get* – don't you see? – from such an opportunity to take hold. Take hold of *us* – take hold of *her*. Make her your duty – make her your life: she'll repay you a thousand-fold!'

It was to Mrs Wix, during this appeal, that Maisie's contemplation transferred itself: partly because, though her heart was in her throat for trepidation, her delicacy deterred her from appearing herself to press the question; partly from the coercion of seeing Mrs Wix come out as Mrs Wix had never come before – not even on the day of her call at Mrs Beale's with the news of mamma's marriage. On that day Mrs Beale had surpassed her in dignity, but nobody could have surpassed her now. There was in fact at this moment a fascination for her pupil in the hint she seemed to give that she had still more of that surprise behind. So the sharpened sense of spectatorship was the child's main support, the long habit, from the first, of seeing herself in discussion and finding in the fury of it – she had had a glimpse of the game of football – a sort of compensation for the doom of a peculiar passivity. It gave her often an odd air of being present at her history in as separate a manner as if she could only get at experience by flattening her nose against a pane of glass. Such she felt to be the application of her nose while she waited for the effect of Mrs Wix's eloquence. Sir Claude, however, didn't keep her long in a position so ungraceful: he sat down and opened his arms to her as he had done the day he came for her at her father's, and while he held her there, looking at her kindly, but as if their companion had brought the blood a good deal to his face, he said:

'Dear Mrs Wix is magnificent, but she's rather too grand about it. I mean the situation isn't after all quite so desperate or quite so simple. But I give you my word before her, and I give it to her before you, that I'll never, never, forsake you. Do you hear that, old fellow, and do you take it in? I'll stick to you through everything.'

Maisie did take it in – took it with a long tremor of all her little being; and then as, to emphasise it, he drew her closer she buried her head on his shoulder and cried without sound and without pain. While she was so engaged she became aware that his own breast was agitated, and gathered from it with rapture that his tears were as silently flowing. Presently she heard a loud sob from Mrs Wix – Mrs Wix was the only one who made a noise.

She was to have made, for some time, none other but this, though within a few days, in conversation with her pupil, she described her intercourse with Ida as little better than the state of being battered. There was as yet nevertheless no attempt to eject her by force, and she recognised that Sir Claude, taking such a stand as never before, had intervened with passion and with success. As Maisie remembered – and remembered wholly without disdain – that he had told her he was afraid of her ladyship, the little girl took this act of resolution as a proof of what, in the spirit of the engagement sealed by all their tears, he was really prepared to do. Mrs Wix spoke to her of the pecuniary sacrifice by which she herself purchased the scant security she enjoyed and which, if it was a defence against the hand of violence, yet left her exposed to incredible rudeness. Didn't her ladyship find every hour of the day some artful means to humiliate and trample upon her? There was a quarter's salary owing her – a great name, even Maisie could suspect, for a small matter; she should never see it as long as she lived, but keeping quiet about it put her ladyship, thank heaven, a little in one's power. Now that he was doing so much else she could never have the grossness to apply for it to Sir Claude. He had sent home for schoolroom consumption a huge frosted cake, a wonderful delectable mountain with geological strata of jam, which might, with economy, see them through many days of their siege; but it was none the less known to Mrs Wix that his affairs were more and more involved, and her fellow partaker looked back tenderly, in the light of these involutions, at the expression of face with which he had greeted the proposal that he should set up another establishment. Maisie felt that if their maintenance should hang by a thread they must still demean themselves with the highest delicacy. What he was doing was simply acting without delay, so far as his embarrassments permitted, on the inspiration of his elder friend. There was at this season a wonderful month of May – as soft as a drop of the wind in a gale that had kept one awake – when he took out his stepdaughter with a fresh alacrity and they rambled the great town in search, as Mrs Wix called it, of combined amusement and instruction.

They rode on the top of 'buses; they visited outlying parks; they went to cricket-matches where Maisie fell asleep; they tried a hundred places for the best one to have tea. This was his direct way of rising to Mrs Wix's grand lesson – of making his little accepted charge his duty and his life. They dropped, under incontrollable impulses, into shops that they agreed were too big, to look at things that they agreed were too small, and it was during these hours that Mrs Wix, alone at home, but a subject of regretful reference as they pulled off their gloves for refreshment, subsequently described herself as least sheltered from the blows her ladyship had achieved such ingenuity in dealing. She again and again repeated that she wouldn't so much have minded having her 'attainments' held up to scorn and her knowledge of every subject denied, hadn't she been branded as 'low' in character and tone. There was by this time no pretence on the part of any one of denying it to be fortunate that her ladyship habitually left London every Saturday and was more and more disposed to a return late in the week. It was almost equally public that she regarded as a preposterous 'pose', and indeed as a direct insult to herself, her husband's attitude of staying behind to look after a child for whom the most elaborate provision had been made. If there was a type Ida despised, Sir Claude communicated to Maisie, it was the man who pottered about town of a Sunday; and he also mentioned how often she had declared to him that if he had a grain of spirit he would be ashamed to accept a menial position about Mr Farange's daughter. It was her lady-ship's contention that he was in craven fear of his predecessor – otherwise he would recognise it as an obligation of plain decency to protect his wife against the outrage of that person's barefaced attempt to swindle her. The swindle was that Mr Farange put upon her the whole intolerable burden; 'and even when I pay for you myself,' Sir Claude averred to his young friend, 'she accuses me the more of truckling and grovelling.' It was Mrs Wix's conviction, they both knew, arrived at on independent grounds, that Ida's weekly excursions were feelers for a more considerable absence. If she came back later each week the week would be sure to arrive when she wouldn't come back at all. This appearance had of course much to do with Mrs Wix's actual valour. Could they but hold out long enough the snug little home with Sir Claude would find itself informally established.

XIII

THIS might moreover have been taken to be the sense of a remark made by her stepfather as – one rainy day when the streets were all splash and two umbrellas unsociable and the wanderers had sought shelter in the National Gallery – Maisie sat beside him staring rather sightlessly at a roomful of pictures which he had mystified her much by speaking of with a bored sigh as a 'silly superstition'. They represented, with patches of gold and cataracts of purple, with stiff saints and angular angels, with ugly Madonnas and uglier babies, strange prayers and prostrations; so that she at first took his words for a protest against devotional idolatry – all the more that he had of late often come with her and with Mrs Wix to morning church, a place of worship of Mrs Wix's own choosing, where there was nothing of that sort; no haloes on heads, but only, during long sermons, beguiling backs of bonnets, and where, as her governess always afterwards observed, he gave the most earnest attention. It presently appeared, however, that his reference was merely to the affectation of admiring such ridiculous works – an admonition that she received from him as submissively as she received everything. What turn it gave to their talk needn't here be recorded: the transition to the colourless schoolroom and lonely Mrs Wix was doubtless an effect of relaxed interest in what was before them. Maisie expressed in her own way the truth that she never went home nowadays without expecting to find the temple of her studies empty and the poor priestess cast out. This conveyed a full appreciation of her peril, and it was in rejoinder that Sir Claude uttered, acknowledging the source of that peril, the reassurance at which I have glanced. 'Don't be afraid, my dear: I've squared her.'

It required indeed a supplement when he saw that it left the child momentarily blank. 'I mean that your mother lets me do what I want so long as I let her do what *she* wants.'

'So you *are* doing what you want?' Maisie asked.

'Rather, Miss Farange!'

Miss Farange turned it over. 'And she's doing the same?'

'Up to the hilt!'

Again she considered. 'Then, please, what may it be?'

'I wouldn't tell you for the whole world.'

She gazed at a gaunt Madonna; after which she broke into a slow smile. 'Well, I don't care, so long as you do let her.'

'Oh you monster!' – and Sir Claude's gay vehemence brought him to his feet.

Another day, in another place – a place in Baker Street where at a hungry hour she had sat down with him to tea and buns – he brought out a question disconnected from previous talk. 'I say, you know, what do you suppose your father *would* do?'

Maisie hadn't long to cast about or to question his pleasant eyes. 'If you were really to go with us? He'd make a great complaint.'

He seemed amused at the term she employed. 'Oh I shouldn't mind a "complaint"!'

'He'd talk to every one about it,' said Maisie.

'Well, I shouldn't mind that either.'

'Of course not,' the child hastened to respond. 'You've told me you're not afraid of him.'

'The question is are you?' said Sir Claude.

Maisie candidly considered; then she spoke resolutely. 'No, not of papa.'

'But of somebody else?'

'Certainly, of lots of people.'

'Of your mother first and foremost of course.'

'Dear, yes; more of mamma than of – than of –'

'Than of what?' Sir Claude asked as she hesitated for a comparison.

She thought over all objects of dread. 'Than of a wild elephant!' she at last declared. 'And you are too,' she reminded him as he laughed.

'Oh yes, I am too.'

Again she meditated. 'Why then did you marry her?'

'Just because I *was* afraid.'

'Even when she loved you?'

'That made her the more alarming.'

For Maisie herself, though her companion seemed to find it droll, this opened up depths of gravity. 'More alarming than she is now?'

'Well, in a different way. Fear, unfortunately, is a very big thing, and there's a great variety of kinds.'

She took this in with complete intelligence. 'Then I think I've got them all.'

'You?' her friend cried. 'Nonsense! You're thoroughly "game".'

'I'm awfully afraid of Mrs Beale,' Maisie objected.

He raised his smooth brows. 'That charming woman?'

'Well,' she answered, 'you can't understand it because you're not in the same state.'

She had been going on with a luminous 'But' when, across the table, he laid his hand on her arm. 'I *can* understand it,' he confessed. 'I *am* in the same state.'

'Oh but she likes you so!' Maisie promptly pleaded.

Sir Claude literally coloured. 'That has something to do with it.'

Maisie wondered again. 'Being liked with being afraid?'

'Yes, when it amounts to adoration.'

'Then why aren't you afraid of *me*?'

'Because with you it amounts to that?' He had kept his hand on her arm. 'Well, what prevents is simply that you're the gentlest spirit on earth. Besides –' he pursued; but he came to a pause.

'Besides –?'

'I *should* be in fear if you were older – there! See – you already make me talk nonsense,' the young man added. 'The question's about your father. Is he likewise afraid of Mrs Beale?'

'I think not. And yet he loves her,' Maisie mused.

'Oh no – he doesn't; not a bit!' After which, as his companion stared, Sir Claude apparently felt that he must make this oddity fit with her recollections. 'There's nothing of that sort *now*.'

But Maisie only stared the more. 'They've changed?'

'Like your mother and me.'

She wondered how he knew. 'Then you've seen Mrs Beale again?'

He demurred. 'Oh no. She has written to me,' he presently subjoined. '*She's* not afraid of your father either. No one at all is – really.' Then he went on while Maisie's little mind, with its filial spring too relaxed from of old for a pang at this want of parental majesty, speculated on the vague relation between Mrs Beale's courage and the question, for Mrs Wix and herself, of a neat lodging with their friend. 'She wouldn't care a bit if Mr Farange should make a row.'

'Do you mean about you and me and Mrs Wix? Why should she care? It wouldn't hurt *her*.'

Sir Claude, with his legs out and his hand diving into his trousers-pocket, threw back his head with a laugh just perceptibly tempered, as she thought, by a sigh. 'My dear stepchild, you're delightful! Look here, we must pay. You've had five buns?'

'How *can* you?' Maisie demanded, crimson under the eye of the young woman who had stepped to their board. 'I've had three.'

Shortly after this Mrs Wix looked so ill that it was to be feared her ladyship had treated her to some unexampled passage. Maisie asked if anything worse than usual had occurred; whereupon the poor woman brought out with infinite gloom: 'He has been seeing Mrs Beale.'

'Sir Claude?' The child remembered what he had said. 'Oh no – not *seeing* her!'

'I beg your pardon. I absolutely know it.' Mrs Wix was as positive as she was dismal.

Maisie nevertheless ventured to challenge her. 'And how, please, do you know it?'

She faltered a moment. 'From herself. I've been to see her.' Then on Maisie's visible surprise: 'I went yesterday while you were out with him. He has seen her repeatedly.'

It was not wholly clear to Maisie why Mrs Wix should be prostrate at this discovery; but her general consciousness of the way things could be both perpetrated and resented always eased off for her the strain of the particular mystery. 'There may be some mistake. He says he hasn't.'

Mrs Wix turned paler, as if this were a still deeper ground for alarm. 'He says so? – he denies that he has seen her?'

'He told me so three days ago. Perhaps she's mistaken,' Maisie suggested.

'Do you mean perhaps she lies? She lies whenever it suits her, I'm very sure. But I know when people lie – and that's what I've loved in you, that *you* never do. Mrs Beale didn't yesterday at any rate. He *has* seen her.'

Maisie was silent a little. 'He says not,' she then repeated. 'Perhaps – perhaps –' Once more she paused.

'Do you mean perhaps *he* lies?'

'Gracious goodness, no!' Maisie shouted.

Mrs Wix's bitterness, however, again overflowed. 'He does, he does,' she cried, 'and it's that that's just the worst of it! They'll take you, they'll take you, and what in the world will then become of me?' She threw herself afresh upon her pupil and wept over her with the inevitable effect of causing the child's own tears to flow. But Maisie couldn't have told you if she had been crying at the image of their separation or at that of Sir Claude's untruth. As regards this deviation it was agreed between them that they were not in a position to bring it home to him. Mrs Wix was in dread of doing anything to make him, as she said, 'worse'; and Maisie was sufficiently initiated to be able to reflect that in speaking to her as he had done he had only wished to be tender of Mrs Beale. It fell in with all her inclinations to think of him as tender, and she forbore to let him know that the two ladies had, as *she* would never do, betrayed him.

She had not long to keep her secret, for the next day, when she went out with him, he suddenly said in reference to some errand he had first proposed: 'No, we won't do that – we'll do something else.' On this, a few steps from the door, he stopped a hansom and helped her in; then following her he gave the driver over the top an address that she lost. When he was seated beside her she asked him where they were going; to which he replied 'My dear child, you'll see.' She saw while she watched and wondered that they took the direction of the Regent's Park; but she didn't know why he should make a mystery of that, and it was not till they passed under a pretty arch and drew up at a white house in a terrace from which the view, she thought, must be lovely that, mystified, she clutched him and broke out: 'I shall see papa?'

He looked down at her with a kind smile. 'No, probably not. I haven't brought you for that.'

'Then whose house is it?'

'It's your father's. They've moved here.'

She looked about: she had known Mr Farange in four or five houses, and there was nothing astonishing in this except that it was the nicest place yet. 'But I shall see Mrs Beale?'

'It's to see her that I brought you.'

She stared, very white, and with her hand on his arm, though they had stopped, kept him sitting in the cab. 'To leave me, do you mean?'

He could scarce bring it out. 'It's not for me to say if you *can* stay. We must look into it.'

'But if I do I shall see papa?'

'Oh some time or other, no doubt.' Then Sir Claude went on: 'Have you really so very great a dread of that?'

Maisie glanced away over the apron of the cab – gazed a minute at the green expanse of the Regent's Park and, at this moment colouring to the roots of her hair, felt the full, hot rush of an emotion more mature than any she had yet known. It consisted of an odd unexpected shame at placing in an inferior light, to so perfect a gentleman and so charming a person as Sir Claude, so very near a relative as Mr Farange. She remembered, however, her friend's telling her that no one was seriously afraid of her father, and she turned round with a small toss of her head. 'Oh I dare say I can manage him!'

Sir Claude smiled, but she noted that the violence with which she had just changed colour had brought into his own face a slight compunctious and embarrassed flush. It was as if he had caught his first glimpse of her sense of responsibility. Neither of them made a movement to get out, and after an instant he said to her: 'Look here, if you say so we won't after all go in.'

'Ah but I want to see Mrs Beale!' the child gently wailed.

'But what if she does decide to take you? Then, you know, you'll have to remain.'

Maisie turned it over. 'Straight on – and give you up?'

'Well – I don't quite know about giving me up.'

'I mean as I gave up Mrs Beale when I last went to mamma's. I couldn't do without you here for anything like so long a time as that.' It struck her as a hundred years since she had seen Mrs Beale, who was on the other side of the door they were so near and whom she yet had not taken the jump to clasp in her arms.

'Oh I dare say you'll see more of me than you've seen of Mrs Beale. It isn't in *me* to be so beautifully discreet,' Sir Claude said. 'But all the same,' he continued, 'I leave the thing, now that we're here, absolutely *with* you. You must settle it. We'll only go in if you say so. If you don't say so we'll turn right round and drive away.'

'So in that case Mrs Beale won't take me?'

'Well – not by any act of ours.'

'And I shall be able to go on with mamma?' Maisie asked.

'Oh I don't say that!'

She considered. 'But I thought you said you had squared her?'

Sir Claude poked his stick at the splashboard of the cab. 'Not, my dear child, to the point she now requires.'

'Then if she turns me out and I don't come here –?'

Sir Claude promptly took her up. 'What do I offer you, you naturally enquire? My poor chick, that's just what I ask myself. I don't see it, I confess, quite as straight as Mrs Wix.'

His companion gazed a moment at what Mrs Wix saw. 'You mean *we* can't make a little family?'

'It's very base of me, no doubt, but I can't wholly chuck your mother.'

Maisie, at this, emitted a low but lengthened sigh, a slight sound of reluctant assent which would certainly have been amusing to an auditor. 'Then there isn't anything else?'

'I vow I don't quite see what there is.'

Maisie waited; her silence seemed to signify that she too had no alternative to suggest. But she made another appeal. 'If I come here you'll come to see me?'

'I won't lose sight of you.'

'But how often will you come?' As he hung fire she pressed him. 'Often and often?'

Still he faltered. 'My dear old woman –' he began. Then he paused again, going on the next moment with a change of tone. 'You're too funny! Yes then,' he said; 'often and often.'

'All right!' Maisie jumped out. Mrs Beale was at home, but not in the drawing-room, and when the butler had gone for her the child suddenly broke out: 'But when I'm here what will Mrs Wix do?'

'Ah you should have thought of that sooner!' said her companion with the first faint note of asperity she had ever heard him sound.

XIV

MRS Beale fairly swooped upon her, and the effect of the whole hour was to show the child how much, how quite formidably indeed, after all, she was loved. This was the more the case as her stepmother, so changed – in the very manner of her mother – that she really struck her as a new acquaintance, somehow recalled more familiarity than Maisie could feel. A rich strong expressive affection in short pounced upon her in the shape of a handsomer, ampler, older Mrs Beale. It was like making a fine friend, and they hadn't been a minute together before she felt elated at the way she had met the choice imposed on her in the cab. There was a whole future in the combination of Mrs Beale's beauty and Mrs Beale's hug. She seemed to Maisie charming to behold, and also to have no connection at all with anybody who had once mended underclothing and had meals in the nursery. The child knew one of her father's wives was a woman of fashion, but she had always dimly made a distinction, not applying that epithet without reserve to the other. Mrs Beale had since their separation acquired a conspicuous right to it, and Maisie's first flush of response to her present delight coloured all her splendour with meanings that this time were sweet. She had told Sir Claude she was afraid of the lady in the Regent's Park; but she had confidence enough to break, on the spot, into the frankest appreciation. 'Why, aren't you beautiful? Isn't she beautiful, Sir Claude, *isn't* she?'

'The handsomest woman in London, simply,' Sir Claude gallantly replied. 'Just as sure as you're the best little girl!'

Well, the handsomest woman in London gave herself up, with

tender lustrous looks and every demonstration of fondness, to a happiness at last clutched again. There was almost as vivid a bloom in her maturity as in mamma's, and it took her but a short time to give her little friend an impression of positive power – an impression that seemed to begin like a long bright day. This was a perception on Maisie's part that neither mamma, nor Sir Claude, nor Mrs Wix, with their immense and so varied respective attractions, had exactly kindled, and that made an immediate difference when the talk, as it promptly did, began to turn to her father. Oh yes, Mr Farange was a complication, but she saw now that he wouldn't be one for his daughter. For Mrs Beale certainly he was an immense one – she speedily made known as much; but Mrs Beale from this moment presented herself to Maisie as a person to whom a great gift had come. The great gift was just for handling complications. Maisie felt how little she made of them when, after she had dropped to Sir Claude some recall of a previous meeting, he made answer, with a sound of consternation and yet an air of relief, that he had denied to their companion their having, since the day he came for her, seen each other till that moment.

Mrs Beale could but vaguely pity it. 'Why did you do anything so silly?'

'To protect your reputation.'

'From Maisie?' Mrs Beale was much amused. 'My reputation with Maisie is too good to suffer.'

'But you believed me, you rascal, didn't you?' Sir Claude asked of the child.

She looked at him; she smiled. 'Her reputation did suffer. I discovered you had been here.'

He was not too chagrined to laugh. 'The way, my dear, you talk of that sort of thing!'

'How should she talk,' Mrs Beale wanted to know, 'after all this wretched time with her mother?'

'It was not mamma who told me,' Maisie explained. 'It was only

Mrs Wix.' She was hesitating whether to bring out before Sir Claude the source of Mrs Wix's information; but Mrs Beale, addressing the young man, showed the vanity of scruples.

'Do you know that preposterous person came to see me a day or two ago? – when I told her I had seen you repeatedly.'

Sir Claude, for once in a way, was disconcerted. 'The old cat! She never told me. Then you thought I had lied?' he demanded of Maisie.

She was flurried by the term with which he had qualified her gentle friend, but she took the occasion for one to which she must in every manner lend herself. 'Oh I didn't mind! But Mrs Wix did,' she added with an intention benevolent to her governess.

Her intention was not very effective as regards Mrs Beale. 'Mrs Wix is too idiotic!' that lady declared.

'But to you, of all people,' Sir Claude asked, 'what had she to say?'

'Why that, like Mrs Micawber – whom she must, I think, rather resemble – she will never, never, never desert Miss Farange.'

'Oh I'll make that all right!' Sir Claude cheerfully returned.

'I'm sure I hope so, my dear man,' said Mrs Beale, while Maisie wondered just how he would proceed. Before she had time to ask Mrs Beale continued: 'That's not all she came to do, if you please. But you'll never guess the rest.'

'Shall *I* guess it?' Maisie quavered.

Mrs Beale was again amused. 'Why you're just the person! It must be quite the sort of thing you've heard at your awful mother's. Have you never seen women there crying to her to "spare" the men they love?'

Maisie, wondering, tried to remember; but Sir Claude was freshly diverted. 'Oh they don't trouble about Ida! Mrs Wix cried to you to spare *me*?'

'She regularly went down on her knees to me.'

'The darling old dear!' the young man exclaimed.

These words were a joy to Maisie – they made up for his

previous description of Mrs Wix. 'And *will* you spare him?' she asked of Mrs Beale.

Her stepmother, seizing her and kissing her again, seemed charmed with the tone of her question. 'Not an inch of him! I'll pick him to the bone!'

'You mean that he'll really come often?' Maisie pressed.

Mrs Beale turned lovely eyes to Sir Claude. 'That's not for me to say – it's for him.'

He said nothing at once, however; with his hands in his pockets and vaguely humming a tune – even Maisie could see he was a little nervous – he only walked to the window and looked out at the Regent's Park. 'Well, he has promised,' Maisie said. 'But how will papa like it?'

'His being in and out? Ah that's a question that, to be frank with you, my dear, hardly matters. In point of fact, however, Beale greatly enjoys the idea that Sir Claude too, poor man, has been forced to quarrel with your mother.'

Sir Claude turned round and spoke gravely and kindly. 'Don't be afraid, Maisie; you won't lose sight of me.'

'Thank you so much!' Maisie was radiant. 'But what I meant – don't you know? – was what papa would say to *me*.'

'Oh I've been having that out with him,' said Mrs Beale. 'He'll behave well enough. You see the great difficulty is that, though he changes every three days about everything else in the world, he has never changed about your mother. It's a caution, the way he hates her.'

Sir Claude gave a short laugh. 'It certainly can't beat the way she still hates *him*!'

'Well,' Mrs Beale went on obligingly, 'nothing can take the place of that feeling with either of them, and the best way they can think of to show it is for each to leave you as long as possible on the hands of the other. There's nothing, as you've seen for yourself, that makes either so furious. It isn't, asking so little as you do, that you're much of an expense or a trouble; it's only that you make each feel so well how nasty the other wants to be. Therefore Beale goes on loathing your mother too much to have any great fury left for any one else. Besides, you know, I've squared him.'

'Oh Lord!' Sir Claude cried with a louder laugh and turning again to the window.

'*I* know how!' Maisie was prompt to proclaim. 'By letting him do what he wants on condition that he lets you also do it.'

'You're too delicious, my own pet!' – she was involved in another hug. 'How in the world have I got on so long without you? I've not been happy, love,' said Mrs Beale with her cheek to the child's.

'Be happy now!' – Maisie throbbed with shy tenderness.

'I think I shall be. You'll save me.'

'As I'm saving Sir Claude?' the little girl asked eagerly.

Mrs Beale, a trifle at a loss, appealed to her visitor, 'Is she really?'

He showed high amusement at Maisie's question. 'It's dear Mrs Wix's idea. There may be something in it.'

'He makes me his duty – he makes me his life,' Maisie set forth to her stepmother.

'Why that's what *I* want to do!' – Mrs Beale, so anticipated, turned pink with astonishment.

'Well, you can do it together. Then he'll *have* to come!'

Mrs Beale by this time had her young friend fairly in her lap and she smiled up at Sir Claude. 'Shall we do it together?'

His laughter had dropped, and for a moment he turned his handsome serious face not to his hostess, but to his stepdaughter. 'Well, it's rather more decent than some things. Upon my soul, the way things are going, it seems to me the only decency!' He had the air of arguing it out to Maisie, of presenting it, through an impulse of conscience, as a connection in which they could honourably see her participate; though his plea of mere 'decency' might well have appeared to fall below her rosy little vision. 'If we're not good for *you*,' he exclaimed, 'I'll be hanged if I know who we shall be good for!'

Mrs Beale showed the child an intenser light. 'I dare say you *will* save us – from one thing and another.'

'Oh I know what she'll save *me* from!' Sir Claude roundly asserted. 'There'll be rows of course,' he went on.

Mrs Beale quickly took him up. 'Yes, but they'll be nothing – for you at least – to the rows your wife makes as it is. I can bear what *I* suffer – I can't bear what you go through.'

'We're doing a good deal for you, you know, young woman,' Sir Claude went on to Maisie with the same gravity.

She coloured with a sense of obligation and the eagerness of her desire it should be remarked how little was lost on her. 'Oh I know!'

'Then you must keep us all right!' This time he laughed.

'How you talk to her!' cried Mrs Beale.

'No worse than you!' he gaily answered.

'Handsome is that handsome does!' she returned in the same spirit. 'You can take off your things,' she went on, releasing Maisie.

The child, on her feet, was all emotion. 'Then I'm just to stop – this way?'

'It will do as well as any other. Sir Claude, tomorrow, will have your things brought.'

'I'll bring them myself. Upon my word I'll see them packed!' Sir Claude promised. 'Come here and unbutton.'

He had beckoned his young companion to where he sat, and he helped to disengage her from her coverings while Mrs Beale, from a little distance, smiled at the hand he displayed. 'There's a stepfather for you! I'm bound to say, you know, that he makes up for the want of other people.'

'He makes up for the want of a nurse!' Sir Claude laughed. 'Don't you remember I told you so the very first time?'

'Remember? It was exactly what made me think so well of you!'

'Nothing would induce me,' the young man said to Maisie, 'to tell you what made me think so well of *her*.' Having divested the child he kissed her gently and gave her a little pat to make her stand off. The pat was accompanied with a vague sigh in which his gravity of a moment before came back. 'All the same, if you hadn't had the fatal gift of beauty –!'

'Well, what?' Maisie asked, wondering why he paused. It was the first time she had heard of her beauty.

'Why, we shouldn't all be thinking so well of each other!'

'He isn't speaking of personal loveliness – you've not *that* vulgar beauty, my dear, at all,' Mrs Beale explained. 'He's just talking of plain dull charm of character.'

'Her character's the most extraordinary thing in all the world,' Sir Claude stated to Mrs Beale.

'Oh I know all about that sort of thing!' – she fairly bridled with the knowledge.

It gave Maisie somehow a sudden sense of responsibility from which she sought refuge. 'Well, you've got it too, "that sort of thing" – you've got the fatal gift: you both really have!' she broke out.

'Beauty of character? My dear boy, we haven't a pennyworth!' Sir Claude protested.

'Speak for yourself, sir!' leaped lightly from Mrs Beale. 'I'm good and I'm clever. What more do you want? For you, I'll spare your blushes and not be personal – I'll simply say that you're as handsome as you can stick together.'

'You're both very lovely; you can't get out of it!' – Maisie felt the need of carrying her point. 'And it's beautiful to see you side by side.'

Sir Claude had taken his hat and stick; he stood looking at her a moment. 'You're a comfort in trouble! But I must go home and pack you.'

'And when will you come back? – tomorrow, tomorrow?'

'You see what we're in for!' he said to Mrs Beale.

'Well, I can bear it if you can.'

Their companion gazed from one of them to the other, thinking that though she had been happy indeed between Sir Claude and Mrs Wix she should evidently be happier still between Sir Claude and Mrs Beale. But it was like being perched on a prancing horse, and she made a movement to hold on to something. 'Then, you know, shan't I bid good-bye to Mrs Wix?'

'Oh I'll make it all right with her,' said Sir Claude.

Maisie considered. 'And with mamma?'

'Ah mamma!' he sadly laughed.

Even for the child this was scarcely ambiguous; but Mrs Beale endeavoured to contribute to its clearness. 'Your mother will crow, she'll crow –'

'Like the early bird!' said Sir Claude as she looked about for a comparison.

'She'll need no consolation,' Mrs Beale went on, 'for having made your father grandly blaspheme.'

Maisie stared. 'Will he grandly blaspheme?' It was impressive, it might have been out of the Bible, and her question produced a fresh play of caresses, in which Sir Claude also engaged. She wondered meanwhile who, if Mrs Wix was disposed of, would represent in her life the element of geography and anecdote; and she presently surmounted the delicacy she felt about asking. 'Won't there be any one to give me lessons?'

Mrs Beale was prepared with a reply that struck her as absolutely magnificent. 'You shall have such lessons as you've never had in all your life. You shall go to courses.'

'Courses?' Maisie had never heard of such things.

'At institutions – on subjects.'

Maisie continued to stare. 'Subjects?'

Mrs Beale was really splendid. 'All the most important ones. French literature – and sacred history. You'll take part in classes – with awfully smart children.'

'I'm going to look thoroughly into the whole thing, you know.' And Sir Claude, with characteristic kindness, gave her a nod of assurance accompanied by a friendly wink.

But Mrs Beale went much further. 'My dear child, you shall attend lectures.'

The horizon was suddenly vast and Maisie felt herself the smaller for it. 'All alone?'

'Oh no; I'll attend them with you,' said Sir Claude. 'They'll teach me a lot I don't know.'

'So they will me,' Mrs Beale gravely admitted. 'We'll go with her together – it will be charming. It's ages,' she confessed to Maisie, 'since I've had any time for study. That's another sweet way in which you'll be a motive to us. Oh won't the good she'll do us be immense?' she broke out uncontrollably to Sir Claude.

He weighed it; then he replied: 'That's certainly our idea.' Of this idea Maisie naturally had less of a grasp, but it inspired her with almost equal enthusiasm. If in so bright a prospect there would be nothing to long for it followed that she wouldn't long for Mrs Wix; but her consciousness of her assent to the absence of that fond figure caused a pair of words that had often sounded in her ears to ring in them again. It showed her in short what her father had always meant by calling her mother a 'low sneak' and her mother by calling her father one. She wondered if she herself shouldn't be a low sneak in learning to be so happy without Mrs Wix. What would Mrs Wix do? – where would Mrs Wix go? Before Maisie knew it, and at the door, as Sir Claude was off, these anxieties, on her lips, grew articulate and her stepfather had stopped long enough to answer them. 'Oh I'll square her!' he cried; and with this he departed.

Face to face with Mrs Beale Maisie, giving a sigh of relief, looked round at what seemed to her the dawn of a higher order. 'Then *every one* will be squared!' she peacefully said. On which her stepmother affectionately bent over her again.

XV

IT was Susan Ash who came to her with the news: 'He's downstairs, miss, and he do look beautiful.'

In the schoolroom at her father's, which had pretty blue curtains, she had been making out at the piano a lovely little thing, as Mrs Beale called it, a 'Moonlight Berceuse' sent her through the post by Sir Claude, who considered that her musical education had been deplorably neglected and who, the last months at her mother's, had been on the point of making arrangements for regular lessons. She knew from him familiarly that the real thing, as he said, was shockingly dear and that anything else was a waste of money, and she therefore rejoiced the more at the sacrifice represented by this composition, of which the price, five shillings, was marked on the cover and which was evidently the real thing. She was already on her feet. 'Mrs Beale has sent up for me?'

'Oh no – it's not that,' said Susan Ash. 'Mrs Beale has been out this hour.'

'Then papa!'

'Dear no – not papa. You'll do, miss, all but them wandering 'airs,' Susan went on. 'Your papa never came 'ome at all,' she added.

'Home from where?' Maisie responded a little absently and very excitedly. She gave a wild manual brush to her locks.

'Oh that, miss, I should be very sorry to tell you! I'd rather tuck away that white thing behind – though I'm blest if it's my work.'

'Do then, please. I know where papa was,' Maisie impatiently continued.

'Well, in your place I wouldn't tell.'

'He was at the club – the Chrysanthemum. So!'

'All night long? Why the flowers shut up at night, you know!' cried Susan Ash.

'Well, I don't care' – the child was at the door. 'Sir Claude asked for me *alone*?'

'The same as if you was a duchess.'

Maisie was aware on her way downstairs that she was now quite as happy as one, and also, a moment later, as she hung round his neck, that even such a personage would scarce commit herself more grandly. There was moreover a hint of the duchess in the infinite point with which, as she felt, she exclaimed: 'And this is what you call coming *often*?'

Sir Claude met her delightfully and in the same fine spirit. 'My dear old man, don't make me a scene – I assure you it's what every woman I look at does. Let us have some fun – it's a lovely day: clap on something smart and come out with me; then we'll talk it over quietly.' They were on their way five minutes later to Hyde Park, and nothing that even in the good days at her mother's they had ever talked over had more of the sweetness of tranquillity than his present prompt explanations. He was at his best in such an office and with the exception of Mrs Wix the only person she had met in her life who ever explained. With him, however, the act had an authority transcending the wisdom of woman. It all came back – all the plans that always failed, all the rewards and bribes that she was perpetually paying for in advance and perpetually out of pocket by afterwards – the whole great stress to be dealt with introduced her on each occasion afresh to the question of money. Even she herself almost knew how it would have expressed the strength of his empire to say that to shuffle away her sense of being duped he had only, from under his lovely moustache, to breathe upon it. It was somehow in the nature of plans to be expensive and in the nature of the expensive to be impossible. To be 'involved' was of the essence of everybody's affairs, and also at every particular moment to be more involved than usual. This had been the case with Sir

Claude's, with papa's, with mamma's, with Mrs Beale's and with Maisie's own at the particular moment, a moment of several weeks, that had elapsed since our young lady had been re-established at her father's. There wasn't 'two-and-tuppence' for anything or for any one, and that was why there had been no sequel to the classes in French literature with all the smart little girls. It was devilish awkward, didn't she see? to try, without even the limited capital mentioned, to mix her up with a remote array that glittered before her after this as the children of the rich. She was to feel henceforth as if she were flattening her nose upon the hard window-pane of the sweetshop of knowledge. If the classes, however, that were select, and accordingly the only ones, were impossibly dear, the lectures at the institutions – at least at some of them – were directly addressed to the intelligent poor, and it therefore had to be easier still to produce on the spot the reason why she had been taken to none. This reason, Sir Claude said, was that she happened to be just going to be, though they had nothing to do with that in now directing their steps to the banks of the Serpentine. Maisie's own park, in the north, had been nearer at hand, but they rolled westward in a hansom because at the end of the sweet June days this was the direction taken by every one that any one looked at. They cultivated for an hour, on the Row and by the Drive, this opportunity for each observer to amuse and for one of them indeed, not a little hilariously, to mystify the other, and before the hour was over Maisie had elicited, in reply to her sharpest challenge, a further account of her friend's long absence.

'Why I've broken my word to you so dreadfully – promising so solemnly and then never coming? Well, my dear, that's a question that, not seeing me day after day, you must very often have put to Mrs Beale.'

'Oh yes,' the child replied; 'again and again.'

'And what has she told you?'

'That you're as bad as you're beautiful.'

'Is that what she says?'

'Those very words.'

'Ah the dear old soul!' Sir Claude was much diverted, and his loud, clear laugh was all his explanation. Those were just the words Maisie had last heard him use about Mrs Wix. She clung to his hand, which was encased in a pearl-grey glove ornamented with the thick black lines that, at her mother's, always used to strike her as connected with the way the bestitched fists of the long ladies carried, with the elbows well out, their umbrellas upside down. The mere sense of his grasp in her own covered the ground of loss just as much as the ground of gain. His presence was like an object brought so close to her face that she couldn't see round its edges. He himself, however, remained showman of the spectacle even after they had passed out of the Park and begun, under the charm of the spot and the season, to stroll in Kensington Gardens. What they had left behind them was, as he said, only a pretty bad circus, and, through prepossessing gates and over a bridge, they had come in a quarter of an hour, as he also remarked, a hundred miles from London. A great green glade was before them, and high old trees, and under the shade of these, in the fresh turf, the crooked course of a rural footpath. 'It's the Forest of Arden,' Sir Claude had just delightfully observed, 'and I'm the banished duke, and you're – what was the young woman called? – the artless country wench. And there,' he went on, 'is the other girl – what's her name, Rosalind? – and (don't you know?) the fellow who was making up to her. Upon my word he is making up to her!'

His allusion was to a couple who, side by side, at the end of the glade, were moving in the same direction as themselves. These distant figures, in their slow stroll (which kept them so close together that their heads, drooping a little forward, almost touched), presented the back of a lady who looked tall, who was evidently a very fine woman, and that of a gentleman whose left hand appeared to be passed well into her arm while his right, behind him, made jerky motions with the stick that it grasped. Maisie's fancy responded for an instant to her friend's idea that the sight was idyllic; then, stopping short, she brought out with all her clearness: 'Why mercy – if it isn't mamma!'

Sir Claude paused with a stare. 'Mamma? But mamma's at Brussels.'

Maisie, with her eyes on the lady, wondered. 'At Brussels?'

'She's gone to play a match.'

'At billiards? You didn't tell me.'

'Of course I didn't!' Sir Claude ejaculated. 'There's plenty I don't tell you. She went on Wednesday.'

The couple had added to their distance, but Maisie's eyes more than kept pace with them. 'Then she has come back.'

Sir Claude watched the lady. 'It's much more likely she never went!'

'It's mamma!' the child said with decision.

They had stood still, but Sir Claude had made the most of his opportunity, and it happened that just at this moment, at the end of the vista, the others halted and, still showing only their backs, seemed to stay talking. 'Right you are, my duck!' he exclaimed at last. 'It's my own sweet wife!'

He had spoken with a laugh, but he had changed colour, and Maisie quickly looked away from him. 'Then who is it with her?'

'Blest if I know!' said Sir Claude.

'Is it Mr Perriam?'

'Oh dear no – Perriam's smashed.'

'Smashed?'

'Exposed – in the City. But there are quantities of others!' Sir Claude smiled.

Maisie appeared to count them; she studied the gentleman's back. 'Then is this Lord Eric?'

For a moment her companion made no answer, and when she turned her eyes again to him he was looking at her, she thought, rather queerly. 'What do you know about Lord Eric?'

She tried innocently to be odd in return. 'Oh I know more than you think! Is it Lord Eric?' she repeated.

'It may be. Blest if I care!'

Their friends had slightly separated and now, as Sir Claude spoke, suddenly faced round, showing all the splendour of her ladyship and all the mystery of her comrade. Maisie held her breath. 'They're coming!'

'Let them come.' And Sir Claude, pulling out his cigarettes, began to strike a light.

'We shall meet them!'

'No. They'll meet *us*.'

Maisie stood her ground. 'They see us. Just look.'

Sir Claude threw away his match. 'Come straight on.' The others, in the return, evidently startled, had half-paused again, keeping well apart, 'She's horribly surprised and wants to slope,' he continued. 'But it's too late.'

Maisie advanced beside him, making out even across the interval that her ladyship was ill at ease. 'Then what will she do?'

Sir Claude puffed his cigarette. 'She's quickly thinking.' He appeared to enjoy it.

Ida had wavered but an instant; her companion clearly gave her moral support. Maisie thought he somehow looked brave, and he had no likeness whatever to Mr Perriam. His face, thin and rather sharp, was smooth, and it was not till they came nearer that she saw he had a remarkably fair little moustache. She could already see that his eyes were of the lightest blue. He was far nicer than Mr Perriam. Mamma looked terrible from afar, but even under her guns the child's curiosity flickered and she appealed again to Sir Claude. 'Is it – *is* it Lord Eric?'

Sir Claude smoked composedly enough. 'I think it's the Count.'

This was a happy solution – it fitted her idea of a count. But what idea, as she now came grandly on, did mamma fit? – unless that of an actress, in some tremendous situation, sweeping down to the footlights as if she would jump them. Maisie felt really so frightened that before she knew it she had passed her hand into Sir Claude's arm. Her pressure caused him to stop, and at the sight of this the other couple came equally to a stand and, beyond the diminished space, remained a moment more in talk. This, however, was the matter of an instant; leaving the Count apparently to come round more circuitously – an outflanking movement, if Maisie had but known – her ladyship resumed the onset. 'What *will* she do now?' her daughter asked.

Sir Claude was at present in a position to say: 'Try to pretend it's me.'

'You?'

'Why that I'm up to something.'

In another minute poor Ida had justified this prediction, erect there before them like a figure of justice in full dress. There were parts of her face that grew whiter while Maisie looked, and other parts in which this change seemed to make other colours reign with more intensity. 'What are you doing with my daughter?' she demanded of her husband; in spite of the indignant tone of which Maisie had a greater sense than ever in her life before of not being personally noticed. It seemed to her Sir Claude also grew pale as an effect of the loud defiance with which Ida twice repeated this question. He put her, instead of answering it, an enquiry of his own: 'Who the devil have you got hold of *now*?' and at this her ladyship turned tremendously to the child, glaring at her as at an equal plotter of sin. Maisie received in petrifaction the full force of her mother's huge painted eyes – they were like Japanese lanterns swung under festal arches. But life came back to her from a tone suddenly and strangely softened. 'Go straight to that gentleman, my dear; I've asked him to take you a few minutes. He's charming – go. I've something to say to *this* creature.'

Maisie felt Sir Claude immediately clutch her. 'No, no – thank you: that won't do. She's mine.'

'Yours?' It was confounding to Maisie to hear her speak quite as if she had never heard of Sir Claude before.

'Mine. You've given her up. You've not another word to say about her. I have her from her father,' said Sir Claude – a statement that startled his companion, who could also measure its lively action on her mother.

There was visibly, however, an influence that made Ida consider; she glanced at the gentleman she had left, who, having strolled with his hands in his pockets to some distance, stood there with unembarrassed vagueness. She directed to him the face that was like an illuminated garden, turnstile and all, for the frequentation of which he had his season-ticket; then she looked again at Sir Claude. 'I've given her up to her father to *keep* – not to get rid of by sending about the town either with you or with any one else. If she's not to mind me let *him* come and tell me so. I decline to take it from another person, and I like your pretending that with your humbug of "interest" you've a leg to stand on. I know your game and have something now to say to you about it.'

Sir Claude gave a squeeze of the child's arm. 'Didn't I tell you she'd have, Miss Farange?'

'You're uncommonly afraid to hear it,' Ida went on; 'but if you think she'll protect you from it you're mightily mistaken.' She gave him a moment. 'I'll give her the benefit as soon as look at you. Should you like her to know, my dear?' Maisie had a sense of her launching the question with effect; yet our young lady was also conscious of hoping that Sir Claude would declare that preference. We have already learned that she had come to like people's liking her to 'know'. Before he could reply at all, none the less, her mother opened a pair of arms of extraordinary elegance, and then she felt the loosening of his grasp. 'My own child,' Ida murmured in a voice – a voice of sudden confused tenderness – that it seemed to her she heard for the first time. She wavered but an instant, thrilled with the first direct appeal, as distinguished from the mere maternal pull, she had ever had from lips that, even in the old vociferous years, had always been sharp. The next moment she was on her mother's breast, where, amid a wilderness of trinkets, she felt as if she had suddenly been thrust, with a smash of glass, into a jeweller's shop-front, but only to be as suddenly ejected with a push and the brisk injunction: 'Now go to the Captain!'

Maisie glanced at the gentleman submissively, but felt the want of more introduction. 'The Captain?'

Sir Claude broke into a laugh. 'I told her it was the Count.'

Ida stared; she rose so superior that she was colossal. 'You're too utterly loathsome,' she then declared. 'Be off!' she repeated to her daughter.

Maisie started, moved backward and, looking at Sir Claude, 'Only for a moment,' she signed to him in her bewilderment.

But he was too angry to heed her – too angry with his wife; as she turned away she heard his anger break out. 'You damned old b—!' – she couldn't quite hear all. It was enough, it was too much: she fled before it, rushing even to a stranger for the shock of such a change of tone.

XVI

AS she met the Captain's light blue eyes the greatest marvel occurred; she felt a sudden relief at finding them reply with anxiety to the horror in her face. 'What in the world has he done?' He put it all on Sir Claude.

'He has called her a damned old brute.' She couldn't help bringing that out.

The Captain, at the same elevation as her ladyship, gaped wide; then of course, like every one else, he was convulsed. But he instantly caught himself up, echoing her bad words. 'A damned old brute – your mother?'

Maisie was already conscious of her second movement. 'I think she tried to make him angry.'

The Captain's stupefaction was fine. 'Angry – *she*? Why she's an angel!'

On the spot, as he said this, his face won her over; it was so bright and kind, and his blue eyes had such a reflection of some mysterious grace that, for him at least, her mother had put forth. Her fund of observation enabled her as she gazed up at him to place him: he was a candid simple soldier; very brave – she came back to that – but not at all terrible. At any rate he struck a note that was new to her and that after a moment made her say: 'Do you like her very much?'

He smiled down at her, hesitating, looking pleasanter and pleasanter. 'Let me tell you about your mother.'

He put out a big military hand which she immediately took, and they turned off together to where a couple of chairs had been placed under one of the trees. 'She told me to come to you,' Maisie explained as they went; and presently she was close to him in a chair, with the prettiest of pictures – the sheen of the lake through other trees – before them, and the sound of birds, the plash of boats, the play of children in the air. The Captain, inclining his military person, sat sideways to be closer and kinder, and as her hand was on the arm of her seat he put his own down on it again to emphasise something he had to say that would be good for her to hear. He had already told her how her mother, from the moment of seeing her so unexpectedly with a person who was – well, not at all the right person, had promptly asked him to take charge of her while she herself tackled, as she said, the real culprit. He gave the child the sense of doing for the time what he liked with her; ten minutes before she had never seen him, but she could now sit there touching him, touched and impressed by him and thinking it nice when a gentleman was thin and brown – brown with a kind of clear depth that made his straw-coloured moustache almost white and his eyes resemble little pale flowers. The most extraordinary thing was the way she didn't appear just then to mind Sir Claude's being tackled. The Captain wasn't a bit like him, for it was an odd part of the pleasantness of mamma's friend that it resided in a manner in this friend's having a face so informally put together that the only kindness could be to call it funny. An odder part still was that it finally made our young lady, to classify him further, say to herself that, of all people in the world, he reminded her most insidiously of Mrs Wix. He had neither straighteners nor a diadem, nor, at least in the same place as the other, a button; he was sun-burnt and deep-voiced and smelt of cigars, yet he marvellously had more in common with her old governess than with her young stepfather. What he had to say to her that was good for her to hear was that her poor mother (didn't she know?) was the best friend he had ever had in all his life. And he added: 'She has told me ever so much about you. I'm awfully glad to know you.'

She had never, she thought, been so addressed as a young lady, not even by Sir Claude the day, so long ago, that she found him with Mrs Beale. It struck her as the way that at balls, by delightful partners, young ladies must be spoken to in the intervals of dances; and she tried to think of something that would meet it at the same high point. But this effort flurried her, and all she could produce was: 'At first, you know, I thought you were Lord Eric.'

The Captain looked vague. 'Lord Eric?'

'And then Sir Claude thought you were the Count.'

At this he laughed out. 'Why he's only five foot high and as red as a lobster!' Maisie laughed, with a certain elegance, in return – the young lady at the ball certainly would – and was on the point, as conscientiously, of pursuing the subject with an agreeable question. But before she could speak her companion challenged her. 'Who in the world's Lord Eric?'

'Don't you know him?' She judged her young lady would say that with light surprise.

'Do you mean a fat man with his mouth always open?' She had to confess that their acquaintance was so limited that she could only describe the bearer of the name as a friend of mamma's; but a light suddenly came to the Captain, who quickly spoke as knowing her man. 'What-do-you-call-him's brother, the fellow that owned Bobolink?' Then, with all his kindness, he contradicted her flat. 'Oh dear no; your mother never knew *him*.'

'But Mrs Wix said so,' the child risked.

'Mrs Wix?'

'My old governess.'

This again seemed amusing to the Captain. 'She mixed him up, your old governess. He's an awful beast. Your mother never looked at him.'

He was as positive as he was friendly, but he dropped for a minute after this into a silence that gave Maisie, confused but ingenious, a chance to redeem the mistake of pretending to know too much by the humility of inviting further correction. 'And doesn't she know the Count?'

'Oh I dare say! But he's another ass.' After which abruptly, with a different look, he put down again on the back of her own the hand he had momentarily removed. Maisie even thought he coloured a little. 'I want tremendously to speak to you. You must never believe any harm of your mother.'

'Oh I assure you I *don't*!' cried the child, blushing, herself, up to her eyes in a sudden surge of deprecation of such a thought.

The Captain, bending his head, raised her hand to his lips with a benevolence that made her wish her glove had been nicer. 'Of course you don't when you know how fond she is of *you*.'

'She's fond of me?' Maisie panted.

'Tremendously. But she thinks you don't like her. You *must* like her. She has had too much to put up with.'

'Oh yes – I know!' She rejoiced that she had never denied it.

'Of course I've no right to speak of her except as a particular friend,' the Captain went on. 'But she's a splendid woman. She has never had any sort of justice.'

'Hasn't she?' – his companion, to hear the words, felt a thrill altogether new.

'Perhaps I oughtn't to say it to you, but she has had everything to suffer.'

'Oh yes – you can *say* it to me!' Maisie hastened to profess.

The Captain was glad. 'Well, you needn't tell. It's all for *you* – do you see?'

Serious and smiling she only wanted to take it from him. 'It's between you and me! Oh there are lots of things I've never told!'

'Well, keep this with the rest. I assure you she has had the most infernal time, no matter what any one says to the contrary. She's the cleverest woman I ever saw in all my life. She's too charming.' She had been touched already by his tone, and now she leaned back in her chair and felt something tremble within her. 'She's tremendous fun – she can do all sorts of things better than I've ever seen any one. She has the pluck of fifty – and I know; I assure you I do. She has the nerve for a tiger-shoot – by Jove I'd *take* her! And

she is awfully open and generous, don't you know? there are
women that are such horrid sneaks. She'll go through anything for
any one she likes.' He appeared to watch for a moment the effect
on his companion of this emphasis; then he gave a small sigh that
mourned the limits of the speakable. But it was almost with the
note of a fresh challenge that he wound up: 'Look here, she's *true*!'

Maisie had so little desire to assert the contrary that she found
herself, in the intensity of her response, throbbing with a joy still
less utterable than the essence of the Captain's admiration. She was
fairly hushed with the sense that he spoke of her mother as she had
never heard any one speak. It came over her as she sat silent that,
after all, this admiration and this respect were quite new words,
which took a distinction from the fact that nothing in the least
resembling them in quality had on any occasion dropped from the
lips of her father, of Mrs Beale, of Sir Claude or even of Mrs Wix.
What it appeared to her to come to was that on the subject of her
ladyship it was the first real kindness she had heard, so that at the
touch of it something strange and deep and pitying surged up
within her – a revelation that, practically and so far as she knew, her
mother, apart from this, had only been disliked. Mrs Wix's original
account of Sir Claude's affection seemed as empty now as the
chorus in a children's game, and the husband and wife, but a little
way off at that moment, were face to face in hatred and with the
dreadful name he had called her still in the air. What was it the
Captain on the other hand had called her? Maisie wanted to hear
that again. The tears filled her eyes and rolled down her cheeks,
which burned under them with the rush of a consciousness that for
her too, five minutes before, the vivid towering beauty whose
assault she awaited had been, a moment long, an object of pure
dread. She became on the spot indifferent to her usual fear of
showing what in children was notoriously most offensive –
presented to her companion, soundlessly but hideously, her wet
distorted face. She cried, with a pang, straight *at* him, cried as she
had never cried at any one in all her life. 'Oh do you love her?' she

brought out with a gulp that was the effect of her trying not to make a noise.

It was doubtless another consequence of the thick mist through which she saw him that in reply to her question the Captain gave her such a queer blurred look. He stammered, yet in his voice there was also the ring of a great awkward insistence. 'Of course I'm tremendously fond of her – I like her better than any woman I ever saw. I don't mind in the least telling you that,' he went on, 'and I should think myself a great beast if I did.' Then to show that his position was superlatively clear he made her, with a kindness that even Sir Claude had never surpassed, tremble again as she had trembled at his first outbreak. He called her by her name, and her name drove it home. 'My dear Maisie, your mother's an angel!'

It was an almost unbelievable balm – it soothed so her impression of danger and pain. She sank back in her chair, she covered her face with her hands. 'Oh mother, mother, mother!' she sobbed. She had an impression that the Captain, beside her, if more and more friendly, was by no means unembarrassed; in a minute, however, when her eyes were clearer, he was erect in front of her, very red and nervously looking about him and whacking his leg with his stick. 'Say you love her, Mr Captain; say it, say it!' she implored.

Mr Captain's blue eyes fixed themselves very hard. 'Of *course* I love her, damn it, you know!'

At this she also jumped up; she had fished out somehow her pocket-handkerchief. 'So do *I* then. I do, I do, I do!' she passionately asseverated.

'Then will you come back to her?'

Maisie, staring, stopped the tight little plug of her handkerchief on the way to her eyes. 'She won't have me.'

'Yes she will. She wants you.'

'Back at the house – with Sir Claude?'

Again he hung fire. 'No, not with him. In another place.'

They stood looking at each other with an intensity unusual as between a Captain and a little girl. 'She won't have me in any place.'

'Oh yes she will if *I* ask her!'

Maisie's intensity continued. 'Shall you be there?'

The Captain's, on the whole, did the same. 'Oh yes – some day.'

'Then you don't mean now?'

He broke into a quick smile. 'Will you come now? – go with us for an hour?'

Maisie considered. 'She wouldn't have me even now.' She could see that he had his idea, but that her tone impressed him. That disappointed her a little, though in an instant he rang out again.

'She will if I ask her,' he repeated. 'I'll ask her this minute.'

Maisie, turning at this, looked away to where her mother and her stepfather had stopped. At first, among the trees, nobody was visible; but the next moment she exclaimed with expression: 'It's over – here he comes!'

The Captain watched the approach of her ladyship's husband, who lounged composedly over the grass, making to Maisie with his closed fingers a little movement in the air. 'I've no desire to avoid him.'

'Well, you mustn't see him,' said Maisie.

'Oh he's in no hurry himself!' Sir Claude had stopped to light another cigarette.

She was vague as to the way it was proper he should feel; but she had a sense that the Captain's remark was rather a free reflection on it. 'Oh he doesn't care!' she replied.

'Doesn't care for what?'

'Doesn't care who you are. He told me so. Go and ask mamma,' she added.

'If you can come with us? Very good. You really want me not to wait for him?'

'*Please* don't.' But Sir Claude was not yet near, and the Captain had with his left hand taken hold of her right, which he familiarly, sociably swung a little. 'Only first,' she continued, 'tell me this. Are you going to *live* with mamma?'

The immemorial note of mirth broke out at her seriousness. 'One of these days.'

She wondered, wholly unperturbed by his laughter. 'Then where will Sir Claude be?'

'He'll have left her of course.'

'Does he really intend to do that?'

'You've every opportunity to ask him.'

Maisie shook her head with decision. 'He won't do it. Not first.'

Her 'first' made the Captain laugh out again. 'Oh he'll be sure to be nasty! But I've said too much to you.'

'Well, you know, I'll never tell,' said Maisie.

'No, it's all for yourself. Good-bye.'

'Good-bye.' Maisie kept his hand long enough to add: 'I like you too.' And then supremely: 'You *do* love her?'

'My dear child –!' The Captain wanted words.

'Then don't do it only for just a little.'

'A little?'

'Like all the others.'

'All the others?' – he stood staring.

She pulled away her hand. 'Do it always!' She bounded to meet Sir Claude, and as she left the Captain she heard him ring out with apparent gaiety:

'Oh I'm in for it!'

As she joined Sir Claude she noted her mother in the distance move slowly off, and, glancing again at the Captain, saw him, swinging his stick, retreat in the same direction.

She had never seen Sir Claude look as he looked just then; flushed yet not excited – settled rather in an immoveable disgust and at once very sick and very hard. His conversation with her mother had clearly drawn blood, and the child's old horror came back to her, begetting the instant moral contraction of the days when her parents had looked to her to feed their love of battle. Her greatest fear for the moment, however, was that her friend would see she had been crying. The next she became aware that he had glanced at her, and it presently occurred to her that he didn't even wish to be looked at. At this she quickly removed her gaze, while he said rather curtly: 'Well, who in the world *is* the fellow?'

She felt herself flooded with prudence. 'Oh *I* haven't found out!' This sounded as if she meant he ought to have done so himself; but she could only face doggedly the ugliness of seeming disagreeable, as she used to face it in the hours when her father, for her blankness, called her a dirty little donkey, and her mother, for her falsity, pushed her out of the room.

'Then what have you been doing all this time?'

'Oh I don't know!' It was of the essence of her method not to be silly by halves.

'Then didn't the beast say anything?' They had got down by the lake and were walking fast.

'Well, not very much.'

'He didn't speak of your mother?'

'Oh yes, a little!'

'Then what I ask you, please, is *how*?' She kept silence – so long that he presently went on: 'I say, you know – don't you hear me?'

At this she produced: 'Well, I'm afraid I didn't attend to him very much.'

Sir Claude, smoking rather hard, made no immediate rejoinder; but finally he exclaimed: 'Then my dear – with such a chance – you were the perfection of a dunce!' He was so irritated – or she took him to be – that for the rest of the time they were in the Gardens he spoke no other word; and she meanwhile subtly abstained from any attempt to pacify him. That would only lead to more questions. At the gate of the Gardens he hailed a four-wheeled cab and, in silence, without meeting her eyes, put her into it, only saying 'Give him *that*' as he tossed half a crown upon the seat. Even when from outside he had closed the door and told the man where to go he never took her departing look. Nothing of this kind had ever yet happened to them, but it had no power to make her love him less; so she could not only bear it, she felt as she drove away – she could rejoice in it. It brought again the sweet sense of success that, ages before, she had had at a crisis when, on the stairs, returning from her father's, she had met a fierce question of her mother's with an imbecility as deep and had in consequence been dashed by Mrs Farange almost to the bottom.

XVII

IF for reasons of her own she could bear the sense of Sir Claude's displeasure her young endurance might have been put to a serious test. The days went by without his knocking at her father's door, and the time would have turned sadly to waste if something hadn't conspicuously happened to give it a new difference. What took place was a marked change in the attitude of Mrs Beale – a change that somehow, even in his absence, seemed to bring Sir Claude again into the house. It began practically with a conversation that occurred between them the day Maisie came home alone in the cab. Mrs Beale had by that time returned, and she was more successful than their friend in extracting from our young lady an account of the extraordinary passage with the Captain. She came back to it repeatedly, and on the very next day it grew distinct to the child that she was already in full possession of what at the same moment had been enacted between her ladyship and Sir Claude. This was the real origin of her final perception that though he didn't come to the house her stepmother had some rare secret for not being quite without him. This led to some rare passages with Mrs Beale, the promptest of which had been – not on Maisie's part – a wonderful outbreak of tears. Mrs Beale was not, as she herself said, a crying creature: she hadn't cried, to Maisie's knowledge, since the lowly governess days, the grey dawn of their connection. But she wept now with passion, professing loudly that it did her good and saying remarkable things to her charge, for whom the occasion was an equal benefit, an addition to all the fine precautionary wisdom stored away. It somehow hadn't violated that wisdom, Maisie felt, for her to have told Mrs Beale what she had not told Sir Claude, inasmuch as the greatest strain, to her sense, was between Sir Claude and Sir Claude's wife, and his wife was just what Mrs Beale was unfortunately not. He sent his stepdaughter three days after the incident in Kensington Gardens a message as frank as it was tender, and that was how Mrs Beale had had to bring out in a manner that seemed half an appeal, half a defiance: 'Well yes, hang it – I *do* see him!'

How and when and where, however, were just what Maisie was not to know – an exclusion moreover that she never questioned in the light of a participation large enough to make him, while she shared the ample void of Mrs Beale's rather blank independence, shine in her yearning eye like the single, the sovereign window-square of a great dim disproportioned room. As far as her father was concerned such hours had no interruption; and then it was clear between them that each was thinking of the absent and thinking the other thought, so that he was an object of conscious reference in everything they said or did. The wretched truth, Mrs Beale had to confess, was that she had hoped against hope and that in the Regent's Park it was impossible Sir Claude should really be in and out. Hadn't they at last to look the fact in the face? – it was too disgustingly evident that no one after all had been squared. Well, if no one had been squared it was because every one had been vile. No one and every one were of course Beale and Ida, the extent of whose power to be nasty was a thing that, to a little girl, Mrs Beale simply couldn't give chapter and verse for. Therefore it was that to keep going at all, as she said, that lady had to make, as she also said, another arrangement – the arrangement in which Maisie was included only to the point of knowing it existed and wondering wistfully what it was. Conspicuously at any rate it had a side that was responsible for Mrs Beale's sudden emotion and sudden confidence – a demonstration this, however, of which the tearfulness was far from deterrent to our heroine's thought of how happy she should be if she could only make an arrangement for herself. Mrs Beale's own operated, it appeared, with regularity and frequency; for it was almost every day or two that she was able to bring Maisie a message and to take one back. It had been over the vision of what, as she called it, he did for her that she broke down; and this vision was kept in a manner before Maisie by a subsequent increase not only of the gaiety, but literally – it seemed not presumptuous to perceive – of the actual virtue of her friend. The friend was herself the first to proclaim it: he had pulled her up immensely – he had quite pulled her round. She had charming tormenting words about him: he was her good fairy, her hidden spring – above all he was just her 'higher' conscience. That was what had particularly come out with her startling tears: he had made her, dear man, think ever so much better of herself. It had been thus rather surprisingly revealed that she had been in a way to think ill, and Maisie was glad to hear of the corrective at the same time that she heard of the ailment.

She presently found herself supposing, and in spite of her envy even hoping, that whenever Mrs Beale was out of the house Sir Claude had in some manner the satisfaction of it. This was now of more frequent occurrence than ever before – so much so that she would have thought of her stepmother as almost extravagantly absent had it not been that, in the first place, her father was a superior specimen of that habit: it was the frequent remark of his present wife, as it had been, before the tribunals of their country, a prominent plea of her predecessor, that he scarce came home even to sleep. In the second place Mrs Beale, when she *was* on the spot, had now a beautiful air of longing to make up for everything. The only shadow in such bright intervals was that, as Maisie put it to herself, she could get nothing by questions. It was in the nature of things to be none of a small child's business, even when a small child had from the first been deluded into a fear that she might be only too much initiated. Things then were in Maisie's experience so true to their nature that questions were almost always improper; but she learned on the other hand soon to recognise how at last, sometimes, patient little silences and intelligent little looks could be

rewarded by delightful little glimpses. There had been years at
Beale Farange's when the monosyllable 'he' meant always, meant
almost violently, the master; but all that was changed at a period at
which Sir Claude's merits were of themselves so much in the air
that it scarce took every two letters to name him. 'He keeps me up
splendidly – he does, my own precious,' Mrs Beale would observe
to her comrade; or else she would say that the situation at the other
establishment had reached a point that could scarcely be believed –
the point, monstrous as it sounded, of his not having laid eyes upon
her for twelve days. 'She' of course at Beale Farange's had never
meant any one but Ida, and there was the difference in this case that
it now meant Ida with renewed intensity. Mrs Beale – it was
striking – was in a position to animadvert more and more upon her
dreadfulness, the moral of all which appeared to be how
abominably yet blessedly little she had to do with her husband. This
flow of information came home to our two friends because, truly,
Mrs Beale had not much more to do with her own; but that was
one of the reflections that Maisie could make without allowing it
to break the spell of her present sympathy. How could such a spell
be anything but deep when Sir Claude's influence, operating from
afar, at last really determined the resumption of his stepdaughter's
studies? Mrs Beale again took fire about them and was quite vivid
for Maisie as to their being the great matter to which the dear
absent one kept her up.

This was the second source – I have just alluded to the first – of
the child's consciousness of something that, very hopefully, she
described to herself as a new phase; and it also presented in the
brightest light the fresh enthusiasm with which Mrs Beale always
reappeared and which really gave Maisie a happier sense than she
had yet had of being very dear at least to two persons. That she had
small remembrance at present of a third illustrates, I am afraid, a
temporary oblivion of Mrs Wix, an accident to be explained only
by a state of unnatural excitement. For what was the form taken by
Mrs Beale's enthusiasm and acquiring relief in the domestic

conditions still left to her but the delightful form of 'reading' with
her little charge on lines directly prescribed and in works profusely
supplied by Sir Claude? He had got hold of an awfully good list –
'mostly essays, don't you know?' Mrs Beale had said; a word always
august to Maisie, but henceforth to be softened by hazy, in fact by
quite languorous edges. There was at any rate a week in which no
less than nine volumes arrived, and the impression was to be
gathered from Mrs Beale that the obscure intercourse she enjoyed
with Sir Claude not only involved an account and a criticism of
studies, but was organised almost for the very purpose of report and
consultation. It was for Maisie's education in short that, as she often
repeated, she closed her door – closed it to the gentlemen who used
to flock there in such numbers and whom her husband's practical
desertion of her would have made it a course of the highest
indelicacy to receive. Maisie was familiar from of old with the
principle at least of the care that a woman, as Mrs Beale phrased it,
attractive and exposed must take of her 'character', and was duly
impressed with the rigour of her stepmother's scruples. There was
literally no one of the other sex whom she seemed to feel at liberty
to see at home, and when the child risked an enquiry about the
ladies who, one by one, during her own previous period, had been
made quite loudly welcome, Mrs Beale hastened to inform her
that, one by one, they had, the fiends, been found out, after all, to
be awful. If she wished to know more about them she was
recommended to approach her father.

Maisie had, however, at the very moment of this injunction
much livelier curiosities, for the dream of lectures at an institution
had at last become a reality, thanks to Sir Claude's now unbounded
energy in discovering what could be done. It stood out in this
connection that when you came to look into things in a spirit of
earnestness an immense deal could be done for very little more than
your fare in the Underground. The institution – there was a
splendid one in a part of the town but little known to the child –
became, in the glow of such a spirit, a thrilling place, and the walk

to it from the station through Glower Street (a pronunciation for which Mrs Beale once laughed at her little friend) a pathway literally strewn with 'subjects'. Maisie imagined herself to pluck them as she went, though they thickened in the great grey rooms where the fountain of knowledge, in the form usually of a high voice that she took at first to be angry, splashed in the stillness of rows of faces thrust out like empty jugs. 'It *must* do us good – it's all so hideous,' Mrs Beale had immediately declared; manifesting a purity of resolution that made these occasions quite the most harmonious of all the many on which the pair had pulled together. Maisie certainly had never, in such an association, felt so uplifted, and never above all been so carried off her feet, as at the moments of Mrs Beale's breathlessly re-entering the house and fairly shrieking upstairs to know if they should still be in time for a lecture. Her stepdaughter, all ready from the earliest hours, almost leaped over the banister to respond, and they dashed out together in quest of learning as hard as they often dashed back to release Mrs Beale for other preoccupations. There had been in short no bustle like these particular spasms, once they had broken out, since that last brief flurry when Mrs Wix, blowing as if she were grooming her, 'made up' for everything previously lost at her father's.

These weeks as well were too few, but they were flooded with a new emotion, part of which indeed came from the possibility that, through the long telescope of Glower Street, or perhaps between the pillars of the institution – which impressive objects were what Maisie thought most made it one – they should some day spy Sir Claude. That was what Mrs Beale, under pressure, had said – doubtless a little impatiently: 'Oh yes, oh yes, some day!' His joining them was clearly far less of a matter of course than was to have been gathered from his original profession of desire to improve in their company his own mind; and this sharpened our young lady's guess that since that occasion either something destructive had happened or something desirable hadn't. Mrs Beale had thrown but a partial light in telling her how it had turned out that nobody had been squared. Maisie wished at any rate that somebody *would* be squared. However, though in every approach to the temple of knowledge she watched in vain for Sir Claude, there was no doubt about the action of his loved image as an incentive and a recompense. When the institution was most on pillars – or, as Mrs Beale put it, on stilts – when the subject was deepest and the lecture longest and the listeners ugliest, then it was they both felt their patron in the background would be most pleased with them.

One day, abruptly, with a glance at this background, Mrs Beale said to her companion: 'We'll go tonight to the thingumbob at Earl's Court'; an announcement putting forth its full lustre when she had made known that she referred to the great Exhibition just opened in that quarter, a collection of extraordinary foreign things in tremendous gardens, with illuminations, bands, elephants, switchbacks and side-shows, as well as crowds of people among whom they might possibly see some one they knew. Maisie flew in the same bound at the neck of her friend and at the name of Sir Claude, on which Mrs Beale confessed that – well, yes, there was just a chance that he would be able to meet them. He never of course, in his terrible position, knew what might happen from hour to hour; but he hoped to be free and he had given Mrs Beale the tip. 'Bring her there on the quiet and I'll try to turn up' – this was clear enough on what so many weeks of privation had made of his desire to see the child: it even appeared to represent on his part a yearning as constant as her own. That in turn was just puzzling enough to make Maisie express a bewilderment. She couldn't see, if they were so intensely of the same mind, why the theory on which she had come back to Mrs Beale, the general reunion, the delightful trio, should have broken down so in fact. Mrs Beale furthermore only gave her more to think about in saying that their disappointment was the result of his having got into his head a kind of idea.

'What kind of idea?'

'Oh goodness knows!' She spoke with an approach to asperity. 'He's so awfully delicate.'

'Delicate?' – that was ambiguous.

'About what he does, don't you know?' said Mrs Beale. She fumbled. 'Well, about what *we* do.'

Maisie wondered. 'You and me?'

'Me and *him*, silly!' cried Mrs Beale with, this time, a real giggle.

'But you don't do any harm – *you* don't,' said Maisie, wondering afresh and intending her emphasis as a decorous allusion to her parents.

'Of course we don't, you angel – that's just the ground *I* take!' her companion exultantly responded. 'He says he doesn't want you mixed up.'

'Mixed up with what?'

'That's exactly what *I* want to know: mixed up with what, and how you are any more mixed –?' Mrs Beale paused without ending her question. She ended after an instant in a different way. 'All you can say is that it's his fancy.'

The tone of this, in spite of its expressing a resignation, the fruit of weariness, that dismissed the subject, conveyed so vividly how much such a fancy was not Mrs Beale's own that our young lady was led by the mere fact of contact to arrive at a dim apprehension of the unuttered and the unknown. The relation between her step-parents had then a mysterious residuum; this was the first time she really had reflected that except as regards herself it was not a relationship. To each other it was only what they might have happened to make it, and she gathered that this, in the event, had been something that led Sir Claude to keep away from her. Didn't he fear she would be compromised? The perception of such a scruple endeared him the more, and it flashed over her that she might simplify everything by showing him how little she made of such a danger. Hadn't she lived with her eyes on it from her third year? It was the condition most frequently discussed at the Faranges', where the word was always in the air and where at the age of five, amid rounds of applause, she could gabble it off. She knew as well in short that a person could be compromised as that a person could be slapped with a hair-brush or left alone in the dark, and it was equally familiar to her that each of these ordeals was in general held to have too little effect. But the first thing was to make absolutely sure of Mrs Beale. This was done by saying to her thoughtfully: 'Well, if you don't mind – and you really don't, do you?'

Mrs Beale, with a dawn of amusement, considered. 'Mixing you up? Not a bit. For what does it mean?'

'Whatever it means I don't in the least mind *being* mixed. Therefore if you don't and I don't,' Maisie concluded, 'don't you think that when I see him this evening I had better just tell him we don't and ask him why in the world *he* should?'

XVIII

THE child, however, was not destined to enjoy much of Sir Claude at the 'thingumbob', which took for them a very different turn indeed. On the spot Mrs Beale, with hilarity, had urged her to the course proposed; but later, at the Exhibition, she withdrew this allowance, mentioning as a result of second thoughts that when a man was so sensitive anything at all frisky usually made him worse. It would have been hard indeed for Sir Claude to be 'worse', Maisie felt, as, in the gardens and the crowd, when the first dazzle had dropped, she looked for him in vain up and down. They had all their time, the couple, for frugal wistful wandering: they had partaken together at home of the light vague meal – Maisie's name for it was a 'jam-supper' – to which they were reduced when Mr Farange sought his pleasure abroad. It was abroad now entirely that Mr Farange pursued this ideal, and it was the actual impression of his daughter, derived from his wife, that he had three days before joined a friend's yacht at Cowes.

The place was full of side-shows, to which Mrs Beale could introduce the little girl only, alas, by revealing to her so attractive, so enthralling a name: the side-shows, each time, were sixpence apiece, and the fond allegiance enjoyed by the elder of our pair had been established from the earliest time in spite of a paucity of sixpences. Small coin dropped from her as half-heartedly as answers from bad children to lessons that had not been looked at. Maisie passed more slowly the great painted posters, pressing with a linked arm closer to her friend's pocket, where she hoped for the audible chink of a shilling. But the upshot of this was but to deepen her yearning: if Sir Claude would only at last come the shillings would begin to ring. The companions paused, for want of one, before the Flowers of the Forest, a large presentment of bright brown ladies – they were brown all over – in a medium suggestive of tropical luxuriance, and there Maisie dolorously expressed her belief that he would never come at all. Mrs Beale hereupon, though discernibly disappointed, reminded her that he had not been promised as a certainty – a remark that caused the child to gaze at the Flowers through a blur in which they became more magnificent, yet oddly more confused, and by which moreover confusion was imparted to the aspect of a gentleman who at that moment, in the company of a lady, came out of the brilliant booth. The lady was so brown that Maisie at first took her for one of the Flowers; but during the few seconds that this required – a few seconds in which she had also desolately given up Sir Claude – she heard Mrs Beale's voice, behind her, gather both wonder and pain into a single sharp little cry.

'Of all the wickedness – *Beale!*'

He had already, without distinguishing them in the mass of strollers, turned another way – it seemed at the brown lady's suggestion. Her course was marked, over heads and shoulders, by an upright scarlet plume, as to the ownership of which Maisie was instantly eager. 'Who is she? – who is she?'

But Mrs Beale for a moment only looked after them. 'The liar – the liar!'

Maisie considered. 'Because he's not – where one thought?' That was also, a month ago in Kensington Gardens, where her mother had not been. 'Perhaps he has come back,' she was quick to contribute.

'He never went – the hound!'

That, according to Sir Claude, had been also what her mother had not done, and Maisie could only have a sense of something that in a maturer mind would be called the way history repeats itself. 'Who is she?' she asked again.

Mrs Beale, fixed to the spot, seemed lost in the vision of an opportunity missed. 'If he had only seen me!' – it came from between her teeth. 'She's a brand-new one. But he must have been with her since Tuesday.'

Maisie took it in. 'She's almost black,' she then reported.

'They're always hideous,' said Mrs Beale.

This was a remark on which the child had again to reflect. 'Oh not his *wives*!' she remonstrantly exclaimed. The words at another moment would probably have set her friend 'off', but Mrs Beale was now, in her instant vigilance, too immensely 'on'. 'Did you ever in your life see such a feather?' Maisie presently continued.

This decoration appeared to have paused at some distance, and in spite of intervening groups they could both look at it. 'Oh that's the way they dress – the vulgarest of the vulgar!'

'They're coming back – they'll see us!' Maisie the next moment cried; and while her companion answered that this was exactly what she wanted and the child returned 'Here they are – here they are!' the unconscious subjects of so much attention, with a change of mind about their direction, quickly retraced their steps and precipitated themselves upon their critics. Their unconsciousness gave Mrs Beale time to leap, under her breath, to a recognition which Maisie caught.

'It must be Mrs Cuddon!'

Maisie looked at Mrs Cuddon hard – her lips even echoed the name. What followed was extraordinarily rapid – a minute of livelier battle than had ever yet, in so short a span at least, been waged round our heroine. The muffled shock – lest people should notice – was violent, and it was only for her later thought that the steps fell into their order, the steps through which, in a bewilderment not so much of sound as of silence, she had come to find herself, too soon for comprehension and too strangely for fear, at the door of the Exhibition with her father. He thrust her into a hansom and got in after her, and then it was – as she drove along with him – that she recovered a little what had happened. Face to face with them in the gardens he had seen them, and there had been a moment of checked concussion during which, in a glare of black eyes and a toss of red plumage, Mrs Cuddon had recognised them, ejaculated and vanished. There had been another moment at which she became aware of Sir Claude, also poised there in surprise, but out of her father's view, as if he had been warned off at the very moment of reaching them. It fell into its place with all the rest that she had heard Mrs Beale say to her father, but whether low or loud was now lost to her, something about his having this time a new one; on which he had growled something indistinct but apparently in the tone and of the sort that the child, from her earliest years, had associated with hearing somebody retort to somebody that somebody was 'another'. 'Oh I stick to the old!' Mrs Beale had then quite loudly pronounced; and her accent, even as the cab got away, was still in the air, Maisie's effective companion having spoken no other word from the moment of whisking her off – none at least save the indistinguishable address which, over the top of the hansom and poised on the step, he had given the driver. Reconstructing these things later Maisie theorised that she at this point would have put a question to him had not the silence into which he charmed her or scared her – she could scarcely tell which – come from his suddenly making her feel his arm about her, feel, as he drew her close, that he was agitated in a way he had never yet shown her. It struck her he trembled, trembled too much to speak, and this had the effect of making her, with an emotion which, though it had begun to throb in an instant, was by no means all dread, conform to his portentous hush. The act of possession that his pressure in a manner advertised came back to her after the longest of the long intermissions that had ever let anything come back. They drove and drove, and he kept her close; she stared straight before her, holding her breath, watching one dark street succeed another and strangely conscious that what it all meant was somehow that papa was less to be left out of everything than she had supposed. It took her but a minute to surrender to this discovery, which, in the form of his present embrace, suggested a purpose in him prodigiously reaffirmed and with that a confused confidence. She neither knew exactly what he had done nor what he was doing; she could only, altogether impressed and rather proud, vibrate with the sense that he had jumped up to do something and that she had as quickly become a part of it. It was a part of it too that here they were at a house that seemed not large, but in the fresh white front of which the street-lamp showed a smartness of flower-boxes. The child had been in thousands of stories – all Mrs Wix's and her own, to say nothing of the richest romances of French Elise – but she had never been in such a story as this. By the time he had helped her out of the cab, which drove away, and she heard in the door of the house the prompt little click of his key, the Arabian Nights had quite closed round her.

From this minute that pitch of the wondrous was in everything, particularly in such an instant 'Open Sesame' and in the departure of the cab, a rattling void filled with relinquished step-parents; it was, with the vividness, the almost blinding whiteness of the light that sprang responsive to papa's quick touch of a little brass knob on the wall, in a place that, at the top of a short soft staircase, struck her as the most beautiful she had ever seen in her life. The next thing she perceived it to be was the drawing-room of a lady – oh of a lady, she could see in a moment, and not of a gentleman, not even of one like papa himself or even like Sir Claude – whose things were as much prettier than mamma's as it had always had to be confessed that mamma's were prettier than Mrs Beale's. In the middle of the small bright room and the presence of more curtains and cushions, more pictures and mirrors, more palm-trees drooping over brocaded and gilded nooks, more little silver boxes scattered over little crooked tables and little oval miniatures hooked upon velvet screens than Mrs Beale and her ladyship together could, in an unnatural alliance, have dreamed of mustering, the child became aware, with a sharp foretaste of compassion, of something that was strangely like a relegation to obscurity of each of those women of taste. It was a stranger operation still that her father should on the spot be presented to her as quite advantageously and even grandly at home in the dazzling scene and himself by so much the more separated from scenes inferior to it. She spent with him in it, while explanations continued to hang back, twenty minutes that, in their sudden drop of danger, affected her, though there were neither buns nor ginger-beer, like an extemporised expensive treat.

'Is she very rich?' He had begun to strike her as almost embarrassed, so shy that he might have found himself with a young lady with whom he had little in common. She was literally moved by this apprehension to offer him some tactful relief.

Beale Farange stood and smiled at his young lady, his back to the fanciful fireplace, his light overcoat – the very lightest in London – wide open, and his wonderful lustrous beard completely concealing the expanse of his shirt-front. It pleased her more than ever to think that papa was handsome and, though as high aloft as mamma and almost, in his specially florid evening-dress, as splendid, of a beauty somehow less belligerent, less terrible. 'The Countess? Why do you ask me that?'

Maisie's eyes opened wider. 'Is she a Countess?'

He seemed to treat her wonder as a positive tribute.

'Oh yes, my dear, but it isn't an English title.'

Her manner appreciated this. 'Is it a French one?'

'No, nor French either. It's American.'

She conversed agreeably. 'Ah then of course she must be rich.' She took in such a combination of nationality and rank. 'I never saw anything so lovely.'

'Did you have a sight of her?' Beale asked.

'At the Exhibition?' Maisie smiled. 'She was gone too quick.'

Her father laughed. 'She did slope!' She had feared he would say something about Mrs Beale and Sir Claude, yet the way he spared them made her rather uneasy too. All he risked was, the next minute, 'She has a horror of vulgar scenes.'

This was something she needn't take up; she could still continue bland. 'But where do you suppose she went?'

'Oh I thought she'd have taken a cab and have been here by this time. But she'll turn up all right.'

'I'm sure I *hope* she will,' Maisie said; she spoke with an earnestness begotten of the impression of all the beauty about them, to which, in person, the Countess might make further contribution. 'We came awfully fast,' she added.

Her father again laughed loud. 'Yes, my dear, I made you step out!' He waited an instant, then pursued: 'I want her to see you.'

Maisie, at this, rejoiced in the attention that, for their evening out, Mrs Beale, even to the extent of personally 'doing up' her old hat, had given her appearance. Meanwhile her father went on: 'You'll like her awfully.'

'Oh I'm sure I shall!' After which, either from the effect of having said so much or from that of a sudden glimpse of the impossibility of saying more, she felt an embarrassment and sought refuge in a minor branch of the subject. 'I thought she was Mrs Cuddon.'

Beale's gaiety rather increased than diminished. 'You mean my wife did? My dear child, my wife's a damned fool!' He had the oddest air of speaking of his wife as of a person whom she might scarcely have known, so that the refuge of her scruple didn't prove particularly happy. Beale on the other hand appeared after an instant himself to feel a scruple. 'What I mean is, to speak seriously, that she doesn't really know anything about anything.' He paused, following the child's charmed eyes and tentative step or two as they brought her nearer to the pretty things on one of the tables. 'She thinks she has good things, don't you know!' He quite jeered at Mrs Beale's delusion.

Maisie felt she must confess that it *was* one; everything she had missed at the side-shows was made up to her by the Countess's luxuries. 'Yes,' she considered; 'she does think that.'

There was again a dryness in the way Beale replied that it didn't matter what she thought; but there was an increasing sweetness for his daughter in being with him so long without his doing anything worse. The whole hour of course was to remain with her, for days and weeks, ineffaceably illumined and confirmed; by the end of which she was able to read into it a hundred things that had been at the moment mere miraculous pleasantness. What they at the moment came to was simply that her companion was still in a good deal of a flutter, yet wished not to show it, and that just in proportion as he succeeded in this attempt he was able to encourage her to regard him as kind. He moved about the room after a little, showed her things, spoke to her as a person of taste, told her the name, which she remembered, of the famous French lady represented in one of the miniatures, and remarked, as if he had caught her wistful over a trinket or a trailing stuff, that he made no doubt the Countess, on coming in, would give her something jolly. He spied a pink satin box with a looking-glass let into the cover, which he raised, with a quick facetious flourish, to offer her the privilege of six rows of chocolate bonbons, cutting out thereby Sir Claude, who had never gone beyond four rows. 'I can do what I like with these,' he said, 'for I don't mind telling you I gave 'em to her myself.' The Countess had evidently appreciated the gift; there were numerous gaps, a ravage now quite unchecked, in the array. Even while they waited together Maisie had her sense, which was the mark of what their separation had become, of her having grown for him, since the last time he had, as it were, noticed her, and by increase of years and of inches if by nothing else, much more of a little person to reckon with. Yes, this was a part of the positive awkwardness that he carried off by being almost foolishly tender. There was a passage during which, on a yellow silk sofa under one of the palms, he had her on his knee, stroking her hair, playfully holding her off while he showed his shining fangs and let her, with a vague affectionate helpless pointless 'Dear old girl, dear little daughter,' inhale the fragrance of his cherished beard. She must have been sorry for him, she afterwards knew, so well could she privately follow his difficulty in being specific to her about anything. She had such possibilities of vibration, of response, that it needed nothing more than this to make up to her in fact for omissions. The tears came into her eyes again as they had done when in the Park that day the Captain told her so 'splendidly' that her mother was good. What was this but splendid too – this still directer goodness of her father and this unexampled shining solitude with him, out of which everything had dropped but that he was papa and that he was magnificent? It didn't spoil it that she finally felt he must have, as he became restless, some purpose he didn't quite see his way to bring out, for in the freshness of their recovered fellowship she would have lent herself gleefully to his suggesting, or even to his pretending, that their relations were easy and graceful. There was something in him that seemed, and quite touchingly, to ask her to help him to pretend – pretend he knew enough about her life and her education, her means of subsistence and her view of himself, to give the questions he couldn't put her a natural domestic tone. She would have pretended with ecstasy if he could only have given her the cue. She waited for it while, between his big teeth, he breathed the sighs she didn't know to be stupid. And as if, though he was so stupid all through, he had let the friendly suffusion of her eyes yet tell him she was ready for anything, he floundered about, wondering what the devil he could lay hold of.

XIX

WHEN he had lighted a cigarette and begun to smoke in her face it
was as if he had struck with the match the note of some queer
clumsy ferment of old professions, old scandals, old duties, a dim
perception of what he possessed in her and what, if everything had
only – damn it! – been totally different, she might still be able to
give him. What she was able to give him, however, as his blinking
eyes seemed to make out through the smoke, would be simply
what he should be able to get from her. To give something, to give
here on the spot, was all her own desire. Among the old things that
came back was her little instinct of keeping the peace; it made her
wonder more sharply what particular thing she could do or not do,
what particular word she could speak or not speak, what particular
line she could take or not take, that might for every one, even for
the Countess, give a better turn to the crisis. She was ready, in this
interest, for an immense surrender, a surrender of everything but
Sir Claude, of everything but Mrs Beale. The immensity didn't
include *them*; but if he had an idea at the back of his head she had
also one in a recess as deep, and for a time, while they sat together,
there was an extraordinary mute passage between her vision of this
vision of his, his vision of her vision, and her vision of his vision of
her vision. What there was no effective record of indeed was the
small strange pathos on the child's part of an innocence so saturated
with knowledge and so directed to diplomacy. What, further,
Beale finally laid hold of while he masked again with his fine
presence half the flounces of the fireplace was: 'Do you know, my
dear, I shall soon be off to America?' It struck his daughter both as
a short cut and as the way he wouldn't have said it to his wife. But

his wife figured with a bright superficial assurance in her response.

'Do you mean with Mrs Beale?'

Her father looked at her hard. 'Don't be a little ass!'

Her silence appeared to represent a concentrated effort not to be. 'Then with the Countess?'

'With her or without her, my dear; that concerns only your poor daddy. She has big interests over there, and she wants me to take a look at them.'

Maisie threw herself into them. 'Will that take very long?'

'Yes; they're in such a muddle — it may take months. Now what I want to hear, you know, is whether you'd like to come along?'

Planted once more before him in the middle of the room she felt herself turning white. 'I?' she gasped, yet feeling as soon as she had spoken that such a note of dismay was not altogether pretty. She felt it still more while her father replied, with a shake of his legs, a toss of his cigarette-ash and a fidgety look — he was for ever taking one — all the length of his waistcoat and trousers, that she needn't be quite so disgusted. It helped her in a few seconds to appear more as he would like her that she saw, in the lovely light of the Countess's splendour, exactly, however she appeared, the right answer to make. 'Dear papa, I'll go with you anywhere.'

He turned his back to her and stood with his nose at the glass of the chimneypiece while he brushed specks of ash out of his beard. Then he abruptly said: 'Do you know anything about your brute of a mother?'

It was just of her brute of a mother that the manner of the question in a remarkable degree reminded her: it had the free flight of one of Ida's fine bridgings of space. With the sense of this was kindled for Maisie at the same time an inspiration. 'Oh yes, I know everything!' and she became so radiant that her father, seeing it in the mirror, turned back to her and presently, on the sofa, had her at his knee again and was again particularly affecting. Maisie's inspiration instructed her, pressingly, that the more she should be able to say about mamma the less she would be called upon to speak of her step-parents. She kept hoping the Countess would come in before her power to protect them was exhausted; and it was now, in closer quarters with her companion, that the idea at the back of her head shifted its place to her lips. She told him she had met her mother in the Park with a gentleman who, while Sir Claude had strolled with her ladyship, had been kind and had sat and talked to her; narrating the scene with a remembrance of her pledge of secrecy to the Captain quite brushed away by the joy of seeing Beale listen without profane interruption. It was almost an amazement, but it was indeed all a joy, thus to be able to guess that papa was at last quite tired of his anger – of his anger at any rate about mamma. He was only bored with her now. That made it, however, the more imperative that his spent displeasure shouldn't be blown out again. It charmed the child to see how much she could interest him; and the charm remained even when, after asking her a dozen questions, he observed musingly and a little obscurely: 'Yes, damned if she won't!' For in this too there was a detachment, a wise weariness that made her feel safe. She had had to mention Sir Claude, though she mentioned him as little as possible and Beale only appeared to look quite over his head. It pieced itself together for her that this was the mildness of general indifference, a source of profit so great for herself personally that if the Countess was the author of it she was prepared literally to hug the Countess. She betrayed that eagerness by a restless question about her, to which her father replied:

'Oh she has a head on her shoulders. I'll back her to get out of anything!' He looked at Maisie quite as if he could trace the connection between her enquiry and the impatience of her gratitude. 'Do you mean to say you'd really come with me?'

She felt as if he were now looking at her very hard indeed, and also as if she had grown ever so much older. 'I'll do anything in the world you ask me, papa.'

He gave again, with a laugh and with his legs apart, his proprietary glance at his waistcoat and trousers. 'That's a way, my dear, of saying "No, thank you!" You know you don't want to go the least little mite. You can't humbug *me*!' Beale Farange laid down. 'I don't want to bully you – I never bullied you in my life; but I make you the offer, and it's to take or to leave. Your mother will never again have any more to do with you than if you were a kitchenmaid she had turned out for going wrong. Therefore of course I'm your natural protector and you've a right to get everything out of me you can. Now's your chance, you know – you won't be half-clever if you don't. You can't say I don't put it before you – you can't say I ain't kind to you or that I don't play fair. Mind you never say that, you know – it *would* bring me down on you. I know what's proper. I'll take you again, just as I *have* taken you again and again. And I'm much obliged to you for making up such a face.'

She was conscious enough that her face indeed couldn't please him if it showed any sign – just as she hoped it didn't – of her sharp impression of what he now really wanted to do. Wasn't he trying to turn the tables on her, embarrass her somehow into admitting that what would really suit her little book would be, after doing so much for good manners, to leave her wholly at liberty to arrange for herself? She began to be nervous again: it rolled over her that this was their parting, their parting for ever, and that he had brought her there for so many caresses only because it was important such an occasion should look better for him than any other. For her to spoil it by the note of discord would certainly give him ground for complaint; and the child was momentarily bewildered between her alternatives of agreeing with him about her wanting to get rid of him and displeasing him by pretending to stick to him. So she found for the moment no solution but to murmur very helplessly: 'Oh papa – oh papa!'

'I know what you're up to – don't tell *me*!' After which he came straight over and, in the most inconsequent way in the world, clasped her in his arms a moment and rubbed his beard against her cheek. Then she understood as well as if he had spoken it that what he wanted, hang it, was that she should let him off with all the honours – with all the appearance of virtue and sacrifice on his side. It was exactly as if he had broken out to her: 'I say, you little booby, help me to be irreproachable, to be noble, and yet to have none of the beastly bore of it. There's only impropriety enough for one of us; so *you* must take it all. *Repudiate* your dear old daddy – in the face, mind you, of his tender supplications. He can't be rough with you – it isn't in his nature: therefore you'll have successfully chucked him because he was too generous to be as firm with you, poor man, as was, after all, his duty.' This was what he communicated in a series of tremendous pats on the back; that portion of her person had never been so thumped since Moddle thumped her when she choked. After a moment he gave her the further impression of having become sure enough of her to be able very gracefully to say out: 'You know your mother loathes you, loathes you simply. And I've been thinking over your precious man – the fellow you told me about.'

'Well,' Maisie replied with competence, 'I'm sure of *him*.'

Her father was vague for an instant. 'Do you mean sure of his liking you?'

'Oh no; of his liking *her*!'

Beale had a return of gaiety. 'There's no accounting for tastes! It's what they all say, you know.'

'I don't care – I'm sure of him!' Maisie repeated.

'Sure, you mean, that she'll bolt?'

Maisie knew all about bolting, but, decidedly, she *was* older, and there was something in her that could wince at the way her father made the ugly word – ugly enough at best – sound flat and low. It prompted her to amend his allusion, which she did by saying: 'I don't know what she'll do. But she'll be happy.'

'Let us hope so,' said Beale – almost as for edification. 'The more happy she is at any rate the less she'll want you about. That's why I press you,' he agreeably pursued, 'to consider this handsome offer – I mean seriously, you know – of your sole surviving parent.'

Their eyes, at this, met again in a long and extraordinary communion which terminated in his ejaculating: 'Ah you little scoundrel!' She took it from him in the manner it seemed to her he would like best and with a success that encouraged him to go on: 'You *are* a deep little devil!' Her silence, ticking like a watch, acknowledged even this, in confirmation of which he finally brought out: 'You've settled it with the other pair!'

'Well, what if I have?' She sounded to herself most bold.

Her father, quite as in the old days, broke into a peal. 'Why, don't you know they're awful?'

She grew bolder still. 'I don't care – not a bit!'

'But they're probably the worst people in the world and the very greatest criminals,' Beale pleasantly urged. 'I'm not the man, my dear, not to let you know it.'

'Well, it doesn't prevent them from loving me. They love me tremendously.' Maisie turned crimson to hear herself.

Her companion fumbled; almost any one – let alone a daughter – would have seen how conscientious he wanted to be. 'I dare say. But do you know why?' She braved his eyes and he added: 'You're a jolly good pretext.'

'For what?' Maisie asked.

'Why, for their game. I needn't tell you what that is.'

The child reflected. 'Well then that's all the more reason.'

'Reason for what, pray?'

'For their being kind to me.'

'And for your keeping in with them?' Beale roared again; it was as if his spirits rose and rose. 'Do you realise, pray, that in saying that you're a monster?'

She turned it over. 'A monster?'

'They've *made* one of you. Upon my honour it's quite awful. It shows the kind of people they are. Don't you understand,' Beale pursued, 'that when they've made you as horrid as they can – as horrid as themselves – they'll just simply chuck you?'

She had at this a flicker of passion. 'They *won't* chuck me!'

'I beg your pardon,' her father courteously insisted; 'it's my duty to put it before you. I shouldn't forgive myself if I didn't point out to you that they'll cease to require you.' He spoke as if with an appeal to her intelligence that she must be ashamed not adequately to meet, and this gave a real distinction to his superior delicacy.

It cleared the case as he had wished. 'Cease to require me because they won't care?' She paused with that sketch of her idea.

'*Of course* Sir Claude won't care if his wife bolts. That's his game. It will suit him down to the ground.'

This was a proposition Maisie could perfectly embrace, but it still left a loophole for triumph. She turned it well over. 'You mean if mamma doesn't come back ever at all?' The composure with which her face was presented to that prospect would have shown a spectator the long road she had travelled. 'Well, but that won't put Mrs Beale –'

'In the same comfortable position –?' Beale took her up with relish; he had sprung to his feet again, shaking his legs and looking at his shoes. 'Right you are, darling! Something more will be wanted for Mrs Beale.' He just paused, then he added: 'But she may not have long to wait for it.'

Maisie also for a minute looked at his shoes, though they were not the pair she most admired, the laced yellow 'uppers' and patent-leather complement. At last, with a question, she raised her eyes. 'Aren't you coming back?'

Once more he hung fire; after which he gave a small laugh that in the oddest way in the world reminded her of the unique sounds she had heard emitted by Mrs Wix. 'It may strike you as extraordinary that I should make you such an admission; and in point of fact you're not to understand that I do. But we'll put it that way to help your decision. The point is that that's the way my wife will presently be sure to put it. You'll hear her shrieking that she's deserted, so that she may just pile up her wrongs. She'll be as free as she likes then – as free, you see, as your mother's muff of a husband. They won't have anything more to consider and they'll just put you into the street. Do I understand,' Beale enquired, 'that, in the face of what I press on you, you still prefer to take the risk of that?' It was the most wonderful appeal any gentleman had ever addressed to his daughter, and it had placed Maisie in the middle of the room again while her father moved slowly about her with his hands in his pockets and something in his step that seemed, more than anything else he had done, to show the habit of the place. She turned her fevered little eyes over his friend's brightnesses, as if, on her own side, to press for some help in a quandary unexampled. As if also the pressure reached him he after an instant stopped short, completing the prodigy of his attitude and the pride of his loyalty by a supreme formulation of the general inducement. 'You've an eye, love! Yes, there's money. No end of money.'

This affected her at first in the manner of some great flashing dazzle in one of the pantomimes to which Sir Claude had taken her: she saw nothing in it but what it directly conveyed. 'And shall I never, never see you again –?'

'If I do go to America?' Beale brought it out like a man. 'Never, never, never!'

Hereupon, with the utmost absurdity, she broke down; everything gave way, everything but the horror of hearing herself definitely utter such an ugliness as the acceptance of that. So she only stiffened herself and said: 'Then I can't give you up.'

She held him some seconds looking at her, showing her a strained grimace, a perfect parade of all his teeth, in which it seemed to her she could read the disgust he didn't quite like to express at this departure from the pliability she had practically promised. But before she could attenuate in any way the crudity of her collapse he gave an impatient jerk which took him to the window. She heard a vehicle stop; Beale looked out; then he freshly faced her. He still said nothing, but she knew the Countess had come back. There was a silence again between them, but with a different shade of embarrassment from that of their united arrival; and it was still without speaking that, abruptly repeating one of the embraces of which he had already been so prodigal, he whisked her back to the lemon sofa just before the door of the room was thrown open. It was thus in renewed and intimate union with him that she was presented to a person whom she instantly recognised as the brown lady.

The brown lady looked almost as astonished, though not quite as alarmed, as when, at the Exhibition, she had gasped in the face of Mrs Beale. Maisie in truth almost gasped in her own; this was with the fuller perception that she was brown indeed. She literally struck the child more as an animal than as a 'real' lady; she might have been a clever frizzled poodle in a frill or a dreadful human monkey in a spangled petticoat. She had a nose that was far too big and eyes that were far too small and a moustache that was, well, not so happy a feature as Sir Claude's. Beale jumped up to her; while, to the child's astonishment, though as if in a quick intensity of thought, the Countess advanced as gaily as if, for many a day, nothing awkward had happened for any one. Maisie, in spite of a large acquaintance with the phenomenon, had never seen it so promptly established that nothing awkward was to be mentioned. The next minute the Countess had kissed her and exclaimed to Beale with bright tender reproach: 'Why, you never told me *half*! My dear child,' she cried, 'it was awfully nice of you to come!'

'But she hasn't come – she won't come!' Beale answered. 'I've put it to her how much you'd like it, but she declines to have anything to do with us.'

The Countess stood smiling, and after an instant that was mainly taken up with the shock of her weird aspect Maisie felt herself reminded of another smile, which was not ugly, though also interested – the kind light thrown, that day in the Park, from the clean fair face of the Captain. Papa's Captain – yes – was the Countess; but she wasn't nearly so nice as the other: it all came back, doubtless, to Maisie's minor appreciation of ladies. 'Shouldn't you like me,' said this one endearingly, 'to take you to Spa?'

'To Spa?' The child repeated the name to gain time, not to show

how the Countess brought back to her a dim remembrance of a
strange woman with a horrid face who once, years before, in an
omnibus, bending to her from an opposite seat, had suddenly
produced an orange and murmured 'Little dearie, won't you have
it?' She had felt then, for some reason, a small silly terror, though
afterwards conscious that her interlocutress, unfortunately hideous,
had particularly meant to be kind. This was also what the Countess
meant; yet the few words she had uttered and the smile with which
she had uttered them immediately cleared everything up. Oh no,
she wanted to go nowhere with *her*, for her presence had already,
in a few seconds, dissipated the happy impression of the room and
put an end to the pleasure briefly taken in Beale's command of such
elegance. There was no command of elegance in his having
exposed her to the approach of the short fat wheedling whiskered
person in whom she had now to recognise the only figure wholly
without attraction involved in any of the intimate connections her
immediate circle had witnessed the growth of. She was abashed
meanwhile, however, at having appeared to weigh in the balance
the place to which she had been invited; and she added as quickly
as possible: 'It isn't to America then?' The Countess, at this, looked
sharply at Beale, and Beale, airily enough, asked what the deuce it
mattered when she had already given him to understand she
wanted to have nothing to do with them. There followed between
her companions a passage of which the sense was drowned for her
in the deepening inward hum of her mere desire to get off; though
she was able to guess later on that her father must have put it to his
friend that it was no use talking, that she was an obstinate little pig
and that, besides, she was really old enough to choose for herself.
It glimmered back to her indeed that she must have failed quite
dreadfully to seem ideally other than rude, inasmuch as before she
knew it she had visibly given the impression that if they didn't
allow her to go home she should cry. Oh if there had ever been a
thing to cry about it was being so consciously and gawkily below
the handsomest offers any one could ever have received. The great

pain of the thing was that she could see the Countess liked her enough to wish to be liked in return, and it was from the idea of a return she sought utterly to flee. It was the idea of a return that after a confusion of loud words had broken out between the others brought to her lips with the tremor preceding disaster: 'Can't I, please, be sent home in a cab?' Yes, the Countess wanted her and the Countess was wounded and chilled, and she couldn't help it, and it was all the more dreadful because it only made the Countess more coaxing and more impossible. The only thing that sustained either of them perhaps till the cab came – Maisie presently saw it would come – was its being in the air somehow that Beale had done what he wanted. He went out to look for a conveyance; the servants, he said, had gone to bed, but she shouldn't be kept beyond her time. The Countess left the room with him, and, alone in the possession of it, Maisie hoped she wouldn't come back. It was all the effect of her face – the child simply couldn't look at it and meet its expression halfway. All in a moment too that queer expression had leaped into the lovely things – all in a moment she had to accept her father as liking some one whom she was sure neither her mother, nor Mrs Beale, nor Mrs Wix, nor Sir Claude, nor the Captain, nor even Mr Perriam and Lord Eric could possibly have liked. Three minutes later, downstairs, with the cab at the door, it was perhaps as a final confession of not having much to boast of that, on taking leave of her, he managed to press her to his bosom without her seeing his face. For herself she was so eager to go that their parting reminded her of nothing, not even of a single one of all the 'nevers' that above, as the penalty of not cleaving to him, he had attached to the question of their meeting again. There was something in the Countess that falsified everything, even the great interests in America and yet more the first flush of that superiority to Mrs Beale and to mamma which had been expressed in Sevres sets and silver boxes. These were still there, but perhaps there were no great interests in America. Mamma had known an American who was not a bit like this one. She was not, however,

of noble rank; her name was only Mrs Tucker. Maisie's detachment would none the less have been more complete if she had not
suddenly had to exclaim: 'Oh dear, I haven't any money!'

Her father's teeth, at this, were such a picture of appetite without
action as to be a match for any plea of poverty. 'Make your
stepmother pay.'

'Stepmothers *don't* pay!' cried the Countess. 'No stepmother
ever paid in her life!' The next moment they were in the street
together, and the next the child was in the cab, with the Countess,
on the pavement, but close to her, quickly taking money from a
purse whisked out of a pocket. Her father had vanished and there
was even yet nothing in that to reawaken the pang of loss. 'Here's
money,' said the brown lady: 'go!' The sound was commanding:
the cab rattled off. Maisie sat there with her hand full of coin. All
that for a cab? As they passed a street-lamp she bent to see how
much. What she saw was a cluster of sovereigns. There *must* then
have been great interests in America. It was still at any rate the
Arabian Nights.

XX

THE money was far too much even for a fee in a fairy-tale, and in
the absence of Mrs Beale, who, though the hour was now late, had
not yet returned to the Regent's Park, Susan Ash, in the hall, as
loud as Maisie was low and as bold as she was bland, produced, on
the exhibition offered under the dim vigil of the lamp that made
the place a contrast to the child's recent scene of light, the half-
crown that an unsophisticated cabman could pronounce to be the
least he would take. It was apparently long before Mrs Beale would
arrive, and in the interval Maisie had been induced by the prompt
Susan not only to go to bed like a darling dear, but, in still richer
expression of that character, to devote to the repayment of
obligations general as well as particular one of the sovereigns in the
ordered array that, on the dressing-table upstairs, was naturally not
less dazzling to a lone orphan of a housemaid than to the subject of
the manoeuvres of a quartette. This subject went to sleep with her
property gathered into a knotted handkerchief, the largest that
could be produced and lodged under her pillow; but the explanations that on the morrow were inevitably more complete with Mrs
Beale than they had been with her humble friend found their
climax in a surrender also more becomingly free. There were
explanations indeed that Mrs Beale had to give as well as to ask, and
the most striking of these was to the effect that it was dreadful for
a little girl to take money from a woman who was simply the vilest
of their sex. The sovereigns were examined with some attention,
the result of which, however, was to make the author of that
statement desire to know what, if one really went into the matter,
they could be called but the wages of sin. Her companion went

into it merely so far as the question of what then they were to do with them; on which Mrs Beale, who had by this time put them into her pocket, replied with dignity and with her hand on the place: 'We're to send them back on the spot!' Susan, the child soon afterwards learnt, had been invited to contribute to this act of restitution her one appropriated coin; but a closer clutch of the treasure showed in her private assurance to Maisie that there was a limit to the way she could be 'done'. Maisie had been open with Mrs Beale about the whole of last night's transaction; but she now found herself on the part of their indignant inferior a recipient of remarks that were so many ringing tokens of that lady's own suppressions. One of these bore upon the extraordinary hour – it was three in the morning if she really wanted to know – at which Mrs Beale had re-entered the house; another, in accents as to which Maisie's criticism was still intensely tacit, characterised her appeal as such a 'gime', such a 'shime', as one had never had to put up with; a third treated with some vigour the question of the enormous sums due belowstairs, in every department, for gratuitous labour and wasted zeal. Our young lady's consciousness was indeed mainly filled for several days with the apprehension created by the too slow subsidence of her attendant's sense of wrong. These days would become terrific like the Revolutions she had learnt by heart in Histories if an outbreak in the kitchen should crown them; and to promote that prospect she had through Susan's eyes more than one glimpse of the way in which Revolutions are prepared. To listen to Susan was to gather that the spark applied to the inflammables and already causing them to crackle would prove to have been the circumstance of one's being called a horrid low thief for refusing to part with one's own.

The redeeming point of this tension was, on the fifth day, that it actually appeared to have had to do with a breathless perception in our heroine's breast that scarcely more as the centre of Sir Claude's than as that of Susan's energies she had soon after breakfast been conveyed from London to Folkestone and established at a lovely

hotel. These agents, before her wondering eyes, had combined to
carry through the adventure and to give it the air of having owed
its success to the fact that Mrs Beale had, as Susan said, but just
stepped out. When Sir Claude, watch in hand, had met this fact
with the exclamation 'Then pack Miss Farange and come off with
us!' there had ensued on the stairs a series of gymnastics of a nature
to bring Miss Farange's heart into Miss Farange's mouth. She sat
with Sir Claude in a four-wheeler while he still held his watch;
held it longer than any doctor who had ever felt her pulse; long
enough to give her a vision of something like the ecstasy of ne-
glecting such an opportunity to show impatience. The ecstasy had
begun in the schoolroom and over the Berceuse, quite in the
manner of the same foretaste on the day, a little while back, when
Susan had panted up and she herself, after the hint about the
duchess, had sailed down; for what harm then had there been in
drops and disappointments if she could still have, even only a
moment, the sensation of such a name 'brought up'? It had
remained with her that her father had foretold her she would some
day be in the street, but it clearly wouldn't be this day, and she felt
justified of the preference betrayed to that parent as soon as her
visitor had set Susan in motion and laid his hand, while she waited
with him, kindly on her own. This was what the Captain, in
Kensington Gardens, had done; her present situation reminded her
a little of that one and renewed the dim wonder of the fashion after
which, from the first, such pats and pulls had struck her as the steps
and signs of other people's business and even a little as the wriggle
or the overflow of their difficulties. What had failed her and what
had frightened her on the night of the Exhibition lost themselves
at present alike in the impression that any 'surprise' now about to
burst from Sir Claude would be too big to burst all at once. Any
awe that might have sprung from his air of leaving out her
stepmother was corrected by the force of a general rule, the odd
truth that if Mrs Beale now never came nor went without making
her think of him, it was never, to balance that, the main mark of

his own renewed reality to appear to be a reference to Mrs Beale.
To be with Sir Claude was to think of Sir Claude, and that law
governed Maisie's mind until, through a sudden lurch of the cab,
which had at last taken in Susan and ever so many bundles and
almost reached Charing Cross, it popped again somehow into her
dizzy head the long-lost image of Mrs Wix.

It was singular, but from this time she understood and she
followed, followed with the sense of an ample filling-out of any
void created by symptoms of avoidance and of flight. Her ecstasy
was a thing that had yet more of a face than of a back to turn, a pair
of eyes still directed to Mrs Wix even after the slight surprise of
their not finding her, as the journey expanded, either at the
London station or at the Folkestone hotel. It took few hours to
make the child feel that if she was in neither of these places she was
at least everywhere else. Maisie had known all along a great deal,
but never so much as she was to know from this moment on and
as she learned in particular during the couple of days that she was
to hang in the air, as it were, over the sea which represented in
breezy blueness and with a summer charm a crossing of more spaces
than the Channel. It was granted her at this time to arrive at
divinations so ample that I shall have no room for the goal if I
attempt to trace the stages; as to which therefore I must be content
to say that the fullest expression we may give to Sir Claude's
conduct is a poor and pale copy of the picture it presented to his
young friend. Abruptly, that morning, he had yielded to the action
of the idea pumped into him for weeks by Mrs Wix on lines of
approach that she had been capable of the extraordinary art of
preserving from entanglement in the fine network of his relations
with Mrs Beale. The breath of her sincerity, blowing without a
break, had puffed him up to the flight by which, in the degree I
have indicated, Maisie too was carried off her feet. This consisted
neither in more nor in less than the brave stroke of his getting off
from Mrs Beale as well as from his wife – of making with the child
straight for some such foreign land as would give a support to Mrs

Wix's dream that she might still see his errors renounced and his delinquencies redeemed. It would all be a sacrifice − under eyes that would miss no faintest shade − to what even the strange frequenters of her ladyship's earlier period used to call the real good of the little unfortunate. Maisie's head held a suspicion of much that, during the last long interval, had confusedly, but quite candidly, come and gone in his own; a glimpse, almost awe-stricken in its gratitude, of the miracle her old governess had wrought. That functionary could not in this connection have been more impressive, even at second-hand, if she had been a prophetess with an open scroll or some ardent abbess speaking with the lips of the Church. She had clung day by day to their plastic associate, plying him with her deep, narrow passion, doing her simple utmost to convert him, and so working on him that he had at last really embraced his fine chance. That the chance was not delusive was sufficiently guaranteed by the completeness with which he could finally figure it out that, in case of his taking action, neither Ida nor Beale, whose book, on each side, it would only too well suit, would make any sort of row.

It sounds, no doubt, too penetrating, but it was not all as an effect of Sir Claude's betrayals that Maisie was able to piece together the beauty of the special influence through which, for such stretches of time, he had refined upon propriety by keeping, so far as possible, his sentimental interests distinct. She had ever of course in her mind fewer names than conceptions, but it was only with this drawback that she now made out her companion's absences to have had for their ground that he was the lover of her stepmother and that the lover of her stepmother could scarce logically pretend to a superior right to look after her. Maisie had by this time embraced the implication of a kind of natural divergence between lovers and little girls. It was just this indeed that could throw light on the probable contents of the pencilled note deposited on the hall-table in the Regent's Park and which would greet Mrs Beale on her return. Maisie freely figured it as

provisionally jocular in tone, even though to herself on this
occasion Sir Claude turned a graver face than he had shown in any
crisis but that of putting her into the cab when she had been horrid
to him after her parting with the Captain. He might really be
embarrassed, but he would be sure, to her view, to have muffled in
some bravado of pleasantry the disturbance produced at her father's
by the removal of a valued servant. Not that there wasn't a great
deal too that wouldn't be in the note – a great deal for which a
more comfortable place was Maisie's light little brain, where it
hummed away hour after hour and caused the first outlook at
Folkestone to swim in a softness of colour and sound. It became
clear in this medium that her stepfather had really now only to take
into account his entanglement with Mrs Beale. Wasn't he at last
disentangled from every one and every thing else? The obstacle to
the rupture pressed upon him by Mrs Wix in the interest of his
virtue would be simply that he was in love, or rather, to put it more
precisely, that Mrs Beale had left him no doubt of the degree in
which *she* was. She was so much so as to have succeeded in making
him accept for a time her infatuated grasp of him and even to some
extent the idea of what they yet might do together with a little
diplomacy and a good deal of patience. I may not even answer for
it that Maisie was not aware of how, in this, Mrs Beale failed to
share his all but insurmountable distaste for their allowing their
little charge to breathe the air of their gross irregularity – his
contention, in a word, that they should either cease to be irregular
or cease to be parental. Their little charge, for herself, had long ago
adopted the view that even Mrs Wix had at one time not thought
prohibitively coarse – the view that she was after all, *as* a little
charge, morally at home in atmospheres it would be appalling to
analyse. If Mrs Wix, however, ultimately appalled, had now set her
heart on strong measures, Maisie, as I have intimated, could also
work round both to the reasons for them and to the quite other
reasons for that lady's not, as yet at least, appearing in them at first-
hand.

Oh decidedly I shall never get you to believe the number of things she saw and the number of secrets she discovered! Why in the world, for instance, couldn't Sir Claude have kept it from her – except on the hypothesis of his not caring to – that, when you came to look at it and so far as it was a question of vested interests, he had quite as much right in her as her stepmother, not to say a right that Mrs Beale was in no position to dispute? He failed at all events of any such successful ambiguity as could keep her, when once they began to look across at France, from regarding even what was least explained as most in the spirit of their old happy times, their rambles and expeditions in the easier better days of their first acquaintance. Never before had she had so the sense of giving him a lead, for the sort of treatment of what was between them that would best carry it off, or of his being grateful to her for meeting him so much in the right place. She met him literally at the very point where Mrs Beale was most to be reckoned with, the point of the jealousy that was sharp in that lady and of the need of their keeping it as long as possible obscure to her that poor Mrs Wix had still a hand. Yes, she met him too in the truth of the matter that, as her stepmother had had no one else to be jealous of, she had made up for so gross a privation by directing the sentiment to a moral influence. Sir Claude appeared absolutely to convey in a wink that a moral influence capable of pulling a string was after all a moral influence exposed to the scratching out of its eyes; and that, this being the case, there was somebody they couldn't afford to leave unprotected before they should see a little better what Mrs Beale was likely to do. Maisie, true enough, had not to put it into words to rejoin, in the coffee-room, at luncheon: 'What *can* she do but come to you if papa does take a step that will amount to legal desertion?' Neither had he then, in answer, to articulate anything but the jollity of their having found a table at a window from which, as they partook of cold beef and apollinaris – for he hinted they would have to save lots of money – they could let their eyes hover tenderly on the far-off white cliffs that so often had signalled to the embarrassed English a promise of safety. Maisie stared at them as if she might really make out after a little a queer dear figure perched on them – a figure as to which she had already the subtle sense that, wherever perched, it would be the very oddest yet seen in France. But it was at least as exciting to feel where Mrs Wix wasn't as it would have been to know where she was, and if she wasn't yet at Boulogne this only thickened the plot.

If she was not to be seen that day, however, the evening was marked by an apparition before which, none the less, overstrained suspense folded on the spot its wings. Adjusting her respirations and attaching, under dropped lashes, all her thoughts to a smartness of frock and frill for which she could reflect that she had not appealed in vain to a loyalty in Susan Ash triumphant over the nice things their feverish flight had left behind, Maisie spent on a bench in the garden of the hotel the half-hour before dinner, that mysterious ceremony of the *table d'hôte* for which she had prepared with a punctuality of flutter. Sir Claude, beside her, was occupied with a cigarette and the afternoon papers; and though the hotel was full the garden showed the particular void that ensues upon the sound of the dressing-bell. She had almost had time to weary of the human scene; her own humanity at any rate, in the shape of a smutch on her scanty skirt, had held her so long that as soon as she raised her eyes they rested on a high fair drapery by which smutches were put to shame and which had glided toward her over the grass without her rioting its rustle. She followed up its stiff sheen – up and up from the ground, where it had stopped – till at the end of a considerable journey her impression felt the shock of the fixed face which, surmounting it, seemed to offer the climax of the dressed condition. 'Why mamma!' she cried the next instant – cried in a tone that, as she sprang to her feet, brought Sir Claude to his own beside her and gave her ladyship, a few yards off, the advantage of their momentary confusion. Poor Maisie's was immense; her mother's drop had the effect of one of the iron shutters that, in evening walks with Susan Ash, she had seen suddenly, at the touch of a spring, rattle down over shining shop-fronts. The light of foreign travel was darkened at a stroke; she had a horrible sense that they were caught; and for the first time of her life in Ida's presence she so far translated an impulse into an invidious act as to clutch straight at the hand of her responsible confederate. It didn't help her that he appeared at first equally hushed with horror; a minute during which, in the empty garden, with its long shadows on the lawn, its blue sea over the hedge and its startled peace in the air, both her elders remained as stiff as tall tumblers filled to the brim and held straight for fear of a spill. At last, in a tone that enriched the whole surprise by its unexpected softness, her mother said to Sir Claude: 'Do you mind at all my speaking to her?'

'Oh no; *do* you?' His reply was so long in coming that Maisie was the first to find the right note.

He laughed as he seemed to take it from her, and she felt a sufficient concession in his manner of addressing their visitor. 'How in the world did you know we were here?'

His wife, at this, came the rest of the way and sat down on the bench with a hand laid on her daughter, whom she gracefully drew to her and in whom, at her touch, the fear just kindled gave a second jump, but now in quite another direction. Sir Claude, on the further side, resumed his seat and his newspapers, so that the three grouped themselves like a family party; his connection, in the oddest way in the world, almost cynically and in a flash acknowledged, and the mother patting the child into conformities unspeakable. Maisie could already feel how little it was Sir Claude and she who were caught. She had the positive sense of their catching their relative, catching her in the act of getting rid of her burden with a finality that showed her as unprecedentedly relaxed. Oh yes, the fear had dropped, and she had never been so irrevocably parted with as in the pressure of possession now supremely exerted by Ida's long-gloved and much-bangled arm. 'I went to the Regent's Park' – this was presently her ladyship's answer to Sir Claude.

'Do you mean today?'

'This morning, just after your own call there. That's how I found you out; that's what has brought me.'

Sir Claude considered and Maisie waited. 'Whom then did you see?'

Ida gave a sound of indulgent mockery. 'I like your scare. I know your game. I didn't see the person I risked seeing, but I had been ready to take my chance of her.' She addressed herself to Maisie; she had encircled her more closely. 'I asked for *you*, my dear, but I saw no one but a dirty parlour-maid. She was red in the face with the great things that, as she told me, had just happened in the absence of her mistress; and she luckily had the sense to have made out the place to which Sir Claude had come to take you. If he hadn't given a false scent I should find you here: that was the supposition on which I've proceeded.' Ida had never been so explicit about proceeding or supposing, and Maisie, drinking this in, noted too how Sir Claude shared her fine impression of it. 'I wanted to see you,' his wife continued, 'and now you can judge of the trouble I've taken. I had everything to do in town today, but I managed to get off.'

Maisie and her companion, for a moment, did justice to this achievement; but Maisie was the first to express it. 'I'm glad you wanted to see me, mamma.' Then after a concentration more deep and with a plunge more brave: 'A little more and you'd have been too late.' It stuck in her throat, but she brought it out: 'We're going to France.'

Ida was magnificent; Ida kissed her on the forehead. 'That's just what I thought likely; it made me decide to run down. I fancied that in spite of your scramble you'd wait to cross, and it added to the reason I have for seeing you.'

Maisie wondered intensely what the reason could be, but she knew ever so much better than to ask. She was slightly surprised indeed to perceive that Sir Claude didn't, and to hear him immediately enquire: 'What in the name of goodness can you have to say to her?'

His tone was not exactly rude, but it was impatient enough to make his wife's response a fresh specimen of the new softness. 'That, my dear man, is all my own business.'

'Do you mean,' Sir Claude asked, 'that you wish me to leave you with her?'

'Yes, if you'll be so good; that's the extraordinary request I take the liberty of making.' Her ladyship had dropped to a mildness of irony by which, for a moment, poor Maisie was mystified and charmed, puzzled with a glimpse of something that in all the years had at intervals peeped out. Ida smiled at Sir Claude with the strange air she had on such occasions of defying an interlocutor to keep it up as long; her huge eyes, her red lips, the intense marks in her face formed an *éclairage* as distinct and public as a lamp set in a window. The child seemed quite to see in it the very beacon that had lighted her path; she suddenly found herself reflecting that it was no wonder the gentlemen were guided. This must have been the way mamma had first looked at Sir Claude; it brought back the lustre of the time they had outlived. It must have been the way she looked also at Mr Perriam and Lord Eric; above all it contributed in Maisie's mind to a completer view of that satisfied state of the Captain. Our young lady grasped this idea with a quick lifting of the heart; there was a stillness during which her mother flooded her with a wealth of support to the Captain's striking tribute. This stillness remained long enough unbroken to represent that Sir Claude too might but be gasping again under the spell originally strong for him; so that Maisie quite hoped he would at least say something to show a recognition of how charming she could be.

What he presently said was: 'Are you putting up for the night?'

His wife cast grandly about. 'Not here – I've come from Dover.'

Over Maisie's head, at this, they still faced each other. 'You spend the night there?'

'Yes, I brought some things. I went to the hotel and hastily arranged; then I caught the train that whisked me on here. You see what a day I've had of it.'

The statement may surprise, but these were really as obliging if not as lucid words as, into her daughter's ears at least, Ida's lips had ever dropped; and there was a quick desire in the daughter that for the hour at any rate they should duly be welcomed as a ground of intercourse. Certainly mamma had a charm which, when turned on, became a large explanation; and the only danger now in an impulse to applaud it would be that of appearing to signalise its rarity. Maisie, however, risked the peril in the geniality of an admission that Ida had indeed had a rush; and she invited Sir Claude to expose himself by agreeing with her that the rush had been even worse than theirs. He appeared to meet this appeal by saying with detachment enough: 'You go back there tonight?'

'Oh yes – there are plenty of trains.'

Again Sir Claude hesitated; it would have been hard to say if the child, between them, more connected or divided them. Then he brought out quietly: 'It will be late for you to knock about. I'll see you over.'

'You needn't trouble, thank you. I think you won't deny that I can help myself and that it isn't the first time in my dreadful life that I've somehow managed it.' Save for this allusion to her dreadful life they talked there, Maisie noted, as if they were only rather superficial friends; a special effect that she had often wondered at before in the midst of what she supposed to be intimacies. This effect was augmented by the almost casual manner in which her ladyship went on: 'I dare say I shall go abroad.'

'From Dover do you mean, straight?'

'How straight I can't say. I'm excessively ill.'

This for a minute struck Maisie as but a part of the conversation; at the end of which time she became aware that it ought to strike her – though it apparently didn't strike Sir Claude – as a part of something graver. It helped her to twist nearer. 'Ill, mamma – really ill?'

She regretted her 'really' as soon as she had spoken it; but there couldn't be a better proof of her mother's present polish than that

Ida showed no gleam of a temper to take it up. She had taken up at other times much tinier things. She only pressed Maisie's head against her bosom and said: 'Shockingly, my dear. I must go to that new place.'

'What new place?' Sir Claude enquired.

Ida thought, but couldn't recall it. 'Oh "Chose", don't you know? – where every one goes. I want some proper treatment. It's all I've ever asked for on earth. But that's not what I came to say.'

Sir Claude, in silence, folded one by one his newspapers; then he rose and stood whacking the palm of his hand with the bundle. 'You'll stop and dine with us?'

'Dear no – I can't dine at this sort of hour. I ordered dinner at Dover.'

Her ladyship's tone in this one instance showed a certain superiority to those conditions in which her daughter had artlessly found Folkestone a paradise. It was yet not so crushing as to nip in the bud the eagerness with which the latter broke out: 'But won't you at least have a cup of tea?'

Ida kissed her again on the brow. 'Thanks, love. I had tea before coming.' She raised her eyes to Sir Claude. 'She *is* sweet!' He made no more answer than if he didn't agree; but Maisie was at ease about that and was still taken up with the joy of this happier pitch of their talk, which put more and more of a meaning into the Captain's version of her ladyship and literally kindled a conjecture that such an admirer might, over there at the other place, be waiting for her to dine. Was the same conjecture in Sir Claude's mind? He partly puzzled her, if it had risen there, by the slight perversity with which he returned to a question that his wife evidently thought she had disposed of.

He whacked his hand again with his paper. 'I had really much better take you.'

'And leave Maisie here alone?'

Mamma so clearly didn't want it that Maisie leaped at the vision of a Captain who had seen her on from Dover and who, while he waited to take her back, would be hovering just at the same distance at which, in Kensington Gardens, the companion of his walk had herself hovered. Of course, however, instead of breathing any such guess she let Sir Claude reply; all the more that his reply could contribute so much to her own present grandeur. 'She won't be alone when she has a maid in attendance.'

Maisie had never before had so much of a retinue, and she waited also to enjoy the action of it on her ladyship. 'You mean the woman you brought from town?' Ida considered. 'The person at the house spoke of her in a way that scarcely made her out company for my child.' Her tone was that her child had never wanted, in her hands, for prodigious company. But she as distinctly continued to decline Sir Claude's. 'Don't be an old goose,' she said charmingly. 'Let us alone.'

In front of them on the grass he looked graver than Maisie at all now thought the occasion warranted. 'I don't see why you can't say it before me.'

His wife smoothed one of her daughter's curls. 'Say what, dear?'

'Why what you came to say.'

At this Maisie at last interposed: she appealed to Sir Claude. 'Do let her say it to me.'

He looked hard for a moment at his little friend. 'How do you know what she may say?'

'She must risk it,' Ida remarked.

'I only want to protect you,' he continued to the child.

'You want to protect yourself – that's what you mean,' his wife replied. 'Don't be afraid. I won't touch you.'

'She won't touch you – she *won't*!' Maisie declared. She felt by this time that she could really answer for it, and something of the emotion with which she had listened to the Captain came back to her. It made her so happy and so secure that she could positively patronise mamma. She did so in the Captain's very language. 'She's good, she's good!' she proclaimed.

'Oh Lord!' – Sir Claude, at this, let himself go. He appeared to have emitted some sound of derision that was smothered, to Maisie's ears, by her being again embraced by his wife. Ida released her and held her off a little, looking at her with a very queer face. Then the child became aware that their companion had left them and that from the face in question a confirmatory remark had proceeded.

'I *am* good, love,' said her ladyship.

XXI

A GOOD deal of the rest of Ida's visit was devoted to explaining, as it were, so extraordinary a statement. This explanation was more copious than any she had yet indulged in, and as the summer twilight gathered and she kept her child in the garden she was conciliatory to a degree that let her need to arrange things a little perceptibly peep out. It was not merely that she explained; she almost conversed; all that was wanting to that was that she should have positively chattered a little less. It was really the occasion of Maisie's life on which her mother was to have most to say to her. That alone was an implication of generosity and virtue, and no great stretch was required to make our young lady feel that she should best meet her and soonest have it over by simply seeming struck with the propriety of her contention. They sat together while the parent's gloved hand sometimes rested sociably on the child's and sometimes gave a corrective pull to a ribbon too meagre or a tress too thick; and Maisie was conscious of the effort to keep out of her eyes the wonder with which they were occasionally moved to blink. Oh there would have been things to blink at if one had let one's self go; and it was lucky they were alone together, without Sir Claude or Mrs Wix or even Mrs Beale to catch an imprudent glance. Though profuse and prolonged her ladyship was not exhaustively lucid, and her account of her situation, so far as it could be called descriptive, was a muddle of inconsequent things, bruised fruit of an occasion she had rather too lightly affronted. None of them were really thought out and some were even not wholly insincere. It was as if she had asked outright what better proof could have been wanted of her goodness and her greatness than just this marvellous consent to give up what she had so cherished. It was as if she had said in so many words: 'There have been things between us – between Sir Claude and me – which I needn't go into, you little nuisance, because you wouldn't understand them.' It suited her to convey that Maisie had been kept, so far as *she* was concerned or could imagine, in a holy ignorance and that she must take for granted a supreme simplicity. She turned this way and that in the predicament she had sought and from which she could neither retreat with grace nor emerge with credit: she draped herself in the tatters of her impudence, postured to her utmost before the last little triangle of cracked glass to which so many fractures had reduced the polished plate of filial superstition. If neither Sir Claude nor Mrs Wix was there this was perhaps all the more a pity: the scene had a style of its own that would have qualified it for presentation, especially at such a moment as that of her letting it betray that she quite did think her wretched offspring better placed with Sir Claude than in her own soiled hands. There was at any rate nothing scant either in her admissions or her perversions, the mixture of her fear of what Maisie might undiscoverably think and of the support she at the same time gathered from a necessity of selfishness and a habit of brutality. This habit flushed through the merit she now made, in terms explicit, of not having come to Folkestone to kick up a vulgar row. She had not come to box any ears or to bang any doors or even to use any language: she had come at the worst to lose the thread of her argument in an occasional dumb disgusted twitch of the toggery in which Mrs Beale's low domestic had had the impudence to serve up Miss Farange. She checked all criticism, not committing herself even so far as for those missing comforts of the schoolroom on which Mrs Wix had presumed.

'I *am* good – I'm crazily, I'm criminally good. But it won't do for *you* any more, and if I've ceased to contend with him, and with you too, who have made most of the trouble between us, it's for reasons that you'll understand one of these days but too well – one of these days when I hope you'll know what it is to have lost a mother. I'm awfully ill, but you mustn't ask me anything about it. If I don't get off somewhere my doctor won't answer for the consequences. He's stupefied at what I've borne – he says it has been put on me because I was formed to suffer. I'm thinking of South Africa, but that's none of your business. You must take your choice – you can't ask me questions if you're so ready to give me up. No, I won't tell you; you can find out for yourself. South Africa's wonderful, they say, and if I do go it must be to give it a fair trial. It must be either one thing or the other; if he takès you, you know, he takes you. I've struck my last blow for you; I can follow you no longer from pillar to post. I must live for myself at last, while there's still a handful left of me. I'm very, very ill; I'm very, very tired; I'm very, very determined. There you have it. Make the most of it. Your frock's too filthy; but I came to sacrifice myself.' Maisie looked at the peccant places; there were moments when it was a relief to her to drop her eyes even on anything so sordid. All her interviews, all her ordeals with her mother had, as she had grown older, seemed to have, before any other, the hard quality of duration; but longer than any, strangely, were these minutes offered to her as so pacific and so agreeably winding up the connection. It was her anxiety that made them long, her fear of some hitch, some check of the current, one of her ladyship's famous quick jumps. She held her breath; she only wanted, by playing into her visitor's hands, to see the thing through. But her impatience itself made at instants the whole situation swim; there were things Ida said that she perhaps didn't hear, and there were things she heard that Ida perhaps didn't say. 'You're all I have, and yet I'm capable of this. Your father wishes you were dead – that, my dear, is what your father wishes. You'll have to get used to it as I've done – I mean to his wishing that *I'm* dead. At all events you see for yourself how wonderful I am to Sir Claude. He wishes me dead quite as much; and I'm sure that if making me scenes about *you* could have killed me –!' It was the mark of Ida's eloquence that she started more hares than she followed, and she gave but a glance in the direction of this one; going on to say that the very proof of her treating her husband like an angel was that he had just stolen off not to be fairly shamed. She spoke as if he had retired on tiptoe, as he might have withdrawn from a place of worship in which he was not fit to be present. 'You'll never know what I've been through about you – never, never, never. I spare you everything, as I always have; though I dare say you know things that, if I did (I mean if I knew them) would make me – well, no matter! You're old enough at any rate to know there are a lot of things I don't say that I easily might; though it would do me good, I assure you, to have spoken my mind for once in my life. I don't speak of your father's infamous wife: that may give you a notion of the way I'm letting you off. When I say "you" I mean your precious friends and backers. If you don't do justice to my forbearing, out of delicacy, to mention, just as a last word, about your stepfather, a little fact or two of a land that really I should only *have* to mention to shine myself in comparison, and after every calumny, like pure gold: if you don't do me *that* justice you'll never do me justice at all!'

Maisie's desire to show what justice she did her had by this time become so intense as to have brought with it an inspiration. The great effect of their encounter had been to confirm her sense of being launched with Sir Claude, to make it rich and full beyond anything she had dreamed, and everything now conspired to suggest that a single soft touch of her small hand would complete the good work and set her ladyship so promptly and majestically afloat as to leave the great seaway clear for the morrow. This was the more the case as her hand had for some moments been rendered free by a marked manoeuvre of both of her mother's. One of these capricious members had fumbled with visible impatience in some backward depth of drapery and had presently reappeared with a small article in its grasp. The act had a significance for a little person trained, in that relation, from an early age, to keep an eye on manual motions, and its possible bearing was not darkened by the memory of the handful of gold that Susan Ash would never, never believe Mrs Beale had sent back – 'not she; she's too false and too greedy!' – to the munificent Countess. To have guessed, none the less, that her ladyship's purse might be the real figure of the object extracted from the rustling covert at her rear – this suspicion gave on the spot to the child's eyes a direction carefully distant. It added moreover to the optimism that for an hour could ruffle the surface of her deep diplomacy, ruffle it to the point of making her forget that she had never been safe unless she had also been stupid. She in short forgot her habitual caution in her impulse to adopt her ladyship's practical interests and show her ladyship how perfectly she understood them. She saw without looking that her mother pressed a little clasp; heard, without wanting to, the sharp click that marked the closing portemonnaie from which something had been taken. What this was she just didn't see; it was not too substantial to be locked with ease in the fold of her ladyship's fingers. Nothing was less new to Maisie than the art of not thinking singly, so that at this instant she could both bring out what was on her tongue's end and weigh, as to the object in her mother's palm, the question of its being a sovereign against the question of its being a shilling. No sooner had she begun to speak than she saw that within a few seconds this question would have been settled: she had foolishly checked the rising words of the little speech of presentation to which, under the circumstances, even such a high pride as Ida's had had to give some thought. She had checked it completely – that was the next thing she felt: the note she sounded brought into her companion's eyes a look that quickly enough seemed at variance with presentations.

'That was what the Captain said to me that day, mamma. I think it would have given you pleasure to hear the way he spoke of you.'

The pleasure, Maisie could now in consternation reflect, would have been a long time coming if it had come no faster than the response evoked by her allusion to it. Her mother gave her one of the looks that slammed the door in her face; never in a career of unsuccessful experiments had Maisie had to take such a stare. It reminded her of the way that once, at one of the lectures in Glower Street, something in a big jar that, amid an array of strange glasses and bad smells, had been promised as a beautiful yellow was produced as a beautiful black. She had been sorry on that occasion for the lecturer, but she was at this moment sorrier for herself. Oh nothing had ever made for twinges like mamma's manner of saying: 'The Captain? What Captain?'

'Why when we met you in the Gardens – the one who took me to sit with him. That was exactly what *he* said.'

Ida let it come on so far as to appear for an instant to pick up a lost thread. 'What on earth did he say?'

Maisie faltered supremely, but supremely she brought it out. 'What you say, mamma – that you're so good.'

'What "I" say?' Ida slowly rose, keeping her eyes on her child, and the hand that had busied itself in her purse conformed at her side and amid the folds of her dress to a certain stiffening of the arm. 'I say you're a precious idiot, and I won't have you put words into my mouth!' This was much more peremptory than a mere contradiction. Maisie could only feel on the spot that everything had broken short off and that their communication had abruptly ceased. That was presently proved. 'What business have you to speak to me of him?'

Her daughter turned scarlet. 'I thought you liked him.'

'Him! – the biggest cad in London!' Her ladyship towered again, and in the gathering dusk the whites of her eyes were huge.

Maisie's own, however, could by this time pretty well match them; and she had at least now, with the first flare of anger that had ever yet lighted her face for a foe, the sense of looking up quite as hard as any one could look down. 'Well, he was kind about you then; he *was*, and it made me like him. He said things – they were beautiful, they were, they were!' She was almost capable of the violence of forcing this home, for even in the midst of her surge of passion – of which in fact it was a part – there rose in her a fear, a pain, a vision ominous, precocious, of what it might mean for her mother's fate to have forfeited such a loyalty as that. There was literally an instant in which Maisie fully saw – saw madness and desolation, saw ruin and darkness and death. 'I've thought of him often since, and I hoped it was with him – with him –!' Here, in her emotion, it failed her, the breath of her filial hope.

But Ida got it out of her. 'You hoped, you little horror –?'

'That it was he who's at Dover, that it was he who's to take you. I mean to South Africa,' Maisie said with another drop.

Ida's stupefaction, on this, kept her silent unnaturally long, so long that her daughter could not only wonder what was coming, but perfectly measure the decline of every symptom of her liberality. She loomed there in her grandeur, merely dark and dumb; her wrath was clearly still, as it had always been, a thing of resource and variety. What Maisie least expected of it was by this law what now occurred. It melted, in the summer twilight, gradually into pity, and the pity after a little found a cadence to which the renewed click of her purse gave an accent. She had put back what she had taken out. 'You're a dreadful dismal deplorable little thing,' she murmured. And with this she turned back and rustled away over the lawn.

After she had disappeared Maisie dropped upon the bench again and for some time, in the empty garden and the deeper dusk, sat and stared at the image her flight had still left standing. It had ceased to be her mother only, in the strangest way, that it might become her father, the father of whose wish that she were dead the announcement still lingered in the air. It was a presence with vague edges – it continued to front her, to cover her. But what reality that she need reckon with did it represent if Mr Farange were, on his side, also going off – going off to America with the Countess, or even only to Spa? That question had, from the house, a sudden gay answer in the great roar of a gong, and at the same moment she saw Sir Claude look out for her from the wide lighted doorway. At this she went to him and he came forward and met her on the lawn.

For a minute she was with him there in silence as, just before, at the last, she had been with her mother.

'She's gone?'

'She's gone.'

Nothing more, for the instant, passed between them but to move together to the house, where, in the hall, he indulged in one of those sudden pleasantries with which, to the delight of his stepdaughter, his native animation overflowed. 'Will Miss Farange do me the honour to accept my arm?'

There was nothing in all her days that Miss Farange had accepted with such bliss, a bright rich element that floated them together to their feast; before they reached which, however, she uttered, in the spirit of a glad young lady taken in to her first dinner, a sociable word that made him stop short. 'She goes to South Africa.'

'To South Africa?' His face, for a moment, seemed to swing for a jump; the next it took its spring into the extreme of hilarity. 'Is that what she said?'

'Oh yes, I didn't *mistake*!' Maisie took to herself *that* credit. 'For the climate.'

Sir Claude was now looking at a young woman with black hair, a red frock and a tiny terrier tucked under her elbow. She swept past them on her way to the dining-room, leaving an impression of a strong scent which mingled, amid the clatter of the place, with the hot aroma of food. He had become a little graver; he still stopped to talk. 'I see – I see.' Other people brushed by; he was not too grave to notice them. 'Did she say anything else?'

'Oh yes, a lot more.'

On this he met her eyes again with some intensity, but only repeating: 'I see – I see.'

Maisie had still her own vision, which she brought out. 'I thought she was going to give me something.'

'What kind of a thing?'

'Some money that she took out of her purse and then put back.'

Sir Claude's amusement reappeared. 'She thought better of it.

Dear thrifty soul! How much did she make by that manoeuvre?'

Maisie considered. 'I didn't see. It was very small.'

Sir Claude threw back his head. 'Do you mean very little? Sixpence?'

Maisie resented this almost as if, at dinner, she were already bandying jokes with an agreeable neighbour. 'It may have been a sovereign.'

'Or even,' Sir Claude suggested, 'a ten-pound note.' She flushed at this sudden picture of what she perhaps had lost, and he made it more vivid by adding: 'Rolled up in a tight little ball, you know – her way of treating banknotes as if they were curlpapers!' Maisie's flush deepened both with the immense plausibility of this and with a fresh wave of the consciousness that was always there to remind her of his cleverness – the consciousness of how immeasurably more after all he knew about mamma than she. She had lived with her so many times without discovering the material of her curlpapers or assisting at any other of her dealings with banknotes. The tight little ball had at any rate rolled away from her for ever – quite like one of the other balls that Ida's cue used to send flying. Sir Claude gave her his arm again, and by the time she was seated at table she had perfectly made up her mind as to the amount of the sum she had forfeited. Everything about her, however – the crowded room, the bedizened banquet, the savour of dishes, the drama of figures – ministered to the joy of life. After dinner she smoked with her friend – for that was exactly what she felt she did – on a porch, a kind of terrace, where the red tips of cigars and the light dresses of ladies made, under the happy stars, a poetry that was almost intoxicating. They talked but little, and she was slightly surprised at his asking for no more news of what her mother had said; but she had no need of talk – there were a sense and a sound in everything to which words had nothing to add. They smoked and smoked, and there was a sweetness in her stepfather's silence. At last he said: 'Let us take another turn – but you must go to bed soon. Oh you know, we're going to have a system!' Their turn was back into the garden, along the dusky paths from which they could see the black masts and the red lights of boats and hear the calls and cries that evidently had to do with happy foreign travel; and their system was once more to get on beautifully in this further lounge without a definite exchange. Yet he finally spoke – he broke out as he tossed away the match from which he had taken a fresh light: 'I must go for a stroll. I'm in a fidget – I must walk it off.' She fell in with this as she fell in with everything; on which he went on: 'You go up to Miss Ash' – it was the name they had started; 'you must see she's not in mischief. Can you find your way alone?'

'Oh yes; I've been up and down seven times.' She positively enjoyed the prospect of an eighth.

Still they didn't separate; they stood smoking together under the stars. Then at last Sir Claude produced it. 'I'm free – I'm free.'

She looked up at him; it was the very spot on which a couple of hours before she had looked up at her mother. 'You're free – you're free.'

'Tomorrow we go to France.' He spoke as if he hadn't heard her; but it didn't prevent her again concurring.

'Tomorrow we go to France.'

Again he appeared not to have heard her; and after a moment – it was an effect evidently of the depth of his reflections and the agitation of his soul – he also spoke as if he had not spoken before. 'I'm free – I'm free!'

She repeated her form of assent. 'You're free – you're free.'

This time he did hear her; he fixed her through the darkness with a grave face. But he said nothing more; he simply stooped a little and drew her to him – simply held her a little and kissed her good-night; after which, having given her a silent push upstairs to Miss Ash, he turned round again to the black masts and the red lights. Maisie mounted as if France were at the top.

XXII

THE next day it seemed to her indeed at the bottom – down too far, in shuddering plunges, even to leave her a sense, on the Channel boat, of the height at which Sir Claude remained and which had never in every way been so great as when, much in the wet, though in the angle of a screen of canvas, he sociably sat with his stepdaughter's head in his lap and that of Mrs Beale's housemaid fairly pillowed on his breast. Maisie was surprised to learn as they drew into port that they had had a lovely passage; but this emotion, at Boulogne, was speedily quenched in others, above all in the great ecstasy of a larger impression of life. She was 'abroad' and she gave herself up to it, responded to it, in the bright air, before the pink houses, among the bare-legged fishwives and the red-legged soldiers, with the instant certitude of a vocation. Her vocation was to see the world and to thrill with enjoyment of the picture; she had grown older in five minutes and had by the time they reached the hotel recognised in the institutions and manners of France a multitude of affinities and messages. Literally in the course of an hour she found her initiation; a consciousness much quickened by the superior part that, as soon as they had gobbled down a French breakfast – which was indeed a high note in the concert – she observed herself to play to Susan Ash. Sir Claude, who had already bumped against people he knew and who, as he said, had business and letters, sent them out together for a walk, a walk in which the child was avenged, so far as poetic justice required, not only for the loud giggles that in their London trudges used to break from her attendant, but for all the years of her tendency to produce socially that impression of an excess of the queer something which had seemed to waver so widely between innocence and guilt. On the spot, at Boulogne, though there might have been excess there was at least no wavering; she recognised, she understood, she adored and took possession; feeling herself attuned to everything and laying her hand, right and left, on what had simply been waiting for her. She explained to Susan, she laughed at Susan, she towered over Susan; and it was somehow Susan's stupidity, of which she had never yet been so sure, and Susan's bewilderment and ignorance and antagonism, that gave the liveliest rebound to her immediate perceptions and adoptions. The place and the people were all a picture together, a picture that, when they went down to the wide sands, shimmered, in a thousand tints, with the pretty organisation of the *plage*, with the gaiety of spectators and bathers, with that of the language and the weather, and above all with that of our young lady's unprecedented situation. For it appeared to her that no one since the beginning of time could have had such an adventure or, in an hour, so much experience; as a sequel to which she only needed, in order to feel with conscious wonder how the past was changed, to hear Susan, inscrutably aggravated, express a preference for the Edgware Road. The past was so changed and the circle it had formed already so overstepped that on that very afternoon, in the course of another walk, she found herself enquiring of Sir Claude — and without a single scruple — if he were prepared as yet to name the moment at which they should start for Paris. His answer, it must be said, gave her the least little chill.

'Oh Paris, my dear child — I don't quite know about Paris!'

This required to be met, but it was much less to challenge him than for the rich joy of her first discussion of the details of a tour that, after looking at him a minute, she replied: 'Well, isn't that the *real* thing, the thing that when one does come abroad —?'

He had turned grave again, and she merely threw that out: it was a way of doing justice to the seriousness of their life. She couldn't moreover be so much older since yesterday without reflecting that if by this time she probed a little he would recognise that she had done enough for mere patience. There was in fact something in his eyes that suddenly, to her own, made her discretion shabby. Before she could remedy this he had answered her last question, answered it in the way that, of all ways, she had least expected. 'The thing it doesn't do not to do? Certainly Paris is charming. But, my dear fellow, Paris eats your head off. I mean it's so beastly expensive.'

That note gave her a pang – it suddenly let in a harder light. Were they poor then, that is was *he* poor, really poor beyond the pleasantry of apollinaris and cold beef? They had walked to the end of the long jetty that enclosed the harbour and were looking out at the dangers they had escaped, the grey horizon that was England, the tumbled surface of the sea and the brown smacks that bobbed upon it. Why had he chosen an embarrassed time to make this foreign dash? unless indeed it was just the dash economic, of which she had often heard and on which, after another look at the grey horizon and the bobbing boats, she was ready to turn round with elation. She replied to him quite in his own manner: 'I see, I see.' She smiled up at him. 'Our affairs are involved.'

'That's it.' He returned her smile. 'Mine are not quite so bad as yours; for yours are really, my dear man, in a state I can't see through at all. But mine will do – for a mess.'

She thought this over. 'But isn't France cheaper than England?'

England, over there in the thickening gloom, looked just then remarkably dear. 'I dare say; some parts.'

'Then can't we live in those parts?'

There was something that for an instant, in satisfaction of this, he had the air of being about to say and yet not saying. What he presently said was: 'This very place is one of them.'

'Then we shall live here?'

He didn't treat it quite so definitely as she liked. 'Since we've come to save money!'

This made her press him more. 'How long shall we stay?'

'Oh three or four days.'

It took her breath away. 'You can save money in that time?'

He burst out laughing, starting to walk again and taking her under his arm. He confessed to her on the way that she too had put a finger on the weakest of all his weaknesses, the fact, of which he was perfectly aware, that he probably might have lived within his means if he had never done anything for thrift. 'It's the happy thoughts that do it,' he said; 'there's nothing so ruinous as putting in a cheap week.' Maisie heard afresh among the pleasant sounds of the closing day that steel click of Ida's change of mind. She thought of the ten-pound note it would have been delightful at this juncture to produce for her companion's encouragement. But the idea was dissipated by his saying irrelevantly, in presence of the next thing they stopped to admire: 'We shall stay till she arrives.'

She turned upon him. 'Mrs Beale?'

'Mrs Wix. I've had a wire,' he went on. 'She has seen your mother.'

'Seen mamma?' Maisie stared. 'Where in the world?'

'Apparently in London. They've been together.'

For an instant this looked ominous – a fear came into her eyes. 'Then she hasn't gone?'

'Your mother? – to South Africa? I give it up, dear boy,' Sir Claude said; and she seemed literally to see him give it up as he stood there and with a kind of absent gaze – absent, that is, from *her* affairs – followed the fine stride and shining limbs of a young fishwife who had just waded out of the sea with her basketful of shrimps. His thought came back to her sooner than his eyes. 'But I dare say it's all right. She wouldn't come if it wasn't, poor old thing: she knows rather well what she's about.'

This was so reassuring that Maisie, after turning it over, could make it fit into her dream. 'Well, what *is* she about?'

He finally stopped looking at the fishwife – he met his companion's enquiry. 'Oh you know!' There was something in the way he said it that made, between them, more of an equality than she had yet imagined; but it had also more the effect of raising her up than of letting him down, and what it did with her was shown by the sound of her assent.

'Yes – I know!' What she knew, what she *could* know is by this time no secret to us: it grew and grew at any rate, the rest of that day, in the air of what he took for granted. It was better he should do that than attempt to test her knowledge; but there at the worst was the gist of the matter: it was open between them at last that their great change, as, speaking as if it had already lasted weeks, Maisie called it, was somehow built up round Mrs Wix. Before she went to bed that night she knew further that Sir Claude, since as *he* called it, they had been on the rush, had received more telegrams than one. But they separated again without speaking of Mrs Beale.

Oh what a crossing for the straighteners and the old brown dress – which latter appurtenance the child saw thriftily revived for the possible disasters of travel! The wind got up in the night and from her little room at the inn Maisie could hear the noise of the sea. The next day it was raining and everything different: this was the case even with Susan Ash, who positively crowed over the bad weather, partly, it seemed, for relish of the time their visitor would have in the boat, and partly to point the moral of the folly of coming to such holes. In the wet, with Sir Claude, Maisie went to the Folkestone packet, on the arrival of which, with many signs of the fray, he made her wait under an umbrella by the quay; whence almost ere the vessel touched, he was to be descried, in quest of their friend, wriggling – that had been his word – through the invalids massed upon the deck. It was long till he reappeared – it was not indeed till every one had landed; when he presented the object of his benevolence in a light that Maisie scarce knew whether to suppose the depth of prostration or the flush of triumph. The lady on his arm, still bent beneath her late ordeal, was muffled in such draperies as had never before offered so much support to so much woe. At the hotel, an hour later, this ambiguity dropped: assisting Mrs Wix in private to refresh and reinvest herself, Maisie heard from her in detail how little she could have

achieved if Sir Claude hadn't put it in her power. It was a phrase
that in her room she repeated in connections indescribable: he had
put it in her power to have 'changes', as she said, of the most
intimate order, adapted to climates and occasions so various as to
foreshadow in themselves the stages of a vast itinerary. Cheap
weeks would of course be in their place after so much money spent
on a governess; sums not grudged, however, by this lady's pupil,
even on her feeling her own appearance give rise, through the
straighteners, to an attention perceptibly mystified. Sir Claude in
truth had had less time to devote to it than to Mrs Wix's; and
moreover she would rather be in her own shoes than in her friend's
creaking new ones in the event of an encounter with Mrs Beale.
Maisie was too lost in the idea of Mrs Beale's judgement of so
much newness to pass any judgement herself. Besides, after much
luncheon and many endearments, the question took quite another
turn, to say nothing of the pleasure of the child's quick view that
there were other eyes than Susan Ash's to open to what she could
show. She couldn't show much, alas, till it stopped raining, which
it declined to do that day; but this had only the effect of leaving
more time for Mrs Wix's own demonstration. It came as they sat
in the little white and gold salon which Maisie thought the loveliest
place she had ever seen except perhaps the apartment of the
Countess; it came while the hard summer storm lashed the
windows and blew in such a chill that Sir Claude, with his hands
in his pockets and cigarettes in his teeth, fidgeting, frowning,
looking out and turning back, ended by causing a smoky little fire
to be made in the dressy little chimney. It came in spite of something that could only be named his air of wishing to put it off; an
air that had served him – oh as all his airs served him! – to the extent
of his having for a couple of hours confined the conversation to
gratuitous jokes and generalities, kept it on the level of the little
empty coffee-cups and *petits verres* (Mrs Wix had two of each!) that
struck Maisie, through the fumes of the French fire and the English
tobacco, as a token more than ever that they were launched. She

felt now, in close quarters and as clearly as if Mrs Wix had told her, that what this lady had come over for was not merely to be chaffed and to hear her pupil chaffed; not even to hear Sir Claude, who knew French in perfection, imitate the strange sounds emitted by the English folk at the hotel. It was perhaps half an effect of her present renovations, as if her clothes had been somebody's else; she had at any rate never produced such an impression of high colour, of a redness associated in Maisie's mind at *that* pitch either with measles or with 'habits'. Her heart was not at all in the gossip about Boulogne; and if her complexion was partly the result of the déjeuner and the *petits verres* it was also the brave signal of what she was there to say. Maisie knew when this did come how anxiously it had been awaited by the youngest member of the party. 'Her ladyship packed me off – she almost put me into the cab!' That was what Mrs Wix at last brought out.

XXIII

SIR Claude was stationed at the window; he didn't so much as turn round, and it was left to the youngest of the three to take up the remark. 'Do you mean you went to see her yesterday?'

'She came to see *me*. She knocked at my shabby door. She mounted my squalid stair. She told me she had seen you at Folkestone.'

Maisie wondered. 'She went back that evening?'

'No; yesterday morning. She drove to me straight from the station. It was most remarkable. If I had a job to get off she did nothing to make it worse – she did a great deal to make it better.' Mrs Wix hung fire, though the flame in her face burned brighter; then she became capable of saying: 'Her ladyship's kind! She did what I didn't expect.'

Maisie, on this, looked straight at her stepfather's back; it might well have been for her at that hour a monument of her ladyship's kindness. It remained, as such, monumentally still, and for a time that permitted the child to ask of their companion: 'Did she really help you?'

'Most practically.' Again Mrs Wix paused; again she quite resounded. 'She gave me a ten-pound note.'

At that, still looking out, Sir Claude, at the window, laughed loud. 'So you see, Maisie, we've not quite lost it!'

'Oh no,' Maisie responded. 'Isn't that too charming?' She smiled at Mrs Wix. 'We know all about it.' Then on her friend's showing such blankness as was compatible with such a flush she pursued: 'She does want me to have you?'

Mrs Wix showed a final hesitation, which, however, while Sir

Claude drummed on the window-pane, she presently surmounted. It came to Maisie that in spite of his drumming and of his not turning round he was really so much interested as to leave himself in a manner in her hands; which somehow suddenly seemed to her a greater proof than he could have given by interfering. 'She wants me to have *you*!' Mrs Wix declared.

Maisie answered this bang at Sir Claude. 'Then that's nice for all of us.'

Of course it was, his continued silence sufficiently admitted while Mrs Wix rose from her chair and, as if to take more of a stand, placed herself, not without majesty, before the fire. The incongruity of her smartness, the circumference of her stiff frock, presented her as really more ready for Paris than any of them. She also gazed hard at Sir Claude's back. 'Your wife was different from anything she had ever shown me. She recognises certain proprieties.'

'Which? Do you happen to remember?' Sir Claude asked.

Mrs Wix's reply was prompt. 'The importance for Maisie of a gentlewoman, of some one who's not – well, so bad! She objects to a mere maid, and I don't in the least mind telling you what she wants me to do.' One thing was clear – Mrs Wix was now bold enough for anything. 'She wants me to persuade you to get rid of the person from Mrs Beale's.'

Maisie waited for Sir Claude to pronounce on this; then she could only understand that he on his side waited, and she felt particularly full of common sense as she met her responsibility. 'Oh I don't want Susan with *you*!' she said to Mrs Wix.

Sir Claude, always from the window, approved. 'That's quite simple. I'll take her back.'

Mrs Wix gave a positive jump; Maisie caught her look of alarm. '"Take" her? You don't mean to go over on purpose?'

Sir Claude said nothing for a moment; after which, 'Why shouldn't I leave you here?' he enquired.

Maisie, at this, sprang up. 'Oh do, oh do, oh do!' The next

moment she was interlaced with Mrs Wix, and the two, on the hearth-rug, their eyes in each other's eyes, considered the plan with intensity. Then Maisie felt the difference of what they saw in it.

'She can surely go back alone: why should you put yourself out?' Mrs Wix demanded.

'Oh she's an idiot – she's incapable. If anything should happen to her it would be awkward: it was I who brought her – without her asking. If I turn her away I ought with my own hand to place her again exactly where I found her.'

Mrs Wix's face appealed to Maisie on such folly, and her manner, as directed to their companion, had, to her pupil's surprise, an unprecedented firmness. 'Dear Sir Claude, I think you're perverse. Pay her fare and give her a sovereign. She has had an experience that she never dreamed of and that will be an advantage to her through life. If she goes wrong on the way it will be simply because she wants to, and, with her expenses and her remuneration – make it even what you like! – you'll have treated her as handsomely as you always treat every one.'

This was a new tone – as new as Mrs Wix's cap; and it could strike a young person with a sharpened sense for latent meanings as the upshot of a relation that had taken on a new character. It brought out for Maisie how much more even than she had guessed her friends were fighting side by side. At the same time it needed so definite a justification that as Sir Claude now at last did face them she at first supposed him merely resentful of excessive familiarity. She was therefore yet more puzzled to see him show his serene beauty untroubled, as well as an equal interest in a matter quite distinct from any freedom but her ladyship's. 'Did my wife come alone?' He could ask even that good-humouredly.

'When she called on me?' Mrs Wix *was* red now: his good humour wouldn't keep down her colour, which for a minute glowed there like her ugly honesty. 'No – there was some one in the cab.' The only attenuation she could think of was after a minute to add: 'But they didn't come up.'

Sir Claude broke into a laugh – Maisie herself could guess what it was at: while he now walked about, still laughing, and at the fireplace gave a gay kick to a displaced log, she felt more vague about almost everything than about the drollery of such a 'they'. She in fact could scarce have told you if it was to deepen or to cover the joke that she bethought herself to observe: 'Perhaps it was her maid.'

Mrs Wix gave her a look that at any rate deprecated the wrong tone. 'It was not her maid.'

'Do you mean there are this time two?' Sir Claude asked as if he hadn't heard.

'Two maids?' Maisie went on as if she might assume he had.

The reproach of the straighteners darkened; but Sir Claude cut across it with a sudden: 'See here; what do you mean? And what do you suppose *she* meant?'

Mrs Wix let him for a moment, in silence, understand that the answer to his question, if he didn't take care, might give him more than he wanted. It was as if, with this scruple, she measured and adjusted all she gave him in at last saying: 'What she meant was to make me know that you're definitely free. To have that straight from her was a joy I of course hadn't hoped for: it made the assurance, and my delight at it, a thing I could really proceed upon. You already know how certainly I'd have started even if she hadn't pressed me; you already know what, so long, we've been looking for and what, as soon as she told me of her step taken at Folkestone, I recognised with rapture that we *have*. It's your freedom that makes me right' – she fairly bristled with her logic. 'But I don't mind telling you that it's her action that makes me happy!'

'Her action?' Sir Claude echoed. 'Why, my dear woman, her action is just a hideous crime. It happens to satisfy our sympathies in a way that's quite delicious; but that doesn't in the least alter the fact that it's the most abominable thing ever done. She has chucked our friend here overboard not a bit less than if she had shoved her, shrieking and pleading, out of that window and down two floors to the paving-stones.'

Maisie surveyed serenely the parties to the discussion. 'Oh your friend here, dear Sir Claude, doesn't plead and shriek!'

He looked at her a moment. 'Never. Never. That's one, only one, but charming so far as it goes, of about a hundred things we love her for.' Then he pursued to Mrs Wix: 'What I can't for the life of me make out is what Ida is *really* up to, what game she was playing in turning to you with that cursed cheek after the beastly way she has used you. Where – to explain her at all – does she fancy she can presently, when we least expect it, take it out of us?'

'She doesn't fancy anything, nor want anything out of any one. Her cursed cheek, as you call it, is the best thing I've ever seen in her. I don't care a fig for the beastly way she used me – I forgive it all a thousand times over!' Mrs Wix raised her voice as she had never raised it; she quite triumphed in her lucidity. 'I understand her, I almost admire her!' she quavered. She spoke as if this might practically suffice; yet in charity to fainter lights she threw out an explanation. 'As I've said, she was different; upon my word I wouldn't have known her. She had a glimmering, she had an instinct; they brought her. It was a kind of happy thought, and if you couldn't have supposed she would ever have had such a thing, why of course I quite agree with you. But she did have it! There!'

Maisie could feel again how a certain rude lightness in this plea might have been found exasperating; but as she had often watched Sir Claude in apprehension of displeasures that didn't come, so now, instead of saying 'Oh hell!' as her father used, she observed him only to take refuge in a question that at the worst was abrupt.

'Who *is* it this time, do you know?'

Mrs Wix tried blind dignity. 'Who is what, Sir Claude?'

'The man who stands the cabs. Who was in the one that waited at your door?'

At this challenge she faltered so long that her young friend's pitying conscience gave her a hand. 'It wasn't the Captain.'

This good intention, however, only converted the excellent woman's scruple to a more ambiguous stare; besides of course making Sir Claude go off. Mrs Wix fairly appealed to him. 'Must I really tell you?'

His amusement continued. 'Did she make you promise not to?'

Mrs Wix looked at him still harder. 'I mean before Maisie.'

Sir Claude laughed again. 'Why *she* can't hurt him!'

Maisie felt herself, as it passed, brushed by the light humour of this. 'Yes, I can't hurt him.'

The straighteners again roofed her over; after which they seemed to crack with the explosion of their wearer's honesty. Amid the flying splinters Mrs Wix produced a name. 'Mr Tischbein.'

There was for an instant a silence that, under Sir Claude's influence and while he and Maisie looked at each other, suddenly pretended to be that of gravity. 'We don't know Mr Tischbein, do we, dear?'

Maisie gave the point all needful thought. 'No, I can't place Mr Tischbein.'

It was a passage that worked visibly on their friend. 'You must pardon me, Sir Claude,' she said with an austerity of which the note was real, 'if I thank God to your face that he has in his mercy – I mean his mercy to our charge – allowed me to achieve this act.' She gave out a long puff of pain. 'It was time!' Then as if still more to point the moral: 'I said just now I understood your wife. I said just now I admired her. I stand to it: I did both of those things when I saw how even *she*, poor thing, saw. If you want the dots on the i's you shall have them. What she came to me for, in spite of everything, was that I'm just' – she quavered it out – 'well, just clean! What she saw for her daughter was that there must at last be a *decent* person!'

Maisie was quick enough to jump a little at the sound of this implication that such a person was what Sir Claude was not; the next instant, however, she more profoundly guessed against whom the discrimination was made. She was therefore left the more surprised at the complete candour with which he embraced the worst. 'If she's bent on decent persons why has she given her to *me*? You don't call me a decent person, and I'll do Ida the justice that *she* never did. I think I'm as indecent as any one and that there's nothing in my behaviour that makes my wife's surrender a bit less ignoble!'

'Don't speak of your behaviour!' Mrs Wix cried. 'Don't say such horrible things; they're false and they're wicked and I forbid you! It's to *keep* you decent that I'm here and that I've done everything I have done. It's to save you – I won't say from yourself, because in yourself you're beautiful and good! It's to save you from the worst person of all. I haven't, after all, come over to be afraid to speak of her! That's the person in whose place her ladyship wants such a person as even me; and if she thought herself, as she as good as told me, not fit for Maisie's company, it's not, as you may well suppose, that she may make room for Mrs Beale!'

Maisie watched his face as it took this outbreak, and the most she saw in it was that it turned a little white. That indeed made him look, as Susan Ash would have said, queer; and it was perhaps a part of the queerness that he intensely smiled. 'You're too hard on Mrs Beale. She has great merits of her own.'

Mrs Wix, at this, instead of immediately replying, did what Sir Claude had been doing before: she moved across to the window and stared a while into the storm. There was for a minute, to Maisie's sense, a hush that resounded with wind and rain. Sir Claude, in spite of these things, glanced about for his hat; on which Maisie spied it first and, making a dash for it, held it out to him. He took it with a gleam of a 'thank-you' in his face, and then something moved her still to hold the other side of the brim; so that, united by their grasp of this object, they stood some seconds looking many things at each other. By this time Mrs Wix had turned round. 'Do you mean to tell me,' she demanded, 'that you *are* going back?'

'To Mrs Beale?' Maisie surrendered his hat, and there was

something that touched her in the embarrassed, almost humiliated way their companion's challenge made him turn it round and round. She had seen people do that who, she was sure, did nothing else that Sir Claude did. 'I can't just say, my dear thing. We'll see about it – we'll talk of it tomorrow. Meantime I must get some air.'

Mrs Wix, with her back to the window, threw up her head to a height that, still for a moment, had the effect of detaining him. 'All the air in France, Sir Claude, won't, I think, give you the courage to deny that you're simply afraid of her!'

Oh this time he did look queer; Maisie had no need of Susan's vocabulary to note it! It would have come to her of itself as, with his hand on the door, he turned his eyes from his stepdaughter to her governess and then back again. Resting on Maisie's, though for ever so short a time, there was something they gave up to her and tried to explain. His lips, however, explained nothing; they only surrendered to Mrs Wix. 'Yes. I'm simply afraid of her!' He opened the door and passed out.

It brought back to Maisie his confession of fear of her mother; it made her stepmother then the second lady about whom he failed of the particular virtue that was supposed most to mark a gentleman. In fact there were three of them, if she counted in Mrs Wix, before whom he had undeniably quailed. Well, his want of valour was but a deeper appeal to her tenderness. To thrill with response to it she had only to remember all the ladies she herself had, as they called it, funked.

XXIV

IT continued to rain so hard that our young lady's private dream of explaining the Continent to their visitor had to contain a provision for some adequate treatment of the weather. At the *table d'hôte* that evening she threw out a variety of lights: this was the second ceremony of the sort she had sat through, and she would have neglected her privilege and dishonoured her vocabulary – which indeed consisted mainly of the names of dishes – if she had not been proportionately ready to dazzle with interpretations. Preoccupied and overawed, Mrs Wix was apparently dim: she accepted her pupil's version of the mysteries of the *menu* in a manner that might have struck the child as the depression of a credulity conscious not so much of its needs as of its dimensions. Maisie was soon enough – though it scarce happened before bedtime – confronted again with the different sort of programme for which she reserved her criticism. They remounted together to their sitting-room while Sir Claude, who said he would join them later, remained below to smoke and to converse with the old acquaintances that he met wherever he turned. He had proposed his companions, for coffee, the enjoyment of the *salon de lecture*, but Mrs Wix had replied promptly and with something of an air that it struck her their own apartments offered them every convenience. They offered the good lady herself, Maisie could immediately observe, not only that of this rather grand reference, which, already emulous, so far as it went, of her pupil, she made as if she had spent her life in salons; but that of a stiff French sofa where she could sit and stare at the faint French lamp, in default of the French clock that had stopped, as for some account of the time Sir Claude would so markedly interpose. Her demeanour accused him so directly of hovering beyond her reach that Maisie sought to divert her by a report of Susan's quaint attitude on the matter of their conversation after lunch. Maisie had mentioned to the young woman for sympathy's sake the plan for her relief, but her disapproval of alien ways appeared, strange to say, only to prompt her to hug her gloom; so that between Mrs Wix's effect of displacing her and the visible stiffening of her back the child had the sense of a double office and enlarged play for pacific powers.

These powers played to no great purpose, it was true, in keeping before Mrs Wix the vision of Sir Claude's perversity, which hung there in the pauses of talk and which he himself, after unmistakeable delays, finally made quite lurid by bursting in – it was near ten o'clock – with an object held up in his hand. She knew before he spoke what it was; she knew at least from the underlying sense of all that, since the hour spent after the Exhibition with her father, had not sprung up to reinstate Mr Farange – she knew it meant a triumph for Mrs Beale. The mere present sight of Sir Claude's face caused her on the spot to drop straight through her last impression of Mr Farange a plummet that reached still deeper down than the security of these days of flight. She had wrapped that impression in silence – a silence that had parted with half its veil to cover also, from the hour of Sir Claude's advent, the image of Mr Farange's wife. But if the object in Sir Claude's hand revealed itself as a letter which he held up very high, so there was something in his mere motion that laid Mrs Beale again bare. 'Here we are!' he cried almost from the door, shaking his trophy at them and looking from one to the other. Then he came straight to Mrs Wix; he had pulled two papers out of the envelope and glanced at them again to see which was which. He thrust one out open to Mrs Wix. 'Read that.' She looked at him hard, as if in fear: it was impossible not to see he was excited. Then she took the letter, but it was not her face that Maisie watched while she read. Neither, for that matter, was it this countenance that Sir Claude scanned: he stood before the fire and, more calmly, now that he had acted, communed in silence with his stepdaughter.

The silence was in truth quickly broken; Mrs Wix rose to her feet with the violence of the sound she emitted. The letter had dropped from her and lay upon the floor; it had made her turn ghastly white and she was speechless with the effect of it. 'It's too abominable – it's too unspeakable!' she then cried.

'Isn't it a charming thing?' Sir Claude asked. 'It has just arrived, enclosed in a word of her own. She sends it on to me with the remark that comment's superfluous. I really think it is. That's all you can say.'

'She oughtn't to pass such a horror about,' said Mrs Wix. 'She ought to put it straight in the fire.'

'My dear woman, she's not such a fool! It's much too precious.' He had picked the letter up and he gave it again a glance of complacency which produced a light in his face. 'Such a document' – he considered, then concluded with a slight drop – 'such a document is, in fine, a basis!'

'A basis for what?'

'Well – for proceedings.'

'Hers?' Mrs Wix's voice had become outright the voice of derision. 'How can *she* proceed?'

Sir Claude turned it over. 'How can she get rid of him? Well – she *is* rid of him.'

'Not legally.' Mrs Wix had never looked to her pupil so much as if she knew what she was talking about.

'I dare say,' Sir Claude laughed; 'but she's not a bit less deprived than I!'

'Of the power to get a divorce? It's just your want of the power that makes the scandal of your connection with her. Therefore it's just her want of it that makes that of hers with you. That's all I contend!' Mrs Wix concluded with an unparalleled neigh of battle. Oh she did know what she was talking about!

Maisie had meanwhile appealed mutely to Sir Claude, who

judged it easier to meet what she didn't say than to meet what Mrs Wix did.

'It's a letter to Mrs Beale from your father, my dear, written from Spa and making the rupture between them perfectly irrevocable. It lets her know, and not in pretty language, that, as we technically say, he deserts her. It puts an end for ever to their relations.' He ran his eyes over it again, then appeared to make up his mind. 'In fact it concerns you, Maisie, so nearly and refers to you so particularly that I really think you ought to see the terms in which this new situation is created for you.' And he held out the letter.

Mrs Wix, at this, pounced upon it; she had grabbed it too soon even for Maisie to become aware of being rather afraid of it. Thrusting it instantly behind her she positively glared at Sir Claude. 'See it, wretched man? – the innocent child *see* such a thing? I think you must be mad, and she shall not have a glimpse of it while I'm here to prevent!'

The breadth of her action had made Sir Claude turn red – he even looked a little foolish. 'You think it's too bad, eh? But it's precisely because it's bad that it seemed to me it would have a lesson and a virtue for her.'

Maisie could do a quick enough justice to his motive to be able clearly to interpose. She fairly smiled at him. 'I assure you I can quite believe how bad it is!' She thought of something, kept it back a moment, and then spoke. 'I know what's in it!'

He of course burst out laughing and, while Mrs Wix groaned an 'Oh heavens!' replied: 'You wouldn't say that, old boy, if you did! The point I make is,' he continued to Mrs Wix with a blandness now re-established – 'the point I make is simply that it sets Mrs Beale free.'

She hung fire but an instant. 'Free to live with *you*?'

'Free not to live, not to pretend to live, with her husband.'

'Ah they're mighty different things!' – a truth as to which her earnestness could now with a fine inconsequent look invite the participation of the child.

Before Maisie could commit herself, however, the ground was occupied by Sir Claude, who, as he stood before their visitor with an expression half rueful, half persuasive, rubbed his hand sharply up and down the back of his head. 'Then why the deuce do you grant so – do you, I may even say, rejoice so – that by the desertion of my own precious partner I'm free?'

Mrs Wix met this challenge first with silence, then with a demonstration the most extraordinary, the most unexpected. Maisie could scarcely believe her eyes as she saw the good lady, with whom she had associated no faintest shade of any art of provocation, actually, after an upward grimace, give Sir Claude a great giggling insinuating naughty slap. 'You wretch – you *know* why!' And she turned away. The face that with this movement she left him to present to Maisie was to abide with his step-daughter as the very image of stupefaction; but the pair lacked time to communicate either amusement or alarm before their admonisher was upon them again. She had begun in fact to show infinite variety and she flashed about with a still quicker change of tone. 'Have you brought me that thing as a pretext for your going over?'

Sir Claude braced himself. 'I can't, after such news, in common decency not go over. I mean, don't you know, in common courtesy and humanity. My dear lady, you can't chuck a woman that way, especially taking the moment when she has been most insulted and wronged. A fellow must behave like a gentleman, damn it, dear good Mrs Wix. We didn't come away, we two, to hang right on, you know: it was only to try our paces and just put in a few days that might prove to every one concerned that we're in earnest. It's exactly because we're in earnest that, dash it, we needn't be so awfully particular. I mean, don't you know, we needn't be so awfully afraid.' He showed a vivacity, an intensity of argument, and if Maisie counted his words she was all the more ready to swallow after a single swift gasp those that, the next thing, she became conscious he paused for a reply to. 'We didn't come, old girl, did we,' he pleaded straight, 'to stop right away for ever and put it all in *now*?'

Maisie had never doubted she could be heroic for him. 'Oh no!' It was as if she had been shocked at the bare thought. 'We're just taking it as we find it.' She had a sudden inspiration, which she backed up with a smile. 'We're just seeing what we can afford.' She had never yet in her life made any claim for herself, but she hoped that this time, frankly, what she was doing would somehow be counted to her. Indeed she felt Sir Claude *was* counting it, though she was afraid to look at him – afraid she should show him tears. She looked at Mrs Wix; she reached her maximum. 'I don't think I ought to be bad to Mrs Beale.'

She heard, on this, a deep sound, something inarticulate and sweet, from Sir Claude; but tears were what Mrs Wix didn't scruple to show. 'Do you think you ought to be bad to *me*?' The question was the more disconcerting that Mrs Wix's emotion didn't deprive her of the advantage of her effect. 'If you see that woman again you're lost!' she declared to their companion.

Sir Claude looked at the moony globe of the lamp; he seemed to see for an instant what seeing Mrs Beale would consist of. It was also apparently from this vision that he drew strength to return: 'Her situation, by what has happened, is completely changed; and it's no use your trying to prove to me that I needn't take any account of that.'

'If you see that woman you're lost!' Mrs Wix with greater force repeated.

'Do you think she'll not let me come back to you? My dear lady, I leave you here, you and Maisie, as a hostage to fortune, and I promise you by all that's sacred that I shall be with you again at the very latest on Saturday. I provide you with funds; I install you in these lovely rooms; I arrange with the people here that you be treated with every attention and supplied with every luxury. The weather, after this, will mend; it will be sure to be exquisite. You'll both be as free as air and you can roam all over the place and have tremendous larks. You shall have a carriage to drive you; the whole house shall be at your call. You'll have a magnificent position.' He paused, he looked from one of his companions to the other as to see the impression he had made. Whether or no he judged it adequate he subjoined after a moment: 'And you'll oblige me above all by not making a fuss.'

Maisie could only answer for the impression on herself, though indeed from the heart even of Mrs Wix's rigour there floated to her sense a faint fragrance of depraved concession. Maisie had her dumb word for the show such a speech could make, for the irresistible charm it could take from his dazzling sincerity; and before she could do anything but blink at excess of light she heard this very word sound on Mrs Wix's lips, just as if the poor lady had guessed it and wished, snatching it from her, to blight it like a crumpled flower. 'You're dreadful, you're terrible, for you know but too well that it's not a small thing to me that you should address me in terms that are princely!' Princely was what he stood there and looked and sounded; that was what Maisie for the occasion found herself reduced to simple worship of him for being. Yet strange to say too, as Mrs Wix went on, an echo rang within her that matched the echo she had herself just produced. 'How much you must *want* to see her to say such things as that and to be ready to do so much for the poor little likes of Maisie and me! She has a hold on you, and you know it, and you want to feel it again and – God knows, or at least *I* do, what's your motive and desire – enjoy it once more and give yourself up to it! It doesn't matter if it's one day or three: enough is as good as a feast and the lovely time you'll have with her is something you're willing to pay for! I dare say you'd like me to believe that your pay is to get her to give you up; but that's a matter on which I strongly urge you not to put down your money in advance. Give *her* up first. Then pay her what you please!'

Sir Claude took this to the end, though there were things in it that made him colour, called into his face more of the apprehension

than Maisie had ever perceived there of a particular sort of shock.
She had an odd sense that it was the first time she had seen any one
but Mrs Wix really and truly scandalised, and this fed her inference,
which grew and grew from moment to moment, that Mrs Wix was
proving more of a force to reckon with than either of them had
allowed so much room for. It was true that, long before, she had
obtained a 'hold' of him, as she called it, different in kind from that
obtained by Mrs Beale and originally by her ladyship. But Maisie
could quite feel with him now that he had really not expected this
advantage to be driven so home. Oh they hadn't at all got to where
Mrs Wix would stop, for the next minute she was driving harder
than ever. It was the result of his saying with a certain dryness,
though so kindly that what most affected Maisie in it was his
patience: 'My dear friend, it's simply a matter in which I must
judge for myself. You've judged *for* me, I know, a good deal, of
late, in a way that I appreciate, I assure you, down to the ground.
But you can't do it always; no one can do that for another, don't
you see, in every case. There are exceptions, particular cases that
turn up and that are awfully delicate. It would be too easy if I could
shift it all off on you: it would be allowing you to incur an amount
of responsibility that I should simply become quite ashamed of.
You'll find, I'm sure, that you'll have quite as much as you'll enjoy
if you'll be so good as to accept the situation as circumstances
happen to make it for you and to stay here with our friend, till I
rejoin you, on the footing of as much pleasantness and as much
comfort – and I think I have a right to add, to both of you, of as
much faith in *me* – as possible.'

Oh he was princely indeed: that came out more and more with
every word he said and with the particular way he said it, and
Maisie could feel his monitress stiffen almost with anguish against
the increase of his spell and then hurl herself as a desperate defence
from it into the quite confessed poorness of violence, of iteration.
'You're afraid of her – afraid, afraid, afraid! Oh dear, oh dear, oh
dear!' Mrs Wix wailed it with a high quaver, then broke down into

a long shudder of helplessness and woe. The next minute she had flung herself again on the lean sofa and had burst into a passion of tears.

Sir Claude stood and looked at her a moment; he shook his head slowly, altogether tenderly. 'I've already admitted it – I'm in mortal terror; so we'll let that settle the question. I think you had best go to bed,' he added; 'you've had a tremendous day and you must both be tired to death. I shall not expect you to concern yourselves in the morning with my movements. There's an early boat on; I shall have cleared out before you're up; and I shall moreover have dealt directly and most effectively, I assure you, with the haughty but not quite hopeless Miss Ash.' He turned to his stepdaughter as if at once to take leave of her and give her a sign of how, through all tension and friction, they were still united in such a way that she at least needn't worry. 'Maisie boy!' – he opened his arms to her. With her culpable lightness she flew into them and, while he kissed her, chose the soft method of silence to satisfy him, the silence that after battles of talk was the best balm she could offer his wounds. They held each other long enough to reaffirm intensely their vows; after which they were almost forced apart by Mrs Wix's jumping to her feet.

Her jump, either with a quick return or with a final lapse of courage, was also to supplication almost abject. 'I beseech you not to take a step so miserable and so fatal. I know her but too well, even if you jeer at me for saying it; little as I've seen her I know her, I know her. I know what she'll do – I see it as I stand here. Since you're afraid of her it's the mercy of heaven. Don't, for God's sake, be afraid to show it, to profit by it and to arrive at the very safety that it gives you. I'm not afraid of her, I assure you; you must already have seen for yourself that there's nothing I'm afraid of now. Let me go to her – I'll settle her and I'll take that woman back without a hair of her touched. Let me put in the two or three days – let me wind up the connection. You stay here with Maisie, with the carriage and the larks and the luxury; then I'll return to you and we'll go off together – we'll live together without a cloud. Take me, take me,' she went on and on – the tide of her eloquence was high. 'Here I am; I know what I am and what I ain't; but I say boldly to the face of you both that I'll do better for you, far, than ever she'll even try to. I say it to yours, Sir Claude, even though I owe you the very dress on my back and the very shoes on my feet. I owe you everything – that's just the reason; and to pay it back, in profusion, what can that be but what I want? Here I am, here I am!' – she spread herself into an exhibition that, combined with her intensity and her decorations, appeared to suggest her for strange offices and devotions, for ridiculous replacements and substitutions. She manipulated her gown as she talked, she insisted on the items of her debt. 'I have nothing of my own, I know – no money, no clothes, no appearance, no anything, nothing but my hold of this little one truth, which is all in the world I can bribe you with: that the pair of you are more to me than all besides, and that if you'll let me help you and save you, make what you both want possible in the one way it *can* be, why, I'll work myself to the bone in your service!'

Sir Claude wavered there without an answer to this magnificent appeal; he plainly cast about for one, and in no small agitation and pain. He addressed himself in his quest, however, only to vague quarters until he met again, as he so frequently and actively met it, the more than filial gaze of his intelligent little charge. That gave him – poor plastic and dependent male – his issue. If she was still a child she was yet of the sex that could help him out. He signified as much by a renewed invitation to an embrace. She freshly sprang to him and again they inaudibly conversed. 'Be nice to her, be nice to her,' he at last distinctly articulated; 'be nice to her as you've not even been to *me!*' On which, without another look at Mrs Wix, he somehow got out of the room, leaving Maisie under the slight oppression of these words as well as of the idea that he had unmistakeably once more dodged.

XXV

EVERY single thing he had prophesied came so true that it was after all no more than fair to expect quite as much for what he had as good as promised. His pledges they could verify to the letter, down to his very guarantee that a way would be found with Miss Ash. Roused in the summer dawn and vehemently squeezed by that interesting exile, Maisie fell back upon her couch with a renewed appreciation of his policy, a memento of which, when she rose later on to dress, glittered at her from the carpet in the shape of a sixpence that had overflowed from Susan's pride of possession. Sixpences really, for the forty-eight hours that followed, seemed to abound in her life; she fancifully computed the number of them represented by such a period of 'larks'. The number was not kept down, she presently noticed, by any scheme of revenge for Sir Claude's flight which should take on Mrs Wix's part the form of a refusal to avail herself of the facilities he had so bravely ordered. It was in fact impossible to escape them; it was in the good lady's own phrase ridiculous to go on foot when you had a carriage prancing at the door. Everything about them pranced: the very waiters even as they presented the dishes to which, from a similar sense of the absurdity of perversity, Mrs Wix helped herself with a freedom that spoke to Maisie quite as much of her depletion as of her logic. Her appetite was a sign to her companion of a great many things and testified no less on the whole to her general than to her particular condition. She had arrears of dinner to make up, and it was touching that in a dinnerless state her moral passion should have burned so clear. She partook largely as a refuge from depression, and yet the opportunity to partake was just a mark of the sinister symptoms that depressed her. The affair was in short a combat, in which the baser element triumphed, between her refusal to be bought off and her consent to be clothed and fed. It was not at any rate to be gainsaid that there was comfort for her in the developments of France; comfort so great as to leave Maisie free to take with her all the security for granted and brush all the danger aside. That was the way to carry out in detail Sir Claude's injunction to be 'nice'; that was the way, as well, to look, with her, in a survey of the pleasures of life abroad, straight over the head of any doubt.

They shrank at last, all doubts, as the weather cleared up: it had an immense effect on them and became quite as lovely as Sir Claude had engaged. This seemed to have put him so into the secret of things, and the joy of the world so waylaid the steps of his friends, that little by little the spirit of hope filled the air and finally took possession of the scene. To drive on the long cliff was splendid, but it was perhaps better still to creep in the shade – for the sun was strong – along the many-coloured and many-odoured *port* and through the streets in which, to English eyes, everything that was the same was a mystery and everything that was different a joke. Best of all was to continue the creep up the long Grand' Rue to the gate of the *haute ville* and, passing beneath it, mount to the quaint and crooked rampart, with its rows of trees, its quiet corners and friendly benches where brown old women in such white-frilled caps and such long gold earrings sat and knitted or snoozed, its little yellow-faced houses that looked like the homes of misers or of priests and its dark château where small soldiers lounged on the bridge that stretched across an empty moat and military washing hung from the windows of towers. This was a part of the place that could lead Maisie to enquire if it didn't just meet one's idea of the middle ages; and since it was rather a satisfaction than a shock to perceive, and not for the first time, the limits in Mrs Wix's mind of the historic imagination, that only added one more to the variety of kinds of insight that she felt it her own present mission to show. They sat together on the old grey bastion; they looked down on the little new town which seemed to them quite as old, and across at the great dome and the high gilt Virgin of the church that, as they gathered, was famous and that pleased them by its unlikeness to any place in which they had worshipped. They wandered in this temple afterwards and Mrs Wix confessed that for herself she had probably made a fatal mistake early in life in not being a Catholic. Her confession in its turn caused Maisie to wonder rather interestedly what degree of lateness it was that shut the door against an escape from such an error. They went back to the rampart on the second morning – the spot on which they appeared to have come furthest in the journey that was to separate them from everything objectionable in the past: it gave them afresh the impression that had most to do with their having worked round to a confidence that on Maisie's part was determined and that she could see to be on her companion's desperate. She had had for many hours the sense of showing Mrs Wix so much that she was comparatively slow to become conscious of being at the same time the subject of a like aim. The business went the faster, however, from the moment she got her glimpse of it; it then fell into its place in her general, her habitual view of the particular phenomenon that, had she felt the need of words for it, she might have called her personal relation to her knowledge. This relation had never been so lively as during the time she waited with her old governess for Sir Claude's reappearance, and what made it so was exactly that Mrs Wix struck her as having a new suspicion of it. Mrs Wix had never yet had a suspicion – this was certain – so calculated to throw her pupil, in spite of the closer union of such adventurous hours, upon the deep defensive. Her pupil made out indeed as many marvels as she had made out on the rush to Folkestone; and if in Sir Claude's company on that occasion Mrs Wix was the constant implication, so in Mrs Wix's, during these hours, Sir Claude was – and most of all through long pauses – the perpetual, the insurmountable theme. It all took them back to the first flush of his

marriage and to the place he held in the schoolroom at that crisis
of love and pain; only he had himself blown to a much bigger
balloon the large consciousness he then filled out.

They went through it all again, and indeed while the interval
dragged by the very weight of its charm they went, in spite of
defences and suspicions, through everything. Their intensified
clutch of the future throbbed like a clock ticking seconds; but this
was a timepiece that inevitably, as well, at the best, rang
occasionally a portentous hour. Oh there were several of these, and
two or three of the worst on the old city-wall where everything
else so made for peace. There was nothing in the world Maisie
more wanted than to be as nice to Mrs Wix as Sir Claude had
desired, but it was exactly because this fell in with her inveterate
instinct of keeping the peace that the instinct itself was quickened.
From the moment it was quickened, however, it found other
work, and that was how, to begin with, she produced the very
complication she most sought to avert. What she had essentially
done, these days, had been to read the unspoken into the spoken;
so that thus, with accumulations, it had become more definite to
her that the unspoken was, unspeakably, the completeness of the
sacrifice of Mrs Beale. There were times when every minute that
Sir Claude stayed away was like a nail in Mrs Beale's coffin. That
brought back to Maisie – it was a roundabout way – the beauty and
antiquity of her connection with the flower of the Overmores as
well as that lady's own grace and charm, her peculiar prettiness and
cleverness and even her peculiar tribulations. A hundred things
hummed at the back of her head, but two of these were simple
enough. Mrs Beale was by the way, after all, just her stepmother
and her relative. She was just – and partly for that very reason – Sir
Claude's greatest intimate ('lady-intimate' was Maisie's term) so
that what together they were on Mrs Wix's prescription to give up
and break short off with was for one of them his particular favourite
and for the other her father's wife. Strangely, indescribably her
perception of reasons kept pace with her sense of trouble; but there

was something in her that, without a supreme effort not to be shabby, couldn't take the reasons for granted. What it comes to perhaps for ourselves is that, disinherited and denuded as we have seen her, there still lingered in her life an echo of parental influence – she was still reminiscent of one of the sacred lessons of home. It was the only one she retained, but luckily she retained it with force. She enjoyed in a word an ineffaceable view of the fact that there were things papa called mamma and mamma called papa a low sneak for doing or for not doing. Now this rich memory gave her a name that she dreaded to invite to the lips of Mrs Beale: she should personally wince so just to hear it. The very sweetness of the foreign life she was steeped in added with each hour of Sir Claude's absence to the possibility of such pangs. She watched beside Mrs Wix the great golden Madonna, and one of the ear-ringed old women who had been sitting at the end of their bench got up and pottered away.

'Adieu mesdames!' said the old woman in a little cracked civil voice – a demonstration by which our friends were so affected that they bobbed up and almost curtseyed to her. They subsided again, and it was shortly after, in a summer hum of French insects and a phase of almost somnolent reverie, that Maisie most had the vision of what it was to shut out from such a perspective so appealing a participant. It had not yet appeared so vast as at that moment, this prospect of statues shining in the blue and of courtesy in romantic forms.

'Why after all should we have to choose between you? Why shouldn't we be four?' she finally demanded.

Mrs Wix gave the jerk of a sleeper awakened or the start even of one who hears a bullet whiz at the flag of truce. Her stupefaction at such a breach of the peace delayed for a moment her answer. 'Four improprieties, do you mean? Because two of us happen to be decent people! Do I gather you to wish that I should stay on with you even if that woman *is* capable –?'

Maisie took her up before she could further phrase Mrs Beale's capability. 'Stay on as *my* companion – yes. Stay on as just what you were at mamma's. Mrs Beale *would* let you!' the child said.

Mrs Wix had by this time fairly sprung to her arms. 'And who, I'd like to know, would let Mrs Beale? Do you mean, little unfortunate, that *you* would?'

'Why not, if now she's free?'

'Free? Are you imitating *him*? Well, if Sir Claude's old enough to know better, upon my word I think it's right to treat you as if you also were. You'll have to, at any rate – to know better – if that's the line you're proposing to take.' Mrs Wix had never been so harsh; but on the other hand Maisie could guess that she herself had never appeared so wanton. What was underlying, however, rather overawed than angered her; she felt she could still insist – not for contradiction, but for ultimate calm. Her wantonness meanwhile continued to work upon her friend, who caught again, on the rebound, the sound of deepest provocation. 'Free, free, free? If she's as free as *you* are, my dear, she's free enough, to be sure!'

'As I am?' – Maisie, after reflection and despite whatever of portentous this seemed to convey, risked a critical echo.

'Well,' said Mrs Wix, 'nobody, you know, is free to commit a crime.'

'A crime!' The word had come out in a way that made the child sound it again.

'You'd commit as great a one as their own – and so should I – if we were to condone their immorality by our presence.'

Maisie waited a little; this seemed so fiercely conclusive. 'Why is it immorality?' she nevertheless presently enquired.

Her companion now turned upon her with a reproach softer because it was somehow deeper. 'You're too unspeakable! Do you know what we're talking about?'

In the interest of ultimate calm Maisie felt that she must be above all clear. 'Certainly; about their taking advantage of their freedom.'

'Well, to do what?'

'Why, to live with us.'

Mrs Wix's laugh, at this, was literally wild. ' "Us?" Thank you!'

'Then to live with *me*.'

The words made her friend jump. 'You give me up? You break with me for ever? You turn me into the street?'

Maisie, though gasping a little, bore up under the rain of challenges. 'Those, it seems to me, are the things you do to *me*.'

Mrs Wix made little of her valour. 'I can promise you that, whatever I do, I shall never let you out of my sight! You ask me why it's immorality when you've seen with your own eyes that Sir Claude has felt it to be so to that dire extent that, rather than make you face the shame of it, he has for months kept away from you altogether? Is it any more difficult to see that the first time he tries to do his duty he washes his hands of *her* – takes you straight away from her?'

Maisie turned this over, but more for apparent consideration than from any impulse to yield too easily. 'Yes, I see what you mean. But at that time they weren't free.' She felt Mrs Wix rear up again at the offensive word, but she succeeded in touching her with a remonstrant hand. 'I don't think you know how free they've become.'

'I know, I believe, at least as much as you do!'

Maisie felt a delicacy but overcame it. 'About the Countess?'

'Your father's – temptress?' Mrs Wix gave her a sidelong squint. 'Perfectly. She pays him!'

'Oh *does* she?' At this the child's countenance fell: it seemed to give a reason for papa's behaviour and place it in a more favourable light. She wished to be just. 'I don't say she's not generous. She was so to me.'

'How, to you?'

'She gave me a lot of money.'

Mrs Wix stared. 'And pray what did you do with a lot of money?'

'I gave it to Mrs Beale.'

'And what did Mrs Beale do with it?'

'She sent it back.'

'To the Countess? Gammon!' said Mrs Wix. She disposed of that plea as effectually as Susan Ash.

'Well, I don't care!' Maisie replied. 'What I mean is that you don't know about the rest.'

'The rest? What rest?'

Maisie wondered how she could best put it. 'Papa kept me there an hour.'

'I do know – Sir Claude told me. Mrs Beale had told him.'

Maisie looked incredulity. 'How could she – when I didn't speak of it?'

Mrs Wix was mystified. 'Speak of what?'

'Why, of her being so frightful.'

'The Countess? Of course she's frightful!' Mrs Wix returned. After a moment she added: 'That's why she pays him.'

Maisie pondered. 'It's the best thing about her then – if she gives him as much as she gave *me*.'

'Well, it's not the best thing about *him*! Or rather perhaps it *is* too!' Mrs Wix subjoined.

'But she's awful – really and truly,' Maisie went on.

Mrs Wix arrested her. 'You needn't go into details!' It was visibly at variance with this injunction that she yet enquired: 'How does that make it any better?'

'Their living with me? Why for the Countess – and for her whiskers! – he has put me off on them. I understood him,' Maisie profoundly said.

'I hope then he understood you. It's more than I do!' Mrs Wix admitted.

This was a real challenge to be plainer, and our young lady immediately became so. 'I mean it isn't a crime.'

'Why then did Sir Claude steal you away?'

'He didn't steal – he only borrowed me. I knew it wasn't for long,' Maisie audaciously professed.

'You must allow me to reply to that,' cried Mrs Wix, 'that you knew nothing of the sort, and that you rather basely failed to back me up last night when you pretended so plump that you did! You hoped in fact, exactly as much as I did and as in my senseless passion I even hope now, that this may be the beginning of better things.'

Oh yes, Mrs Wix was indeed, for the first time, sharp; so that there at last stirred in our heroine the sense not so much of being proved disingenuous as of being precisely accused of the meanness that had brought everything down on her through her very desire to shake herself clear of it. She suddenly felt herself swell with a passion of protest. 'I never, *never* hoped I wasn't going again to see Mrs Beale! I didn't, I didn't, I didn't!' she repeated. Mrs Wix bounced about with a force of rejoinder of which she also felt that she must anticipate the concussion and which, though the good lady was evidently charged to the brim, hung fire long enough to give time for an aggravation. 'She's beautiful and I love her! I love her and she's beautiful!'

'And I'm hideous and you hate *me*?' Mrs Wix fixed her a moment, then caught herself up. 'I won't embitter you by absolutely accusing you of that; though, as for my being hideous, it's hardly the first time I've been told so! I know it so well that even if I haven't whiskers – have I? – I dare say there are other ways in which the Countess is a Venus to me! My pretensions must therefore seem to you monstrous – which comes to the same thing as your not liking me. But do you mean to go so far as to tell me that you *want* to live with them in their sin?'

'You know what I want, you know what I want!' – Maisie spoke with the shudder of rising tears.

'Yes, I do; you want me to be as bad as yourself! Well, I won't. There! Mrs Beale's as bad as your father!' Mrs Wix went on.

'She's not! – she's not!' her pupil almost shrieked in retort.

'You mean because Sir Claude at least has beauty and wit and grace? But he pays just as the Countess pays!' Mrs Wix, who now rose as she spoke, fairly revealed a latent cynicism.

It raised Maisie also to her feet; her companion had walked off a few steps and paused. The two looked at each other as they had never looked, and Mrs Wix seemed to flaunt there in her finery. 'Then doesn't he pay *you* too?' her unhappy charge demanded.

At this she bounded in her place. 'Oh you incredible little waif!' She brought it out with a wail of violence; after which, with another convulsion, she marched straight away.

Maisie dropped back on the bench and burst into sobs.

XXVI

NOTHING so dreadful of course could be final or even for many minutes prolonged: they rushed together again too soon for either to feel that either had kept it up, and though they went home in silence it was with a vivid perception for Maisie that her companion's hand had closed upon her. That hand had shown altogether, these twenty-four hours, a new capacity for closing, and one of the truths the child could least resist was that a certain greatness had now come to Mrs Wix. The case was indeed that the quality of her motive surpassed the sharpness of her angles; both the combination and the singularity of which things, when in the afternoon they used the carriage, Maisie could borrow from the contemplative hush of their grandeur the freedom to feel to the utmost. She still bore the mark of the tone in which her friend had thrown out that threat of never losing sight of her. This friend had been converted in short from feebleness to force; and it was the light of her new authority that showed from how far she had come. The threat in question, sharply exultant, might have produced defiance; but before anything so ugly could happen another process had insidiously forestalled it. The moment at which this process had begun to mature was that of Mrs Wix's breaking out with a dignity attuned to their own apartments and with an advantage now measurably gained. They had ordered coffee after luncheon, in the spirit of Sir Claude's provision, and it was served to them while they awaited their equipage in the white and gold saloon. It was flanked moreover with a couple of liqueurs, and Maisie felt that Sir Claude could scarce have been taken more at his word had it been followed by anecdotes and cigarettes. The influence of these

luxuries was at any rate in the air. It seemed to her while she tiptoed
at the chimney-glass, pulling on her gloves and with a motion of
her head shaking a feather into place, to have had something to do
with Mrs Wix's suddenly saying: 'Haven't you really and truly *any*
moral sense?'

Maisie was aware that her answer, though it brought her down
to her heels, was vague even to imbecility, and that this was the first
time she had appeared to practise with Mrs Wix an intellectual
inaptitude to meet her – the infirmity to which she had owed so
much success with papa and mamma. The appearance did her
injustice, for it was not less through her candour than through her
playfellow's pressure that after this the idea of a moral sense mainly
coloured their intercourse. She began, the poor child, with scarcely
knowing what it was; but it proved something that, with scarce an
outward sign save her surrender to the swing of the carriage, she
could, before they came back from their drive, strike up a sort of
acquaintance with. The beauty of the day only deepened, and the
splendour of the afternoon sea, and the haze of the far headlands,
and the taste of the sweet air. It was the coachman indeed who,
smiling and cracking his whip, turning in his place, pointing to
invisible objects and uttering unintelligible sounds – all, our tourists
recognised, strict features of a social order principally devoted to
language: it was this polite person, I say, who made their excursion
fall so much short that their return left them still a stretch of the long
daylight and an hour that, at his obliging suggestion, they spent on
foot by the shining sands. Maisie had seen the *plage* the day before
with Sir Claude, but that was a reason the more for showing on the
spot to Mrs Wix that it was, as she said, another of the places on her
list and of the things of which she knew the French name. The
bathers, so late, were absent and the tide was low; the sea-pools
twinkled in the sunset and there were dry places as well, where they
could sit again and admire and expatiate: a circumstance that, while
they listened to the lap of the waves, gave Mrs Wix a fresh support
for her challenge. 'Have you absolutely none at all?'

She had no need now, as to the question itself at least, to be specific; that on the other hand was the eventual result of their quiet conjoined apprehension of the thing that – well, yes, since they must face it – Maisie absolutely and appallingly had so little of. This marked more particularly the moment of the child's perceiving that her friend had risen to a level which might – till superseded at all events – pass almost for sublime. Nothing more remarkable had taken place in the first heat of her own departure, no act of perception less to be overtraced by our rough method, than her vision, the rest of that Boulogne day, of the manner in which she figured. I so despair of courting her noiseless mental footsteps here that I must crudely give you my word for its being from this time forward a picture literally present to her. Mrs Wix saw her as a little person knowing so extraordinarily much that, for the account to be taken of it, what she still didn't know would be ridiculous if it hadn't been embarrassing. Mrs Wix was in truth more than ever qualified to meet embarrassment; I am not sure that Maisie had not even a dim discernment of the queer law of her own life that made her educate to that sort of proficiency those elders with whom she was concerned. She promoted, as it were, their development; nothing could have been more marked for instance than her success in promoting Mrs Beale's. She judged that if her whole history, for Mrs Wix, had been the successive stages of her knowledge, so the very climax of the concatenation would, in the same view, be the stage at which the knowledge should over-flow. As she was condemned to know more and more, how could it logically stop before she should know Most? It came to her in fact as they sat there on the sands that she was distinctly on the road to know Everything. She had not had governesses for nothing: what in the world had she ever done but learn and learn and learn? She looked at the pink sky with a placid foreboding that she soon should have learnt All. They lingered in the flushed air till at last it turned to grey and she seemed fairly to receive new information from every brush of the breeze. By the time they moved homeward it was as if this inevitability had become for Mrs Wix a long, tense cord, twitched by a nervous hand, on which the valued pearls of intelligence were to be neatly strung.

In the evening upstairs they had another strange sensation, as to which Maisie couldn't afterwards have told you whether it was bang in the middle or quite at the beginning that her companion sounded with fresh emphasis the note of the moral sense. What mattered was merely that she did exclaim, and again, as at first appeared, most disconnectedly: 'God help me, it does seem to peep out!' Oh the queer confusions that had wooed it at last to such peeping! None so queer, however, as the words of woe, and it might verily be said of rage, in which the poor lady bewailed the tragic end of her own rich ignorance. There was a point at which she seized the child and hugged her as close as in the old days of partings and returns; at which she was visibly at a loss how to make up to such a victim for such contaminations: appealing, as to what she had done and was doing, in bewilderment, in explanation, in supplication, for reassurance, for pardon and even outright for pity.

'I don't know what I've said to you, my own: I don't know what I'm saying or what the turn you've given my life has rendered me, heaven forgive me, capable of saying. Have I lost all delicacy, all decency, all measure of how far and how bad? It seems to me mostly that I have, though I'm the last of whom you would ever have thought it. I've just done it for *you*, precious – not to lose you, which would have been worst of all: so that I've had to pay with my own innocence, if you do laugh! for clinging to you and keeping you. Don't let me pay for nothing; don't let me have been thrust for nothing into such horrors and such shames. I never knew anything about them and I never wanted to know! Now I know too much, too much!' the poor woman lamented and groaned. 'I know so much that with hearing such talk I ask myself where I am; and with uttering it too, which is worse, say to myself that I'm far, too far, from where I started! I ask myself what I should have thought with my lost one if I had heard myself cross the line. There are lines I've crossed with *you* where I should have fancied I had come to a pretty pass –!' She gasped at the mere supposition. 'I've gone from one thing to another, and all for the real love of you; and now what would any one say – I mean any one but *them* – if they were to hear the way I go on? I've had to keep up with you, haven't I? – and therefore what could I do less than look to you to keep up with *me*? But it's not *them* that are the worst – by which I mean to say it's not *him*: it's your dreadfully base papa and the one person in the world whom he could have found, I do believe – and she's not the Countess, duck – wickeder than himself. While they were about it at any rate, since they *were* ruining you, they might have done it so as to spare an honest woman. Then I shouldn't have had to do whatever it is that's the worst: throw up at you the badness you haven't taken in, or find my advantage in the vileness you *have*! What I did lose patience at this morning was at how it was that without your seeming to condemn – for you didn't, you remember! – you yet did seem to *know*. Thank God, in his mercy, at last, *if* you do!'

The night, this time, was warm and one of the windows stood open to the small balcony over the rail of which, on coming up from dinner, Maisie had hung a long time in the enjoyment of the chatter, the lights, the life of the quay made brilliant by the season and the hour. Mrs Wix's requirements had drawn her in from this posture and Mrs Wix's embrace had detained her even though midway in the outpouring her confusion and sympathy had permitted, or rather had positively helped, her to disengage herself. But the casement was still wide, the spectacle, the pleasure were still there, and from her place in the room, which, with its polished floor and its panels of elegance, was lighted from without more than from within, the child could still take account of them. She appeared to watch and listen; after which she answered Mrs Wix with a question. 'If I do know –?'

'If you do condemn.' The correction was made with some austerity.

It had the effect of causing Maisie to heave a vague sigh of oppression and then after an instant and as if under cover of this ambiguity pass out again upon the balcony. She hung again over the rail; she felt the summer night; she dropped down into the manners of France. There was a café below the hotel, before which, with little chairs and tables, people sat on a space enclosed by plants in tubs; and the impression was enriched by the flash of the white aprons of waiters and the music of a man and a woman who, from beyond the precinct, sent up the strum of a guitar and the drawl of a song about 'amour'. Maisie knew what 'amour' meant too, and wondered if Mrs Wix did: Mrs Wix remained within, as still as a mouse and perhaps not reached by the performance. After a while, but not till the musicians had ceased and begun to circulate with a little plate, her pupil came back to her. '*Is* it a crime?' Maisie then asked.

Mrs Wix was as prompt as if she had been crouching in a lair. 'Branded by the Bible.'

'Well, he won't commit a crime.'

Mrs Wix looked at her gloomily. 'He's committing one now.'

'Now?'

'In being with her.'

Maisie had it on her tongue's end to return once more: 'But now he's free.' She remembered, however, in time that one of the things she had known for the last entire hour was that this made no difference. After that, and as if to turn the right way, she was on the point of a blind dash, a weak reversion to the reminder that it might make a difference, might diminish the crime for Mrs Beale; till such a reflection was in its order also quashed by the visibility in Mrs Wix's face of the collapse produced by her inference from her pupil's manner that after all her pains her pupil didn't even yet adequately understand. Never so much as when confronted had Maisie wanted to understand, and all her thought for a minute centred in the effort to come out with something which should be a disproof of her simplicity. 'Just *trust* me, dear; that's all!' – she came out finally with that; and it was perhaps a good sign of her action that with a long, impartial moan Mrs Wix floated her to bed.

There was no letter the next morning from Sir Claude – which Mrs Wix let out that she deemed the worst of omens; yet it was just for the quieter communion they so got with him that, when after the coffee and rolls which made them more foreign than ever, it came to going forth for fresh drafts upon his credit they wandered again up the hill to the rampart instead of plunging into distraction with the crowd on the sands or into the sea with the semi-nude bathers. They gazed once more at their gilded Virgin; they sank once more upon their battered bench; they felt once more their distance from the Regent's Park. At last Mrs Wix became definite about their friend's silence. 'He *is* afraid of her! She has forbidden him to write.' The fact of his fear Maisie already knew; but her companion's mention of it had at this moment two unexpected results. The first was her wondering in dumb remonstrance how Mrs Wix, with a devotion not after all inferior to her own, could put into such an allusion such a grimness of derision; the second was that she found herself suddenly drop into a deeper view of it. She too had been afraid, as we have seen, of the people of whom Sir Claude was afraid, and by that law she had had her due measure of latest apprehension of Mrs Beale. What occurred at present, however, was that, whereas this sympathy appeared vain as for him, the ground of it loomed dimly as a reason for selfish alarm. That uneasiness had not carried her far before Mrs Wix spoke again and with an abruptness so great as almost to seem irrelevant. 'Has it never occurred to you to be jealous of her?'

It never had in the least; yet the words were scarce in the air before Maisie had jumped at them. She held them well, she looked at them hard; at last she brought out with an assurance which there was no one, alas, but herself to admire: 'Well, yes – since you ask me.' She debated, then continued: 'Lots of times!'

Mrs Wix glared askance an instant; such approval as her look expressed was not wholly unqualified. It expressed at any rate something that presumably had to do with her saying once more: 'Yes. He's afraid of her.'

Maisie heard, and it had afresh its effect on her even through the blur of the attention now required by the possibility of that idea of jealousy – a possibility created only by her feeling she had thus found the way to show she was not simple. It struck out of Mrs Wix that this lady still believed her moral sense to be interested and feigned; so what could be such a gage of her sincerity as a peep of the most restless of the passions? Such a revelation would baffle discouragement, and discouragement was in fact so baffled that, helped in some degree by the mere intensity of their need to hope, which also, according to its nature, sprang from the dark portent of the absent letter, the real pitch of their morning was reached by the note, not of mutual scrutiny, but of unprecedented frankness. There were broodings indeed and silences, and Maisie sank deeper into the vision that for her friend she was, at the most, superficial, and that also, positively, she was the more so the more she tried to appear complete. Was the sum of all knowledge only to know how little in this presence one would ever reach it? The answer to that question luckily lost itself in the brightness suffusing the scene as soon as Maisie had thrown out in regard to Mrs Beale such a remark as she had never dreamed she should live to make. 'If I thought she was unkind to him – I don't know *what* I should do!'

Mrs Wix dropped one of her squints; she even confirmed it by a wild grunt. 'I know what *I* should!'

Maisie at this felt that she lagged. 'Well, I can think of *one* thing.'

Mrs Wix more directly challenged her. 'What is it then?'

Maisie met her expression as if it were a game with forfeits for winking. 'I'd *kill* her!' That at least, she hoped as she looked away, would guarantee her moral sense. She looked away, but her companion said nothing for so long that she at last turned her head again. Then she saw the straighteners all blurred with tears which after a little seemed to have sprung from her own eyes. There were tears in fact on both sides of the spectacles, and they were even so thick that it was presently all Maisie could do to make out through them that slowly, finally Mrs Wix put forth a hand. It was the material pressure that settled this and even at the end of some minutes more things besides. It settled in its own way one thing in particular, which, though often, between them, heaven knew, hovered round and hung over, was yet to be established without the shadow of an attenuating smile. Oh there was no gleam of levity, as little of humour as of deprecation, in the long time they now sat together or in the way in which at some unmeasured point of it Mrs Wix became distinct enough for her own dignity and yet not loud enough for the snoozing old women.

'I adore him. I adore him.'

Maisie took it well in; so well that in a moment more she would have answered profoundly: 'So do I.' But before that moment passed something took place that brought other words to her lips; nothing more, very possibly, than the closer consciousness in her hand of the significance of Mrs Wix's. Their hands remained linked in unutterable sign of their union, and what Maisie at last said was simply and serenely: 'Oh I know!'

Their hands were so linked and their union was so confirmed that it took the far deep note of a bell, borne to them on the summer air, to call them back to a sense of hours and proprieties. They had touched bottom and melted together, but they gave a start at last: the bell was the voice of the inn and the inn was the image of luncheon. They should be late for it; they got up, and their quickened step on the return had something of the swing of confidence. When they reached the hotel the *table d'hôte* had begun; this was clear from the threshold, clear from the absence in the hall and on the stairs of the 'personnel', as Mrs Wix said – she had picked *that* up – all collected in the dining-room. They mounted to their apartments for a brush before the glass, and it was Maisie who, in passing and from a vain impulse, threw open the white and gold door. She was thus first to utter the sound that brought Mrs Wix almost on top of her, as by the other accident it would have brought her on top of Mrs Wix. It had at any rate the effect of leaving them bunched together in a strained stare at their new situation. This situation had put on in a flash the bright form of Mrs Beale: she stood there in her hat and her jacket, amid bags and shawls, smiling and holding out her arms. If she had just arrived it was a different figure from either of the two that for *their* benefit, wan and tottering and none too soon to save life, the Channel had recently disgorged. She was as lovely as the day that had brought her over, as fresh as the luck and the health that attended her: it came to Maisie on the spot that she was more beautiful than she had ever been. All this was too quick to count, but there was still time in it to give the child the sense of what had kindled the light. That leaped out of the open arms, the open eyes, the open mouth; it leaped out with Mrs Beale's loud cry at her: 'I'm free, I'm free!'

XXVII

THE greatest wonder of all was the way Mrs Beale addressed her announcement, so far as could be judged, equally to Mrs Wix, who, as if from sudden failure of strength, sank into a chair while Maisie surrendered to the visitor's embrace. As soon as the child was liberated she met with profundity Mrs Wix's stupefaction and actually was able to see that while in a manner sustaining the encounter her face yet seemed with intensity to say: 'Now, for God's sake, don't crow "I told you so!"' Maisie was somehow on the spot aware of an absence of disposition to crow; it had taken her but an extra minute to arrive at such a quick survey of the objects surrounding Mrs Beale as showed that among them was no appurtenance of Sir Claude's. She knew his dressing-bag now – oh with the fondest knowledge! – and there was an instant during which its not being there was a stroke of the worst news. She was yet to learn what it could be to recognise in some lapse of a sequence the proof of an extinction, and therefore remained unaware that this momentary pang was a foretaste of the experience of death. It of course yielded in a flash to Mrs Beale's brightness, it gasped itself away in her own instant appeal. 'You've come alone?'

'Without Sir Claude?' Strangely, Mrs Beale looked even brighter. 'Yes; in the eagerness to get at you. You abominable little villain!' – and her stepmother, laughing clear, administered to her cheek a pat that was partly a pinch. 'What were you up to and what did you take me for? But I'm glad to be abroad, and after all it's you who have shown me the way. I mightn't, without you, have been able to come – to come, that is, so soon. Well, here I am at any rate and in a moment more I should have begun to worry about you.

This will do very well' – she was good-natured about the place and even presently added that it was charming. Then with a rosier glow she made again her great point: 'I'm free, I'm free!' Maisie made on her side her own: she carried back her gaze to Mrs Wix, whom amazement continued to hold; she drew afresh her old friend's attention to the superior way she didn't take that up. What she did take up the next minute was the question of Sir Claude. 'Where is he? Won't he come?'

Mrs Beale's consideration of this oscillated with a smile between the two expectancies with which she was flanked: it was conspicuous, it was extraordinary, her unblinking acceptance of Mrs Wix, a miracle of which Maisie had even now begun to read a reflection in that lady's long visage. 'He'll come, but we must *make* him!' she gaily brought forth.

'Make him?' Maisie echoed.

'We must give him time. We must play our cards.'

'But he promised us awfully,' Maisie replied.

'My dear child, he has promised *me* awfully; I mean lots of things, and not in every case kept his promise to the letter.' Mrs Beale's good humour insisted on taking for granted Mrs Wix's, to whom her attention had suddenly grown prodigious. 'I dare say he has done the same with you, and not always come to time. But he makes it up in his own way – and it isn't as if we didn't know exactly what he is. There's one thing he is,' she went on, 'which makes everything else only a question, for us, of tact.' They scarce had time to wonder what this was before, as they might have said, it flew straight into their face. 'He's as free as I am!'

'Yes, I know,' said Maisie; as if, however, independently weighing the value of that. She really weighed also the oddity of her stepmother's treating it as news to *her*, who had been the first person literally to whom Sir Claude had mentioned it. For a few seconds, as if with the sound of it in her ears, she stood with him again, in memory and in the twilight, in the hotel garden at Folkestone.

Anything Mrs Beale overlooked was, she indeed divined, but the effect of an exaltation of high spirits, a tendency to soar that showed even when she dropped – still quite impartially – almost to the confidential. 'Well, then – we've only to wait. He can't do without us long. I'm sure, Mrs Wix, he can't do without *you*! He's devoted to you; he has told me so much about you. The extent I count on you, you know, count on you to help me –!' was an extent that even all her radiance couldn't express. What it couldn't express quite as much as what it could made at any rate every instant her presence and even her famous freedom loom larger; and it was this mighty mass that once more led her companions, bewildered and disjoined, to exchange with each other as through a thickening veil confused and ineffectual signs. They clung together at least on the common ground of unpreparedness, and Maisie watched without relief the havoc of wonder in Mrs Wix. It had reduced her to perfect impotence, and, but that gloom was black upon her, she sat as if fascinated by Mrs Beale's high style. It had plunged her into a long deep hush; for what had happened was the thing she had least allowed for and before which the particular rigour she had worked up could only grow limp and sick. Sir Claude was to have reappeared with his accomplice or without her; never, never his accomplice without *him*. Mrs Beale had gained apparently by this time an advantage she could pursue: she looked at the droll dumb figure with jesting reproach. 'You really won't shake hands with me? Never mind; you'll come round!' She put the matter to no test, going on immediately and, instead of offering her hand, raising it, with a pretty gesture that her bent head met, to a long black pin that played a part in her back hair. 'Are hats worn at luncheon? If you're as hungry as I am we must go right down.'

Mrs Wix stuck fast, but she met the question in a voice her pupil scarce recognised. 'I wear mine.'

Mrs Beale, swallowing at one glance her brand-new bravery, which she appeared at once to refer to its origin and to follow in its

flights, accepted this as conclusive. 'Oh but I've not such a beauty!'
Then she turned rejoicingly to Maisie. 'I've got a beauty for *you*,
my dear.'

'A beauty?'

'A love of a hat – in my luggage. I remembered *that*' – she
nodded at the object on her stepdaughter's head – 'and I've
brought you one with a peacock's breast. It's the most gorgeous
blue!'

It was too strange, this talking with her there already not about
Sir Claude but about peacocks – too strange for the child to have
the presence of mind to thank her. But the felicity in which she
had arrived was so proof against everything that Maisie felt more
and more the depth of the purpose that must underlie it. She had
a vague sense of its being abysmal, the spirit with which Mrs Beale
carried off the awkwardness, in the white and gold salon, of such
a want of breath and of welcome. Mrs Wix was more breathless
than ever; the embarrassment of Mrs Beale's isolation was as
nothing to the embarrassment of her grace. The perception of this
dilemma was the germ on the child's part of a new question
altogether. What if *with* this indulgence –? But the idea lost
itself in something too frightened for hope and too conjectured for
fear; and while everything went by leaps and bounds one of the
waiters stood at the door to remind them that the *table d'hôte* was
half over.

'Had you come up to wash hands?' Mrs Beale hereupon asked
them. 'Go and do it quickly and I'll be with you: they've put my
boxes in that nice room – it was Sir Claude's. Trust him,' she
laughed, 'to have a nice one!' The door of a neighbouring room
stood open, and now from the threshold, addressing herself again
to Mrs Wix, she launched a note that gave the very key of what, as
she would have said, she was up to. 'Dear lady, please attend to my
daughter.'

She was up to change of deportment so complete that it
represented – oh for offices still honourably subordinate if not too

explicitly menial – an absolute coercion, an interested clutch of the old woman's respectability. There was response, to Maisie's view, I may say at once, in the jump of that respectability to its feet: it was itself capable of one of the leaps, one of the bounds just mentioned, and it carried its charge, with this momentum and while Mrs Beale popped into Sir Claude's chamber, straight away to where, at the end of the passage, pupil and governess were quartered. The greatest stride of all, for that matter, was that within a few seconds the pupil had, in another relation, been converted into a daughter. Maisie's eyes were still following it when, after the rush, with the door almost slammed and no thought of soap and towels, the pair stood face to face. Mrs Wix, in this position, was the first to gasp a sound. 'Can it ever be that *she* has one?'

Maisie felt still more bewildered. 'One what?'

'Why moral sense.'

They spoke as if you might have two, but Mrs Wix looked as if it were not altogether a happy thought, and Maisie didn't see how even an affirmative from her own lips would clear up what had become most of a mystery. It was to this larger puzzle she sprang pretty straight. '*Is* she my mother now?'

It was a point as to which an horrific glimpse of the responsibility of an opinion appeared to affect Mrs Wix like a blow in the stomach. She had evidently never thought of it; but she could think and rebound. 'If she is, he's equally your father.'

Maisie, however, thought further. 'Then my father and my mother –!'

But she had already faltered and Mrs Wix had already glared back: 'Ought to live together? Don't begin it *again*!' She turned away with a groan, to reach the washing-stand, and Maisie could by this time recognise with a certain ease that that way verily madness did lie. Mrs Wix gave a great untidy splash, but the next instant had faced round. 'She has taken a new line.'

'She was nice to you,' Maisie concurred.

'What *she* thinks so – "go and dress the young lady!" But it's something!' she panted. Then she thought out the rest. 'If he won't have her, why she'll have *you*. She'll be the one.'

'The one to keep me abroad?'

'The one to give you a home.' Mrs Wix saw further; she mastered all the portents. 'Oh she's cruelly clever! It's not a moral sense.' She reached her climax: 'It's a game!'

'A game?'

'Not to lose him. She has sacrificed him – to her duty.'

'Then won't he come?' Maisie pleaded.

Mrs Wix made no answer; her vision absorbed her. 'He has fought. But she has won.'

'Then won't he come?' the child repeated.

Mrs Wix made it out. 'Yes, hang him!' She had never been so profane.

For all Maisie minded! 'Soon – tomorrow?'

'Too soon – whenever. Indecently soon.'

'But then we *shall* be together!' the child went on. It made Mrs Wix look at her as if in exasperation; but nothing had time to come before she precipitated: 'Together with *you*!' The air of criticism continued, but took voice only in her companion's bidding her wash herself and come down. The silence of quick ablutions fell upon them, presently broken, however, by one of Maisie's sudden reversions. 'Mercy, isn't she handsome?'

Mrs Wix had finished; she waited. 'She'll attract attention.' They were rapid, and it would have been noticed that the shock the beauty had given them acted, incongruously, as a positive spur to their preparations for rejoining her. She had none the less, when they returned to the sitting-room, already descended; the open door of her room showed it empty and the chambermaid explained. Here again they were delayed by another sharp thought of Mrs Wix's. 'But what will she live on meanwhile?'

Maisie stopped short. 'Till Sir Claude comes?'

It was nothing to the violence with which her friend had been arrested. 'Who'll pay the bills?'

Maisie thought. 'Can't *she*?'

'She? She hasn't a penny.'

The child wondered. 'But didn't papa –?'

'Leave her a fortune?' Mrs Wix would have appeared to speak of papa as dead had she not immediately added: 'Why he lives on other women!'

Oh yes, Maisie remembered. 'Then can't he send –?' She faltered again; even to herself it sounded queer.

'Some of their money to his wife?' Mrs Wix gave a laugh still stranger than the weird suggestion. 'I dare say she'd take it!'

They hurried on again; yet again, on the stairs, Maisie pulled up. 'Well, if she had stopped in England –!' she threw out.

Mrs Wix considered. 'And he had come over instead?'

'Yes, as we expected.' Maisie launched her speculation. 'What then would she have lived on?'

Mrs Wix hung fire but an instant. 'On other men!' And she marched downstairs.

XXVIII

MRS Beale, at table between the pair, plainly attracted the attention Mrs Wix had foretold. No other lady present was nearly so handsome, nor did the beauty of any other accommodate itself with such art to the homage it produced. She talked mainly to her other neighbour, and that left Maisie leisure both to note the manner in which eyes were riveted and nudges interchanged, and to lose herself in the meanings that, dimly as yet and disconnectedly, but with a vividness that fed apprehension, she could begin to read into her stepmother's independent move. Mrs Wix had helped her by talking of a game; it was a connection in which the move could put on a strategic air. Her notions of diplomacy were thin, but it was a kind of cold diplomatic shoulder and an elbow of more than usual point that, temporarily at least, were presented to her by the averted inclination of Mrs Beale's head. There was a phrase familiar to Maisie, so often was it used by this lady to express the idea of one's getting what one wanted: one got it – Mrs Beale always said *she* at all events always got it or proposed to get it – by 'making love'. She was at present making love, singular as it appeared, to Mrs Wix, and her young friend's mind had never moved in such freedom as on thus finding itself face to face with the question of what she wanted to get. This period of the *omelette aux rognons* and the *poulet sauté*, while her sole surviving parent, her fourth, fairly chattered to her governess, left Maisie rather wondering if her governess would hold out. It was strange, but she became on the spot quite as interested in Mrs Wix's moral sense as Mrs Wix could possibly be in hers: it had risen before her so pressingly that this was something new for Mrs Wix to resist. Resisting Mrs Beale herself promised at such a rate to become a very different business from resisting Sir Claude's view of her. More might come of what had happened – whatever it was – than Maisie felt she could have expected. She put it together with a suspicion that, had she ever in her life had a sovereign changed, would have resembled an impression, baffled by the want of arithmetic, that her change was wrong: she groped about in it that she was perhaps playing the passive part in a case of violent substitution. A victim was what she should surely be if the issue between her step-parents had been settled by Mrs Beale's saying: 'Well, if she can live with but one of us alone, with which in the world should it be but me?' That answer was far from what, for days, she had nursed herself in, and the desolation of it was deepened by the absence of anything from Sir Claude to show he had not had to take it as triumphant. Had not Mrs Beale, upstairs, as good as given out that she had quitted him with the snap of a tension, left him, dropped him in London, after some struggle as a sequel to which her own advent represented that she had practically sacrificed him? Maisie assisted in fancy at the probable episode in the Regent's Park, finding elements almost of terror in the suggestion that Sir Claude had not had fair play. They drew something, as she sat there, even from the pride of an association with such beauty as Mrs Beale's; and the child quite forgot that, though the sacrifice of Mrs Beale herself was a solution she had not invented, she would probably have seen Sir Claude embark upon it without a direct remonstrance.

What her stepmother had clearly now promised herself to wring from Mrs Wix was an assent to the great modification, the change, as smart as a juggler's trick, in the interest of which nothing so much mattered as the new convenience of Mrs Beale. Maisie could positively seize the moral that her elbow seemed to point in ribs thinly defended – the moral of its not mattering a straw which of the step-parents was the guardian. The essence of the question was that a girl wasn't a boy: if Maisie had been a mere rough trousered thing, destined at the best probably to grow up a scamp, Sir Claude

would have been welcome. As the case stood he had simply
tumbled out of it, and Mrs Wix would henceforth find herself in
the employ of the right person. These arguments had really fallen
into their place, for our young friend, at the very touch of that tone
in which she had heard her new title declared. She was still, as a
result of so many parents, a daughter to somebody even after papa
and mamma were to all intents dead. If her father's wife and her
mother's husband, by the operation of a natural or, for all she
knew, a legal rule, were in the shoes of their defunct partners, then
Mrs Beale's partner was exactly as defunct as Sir Claude's and her
shoes the very pair to which, in 'Farange *v.* Farange and Others',
the divorce court had given priority. The subject of that celebrated
settlement saw the rest of her day really filled out with the pomp of
all that Mrs Beale assumed. The assumption rounded itself there
between this lady's entertainers, flourished in a way that left them,
in their bottomless element, scarce a free pair of eyes to exchange
signals. It struck Maisie even a little that there was a rope or two
Mrs Wix might have thrown out if she would, a rocket or two she
might have sent up. They had at any rate never been so long
together without communion or telegraphy, and their companion
kept them apart by simply keeping them with her. From this
situation they saw the grandeur of their intenser relation to her pass
and pass like an endless procession. It was a day of lively movement
and of talk on Mrs Beale's part so brilliant and overflowing as to
represent music and banners. She took them out with her promptly
to walk and to drive, and even – towards night – sketched a plan
for carrying them to the Etablissement, where, for only a franc
apiece, they should listen to a concert of celebrities. It reminded
Maisie, the plan, of the side-shows at Earl's Court, and the franc
sounded brighter than the shillings which had at that time failed;
yet this too, like the other, was a frustrated hope: the francs failed
like the shillings and the side-shows had set an example to the
concert. The Etablissement in short melted away, and it was little
wonder that a lady who from the moment of her arrival had been

so gallantly in the breach should confess herself at last done up. Maisie could appreciate her fatigue; the day had not passed without such an observer's discovering that she was excited and even mentally comparing her state to that of the breakers after a gale. It had blown hard in London, and she would take time to go down. It was of the condition known to the child by report as that of talking against time that her emphasis, her spirit, her humour, which had never dropped, now gave the impression.

She too was delighted with foreign manners; but her daughter's opportunities of explaining them to her were unexpectedly fore-stalled by her own tone of large acquaintance with them. One of the things that nipped in the bud all response to her volubility was Maisie's surprised retreat before the fact that Continental life was what she had been almost brought up on. It was Mrs Beale, disconcertingly, who began to explain it to her friends; it was she who, wherever they turned, was the interpreter, the historian and the guide. She was full of reference to her early travels – at the age of eighteen: she had at that period made, with a distinguished Dutch family, a stay on the Lake of Geneva. Maisie had in the old days been regaled with anecdotes of these adventures, but they had with time become phantasmal, and the heroine's quite showy exemption from bewilderment at Boulogne, her acuteness on some of the very subjects on which Maisie had been acute to Mrs Wix, were a high note of the majesty, of the variety of advantage, with which she had alighted. It was all a part of the wind in her sails and of the weight with which her daughter was now to feel her hand. The effect of it on Maisie was to add already the burden of time to her separation from Sir Claude. This might, to her sense, have lasted for days; it was as if, with their main agitation transferred thus to France and with neither mamma now nor Mrs Beale nor Mrs Wix nor herself at his side, he must be fearfully alone in England. Hour after hour she felt as if she were waiting; yet she couldn't have said exactly for what. There were moments when Mrs Beale's flow of talk was a mere rattle to smother a knock. At no part of the crisis had the rattle so public a purpose as when, instead of letting Maisie go with Mrs Wix to prepare for dinner, she pushed her – with a push at last incontestably maternal – straight into the room inherited from Sir Claude. She titivated her little charge with her own brisk hands; then she brought out: 'I'm going to divorce your father.'

This was so different from anything Maisie had expected that it took some time to reach her mind. She was aware meanwhile that she probably looked rather wan. 'To marry Sir Claude?'

Mrs Beale rewarded her with a kiss. 'It's sweet to hear you put it so.'

This was a tribute, but it left Maisie balancing for an objection. 'How *can* you when he's married?'

'He isn't – practically. He's free, you know.'

'Free to marry?'

'Free, first, to divorce his own fiend.'

The benefit that, these last days, she had felt she owed a certain person left Maisie a moment so ill-prepared for recognising this lurid label that she hesitated long enough to risk: 'Mamma?'

'She isn't your mamma any longer,' Mrs Beale returned. 'Sir Claude has paid her money to cease to be.' Then as if remembering how little, to the child, a pecuniary transaction must represent: 'She lets him off supporting her if he'll let her off supporting you.'

Mrs Beale appeared, however, to have done injustice to her daughter's financial grasp. 'And support me himself?' Maisie asked.

'Take the whole bother and burden of you and never let her hear of you again. It's a regular signed contract.'

'Why that's lovely of her!' Maisie cried.

'It's not so lovely, my dear, but that he'll get his divorce.'

Maisie was briefly silent; after which, 'No – he won't get it,' she said. Then she added still more boldly: 'And you won't get yours.'

Mrs Beale, who was at the dressing-glass, turned round with amusement and surprise. 'How do you know that?'

'Oh I know!' cried Maisie.

'From Mrs Wix?'

Maisie debated, then after an instant took her cue from Mrs Beale's absence of anger, which struck her the more as she had felt how much of her courage she needed. 'From Mrs Wix,' she admitted.

Mrs Beale, at the glass again, made play with a powder-puff. 'My own sweet, she's mistaken!' was all she said.

There was a certain force in the very amenity of this, but our young lady reflected long enough to remember that it was not the answer Sir Claude himself had made. The recollection nevertheless failed to prevent her saying: 'Do you mean then that he won't come till he has got it?'

Mrs Beale gave a last touch; she was ready; she stood there in all her elegance. 'I mean, my dear, that it's because he *hasn't* got it that I left him.'

This opened a view that stretched further than Maisie could reach. She turned away from it, but she spoke before they went out again. 'Do you like Mrs Wix now?'

'Why, my chick, I was just going to ask you if you think she has come at all to like poor bad me!'

Maisie thought, at this hint; but unsuccessfully. 'I haven't the least idea. But I'll find out.'

'Do!' said Mrs Beale, rustling out with her in a scented air and as if it would be a very particular favour.

The child tried promptly at bedtime, relieved now of the fear that their visitor would wish to separate her for the night from her attendant. 'Have you held out?' she began as soon as the two doors at the end of the passage were again closed on them.

Mrs Wix looked hard at the flame of the candle. 'Held out –?'

'Why, she has been making love to you. Has she won you over?'

Mrs Wix transferred her intensity to her pupil's face. 'Over to what?'

'To *her* keeping me instead.'

'Instead of Sir Claude?' Mrs Wix was distinctly gaining time.

'Yes; who else? since it's not instead of you.'

Mrs Wix coloured at this lucidity. 'Yes, that *is* what she means.'

'Well, do you like it?' Maisie asked.

She actually had to wait, for oh her friend was embarrassed! 'My opposition to the connection – theirs – would then naturally to some extent fall. She has treated me today as if I weren't after all quite such a worm; not that I don't know very well where she got the pattern of her politeness. But of course,' Mrs Wix hastened to add, 'I shouldn't like her as *the* one nearly so well as him.'

'"Nearly so well!"' Maisie echoed. 'I should hope indeed not.' She spoke with a firmness under which she was herself the first to quiver. 'I thought you "adored" him.'

'I do,' Mrs Wix sturdily allowed.

'Then have you suddenly begun to adore her too?'

Mrs Wix, instead of directly answering, only blinked in support of her sturdiness. 'My dear, in what a tone you ask that! You're coming out.'

'Why shouldn't I? *You've* come out. Mrs Beale has come out. We each have our turn!' And Maisie threw off the most extraordinary little laugh that had ever passed her young lips.

There passed Mrs Wix's indeed the next moment a sound that more than matched it. 'You're most remarkable!' she neighed.

Her pupil, though wholly without aspirations to pertness, barely faltered. 'I think you've done a great deal to make me so.'

'Very true, I have.' She dropped to humility, as if she recalled her so recent self-arraignment.

'Would you accept her then? That's what I ask,' said Maisie.

'As a substitute?' Mrs Wix turned it over; she met again the child's eyes. 'She has literally almost fawned upon me.'

'She hasn't fawned upon *him*. She hasn't even been kind to him.'

Mrs Wix looked as if she had now an advantage. 'Then do you propose to "kill" her?'

'You don't answer my question,' Maisie persisted. 'I want to know if you accept her.'

Mrs Wix continued to hedge. 'I want to know if *you* do!'

Everything in the child's person, at this, announced that it was easy to know. 'Not for a moment.'

'Not the two now?' Mrs Wix had caught on; she flushed with it. 'Only him alone?'

'Him alone or nobody.'

'Not even *me*?' cried Mrs Wix.

Maisie looked at her a moment, then began to undress. 'Oh you're nobody!'

XXIX

HER sleep was drawn out; she instantly recognised lateness in the way her eyes opened to Mrs Wix, erect, completely dressed, more dressed than ever, and gazing at her from the centre of the room. The next thing she was sitting straight up, wide awake with the fear of the hours of 'abroad' that she might have lost. Mrs Wix looked as if the day had already made itself felt, and the process of catching up with it began for Maisie in hearing her distinctly say: 'My poor dear, he has come!'

'Sir Claude?' Maisie, clearing the little bed-rug with the width of her spring, felt the polished floor under her bare feet.

'He crossed in the night; he got in early.' Mrs Wix's head jerked stiffly backward. 'He's there.'

'And you've seen him?'

'No. He's there – he's there,' Mrs Wix repeated. Her voice came out with a queer extinction that was not a voluntary drop, and she trembled so that it added to their common emotion. Visibly pale, they gazed at each other.

'Isn't it too *beautiful*?' Maisie panted back at her; a challenge with an answer to which, however, she was not ready at once. The term Maisie had used was a flash of diplomacy – to prevent at any rate Mrs Wix's using another. To that degree it was successful; there was only an appeal, strange and mute, in the white old face, which produced the effect of a want of decision greater than could by any stretch of optimism have been associated with her attitude toward what had happened. For Maisie herself indeed what had happened was oddly, as she could feel, less of a simple rapture than any arrival or return of the same supreme friend had ever been before. What had become overnight, what had become while she slept, of the comfortable faculty of gladness? She tried to wake it up a little wider by talking, by rejoicing, by plunging into water and into clothes, and she made out that it was ten o'clock, but also that Mrs Wix had not yet breakfasted. The day before, at nine, they had had together a *café complet* in their sitting-room. Mrs Wix on her side had evidently also a refuge to seek. She sought it in checking the precipitation of some of her pupil's present steps, in recalling to her with an approach to sternness that of such preliminaries those embodied in a thorough use of soap should be the most thorough, and in throwing even a certain reprobation on the idea of hurrying into clothes for the sake of a mere stepfather. She took her in hand with a silent insistence; she reduced the process to sequences more definite than any it had known since the days of Moddle. Whatever it might be that had now, with a difference, begun to belong to Sir Claude's presence was still after all compatible, for our young lady, with the instinct of dressing to see him with almost untidy haste. Mrs Wix meanwhile luckily was not wholly directed to repression. 'He's there – he's there!' she had said over several times. It was her answer to every invitation to mention how long she had been up and her motive for respecting so rigidly the slumber of her companion. It formed for some minutes her only account of the whereabouts of the others and her reason for not having yet seen them, as well as of the possibility of their presently being found in the salon.

'He's there – he's there!' she declared once more as she made, on the child, with an almost invidious tug, a strained undergarment 'meet'.

'Do you mean he's in the salon?' Maisie asked again.

'He's *with* her,' Mrs Wix desolately said. 'He's with her,' she reiterated.

'Do you mean in her own room?' Maisie continued.

She waited an instant. 'God knows!'

Maisie wondered a little why, or how, God should know; this, however, delayed but an instant her bringing out: 'Well, won't she go back?'

'Go back? Never!'

'She'll stay all the same?'

'All the more.'

'Then won't Sir Claude go?' Maisie asked.

'Go back – if *she* doesn't?' Mrs Wix appeared to give this question the benefit of a minute's thought. 'Why should he have come – only to go back?'

Maisie produced an ingenious solution. 'To *make* her go. To take her.'

Mrs Wix met it without a concession. 'If he can make her go so easily, why should he have let her come?'

Maisie considered. 'Oh just to see *me*. She has a right.'

'Yes – she has a right.'

'She's my mother!' Maisie tentatively tittered.

'Yes – she's your mother.'

'Besides,' Maisie went on, 'he didn't let her come. He doesn't like her coming, and if he doesn't like it –'

Mrs Wix took her up. 'He must lump it – that's what he must do! Your mother was right about him – I mean your real one. He has no strength. No – none at all.' She seemed more profoundly to muse. 'He might have had some even with *her* – I mean with her ladyship. He's just a poor sunk slave,' she asserted with sudden energy.

Maisie wondered again. 'A slave?'

'To his passions.'

She continued to wonder and even to be impressed; after which she went on: 'But how do you know he'll stay?'

'Because he likes us!' – and Mrs Wix, with her emphasis of the word, whirled her charge round again to deal with posterior hooks. She had positively never shaken her so.

It was as if she quite shook something out of her. 'But how will that help him if we – in spite of his liking! – don't stay?'

'Do you mean if we go off and leave him with her?' – Mrs Wix put the question to the back of her pupil's head. 'It *won't* help him. It will be his ruin. He'll have got nothing. He'll have lost everything. It will be his utter destruction, for he's certain after a while to loathe her.'

'Then when he loathes her' – it was astonishing how she caught the idea – 'he'll just come right after us!' Maisie announced.

'Never.'

'Never?'

'She'll keep him. She'll hold him for ever.'

Maisie doubted. 'When he "loathes" her?'

'That won't matter. She won't loathe *him*. People don't!' Mrs Wix brought up.

'Some do. Mamma does,' Maisie contended.

'Mamma does *not*!' It was startling – her friend contradicted her flat. 'She loves him – she adores him. A woman knows.' Mrs Wix spoke not only as if Maisie were not a woman, but as if she would never be one. '*I* know!' she cried.

'Then why on earth has she left him?'

Mrs Wix hesitated. 'He hates *her*. Don't stoop so – lift up your hair. You know how I'm affected toward him,' she added with dignity; 'but you must also know that I see clear.'

Maisie all this time was trying hard to do likewise. 'Then if she has left him for that why shouldn't Mrs Beale leave him?'

'Because she's not such a fool!'

'Not such a fool as mamma?'

'Precisely – if you *will* have it. Does it look like her leaving him?' Mrs Wix enquired. She brooded again; then she went on with more intensity: 'Do you want to know really and truly why? So that she may be his wretchedness and his punishment.'

'His punishment?' – this was more than as yet Maisie could quite accept. 'For what?'

'For everything. That's what will happen: he'll be tied to her for ever. She won't mind in the least his hating her, and she won't hate him back. She'll only hate *us*.'

'Us?' the child faintly echoed.

'She'll hate *you*.'

'Me? Why, I brought them together!' Maisie resentfully cried.

'You brought them together.' There was a completeness in Mrs Wix's assent. 'Yes; it was a pretty job. Sit down.' She began to brush her pupil's hair and, as she took up the mass of it with some force of hand, went on with a sharp recall: 'Your mother adored him at first – it might have lasted. But he began too soon with Mrs Beale. As you say,' she pursued with a brisk application of the brush, 'you brought them together.'

'I brought them together' – Maisie was ready to reaffirm it. She felt none the less for a moment at the bottom of a hole; then she seemed to see a way out. 'But I didn't bring mamma together –' She just faltered.

'With all those gentlemen?' – Mrs Wix pulled her up. 'No; it isn't quite so bad as that.'

'I only said to the Captain' – Maisie had the quick memory of it – 'that I hoped he at least (he was awfully nice!) would love her and keep her.'

'And even that wasn't much harm,' threw in Mrs Wix.

'It wasn't much good,' Maisie was obliged to recognise. 'She can't bear him – not even a mite. She told me at Folkestone.'

Mrs Wix suppressed a gasp; then after a bridling instant during which she might have appeared to deflect with difficulty from her odd consideration of Ida's wrongs: 'He was a nice sort of person for her to talk to you about!'

'Oh I *like* him!' Maisie promptly rejoined; and at this, with an inarticulate sound and an inconsequence still more marked, her companion bent over and dealt her on the cheek a rapid peck which had the apparent intention of a kiss.

'Well, if her ladyship doesn't agree with you, what does it only prove?' Mrs Wix demanded in conclusion. 'It proves that she's fond of Sir Claude!'

Maisie, in the light of some of the evidence, reflected on that till her hair was finished, but when she at last started up she gave a sign of no very close embrace of it. She grasped at this moment Mrs Wix's arm. 'He must have got his divorce!'

'Since day before yesterday? Don't talk trash.'

This was spoken with an impatience which left the child nothing to reply; whereupon she sought her defence in a completely different relation to the fact. 'Well, I knew he would come!'

'So did I; but not in twenty-four hours. I gave him a few days!' Mrs Wix wailed.

Maisie, whom she had now released, looked at her with interest. 'How many did *she* give him?'

Mrs Wix faced her a moment; then as if with a bewildered sniff: 'You had better ask her!' But she had no sooner uttered the words than she caught herself up. 'Lord o' mercy, how we talk!'

Maisie felt that however they talked she must see him, but she said nothing more for a time, a time during which she conscientiously finished dressing and Mrs Wix also kept silence. It was as if they each had almost too much to think of, and even as if the child had the sense that her friend was watching her and seeing if she herself were watched. At last Mrs Wix turned to the window and stood – sightlessly, as Maisie could guess – looking away. Then our young lady, before the glass, gave the supreme shake. 'Well, I'm ready. And now to *see* him!'

Mrs Wix turned round, but as if without having heard her. 'It's tremendously grave.' There were slow still tears behind the straighteners.

'It is – it is.' Maisie spoke as if she were now dressed quite up to the occasion; as if indeed with the last touch she had put on the judgement-cap. 'I must see him immediately.'

'How can you see him if he doesn't send for you?'

'Why can't I go and find him?'

'Because you don't know where he is.'

'Can't I just look in the salon?' That still seemed simple to Maisie.

Mrs Wix, however, instantly cut it off. 'I wouldn't have you look in the salon for all the world!' Then she explained a little: 'The salon isn't ours now.'

'Ours?'

'Yours and mine. It's theirs.'

'Theirs?' Maisie, with her stare, continued to echo. 'You mean they want to keep us out?'

Mrs Wix faltered; she sank into a chair and, as Maisie had often enough seen her do before, covered her face with her hands. 'They ought to, at least. The situation's too monstrous!'

Maisie stood there a moment – she looked about the room. 'I'll go to him – I'll find him.'

'*I* won't! I won't go *near* them!' cried Mrs Wix.

'Then I'll see him alone.' The child spied what she had been looking for – she possessed herself of her hat. 'Perhaps I'll take him out!' And with decision she quitted the room.

When she entered the salon it was empty, but at the sound of the opened door some one stirred on the balcony, and Sir Claude, stepping straight in, stood before her. He was in light fresh clothes and wore a straw hat with a bright ribbon; these things, besides striking her in themselves as the very promise of the grandest of grand tours, gave him a certain radiance and, as it were, a tropical ease; but such an effect only marked rather more his having stopped short and, for a longer minute than had ever at such a juncture elapsed, not opened his arms to her. His pause made her pause and enabled her to reflect that he must have been up some time, for there were no traces of breakfast; and that though it was so late he had rather markedly not caused her to be called to him. Had Mrs Wix been right about their forfeiture of the salon? Was it all his now, all his and Mrs Beale's? Such an idea, at the rate her small thoughts throbbed, could only remind her of the way in which what had been hers hitherto was what was exactly most Mrs Beale's and his. It was strange to be standing there and greeting him across a gulf, for he had by this time spoken, smiled and said: 'My dear child, my dear child!' but without coming any nearer. In a flash she saw he was different – more so than he knew or designed. The next minute indeed it was as if he caught an impression from her face: this made him hold out his hand. Then they met, he kissed her, he laughed, she thought he even blushed: something of his affection rang out as usual. 'Here I am, you see, again – as I promised you.'

It was not as he had promised them – he had not promised them Mrs Beale; but Maisie said nothing about that. What she said was simply: 'I knew you had come. Mrs Wix told me.'

'Oh yes. And where is she?'

'In her room. She got me up – she dressed me.'

Sir Claude looked at her up and down; a sweetness of mockery that she particularly loved came out in his face whenever he did that, and it was not wanting now. He raised his eyebrows and his arms to play at admiration; he was evidently after all disposed to be gay. 'Got you up? – I should think so! She has dressed you most beautifully. Isn't she coming?'

Maisie wondered if she had better tell. 'She said not.'

'Doesn't she want to see a poor devil?'

She looked about under the vibration of the way he described himself, and her eyes rested on the door of the room he had previously occupied. 'Is Mrs Beale in there?'

Sir Claude looked blankly at the same object. 'I haven't the least idea!'

'You haven't seen her?'

'Not the tip of her nose.'

Maisie thought: there settled on her, in the light of his beautiful smiling eyes, the faintest purest coldest conviction that he wasn't telling the truth. 'She hasn't welcomed you?'

'Not by a single sign.'

'Then where is she?'

Sir Claude laughed; he seemed both amused and surprised at the point she made of it. 'I give it up!'

'Doesn't she know you've come?'

He laughed again. 'Perhaps she doesn't care!'

Maisie, with an inspiration, pounced on his arm. 'Has she *gone*?'

He met her eyes and then she could see that his own were really much graver than his manner. 'Gone?' She had flown to the door, but before she could raise her hand to knock he was beside her and had caught it. 'Let her be. I don't care about her. I want to see *you*.'

Maisie fell back with him. 'Then she *hasn't* gone?'

He still looked as if it were a joke, but the more she saw of him the more she could make out that he was troubled. 'It wouldn't be like her!'

She stood wondering at him. 'Did you want her to come?'

'How can you suppose –?' He put it to her candidly. 'We had an immense row over it.'

'Do you mean you've quarrelled?'

Sir Claude was at a loss. 'What has she told you?'

'That I'm hers as much as yours. That she represents papa.'

His gaze struck away through the open window and up to the sky; she could hear him rattle in his trousers-pockets his money or his keys. 'Yes – that's what she keeps saying.' It gave him for a moment an air that was almost helpless.

'You say you don't care about her,' Maisie went on. '*Do* you mean you've quarrelled?'

'We do nothing in life but quarrel.'

He rose before her, as he said this, so soft and fair, so rich, in spite of what might worry him, in restored familiarities, that it gave a bright blur to the meaning – to what would otherwise perhaps have been the palpable promise – of the words. 'Oh *your* quarrels!' she exclaimed with discouragement.

'I assure you hers are quite fearful!'

'I don't speak of hers. I speak of yours.'

'Ah don't do it till I've had my coffee! You're growing up

clever,' he added. Then he said: 'I suppose you've breakfasted?'

'Oh no – I've had nothing.'

'Nothing in your room?' – he was all compunction. 'My dear old man! – we'll breakfast then together.' He had one of his happy thoughts. 'I say – we'll go out.'

'That was just what I hoped. I've brought my hat.'

'You *are* clever! We'll go to a café.' Maisie was already at the door; he glanced round the room. 'A moment – my stick.' But there appeared to be no stick. 'No matter; I left it – oh!' He remembered with an odd drop and came out.

'You left it in London?' she asked as they went downstairs.

'Yes – in London: fancy!'

'You were in such a hurry to come,' Maisie explained.

He had his arm round her. 'That must have been the reason.' Halfway down he stopped short again, slapping his leg. 'And poor Mrs Wix?'

Maisie's face just showed a shadow. 'Do you want her to come?'

'Dear no – I want to see you alone.'

'That's the way I want to see *you!*' she replied. 'Like before.'

'Like before!' he gaily echoed. 'But I mean has she had her coffee?'

'No, nothing.'

'Then I'll send it up to her. Madame!' He had already, at the foot of the stair, called out to the stout *patronne*, a lady who turned to him from the bustling, breezy hall a countenance covered with fresh matutinal powder and a bosom as capacious as the velvet shelf of a chimneypiece, over which her round white face, framed in its golden frizzle, might have figured as a showy clock. He ordered, with particular recommendations, Mrs Wix's repast, and it was a charm to hear his easy brilliant French: even his companion's ignorance could measure the perfection of it. The *patronne*, rubbing her hands and breaking in with high swift notes as into a florid duet, went with him to the street, and while they talked a moment longer Maisie remembered what Mrs Wix had said about every one's liking him. It came out enough through the morning powder, it came out enough in the heaving bosom, how the landlady liked him. He had evidently ordered something lovely for Mrs Wix. '*Et bien soigné, n'est-ce-pas?*'

'*Soyez tranquille*' – the *patronne* beamed upon him. '*Et pour Madame?*'

'*Madame?*' he echoed – it just pulled him up a little.

'*Rien encore?*'

'*Rien encore.* Come, Maisie.' She hurried along with him, but on the way to the café he said nothing.

XXX

AFTER they were seated there it was different: the place was not below the hotel, but further along the quay; with wide, clear windows and a floor sprinkled with bran in a manner that gave it for Maisie something of the added charm of a circus. They had pretty much to themselves the painted spaces and the red plush benches; these were shared by a few scattered gentlemen who picked teeth, with facial contortions, behind little bare tables, and by an old personage in particular, a very old personage with a red ribbon in his buttonhole, whose manner of soaking buttered rolls in coffee and then disposing of them in the little that was left of the interval between his nose and chin might at a less anxious hour have cast upon Maisie an almost envious spell. They too had their *café au lait* and their buttered rolls, determined by Sir Claude's asking her if she could with that light aid wait till the hour of déjeuner. His allusion to this meal gave her, in the shaded sprinkled coolness, the scene, as she vaguely felt, of a sort of ordered mirrored licence, the haunt of those – the irregular, like herself – who went to bed or who rose too late, something to think over while she watched the white-aproned waiter perform as nimbly with plates and saucers as a certain conjurer her friend had in London taken her to a music-hall to see. Sir Claude had presently begun to talk again, to tell her how London had looked and how long he had felt himself, on either side, to have been absent; all about Susan Ash too and the amusement as well as the difficulty he had had with her; then all about his return journey and the Channel in the night and the crowd of people coming over and the way there were always too many one knew. He spoke of other matters beside, especially of what she must tell him of the occupations, while he was away, of Mrs Wix and her pupil. Hadn't they had the good time he had promised? – had he exaggerated a bit the arrangements made for their pleasure? Maisie had something – not all there was – to say of his success and of their gratitude: she had a complication of thought that grew every minute, grew with the consciousness that she had never seen him in this particular state in which he had been given back.

Mrs Wix had once said – it was once or fifty times; once was enough for Maisie, but more was not too much – that he was wonderfully various. Well, he was certainly so, to the child's mind, on the present occasion: he was much more various than he was anything else. Besides, the fact that they were together in a shop, at a nice little intimate table as they had so often been in London, only made greater the difference of what they were together about. This difference was in his face, in his voice, in every look he gave her and every movement he made. They were not the looks and the movements he really wanted to show, and she could feel as well that they were not those she herself wanted. She had seen him nervous, she had seen every one she had come in contact with nervous, but she had never seen him so nervous as this. Little by little it gave her a settled terror, a terror that partook of the coldness she had felt just before, at the hotel, to find herself, on his answer about Mrs Beale, disbelieve him. She seemed to see at present, to touch across the table, as if by laying her hand on it, what he had meant when he confessed on those several occasions to fear. Why was such a man so often afraid? It must have begun to come to her now that there was one thing just such a man above all could be afraid of. He could be afraid of himself. His fear at all events was there; his fear was sweet to her, beautiful and tender to her, was having coffee and buttered rolls and talk and laughter that were no talk and laughter at all with her; his fear was in his jesting post-poning perverting voice; it was just in this make-believe way he had brought her out to imitate the old London playtimes, to imitate indeed a relation that had wholly changed, a relation that she had with her very eyes seen in the act of change when, the day before in the salon, Mrs Beale rose suddenly before her. She rose before her, for that matter, now, and even while their refreshment delayed Maisie arrived at the straight question for which, on their entrance, his first word had given opportunity. 'Are we going to have déjeuner with Mrs Beale?'

His reply was anything but straight. 'You and I?'

Maisie sat back in her chair. 'Mrs Wix and me.'

Sir Claude also shifted. 'That's an enquiry, my dear child, that Mrs Beale herself must answer.' Yes, he had shifted; but abruptly, after a moment during which something seemed to hang there between them and, as it heavily swayed, just fan them with the air of its motion, she felt that the whole thing was upon them. 'Do you mind,' he broke out, 'my asking you what Mrs Wix has said to you?'

'Said to me?'

'This day or two – while I was away.'

'Do you mean about you and Mrs Beale?'

Sir Claude, resting on his elbows, fixed his eyes a moment on the white marble beneath them. 'No; I think we had a good deal of that – didn't we? – before I left you. It seems to me we had it pretty well all out. I mean about yourself, about your – don't you know? – associating with us, as I might say, and staying on with us. While you were alone with our friend what did she say?'

Maisie felt the weight of the question; it kept her silent for a space during which she looked at Sir Claude, whose eyes remained bent. 'Nothing,' she returned at last.

He showed incredulity. 'Nothing?'

'Nothing,' Maisie repeated; on which an interruption descended in the form of a tray bearing the preparations for their breakfast.

These preparations were as amusing as everything else; the waiter poured their coffee from a vessel like a watering-pot and then made it froth with the curved stream of hot milk that dropped from the height of his raised arm; but the two looked across at each other through the whole play of French pleasantness with a gravity that had now ceased to dissemble. Sir Claude sent the waiter off again for something and then took up her answer. 'Hasn't she tried to affect you?'

Face to face with him thus it seemed to Maisie that she had tried so little as to be scarce worth mentioning; again therefore an instant she shut herself up. Presently she found her middle course. 'Mrs Beale likes her now; and there's one thing I've found out – a great thing. Mrs Wix enjoys her being so kind. She was tremendously kind all day yesterday.'

'I see. And what did she do?' Sir Claude asked.

Maisie was now busy with her breakfast, and her companion attacked his own; so that it was all, in form at least, even more than their old sociability. 'Everything she could think of. She was as nice to her as you are,' the child said. 'She talked to her all day.'

'And what did she say to her?'

'Oh I don't know.' Maisie was a little bewildered with his pressing her so for knowledge; it didn't fit into the degree of intimacy with Mrs Beale that Mrs Wix had so denounced and that, according to that lady, had now brought him back in bondage. Wasn't he more aware than his stepdaughter of what would be done by the person to whom he was bound? In a moment, however, she added: 'She made love to her.'

Sir Claude looked at her harder, and it was clearly something in her tone that made him quickly say: 'You don't mind my asking you, do you?'

'Not at all; only I should think you'd know better than I.'

'What Mrs Beale did yesterday?'

She thought he coloured a trifle; but almost simultaneously with that impression she found herself answering: 'Yes – if you *have* seen her.'

He broke into the loudest of laughs. 'Why, my dear boy, I told you just now I've absolutely not. I say, don't you believe me?'

There was something she was already so afraid of that it covered up other fears. 'Didn't you come back to see her?' she enquired in a moment. 'Didn't you come back because you always want to so much?'

He received her enquiry as he had received her doubt – with an extraordinary absence of resentment. 'I can imagine of course why you think that. But it doesn't explain my doing what I have. It was, as I said to you just now at the inn, really and truly you I wanted to see.'

She felt an instant as she used to feel when, in the back garden at her mother's, she took from him the highest push of a swing – high, high, high – that he had had put there for her pleasure and that had finally broken down under the weight and the extravagant patronage of the cook. 'Well, that's beautiful. But to see me, you mean, and go away again?'

'My going away again is just the point. I can't tell yet – it all depends.'

'On Mrs Beale?' Maisie asked. '*She* won't go away.' He finished emptying his coffee-cup and then, when he had put it down, leaned back in his chair, where she could see that he smiled on her. This only added to her idea that he was in trouble, that he was turning somehow in his pain and trying different things. He continued to smile and she went on: 'Don't you know that?'

'Yes, I may as well confess to you that as much as that I do know. *She* won't go away. She'll stay.'

'She'll stay. She'll stay,' Maisie repeated.

'Just so. Won't you have some more coffee?'

'Yes, please.'

'And another buttered roll?'

'Yes, please.'

He signed to the hovering waiter, who arrived with the shining spout of plenty in either hand and with the friendliest interest in mademoiselle. '*Les tartines sont là.*' Their cups were replenished and, while he watched almost musingly the bubbles in the fragrant mixture, 'Just so – just so,' Sir Claude said again and again. 'It's awfully awkward!' he exclaimed when the waiter had gone.

'That she won't go?'

'Well – everything! Well, well, well!' But he pulled himself together; he began again to eat. 'I came back to ask you something. That's what I came back for.'

'I know what you want to ask me,' Maisie said.

'Are you very sure?'

'I'm *almost* very.'

'Well then risk it. You mustn't make *me* risk everything.'

She was struck with the force of this. 'You want to know if I should be happy with *them*.'

'With those two ladies only? No, no, old man: *vous n'y êtes pas.* So now – there!' Sir Claude laughed.

'Well then what is it?'

The next minute, instead of telling her what it was, he laid his hand across the table on her own and held her as if under the prompting of a thought. 'Mrs Wix would stay with *her?*'

'Without you? Oh yes – now.'

'On account, as you just intimated, of Mrs Beale's changed manner?'

Maisie, with her sense of responsibility, weighed both Mrs Beale's changed manner and Mrs Wix's human weakness. 'I think she talked her round.'

Sir Claude thought a moment. 'Ah poor dear!'

'Do you mean Mrs Beale?'

'Oh no – Mrs Wix.'

'She likes being talked round – treated like any one else. Oh she likes great politeness,' Maisie expatiated. 'It affects her very much.'

Sir Claude, to her surprise, demurred a little to this. 'Very much – up to a certain point.'

'Oh up to any point!' Maisie returned with emphasis.

'Well, haven't I been polite to her?'

'Lovely – and she perfectly worships you.'

'Then, my dear child, why can't she let me alone?' – this time Sir Claude unmistakeably blushed. Before Maisie, however, could answer his question, which would indeed have taken her long, he went on in another tone: 'Mrs Beale thinks she has probably quite broken her down. But she hasn't.'

Though he spoke as if he were sure, Maisie was strong in the impression she had just uttered and that she now again produced. 'She has talked her round.'

'Ah yes; round to herself, but not round to me.'

Oh she couldn't bear to hear him say that! 'To you? Don't you really believe how she loves you?'

Sir Claude examined his belief. 'Of course I know she's wonderful.'

'She's just every bit as fond of you as *I* am,' said Maisie. 'She told me so yesterday.'

'Ah then,' he promptly exclaimed, 'she *has* tried to affect you! I don't love *her*, don't you see? I do her perfect justice,' he pursued, 'but I mean I don't love her as I do you, and I'm sure you wouldn't seriously expect it. She's not my daughter – come, old chap! She's not even my mother, though I dare say it would have been better for me if she had been. I'll do for her what I'd do for my mother, but I won't do more.' His real excitement broke out in a need to explain and justify himself, though he kept trying to correct and conceal it with laughs and mouthfuls and other vain familiarities. Suddenly he broke off, wiping his moustache with sharp pulls and coming back to Mrs Beale. 'Did she try to talk *you* over?'

'No – to me she said very little. Very little indeed,' Maisie continued.

Sir Claude seemed struck with this. 'She was only sweet to Mrs Wix?'

'As sweet as sugar!' cried Maisie.

He looked amused at her comparison, but he didn't contest it; he uttered on the contrary, in an assenting way, a little inarticulate sound. 'I know what she *can* be. But much good may it have done her! Mrs Wix won't *come* "round". That's what makes it so fearfully awkward.'

Maisie knew it was fearfully awkward; she had known this now, she felt, for some time, and there was something else it more pressingly concerned her to learn. 'What is it you meant, you came over to ask me?'

'Well,' said Sir Claude, 'I was just going to say. Let me tell you it will surprise you.' She had finished breakfast now and she sat back in her chair again: she waited in silence to hear. He had pushed the things before him a little way and had his elbows on the table. This time, she was convinced, she knew what was coming, and once more, for the crash, as with Mrs Wix lately in her room, she held her breath and drew together her eyelids. He was going to say she must give him up. He looked hard at her again; then he made his effort. 'Should you see your way to let her go?'

She was bewildered. 'To let who –?'

'Mrs Wix simply. I put it at the worst. Should you see your way to sacrifice her? Of course I know what I'm asking.'

Maisie's eyes opened wide again; this was so different from what she had expected. 'And stay with you alone?'

He gave another push to his coffee-cup. 'With me and Mrs Beale. Of course it would be rather rum; but everything in our whole story is rather rum, you know. What's more unusual than for any one to be given up, like you, by her parents?'

'Oh nothing is more unusual than *that*!' Maisie concurred, relieved at the contact of a proposition as to which concurrence could have lucidity.

'Of course it would be quite unconventional,' Sir Claude went on – 'I mean the little household we three should make together; but things have got beyond that, don't you see? They got beyond that long ago. We shall stay abroad at any rate – it's ever so much easier and it's our affair and nobody else's: it's no one's business but ours on all the blessed earth. I don't say that for Mrs Wix, poor dear – I do her absolute justice. I respect her; I see what she means; she has done me a lot of good. But there are the facts. There they are, simply. And here am I, and here are you. And she won't come round. She's right from her point of view. I'm talking to you in the most extraordinary way – I'm always talking to you in the most extraordinary way, ain't I? One would think you were about sixty and that I – I don't know what any one would think *I* am. Unless a beastly cad!' he suggested. 'I've been awfully worried, and this's what it has come to. You've done us the most tremendous good, and you'll do it still and always, don't you see? We can't let you go – you're everything. There are the facts as I say. She *is* your mother now, Mrs Beale, by what has happened, and I, in the same way, I'm your father. No one can contradict that, and we can't get out of it. My idea would be a nice little place – somewhere in the South – where she and you would be together and as good as any one else. And I should be as good too, don't you see? for I shouldn't live with you, but I should be close to you – just round the corner, and it would be just the same. My idea would be that it should all be perfectly open and frank. *Honi soit qui mal y pense*, don't you know? You're the best thing – you and what we can do for you – that either of us has ever known:' he came back to that. 'When I say to her "Give her up, come," she lets me have it bang in the face: "Give her up yourself!" It's the same old vicious circle – and when I say vicious I don't mean a pun, a what-d'-ye-call-'em. Mrs Wix is the obstacle; I mean, you know, if she has affected you. She has affected *me*, and yet here I am. I never was in such a tight place: please believe it's only that that makes me put it to you as I do. My dear child, isn't that – to put it so – just the way out of it? That came to me yesterday, in London, after Mrs Beale had gone: I had the most infernal atrocious day. "Go straight over and put it to her: let her choose, freely, her own self." So I do, old girl – I put it to you. *Can* you choose freely?'

This long address, slowly and brokenly uttered, with fidgets and falterings, with lapses and recoveries, with a mottled face and embarrassed but supplicating eyes, reached the child from a quarter so close that after the shock of the first sharpness she could see intensely its direction and follow it from point to point; all the more that it came back to the point at which it had started. There was a word that had hummed all through it. 'Do you call it a "sacrifice"?'

'Of Mrs Wix? I'll call it whatever *you* call it. I won't funk it – I haven't, have I? I'll face it in all its baseness. Does it strike you it is base for me to get you well away from her, to smuggle you off here into a corner and bribe you with sophistries and buttered rolls to betray her?'

'To betray her?'

'Well – to part with her.'

Maisie let the question wait; the concrete image it presented was the most vivid side of it. 'If I part with her where will she go?'

'Back to London.'

'But I mean what will she do?'

'Oh as for that I won't pretend I know. I don't. We all have our difficulties.'

That, to Maisie, was at this moment more striking than it had ever been. 'Then who'll teach me?'

Sir Claude laughed out. 'What Mrs Wix teaches?'

She smiled dimly; she saw what he meant. 'It isn't so very very much.'

'It's so very very little,' he returned, 'that that's a thing we've positively to consider. We probably shouldn't give you another governess. To begin with we shouldn't be able to get one – not of the only kind that would do. It wouldn't do – the kind that *would* do,' he queerly enough explained. 'I mean they wouldn't stay – heigh-ho! We'd do you ourselves. Particularly me. You see I *can* now; I haven't got to mind – what I used to. I won't fight shy as I did – she can show out *with* me. Our relation, all round, is more regular.'

It seemed wonderfully regular, the way he put it; yet none the less, while she looked at it as judiciously as she could, the picture it made persisted somehow in being a combination quite distinct – an old woman and a little girl seated in deep silence on a battered old bench by the rampart of the *haute ville*. It was just at that hour yesterday; they were hand in hand; they had melted together. 'I don't think you yet understand how she clings to you,' Maisie said at last.

'I do – I do. But for all that –!' And he gave, turning in his conscious exposure, an oppressed impatient sigh; the sigh, even his companion could recognise, of the man naturally accustomed to that argument, the man who wanted thoroughly to be reasonable, but who, if really he had to mind so many things, would be always impossibly hampered. What it came to indeed was that he understood quite perfectly. If Mrs Wix clung it was all the more reason for shaking Mrs Wix off.

This vision of what she had brought him to occupied our young lady while, to ask what he owed, he called the waiter and put down a gold piece that the man carried off for change. Sir Claude looked after him, then went on: 'How could a woman have less to reproach a fellow with? I mean as regards herself.'

Maisie entertained the question. 'Yes. How *could* she have less? So why are you so sure she'll go?'

'Surely you heard why – you heard her come out three nights ago? How can she do anything but go – after what she then said? I've done what she warned me of – she was absolutely right. So here we are. Her liking Mrs Beale, as you call it now, is a motive sufficient, with other things, to make her, for your sake, stay on without me; it's not a motive sufficient to make her, even for yours, stay on *with* me – swallow, don't you see? what she can't swallow. And when you say she's as fond of me as you are I think I can, if that's the case, challenge you a little on it. Would *you*, only with those two, stay on without me?' The waiter came back with the change, and that gave her, under this appeal, a moment's respite. But when he had retreated again with the 'tip' gathered in with graceful thanks on a subtle hint from Sir Claude's forefinger, the latter, while pocketing the money, followed the appeal up. 'Would you let her make you live with Mrs Beale?'

'Without you? Never,' Maisie then answered. 'Never,' she said again.

It made him quite triumph, and she was indeed herself shaken by the mere sound of it. 'So you see you're not, like her,' he exclaimed, 'so ready to give me away!' Then he came back to his original question. '*Can* you choose? I mean can you settle it by a word yourself? Will you stay on with us without her?'

Now in truth she felt the coldness of her terror, and it seemed to her that suddenly she knew, as she knew it about Sir Claude, what she was afraid of. She was afraid of herself. She looked at him in such a way that it brought, she could see, wonder into his face, a wonder held in check, however, by his frank pretension to play fair with her, not to use advantages, not to hurry nor hustle her – only to put her chance clearly and kindly before her. 'May I think?' she finally asked.

'Certainly, certainly. But how long?'

'Oh only a little while,' she said meekly.

He had for a moment the air of wishing to look at it as if it were the most cheerful prospect in the world. 'But what shall we do while you're thinking?' He spoke as if thought were compatible with almost any distraction.

There was but one thing Maisie wished to do, and after an instant she expressed it. 'Have we got to go back to the hotel?'

'Do you want to?'

'Oh no.'

'There's not the least necessity for it.' He bent his eyes on his watch; his face was now very grave. 'We can do anything else in the world.' He looked at her again almost as if he were on the point of saying that they might for instance start off for Paris. But even while she wondered if that were not coming he had a sudden drop. 'We can take a walk.'

She was all ready, but he sat there as if he had still something more to say. This too, however, didn't come; so she herself spoke. 'I think I should like to see Mrs Wix first.'

'Before you decide? All right – all right.' He had put on his hat, but he had still to light a cigarette. He smoked a minute, with his head thrown back, looking at the ceiling; then he said: 'There's one thing to remember – I've a right to impress it on you: we stand absolutely in the place of your parents. It's their defection, their extraordinary baseness, that has made our responsibility. Never was a young person more directly committed and confided.' He appeared to say this over, at the ceiling, through his smoke, a little for his own illumination. It carried him after a pause somewhat further. 'Though I admit it was to each of us separately.'

He gave her so at that moment and in that attitude the sense of wanting, as it were, to be on her side – on the side of what would be in every way most right and wise and charming for her – that she felt a sudden desire to prove herself not less delicate and magnanimous, not less solicitous for his own interests. What were these but that of the 'regularity' he had just before spoken of? 'It *was* to each of you separately,' she accordingly with much earnestness remarked. 'But don't you remember? I brought you together.'

He jumped up with a delighted laugh. 'Remember? Rather! You brought us together, you brought us together. Come!'

XXXI

SHE remained out with him for a time of which she could take no measure save that it was too short for what she wished to make of it – an interval, a barrier indefinite, insurmountable. They walked about, they dawdled, they looked in shop-windows; they did all the old things exactly as if to try to get back all the old safety, to get something out of them that they had always got before. This had come before, whatever it was, without their trying, and nothing came now but the intenser consciousness of their quest and their subterfuge. The strangest thing of all was what had really happened to the old safety. What had really happened was that Sir Claude was 'free' and that Mrs Beale was 'free', and yet that the new medium was somehow still more oppressive than the old. She could feel that Sir Claude concurred with her in the sense that the oppression would be worst at the inn, where, till something should be settled, they would feel the want of something – of what could they call it but a footing? The question of the settlement loomed larger to her now: it depended, she had learned, so completely on herself. Her choice, as her friend had called it, was there before her like an impossible sum on a slate, a sum that in spite of her plea for consideration she simply got off from doing while she walked about with him. She must see Mrs Wix before she could do her sum; therefore the longer before she saw her the more distant would be the ordeal. She met at present no demand whatever of her obligation; she simply plunged, to avoid it, deeper into the company of Sir Claude. She saw nothing that she had seen hitherto – no touch in the foreign picture that had at first been always before her. The only touch was that of Sir Claude's hand, and to feel her own in it was her mute resistance to time. She went about as sightlessly as if he had been leading her blindfold. If they were afraid of themselves it was themselves they would find at the inn. She was certain now that what awaited them there would be to lunch with Mrs Beale. All her instinct was to avoid that, to draw out their walk, to find pretexts, to take him down upon the beach, to take him to the end of the pier. He said no other word to her about what they had talked of at breakfast, and she had a dim vision of how his way of not letting her see him definitely wait for anything from her would make any one who should know of it, would make Mrs Wix for instance, think him more than ever a gentleman. It was true that once or twice, on the jetty, on the sands, he looked at her for a minute with eyes that seemed to propose to her to come straight off with him to Paris. That, however, was not to give her a nudge about her responsibility. He evidently wanted to procrastinate quite as much as she did; he was not a bit more in a hurry to get back to the others. Maisie herself at this moment could be secretly merciless to Mrs Wix – to the extent at any rate of not caring if her continued disappearance did make that lady begin to worry about what had become of her, even begin to wonder perhaps if the truants hadn't found their remedy. Her want of mercy to Mrs Beale indeed was at least as great; for Mrs Beale's worry and wonder would be as much greater as the object at which they were directed. When at last Sir Claude, at the far end of the *plage*, which they had already, in the many-coloured crowd, once traversed, suddenly, with a look at his watch, remarked that it was time, not to get back to the *table d'hôte*, but to get over to the station and meet the Paris papers – when he did this she found herself thinking quite with intensity what Mrs Beale and Mrs Wix *would* say. On the way over to the station she had even a mental picture of the stepfather and the pupil established in a little place in the South while the governess and the stepmother, in a little place in the North, remained linked by a community of blankness and by the endless series of remarks it would give birth to. The Paris papers had come in and her companion, with a strange extravagance, purchased no fewer than eleven: it took up time while they hovered at the bookstall on the restless platform, where the little volumes in a row were all yellow and pink and one of her favourite old women in one of her favourite old caps absolutely wheedled him into the purchase of three. They had thus so much to carry home that it would have seemed simpler, with such a provision for a nice straight journey through France, just to 'nip', as she phrased it to herself, into the coupé of the train that, a little further along, stood waiting to start. She asked Sir Claude where it was going.

'To Paris. Fancy!'

She could fancy well enough. They stood there and smiled, he with all the newspapers under his arm and she with the three books, one yellow and two pink. He had told her the pink were for herself and the yellow one for Mrs Beale, implying in an interesting way that these were the natural divisions in France of literature for the young and for the old. She knew how prepared they looked to pass into the train, and she presently brought out to her companion: 'I wish we could go. Won't you take me?'

He continued to smile. 'Would you really come?'

'Oh yes, oh yes. Try.'

'Do you want me to take our tickets?'

'Yes, take them.'

'Without any luggage?'

She showed their two armfuls, smiling at him as he smiled at her, but so conscious of being more frightened than she had ever been in her life that she seemed to see her whiteness as in a glass. Then she knew that what she saw was Sir Claude's whiteness: he was as frightened as herself. 'Haven't we got plenty of luggage?' she asked. 'Take the tickets – haven't you time? When does the train go?'

Sir Claude turned to a porter. 'When does the train go?'

The man looked up at the station-clock. 'In two minutes. *Monsieur est placé?*'

'*Pas encore.*'

'*Et vos billets? – vous n'avez que le temps.*' Then after a look at Maisie, '*Monsieur veut-il que je les prenne?*' the man said.

Sir Claude turned back to her. '*Veux-tu bien qu'il en prenne?*'

It was the most extraordinary thing in the world: in the intensity of her excitement she not only by illumination understood all their French, but fell into it with an active perfection. She addressed herself straight to the porter. '*Prenny, prenny. Oh prenny!*'

'*Ah si mademoiselle le veut –!*' He waited there for the money.

But Sir Claude only stared – stared at her with his white face. 'You *have* chosen then? You'll let her go?'

Maisie carried her eyes wistfully to the train, where, amid cries of '*En voiture, en voiture!*' heads were at windows and doors banging loud. The porter was pressing. '*Ah vous n'avez plus le temps!*'

'It's going – it's going!' cried Maisie.

They watched it move, they watched it start; then the man went his way with a shrug. 'It's gone!' Sir Claude said.

Maisie crept some distance up the platform; she stood there with her back to her companion, following it with her eyes, keeping down tears, nursing her pink and yellow books. She had had a real fright but had fallen back to earth. The odd thing was that in her fall her fear too had been dashed down and broken. It was gone. She looked round at last, from where she had paused, at Sir Claude's, and then saw that his wasn't. It sat there with him on the bench to which against the wall of the station, he had retreated, and where, leaning back and, as she thought, rather queer, he still waited. She came down to him and he continued to offer his ineffectual intention of pleasantry. 'Yes, I've chosen,' she said to him. 'I'll let her go if you – if you –'

She faltered; he quickly took her up. 'If I, if I –?'

'If you'll give up Mrs Beale.'

'Oh!' he exclaimed; on which she saw how much, how hopelessly he was afraid. She had supposed at the café that it was of his rebellion, of his gathering motive; but how could that be when his temptations – that temptation for example of the train they had just lost – were after all so slight? Mrs Wix was right. He was afraid of his weakness – of his weakness.

She couldn't have told you afterwards how they got back to the inn: she could only have told you that even from this point they had not gone straight, but once more had wandered and loitered and, in the course of it, had found themselves on the edge of the quay where – still apparently with half an hour to spare – the boat prepared for Folkestone was drawn up. Here they hovered as they had done at the station; here they exchanged silences again, but only exchanged silences. There were punctual people on the deck, choosing places, taking the best; some of them already contented, all established and shawled, facing to England and attended by the steward, who, confined on such a day to the lighter offices, tucked up the ladies' feet or opened bottles with a pop. They looked down at these things without a word; they even picked out a good place for two that was left in the lee of a lifeboat; and if they lingered rather stupidly, neither deciding to go aboard nor deciding to come away, it was Sir Claude quite as much as she who wouldn't move. It was Sir Claude who cultivated the supreme stillness by which she knew best what he meant. He simply meant that he knew all she herself meant. But there was no pretence of pleasantry now: their faces were grave and tired. When at last they lounged off it was as if his fear, his fear of his weakness, leaned upon her heavily as they followed the harbour. In the hall of the hotel as they passed in she saw a battered old box that she recognised, an ancient receptacle with dangling labels that she knew and a big painted W, lately done over and intensely personal, that seemed to stare at her with a recognition and even with some suspicion of its own. Sir Claude caught it too, and there was agitation for both of them in the sight of this object on the move. Was Mrs Wix going and was the responsibility of giving her up lifted, at a touch, from her pupil? Her pupil and her pupil's companion, transfixed a moment, held, in the presence of the omen, communication more intense than in the presence either of the Paris train or of the Channel steamer; then, and still without a word, they went straight upstairs. There, however, on the landing, out of sight of the people below, they collapsed so that they had to sink down together for support: they simply seated themselves on the uppermost step while Sir Claude grasped the hand of his stepdaughter with a pressure that at another moment would probably have made her squeal. Their books and papers were all scattered. 'She thinks you've given her up!'

'Then I must see her – I must see her,' Maisie said.

'To bid her good-bye?'

'I must see her – I must see her,' the child only repeated.

They sat a minute longer, Sir Claude, with his tight grip of her hand and looking away from her, looking straight down the staircase to where, round the turn, electric bells rattled and the pleasant sea-draught blew. At last, loosening his grasp, he slowly got up while she did the same. They went together along the lobby, but before they reached the salon he stopped again. 'If I give up Mrs Beale –?'

'I'll go straight out with you again and not come back till she has gone.'

He seemed to wonder. 'Till Mrs Beale –?'

He had made it sound like a bad joke. 'I mean till Mrs Wix leaves – in that boat.'

Sir Claude looked almost foolish. 'Is she going in that boat?'

'I suppose so. I won't even bid her good-bye,' Maisie continued. 'I'll stay out till the boat has gone. I'll go up to the old rampart.'

'The old rampart?'

'I'll sit on that old bench where you see the gold Virgin.'

'The gold Virgin?' he vaguely echoed. But it brought his eyes back to her as if after an instant he could see the place and the thing she named – could see her sitting there alone. 'While I break with Mrs Beale?'

'While you break with Mrs Beale.'

He gave a long deep smothered sigh. 'I must see her first.'

'You won't do as I do? Go out and wait?'

'Wait?' – once more he appeared at a loss.

'Till they both have gone,' Maisie said.

'Giving *us* up?'

'Giving *us* up.'

Oh with what a face for an instant he wondered if that could be! But his wonder the next moment only made him go to the door and, with his hand on the knob, stand as if listening for voices. Maisie listened, but she heard none. All she heard presently was Sir Claude's saying with speculation quite choked off, but so as not to be heard in the salon: 'Mrs Beale will never go.' On this he pushed open the door and she went in with him. The salon was empty, but as an effect of their entrance the lady he had just mentioned appeared at the door of the bedroom. 'Is she going?' he then demanded.

Mrs Beale came forward, closing her door behind her. 'I've had the most extraordinary scene with her. She told me yesterday she'd stay.'

'And my arrival has altered it?'

'Oh we took that into account!' Mrs Beale was flushed, which was never quite becoming to her, and her face visibly testified to the encounter to which she alluded. Evidently, however, she had not been worsted, and she held up her head and smiled and rubbed her hands as if in sudden emulation of the *patronne*. 'She promised she'd stay even if you should come.'

'Then why has she changed?'

'Because she's a hound. The reason she herself gives is that you've been out too long.'

Sir Claude stared. 'What has that to do with it?'

'You've been out an age,' Mrs Beale continued; 'I myself couldn't imagine what had become of you. The whole morning,' she exclaimed, 'and luncheon long since over!'

Sir Claude appeared indifferent to that. 'Did Mrs Wix go down with you?' he only asked.

'Not she; she never budged!' – and Mrs Beale's flush, to Maisie's vision, deepened. 'She moped there – she didn't so much as come out to me; and when I sent to invite her she simply declined to appear. She said she wanted nothing, and I went down alone. But when I came up, fortunately a little primed' – and Mrs Beale smiled a fine smile of battle – 'she was in the field!'

'And you had a big row?'

'We had a big row' – she assented with a frankness as large. 'And while you left me to that sort of thing I should like to know where you were!' She paused for a reply, but Sir Claude merely looked at Maisie; a movement that promptly quickened her challenge. 'Where the mischief have you been?'

'You seem to take it as hard as Mrs Wix,' Sir Claude returned.

'I take it as I choose to take it, and you don't answer my question.'

He looked again at Maisie – as if for an aid to this effort; whereupon she smiled at her stepmother and offered: 'We've been everywhere.'

Mrs Beale, however, made her no response, thereby adding to a surprise of which our young lady had already felt the light brush. She had received neither a greeting nor a glance, but perhaps this was not more remarkable than the omission, in respect to Sir Claude, parted with in London two days before, of any sign of a sense of their reunion. Most remarkable of all was Mrs Beale's announcement of the pledge given by Mrs Wix and not hitherto revealed to her pupil. Instead of heeding this witness she went on with acerbity: 'It might surely have occurred to you that something would come up.'

Sir Claude looked at his watch. 'I had no idea it was so late, nor that we had been out so long. We weren't hungry. It passed like a flash. What *has* come up?'

'Oh that she's disgusted,' said Mrs Beale.

'With whom then?'

'With Maisie.' Even now she never looked at the child, who stood there equally associated and disconnected. 'For having no moral sense.'

'How *should* she have?' Sir Claude tried again to shine a little at the companion of his walk. 'How at any rate is it proved by her going out with me?'

'Don't ask *me*; ask that woman. She drivels when she doesn't rage,' Mrs Beale declared.

'And she leaves the child?'

'She leaves the child,' said Mrs Beale with great emphasis and looking more than ever over Maisie's head.

In this position suddenly a change came into her face, caused, as the others could the next thing see, by the reappearance of Mrs Wix in the doorway which, on coming in at Sir Claude's heels, Maisie had left gaping. 'I *don't* leave the child – I don't, I don't!' she thundered from the threshold, advancing upon the opposed three but addressing herself directly to Maisie. She was girded – positively harnessed – for departure, arrayed as she had been arrayed on her advent and armed with a small fat rusty reticule which, almost in the manner of a battle-axe, she brandished in support of her words. She had clearly come straight from her room, where Maisie in an instant guessed she had directed the removal of her minor effects. 'I don't leave you till I've given you another chance. Will you come *with* me?'

Maisie turned to Sir Claude, who struck her as having been removed to a distance of about a mile. To Mrs Beale she turned no more than Mrs Beale had turned: she felt as if already their difference had been disclosed. What had come out about that in the scene between the two women? Enough came out now, at all events, as she put it practically to her stepfather. 'Will *you* come? Won't you?' she enquired as if she had not already seen that she should have to give him up. It was the last flare of her dream. By this time she was afraid of nothing.

'I should think you'd be too proud to ask!' Mrs Wix interposed. Mrs Wix was herself conspicuously too proud.

But at the child's words Mrs Beale had fairly bounded. 'Come away from *me*, Maisie?' It was a wail of dismay and reproach, in which her step-daughter was astonished to read that she had had no hostile consciousness and that if she had been so actively grand it was not from suspicion, but from strange entanglements of modesty.

Sir Claude presented to Mrs Beale an expression positively sick. 'Don't put it to her *that* way!' There had indeed been something in Mrs Beale's tone, and for a moment our young lady was reminded of the old days in which so many of her friends had been 'compromised'.

This friend blushed; she was before Mrs Wix, and though she bridled she took the hint. 'No – it isn't the way.' Then she showed she knew the way. 'Don't be a still bigger fool, dear, but go straight to your room and wait there till I can come to you.'

Maisie made no motion to obey, but Mrs Wix raised a hand that forestalled every evasion. 'Don't move till you've heard me. *I'm* going, but I must first understand. Have you lost it again?'

Maisie surveyed – for the idea of a describable loss – the immensity of space. Then she replied lamely enough: 'I feel as if I had lost everything.'

Mrs Wix looked dark. 'Do you mean to say you *have* lost what we found together with so much difficulty two days ago?' As her pupil failed of response she continued: 'Do you mean to say you've already forgotten what we found together?'

Maisie dimly remembered. 'My moral sense?'

'Your moral sense. *Haven't* I, after all, brought it out?' She spoke as she had never spoken even in the schoolroom and with the book in her hand.

It brought back to the child's recollection how she sometimes couldn't repeat on Friday the sentence that had been glib on Wednesday, and she dealt all feebly and ruefully with the present tough passage. Sir Claude and Mrs Beale stood there like visitors at an 'exam'. She had indeed an instant a whiff of the faint flower that Mrs Wix pretended to have plucked and now with such a peremptory hand thrust at her nose. Then it left her, and, as if she were sinking with a slip from a foothold, her arms made a short jerk. What this jerk represented was the spasm within her of something still deeper than a moral sense. She looked at her examiner; she looked at the visitors; she felt the rising of the tears she had kept down at the station. They had nothing – no, distinctly nothing – to do with her moral sense. The only thing was the old flat shameful schoolroom plea. 'I don't know – I don't know.'

'Then you've lost it.' Mrs Wix seemed to close the book as she fixed the straighteners on Sir Claude. 'You've nipped it in the bud. You've killed it when it had begun to live.'

She was a newer Mrs Wix than ever, a Mrs Wix high and great; but Sir Claude was not after all to be treated as a little boy with a missed lesson. 'I've not killed anything,' he said; 'on the contrary I think I've produced life. I don't know what to call it – I haven't even known how decently to deal with it, to approach it; but, whatever it is, it's the most beautiful thing I've ever met – it's exquisite, it's sacred.' He had his hands in his pockets and, though a trace of the sickness he had just shown perhaps lingered there, his face bent itself with extraordinary gentleness on both the friends he was about to lose. 'Do you know what I came back for?' he asked of the elder.

'I think I do!' cried Mrs Wix, surprisingly unmollified and with the heat of her late engagement with Mrs Beale still on her brow. That lady, as if a little besprinkled by such turns of the tide, uttered a loud inarticulate protest and, averting herself, stood a moment at the window.

'I came back with a proposal,' said Sir Claude.

'To me?' Mrs Wix asked.

'To Maisie. That she should give you up.'

'And does she?'

Sir Claude wavered. 'Tell her!' he then exclaimed to the child, also turning away as if to give her the chance. But Mrs Wix and her pupil stood confronted in silence, Maisie whiter than ever – more awkward, more rigid and yet more dumb. They looked at each other hard, and as nothing came from them Sir Claude faced about again. 'You won't tell her? – you can't?' Still she said nothing; whereupon, addressing Mrs Wix, he broke into a kind of ecstasy. 'She refused – she refused!'

Maisie, at this, found her voice. 'I didn't refuse. I didn't,' she repeated.

It brought Mrs Beale straight back to her. 'You accepted, angel – you accepted!' She threw herself upon the child and, before Maisie could resist, had sunk with her upon the sofa, possessed of her, encircling her. 'You've given her up already, you've given her up for ever, and you're ours and ours only now, and the sooner she's off the better!'

Maisie had shut her eyes, but at a word of Sir Claude's they opened. 'Let her go!' he said to Mrs Beale.

'Never, never, never!' cried Mrs Beale. Maisie felt herself more compressed.

'Let her go!' Sir Claude more intensely repeated. He was looking at Mrs Beale and there was something in his voice. Maisie knew from a loosening of arms that she had become conscious of what it was; she slowly rose from the sofa, and the child stood there again dropped and divided. 'You're free – you're free,' Sir Claude went on; at which Maisie's back became aware of a push that vented resentment and that placed her again in the centre of the room, the cynosure of every eye and not knowing which way to turn.

She turned with an effort to Mrs Wix. 'I didn't refuse to give you up. I said I would if *he'd* give up –!'

'Give up Mrs Beale?' burst from Mrs Wix.

'Give up Mrs Beale. What do you call that but exquisite?' Sir Claude demanded of all of them, the lady mentioned included; speaking with a relish as intense now as if some lovely work of art or of nature had suddenly been set down among them. He was rapidly recovering himself on this basis of fine appreciation. 'She made her condition – with such a sense of what it should be! She made the only right one.'

'The only right one?' – Mrs Beale returned to the charge. She had taken a moment before a snub from him, but she was not to be snubbed on this. 'How can you talk such rubbish and how can you back her up in such impertinence? What in the world have you done to her to make her think of such stuff?' She stood there in righteous wrath; she flashed her eyes round the circle. Maisie took them full in her own, knowing that here at last was the moment she had had most to reckon with. But as regards her stepdaughter Mrs Beale subdued herself to a question deeply mild. '*Have* you made, my own love, any such condition as that?'

Somehow, now that it was there, the great moment was not so bad. What helped the child was that she knew what she wanted. All her learning and learning had made her at last learn that; so that if she waited an instant to reply it was only from the desire to be nice. Bewilderment had simply gone or at any rate was going fast. Finally she answered. 'Will you give *him* up? Will you?'

'Ah leave her alone – leave her, leave her!' Sir Claude in sudden supplication murmured to Mrs Beale.

Mrs Wix at the same instant found another apostrophe. 'Isn't it enough for you, madam, to have brought her to discussing your relations?'

Mrs Beale left Sir Claude unheeded, but Mrs Wix could make her flame. 'My relations? What do you know, you hideous creature, about my relations, and what business on earth have you to speak of them? Leave the room this instant, you horrible old woman!'

'I think you had better go – you must really catch your boat,' Sir Claude said distressfully to Mrs Wix. He was out of it now, or wanted to be; he knew the worst and had accepted it: what now concerned him was to prevent, to dissipate vulgarities. 'Won't you go – won't you just get off quickly?'

'With the child as quickly as you like. Not without her.' Mrs Wix was adamant.

'Then why did you lie to me, you fiend?' Mrs Beale almost

yelled. 'Why did you tell me an hour ago that you had given her up?'

'Because I despaired of her – because I thought she had left me.' Mrs Wix turned to Maisie. 'You were *with* them – in their connection. But now your eyes are open, and I take you!'

'No you don't!' and Mrs Beale made, with a great fierce jump, a wild snatch at her stepdaughter. She caught her by the arm and, completing an instinctive movement, whirled her round in a further leap to the door, which had been closed by Sir Claude the instant their voices had risen. She fell back against it and, even while denouncing and waving off Mrs Wix, kept it closed in an incoherence of passion. 'You don't take her, but you bundle yourself: she stays with her own people and she's rid of you! I never heard anything so monstrous!' Sir Claude had rescued Maisie and kept hold of her; he held her in front of him, resting his hands very lightly on her shoulders and facing the loud adversaries. Mrs Beale's flush had dropped; she had turned pale with a splendid wrath. She kept protesting and dismissing Mrs Wix; she glued her back to the door to prevent Maisie's flight; she drove out Mrs Wix by the window or the chimney. 'You're a nice one – "discussing relations" – with your talk of our "connection" and your insults! What in the world's our connection but the love of the child who's our duty and our life and who holds us together as closely as she originally brought us?'

'I know, I know!' Maisie said with a burst of eagerness. 'I did bring you.'

The strangest of laughs escaped from Sir Claude. 'You did bring us – you did!' His hands went up and down gently on her shoulders.

Mrs Wix so dominated the situation that she had something sharp for every one. 'There you have it, you see!' she pregnantly remarked to her pupil.

'*Will* you give him up?' Maisie persisted to Mrs Beale.

'To *you*, you abominable little horror?' that lady indignantly enquired, 'and to this raving old demon who has filled your dreadful little mind with her wickedness? Have you been a hideous little hypocrite all these years that I've slaved to make you love me and deludedly believed you did?'

'I love Sir Claude – I love *him*,' Maisie replied with an awkward sense that she appeared to offer it as something that would do as well. Sir Claude had continued to pat her, and it was really an answer to his pats.

'She hates you – she hates you,' he observed with the oddest quietness to Mrs Beale.

His quietness made her blaze. 'And you back her up in it and give me up to outrage?'

'No; I only insist that she's free – she's free.'

Mrs Beale stared – Mrs Beale glared. 'Free to starve with this pauper lunatic?'

'I'll do more for her than *you* ever did!' Mrs Wix retorted. 'I'll work my fingers to the bone.'

Maisie, with Sir Claude's hands still on her shoulders, felt, just as she felt the fine surrender in them, that over her head he looked in a certain way at Mrs Wix. 'You needn't do that,' she heard him say. 'She has means.'

'Means? – Maisie?' Mrs Beale shrieked. 'Means that her vile father has stolen!'

'I'll get them back – I'll get them back. I'll look into it.' He smiled and nodded at Mrs Wix.

This had a fearful effect on his other friend. 'Haven't *I* looked into it, I should like to know, and haven't I found an abyss? It's too inconceivable – your cruelty to me!' she wildly broke out. She had hot tears in her eyes.

He spoke to her very kindly, almost coaxingly. 'We'll look into it again; we'll look into it together. It *is* an abyss, but he *can* be made – or Ida can. Think of the money they're getting now!' he laughed. 'It's all right, it's all right,' he continued. 'It wouldn't do – it wouldn't do. We *can't* work her in. It's perfectly true – she's unique. We're not good enough – oh no!' and, quite exuberantly, he laughed again.

'Not good enough, and that beast *is*?' Mrs Beale shouted.

At this for a moment there was a hush in the room, and in the midst of it Sir Claude replied to the question by moving with Maisie to Mrs Wix. The next thing the child knew she was at that lady's side with an arm firmly grasped. Mrs Beale still guarded the door. 'Let them pass,' said Sir Claude at last.

She remained there, however; Maisie saw the pair look at each other. Then she saw Mrs Beale turn to her. 'I'm your mother now, Maisie. And he's your father.'

'That's just where it is!' sighed Mrs Wix with an effect of irony positively detached and philosophic.

Mrs Beale continued to address her young friend, and her effort to be reasonable and tender was in its way remarkable. 'We're representative, you know, of Mr Farange and his former wife. This person represents mere illiterate presumption. We take our stand on the law.'

'Oh the law, the law!' Mrs Wix superbly jeered. 'You had better indeed let the law have a look at you!'

'Let them pass – let them pass!' Sir Claude pressed his friend hard – he pleaded.

But she fastened herself still to Maisie. '*Do* you hate me, dearest?'

Maisie looked at her with new eyes, but answered as she had answered before. 'Will you give him up?'

Mrs Beale's rejoinder hung fire, but when it came it was noble. 'You shouldn't talk to me of such things!' She was shocked, she was scandalised to tears.

For Mrs Wix, however, it was her discrimination that was indelicate. 'You ought to be ashamed of yourself!' she roundly cried.

Sir Claude made a supreme appeal. 'Will you be so good as to allow these horrors to terminate?'

Mrs Beale fixed her eyes on him, and again Maisie watched

them. 'You should do him justice,' Mrs Wix went on to Mrs Beale. 'We've always been devoted to him, Maisie and I — and he has shown how much he likes us. He would like to please her; he would like even, I think, to please me. But he hasn't given you up.'

They stood confronted, the step-parents, still under Maisie's observation. That observation had never sunk so deep as at this particular moment. 'Yes, my dear, I haven't given you up,' Sir Claude said to Mrs Beale at last, 'and if you'd like me to treat our friends here as solemn witnesses I don't mind giving you my word for it that I never never will. There!' he dauntlessly exclaimed.

'He can't!' Mrs Wix tragically commented.

Mrs Beale, erect and alive in her defeat, jerked her handsome face about. 'He can't!' she literally mocked.

'He can't, he can't, he can't!' — Sir Claude's gay emphasis wonderfully carried it off.

Mrs Beale took it all in, yet she held her ground; on which Maisie addressed Mrs Wix. 'Shan't we lose the boat?'

'Yes, we shall lose the boat,' Mrs Wix remarked to Sir Claude.

Mrs Beale meanwhile faced full at Maisie. 'I don't know what to make of you!' she launched.

'Good-bye,' said Maisie to Sir Claude.

'Good-bye, Maisie,' Sir Claude answered.

Mrs Beale came away from the door. 'Good-bye!' she hurled at Maisie; then passed straight across the room and disappeared in the adjoining one.

Sir Claude had reached the other door and opened it. Mrs Wix was already out. On the threshold Maisie paused; she put out her hand to her stepfather. He took it and held it a moment, and their eyes met as the eyes of those who have done for each other what they can. 'Good-bye,' he repeated.

'Good-bye.' And Maisie followed Mrs Wix.

They caught the steamer, which was just putting off, and, hustled across the gulf, found themselves on the deck so breathless and so scared that they gave up half the voyage to letting their emotion sink. It sank slowly and imperfectly; but at last, in mid-channel, surrounded by the quiet sea, Mrs Wix had courage to revert. 'I didn't look back, did you?'

'Yes. He wasn't there,' said Maisie.

'Not on the balcony?'

Maisie waited a moment; then 'He wasn't there' she simply said again.

Mrs Wix also was silent a while. 'He went to *her*,' she finally observed.

'Oh I know!' the child replied.

Mrs Wix gave a sidelong look. She still had room for wonder at what Maisie knew.

THE PUPIL

I

THE poor young man hesitated and procrastinated: it cost him such an effort to broach the subject of terms, to speak of money to a person who spoke only of feelings and, as it were, of the aristocracy. Yet he was unwilling to take leave, treating his engagement as settled, without some more conventional glance in that direction than he could find an opening for in the manner of the large affable lady who sat there drawing a pair of soiled *gants de Suède* through a fat jewelled hand and, at once pressing and gliding, repeated over and over everything but the thing he would have liked to hear. He would have liked to hear the figure of his salary; but just as he was nervously about to sound that note the little boy came back – the little boy Mrs Moreen had sent out of the room to fetch her fan. He came back without the fan, only with the casual observation that he couldn't find it. As he dropped this cynical confession he looked straight and hard at the candidate for the honour of taking his education in hand. This personage reflected somewhat grimly that the first thing he should have to teach his little charge would be to appear to address himself to his mother when he spoke to her – especially not to make her such an improper answer as that.

When Mrs Moreen bethought herself of this pretext for getting rid of their companion Pemberton supposed it was precisely to approach the delicate subject of his remuneration. But it had been only to say some things about her son that it was better a boy of eleven shouldn't catch. They were extravagantly to his advantage save when she lowered her voice to sigh, tapping her left side familiarly, 'And all over-clouded by *this*, you know; all at the mercy of a weakness –!' Pemberton gathered that the weakness was in the region of the heart. He had known the poor child was not robust: this was the basis on which he had been invited to treat, through an English lady, an Oxford acquaintance, then at Nice, who happened to know both his needs and those of the amiable American family looking out for something really superior in the way of a resident tutor.

The young man's impression of his prospective pupil, who had come into the room as if to see for himself the moment Pemberton was admitted was not quite the soft solicitation the visitor had taken for granted. Morgan Moreen was somehow sickly without being 'delicate,' and that he looked intelligent – it is true Pemberton wouldn't have enjoyed his being stupid – only added to the suggestion that, as with his big mouth and big ears he really couldn't be called pretty, he might too utterly fail to please Pemberton was modest, was even timid; and the chance that his small scholar would prove cleverer than himself had quite figured, to his anxiety, among the dangers of an untried experiment. He reflected, however, that these were risks one had to run when one accepted a position, as it was called, in a private family; when as yet one's university honours had, pecuniarily speaking, remained barren. At any rate when Mrs Moreen got up as to intimate that, since it was understood he would enter upon his duties within the week she would let him off now, he succeeded, in spite of the presence of the child, in squeezing out a phrase about the rate of payment. It was not the fault of the conscious smile which seemed a reference to the lady's expensive identity, it was not the fault of this demonstration, which had, in a sort, both vagueness and point, if the allusion didn't sound rather vulgar. This was exactly because she became still more gracious to reply: 'Oh I can assure you that all that will be quite regular.'

Pemberton only wondered, while he took up his hat, what 'all that' was to amount to – people had such different ideas. Mrs Moreen's words, however, seemed to commit the family to a pledge definite enough to elicit from the child a strange little comment in the shape of the mocking foreign ejaculation 'Oh la–la!'

Pemberton, in some confusion, glanced at him as he walked slowly to the window with his back turned, his hands in his pockets and the air in his elderly shoulders of a boy who didn't play. The young man wondered if he should be able to teach him to play, though his mother had said it would never do and that this was why school was impossible. Mrs Moreen exhibited no discomfiture; she only continued blandly: 'Mr Moreen will be delighted to meet your wishes. As I told you, he has been called to London for a week. As soon as he comes back you shall have it out with him.'

This was so frank and friendly that the young man could only reply, laughing as his hostess laughed: 'Oh I don't imagine we shall have much of a battle.'

'They'll give you anything you like,' the boy remarked unexpectedly, returning from the window. 'We don't mind what anything costs – we live awfully well.'

'My darling, you're too quaint!' his mother exclaimed, putting out to caress him a practised but ineffectual hand. He slipped out of it, but looked with intelligent innocent eyes at Pemberton, who had already had time to notice that from one moment to the other his small satiric face seemed to change its time of life. At this moment it was infantine, yet it appeared also to be under the influence of curious intuitions and knowledges. Pemberton rather disliked precocity and was disappointed to find gleams of it in a disciple not yet in his teens. Nevertheless he divined on the spot that Morgan wouldn't prove a bore. He would prove on the contrary a source of agitation. This idea held the young man, in spite of a certain repulsion.

'You pompous little person! We're not extravagant!' Mrs Moreen gaily protested, making another unsuccessful attempt to draw the boy to her side. 'You must know what to expect,' she went on to Pemberton.

'The less you expect the better!' her companion interposed. 'But we *are* people of fashion.'

'Only so far as *you* make us so!' Mrs Moreen tenderly mocked. 'Well then, on Friday – don't tell me you're superstitious – and mind you don't fail us. Then you'll see us all. I'm so sorry the girls are out. I guess you'll like the girls. And, you know, I've another son, quite different from this one.'

'He tries to imitate me,' Morgan said to their friend.

'He tries? Why he's twenty years old!' cried Mrs Moreen.

'You're very witty,' Pemberton remarked to the child – a proposition his mother echoed with enthusiasm, declaring Morgan's sallies to be the delight of the house.

The boy paid no heed to this; he only enquired abruptly of the visitor, who was surprised afterwards that he hadn't struck him as offensively forward: 'Do you *want* very much to come?'

'Can you doubt it after such a description of what I shall hear?' Pemberton replied. Yet he didn't want to come at all; he was coming because he had to go somewhere, thanks to the collapse of his fortune at the end of a year abroad spent on the system of putting his scant patrimony into a single full wave of experience. He had had his full wave but couldn't pay the score at his inn. Moreover he had caught in the boy's eyes the glimpse of a far-off appeal.

'Well, I'll do the best I can for you,' said Morgan; with which he turned away again. He passed out of one of the long windows; Pemberton saw him go and lean on the parapet of the terrace. He remained there while the young man took leave of his mother, who, on Pemberton's looking as if he expected a farewell from him, interposed with: 'Leave him, leave him; he's so strange!' Pemberton supposed her to fear something he might say. 'He's a genius – you'll love him,' she added. 'He's much the most interesting person in the family.' And before he could invent some civility to oppose to this she wound up with: 'But we're all good, you know!'

'He's a genius – you'll love him!' were words that recurred to our aspirant before the Friday, suggesting among many things that geniuses were not invariably loveable. However, it was all the better if there was an element that would make tutorship absorbing: he had perhaps taken too much for granted it would only disgust him. As he left the villa after his interview he looked up at the balcony and saw the child leaning over it. 'We shall have great larks!' he called up.

Morgan hung fire a moment and then gaily returned: 'By the time you come back I shall have thought of something witty!'

This made Pemberton say to himself 'After all he's rather nice.'

II

ON the Friday he saw them all, as Mrs Moreen had promised, for her husband had come back and the girls and the other son were at home. Mr Moreen had a white moustache, a confiding manner and, in his buttonhole, the ribbon of a foreign order – bestowed, as Pemberton eventually learned, for services. For what services he never clearly ascertained: this was a point – one of a large number – that Mr Moreen's manner never confided. What it emphatically did confide was that he was even more a man of the world than you might first make out. Ulick, the firstborn, was in visible training for the same profession – under the disadvantage as yet, however, of a buttonhole but feebly floral and a moustache with no pretensions to type. The girls had hair and figures and manners and small fat feet, but had never been out alone. As for Mrs Moreen Pemberton saw on a nearer view that her elegance was intermittent and her parts didn't always match. Her husband, as she had promised, met with enthusiasm Pemberton's ideas in regard to a salary. The young man had endeavoured to keep these stammerings modest, and Mr Moreen made it no secret that *he* found them wanting in 'style.' He further mentioned that he aspired to be intimate with his children, to be their best friend, and that he was always looking out for them. That was what he went off for, to London and other places – to look out; and this vigilance was the theory of life, as well as the real occupation, of the whole family. They all looked out, for they were very frank on the subject of its being necessary. They desired it to be understood that they were earnest people, and also that their fortune, though quite adequate for earnest people, required the most careful administration. Mr Moreen, as the parent bird, sought sustenance for the nest. Ulick invoked support mainly at the club, where Pemberton guessed that it was usually served on green cloth. The girls used to do up their hair and their frocks themselves, and our young man felt appealed to to be glad, in regard to Morgan's education, that, though it must naturally be of the best, it didn't cost too much. After a little he *was* glad, forgetting at times his own needs in the interest inspired by the child's character and culture and the pleasure of making easy terms for him.

During the first weeks of their acquaintance Morgan had been as puzzling as a page in an unknown language – altogether different from the obvious little Anglo-Saxons who had misrepresented childhood to Pemberton. Indeed the whole mystic volume in which the boy had been amateurishly bound demanded some practice in translation. Today, after a considerable interval, there is something phantasmagoric, like a prismatic reflection or a serial novel, in Pemberton's memory of the queerness of the Moreens. If it were not for a few tangible tokens – a lock of Morgan's hair cut by his own hand, and the half-dozen letters received from him when they were disjoined – the whole episode, and the figures peopling it would seem too inconsequent for anything but dreamland. Their supreme quaintness was their success – as it appeared to him for a while at the time; since he had never seen a family so brilliantly equipped for failure. Wasn't it success to have kept him so hatefully long? Wasn't it success to have drawn him in that first morning at déjeuner, the Friday he came – it was enough to *make* one superstitious – so that he utterly committed himself, and this not by calculation or on a signal, but from a happy instinct which made them, like a band of gipsies, work so neatly together? They amused him as much as if they had really been a band of gipsies. He was still young and had not seen much of the world – his English years had been properly arid; therefore the reversed conventions of the Moreens – for they had *their* desperate proprieties – struck him as topsy-turvy. He had encountered nothing like them at Oxford; still less had any such note been

struck to his younger American ear during the four years at Yale in
which he had richly supposed himself to be reacting against a
Puritan strain. The reaction of the Moreens, at any rate, went ever
so much further. He had thought himself very sharp that first day
in hitting them all off in his mind with the 'cosmopolite' label.
Later it seemed feeble and colourless – confessedly helplessly
provisional.

He yet when he first applied it felt a glow of joy – for an
instructor he was still empirical – rise from the apprehension that
living with them would really be to see life. Their sociable
strangeness was an intimation of that – their chatter of tongues,
their gaiety and good humour, their infinite dawdling (they were
always getting themselves up, but it took for ever, and Pemberton
had once found Mr Moreen shaving in the drawing-room), their
French, their Italian and, cropping up in the foreign fluencies, their
cold tough slices of American. They lived on maccaroni and coffee
– they had these articles prepared in perfection – but they knew
recipes for a hundred other dishes. They overflowed with music
and song, were always humming and catching each other up, and
had a sort of professional acquaintance with Continental cities.
They talked of 'good places' as if they had been pickpockets or
strolling players. They had at Nice a villa, a carriage, a piano and a
banjo, and they went to official parties. They were a perfect
calendar of the 'days' of their friends, which Pemberton knew
them, when they were indisposed, to get out of bed to go to, and
which made the week larger than life when Mrs Moreen talked of
them with Paula and Amy. Their initiations gave their new inmate
at first an almost dazzling sense of culture. Mrs Moreen had
translated something at some former period – an author whom it
made Pemberton feel *borné* never to have heard of. They could
imitate Venetian and sing Neapolitan, and when they wanted to
say something very particular communicated with each other in an
ingenious dialect of their own, an elastic spoken cipher which
Pemberton at first took for some *patois* of one of their countries,

but which he 'caught on to' as he would not have grasped provincial development of Spanish or German.

'It's the family language – Ultramoreen,' Morgan explained to him drolly enough; but the boy rarely condescended to use it himself, though he dealt in colloquial Latin as if he had been a little prelate.

Among all the 'days' with which Mrs Moreen's memory was taxed she managed to squeeze in one of her own, which her friends sometimes forgot. But the house drew a frequented air from the number of fine people who were freely named there and from several mysterious men with foreign titles and English clothes whom Morgan called the Princes and who, on sofas with the girls, talked French very loud – though sometimes with some oddity of accent – as if to show they were saying nothing improper. Pemberton wondered how the Princes could ever propose in that tone and so publicly: he took for granted cynically that this was what was desired of them. Then he recognised that even for the chance of such an advantage Mrs Moreen would never allow Paula and Amy to receive alone. These young ladies were not at all timid, but it was just the safeguards that made them so candidly free. It was a houseful of Bohemians who wanted tremendously to be Philistines.

In one respect, however, certainly, they achieved no rigour – they were wonderfully amiable and ecstatic about Morgan. It was a genuine tenderness, an artless admiration, equally strong in each. They even praised his beauty, which was small, and were as afraid of him as if they felt him of finer clay. They spoke of him as a little angel and a prodigy – they touched on his want of health with long, vague faces. Pemberton feared at first an extravagance that might make him hate the boy, but before this happened he had become extravagant himself. Later, when he had grown rather to hate the others, it was a bribe to patience for him that they were at any rate nice about Morgan, going on tiptoe if they fancied he was showing symptoms, and even giving up somebody's 'day' to procure him a pleasure. Mixed with this too was the oddest wish to make him independent, as if they had felt themselves not good enough for him. They passed him over to the new members of their circle very much as if wishing to force some charity of adoption on so free an agent and get rid of their own charge. They were delighted when they saw Morgan take so to his kind playfellow, and could think of no higher praise for the young man. It was strange how they contrived to reconcile the appearance, and indeed the essential fact, of adoring the child with their eagerness to wash their hands of him. Did they want to get rid of him before he should find them out? Pemberton was finding them out month by month. The boy's fond family, however this might be, turned their backs with exaggerated delicacy, as if to avoid the reproach of interfering. Seeing in time how little he had in common with them – it was by *them* he first observed it; they proclaimed it with complete humility – his companion was moved to speculate on the mysteries of transmission, the far jumps of heredity. Where his detachment from most of the things they represented had come from was more than an observer could say – it certainly had burrowed under two or three generations.

As for Pemberton's own estimate of his pupil, it was a good while before he got the point of view, so little had he been prepared for it by the smug young barbarians to whom the tradition of tutorship, as hitherto revealed to him, had been adjusted. Morgan was scrappy and surprising, deficient in many properties supposed common to the *genus* and abounding in others that were the portion only of the supernaturally clever. One day his friend made a great stride: it cleared up the question to perceive that Morgan *was* supernaturally clever and that, though the formula was temporarily meagre, this would be the only assumption on which one could successfully deal with him. He had the general quality of a child for whom life had not been simplified by school, a kind of homebred sensibility which might have been bad for himself, but was charming for others, and a whole range of refinement and perception – little musical vibrations as taking as picked-up airs – begotten by wandering about Europe at the tail of his migratory tribe. This might not have been an education to recommend in advance, but its results with so special a subject were as appreciable as the marks on a piece of fine porcelain. There was at the same time in him a small strain of stoicism, doubtless the fruit of having had to begin early to bear pain, which counted for pluck and made it of less consequence that he might have been thought at school rather a polyglot little beast. Pemberton indeed quickly found himself rejoicing that school was out of the question: in any million of boys it was probably good for all but one, and Morgan was that millionth. It would have made him comparative and superior – it might have made him really require kicking. Pemberton would try to be school himself – a bigger seminary than five hundred grazing donkeys, so that, winning no prizes, the boy would remain unconscious and irresponsible and amusing – amusing, because, though life was already intense in his childish nature, freshness still made there a strong draught for jokes. It turned out that even in the still air of Morgan's various disabilities jokes flourished greatly. He was a pale lean acute undeveloped little cosmopolite, who liked intellectual gymnastics and who also, as regards the behaviour of mankind, had noticed more things than you might suppose, but who nevertheless had his proper playroom of superstitions, where he smashed a dozen toys a day.

III

AT Nice once, toward evening, as the pair rested in the open air after a walk, and looked over the sea at the pink western lights, he said suddenly to his comrade: 'Do you like it, you know – being with us all in this intimate way?'

'My dear fellow, why should I stay if I didn't?'

'How do I know you'll stay? I'm almost sure you won't, very long.'

'I hope you don't mean to dismiss me,' said Pemberton.

Morgan debated, looking at the sunset. 'I think if I did right I ought to.'

'Well, I know I'm supposed to instruct you in virtue; but in that case don't do right.'

'You're very young – fortunately,' Morgan went on, turning to him again.

'Oh yes, compared with you!'

'Therefore it won't matter so much if you do lose a lot of time.'

'That's the way to look at it,' said Pemberton accommodatingly.

They were silent a minute; after which the boy asked: 'Do you like my father and my mother very much?'

'Dear me, yes. Charming people.'

Morgan received this with another silence; then unexpectedly, familiarly, but at the same time affectionately, he remarked: 'You're a jolly old humbug!'

For a particular reason the words made our young man change colour. The boy noticed in an instant that he had turned red, whereupon he turned red himself and pupil and master exchanged a longish glance in which there was a consciousness of many more

things than are usually touched upon, even tacitly, in such a
relation. It produced for Pemberton an embarrassment; it raised in
a shadowy form a question – this was the first glimpse of it –
destined to play a singular and, as he imagined, owing to the
altogether peculiar conditions, an unprecedented part in his intercourse with his little companion. Later, when he found himself
talking with the youngster in a way in which few youngsters could
ever have been talked with, he thought of that clumsy moment on
the bench at Nice as the dawn of an understanding that had
broadened. What had added to the clumsiness then was that he
thought it his duty to declare to Morgan that he might abuse him,
Pemberton, as much as he liked, but must never abuse his parents.
To this Morgan had the easy retort that he hadn't dreamed of
abusing them; which appeared to be true: it put Pemberton in the
wrong.

'Then why am I a humbug for saying *I* think them charming?'
the young man asked, conscious of a certain rashness.

'Well – they're not your parents.'

'They love you better than anything in the world – never forget
that,' said Pemberton.

'Is that why you like them so much?'

'They're very kind to me,' Pemberton replied evasively.

'You *are* a humbug!' laughed Morgan, passing an arm into his
tutor's. He leaned against him looking off at the sea again and
swinging his long thin legs.

'Don't kick my shins,' said Pemberton while he reflected 'Hang
it, I can't complain of them to the child!'

'There's another reason too,' Morgan went on, keeping his legs
still.

'Another reason for what?'

'Besides their not being your parents.'

'I don't understand you,' said Pemberton.

'Well, you will before long. All right!'

He did understand fully before long, but he made a fight even

with himself before he confessed it. He thought it the oddest thing
to have a struggle with the child about. He wondered he didn't
hate the hope of the Moreens for bringing the struggle on. But by
the time it began any such sentiment for that scion was closed to
him. Morgan was a special case, and to know him was to accept
him on his own odd terms. Pemberton had spent his aversion to
special cases before arriving at knowledge. When at last he did
arrive his quandary was great. Against every interest he had
attached himself. They would have to meet things together. Before
they went home that evening at Nice the boy had said, clinging to
his arm:

'Well, at any rate you'll hang on to the last.'

'To the last?'

'Till you're fairly beaten.'

'*You* ought to be fairly beaten!' cried the young man, drawing
him closer.

IV

A YEAR after he had come to live with them Mr and Mrs Moreen
suddenly gave up the villa at Nice. Pemberton had got used to
suddenness, having seen it practised on a considerable scale during
two jerky little tours – one in Switzerland the first summer, and the
other late in the winter, when they all ran down to Florence and
then, at the end of ten days, liking it much less than they had
intended, straggled back in mysterious depression. They had
returned to Nice 'for ever', as they said; but this didn't prevent
their squeezing, one rainy muggy May night, into a second-class
railway-carriage – you could never tell by which class they would
travel – where Pemberton helped them to stow away a wonderful
collection of bundles and bags. The explanation of this manoeuvre
was that they had determined to spend the summer 'in some
bracing place'; but in Paris they dropped into a small furnished
apartment – a fourth floor in a third-rate avenue, where there was
a smell on the staircase and the *portier* was hateful – and passed the
next four months in blank indigence.

The better part of this baffled sojourn was for the preceptor and
his pupil, who, visiting the Invalides and Notre Dame, the
Conciergerie and all the museums, took a hundred remunerative
rambles. They learned to know their Paris, which was useful, for
they came back another year for a longer stay, the general character
of which in Pemberton's memory today mixes pitiably and
confusedly with that of the first. He sees Morgan's shabby knicker-
bockers – the everlasting pair that didn't match his blouse and that
as he grew longer could only grow faded. He remembers the
particular holes in his three or four pair of coloured stockings.

Morgan was dear to his mother, but he never was better dressed than was absolutely necessary – partly, no doubt, by his own fault, for he was as indifferent to his appearance as a German philosopher. 'My dear fellow, you *are* coming to pieces,' Pemberton would say to him in sceptical remonstrance; to which the child would reply, looking at him serenely up and down: 'My dear fellow, so are you! I don't want to cast you in the shade.' Pemberton could have no rejoinder for this – the assertion so closely represented the fact. If however the deficiencies of his own wardrobe were a chapter by themselves he didn't like his little charge to look too poor. Later he used to say 'Well, if we're poor, why, after all, shouldn't we look it?' and he consoled himself with thinking there was something rather elderly and gentlemanly in Morgan's disrepair – it differed from the untidiness of the urchin who plays and spoils his things. He could trace perfectly the degrees by which, in proportion as her little son confined himself to his tutor for society, Mrs Moreen shrewdly forbore to renew his garments. She did nothing that didn't show, neglected him because he escaped notice, and then, as he illustrated this clever policy, discouraged at home his public appearances. Her position was logical enough – those members of her family who did show had to be showy.

During this period and several others Pemberton was quite aware of how he and his comrade might strike people; wandering languidly through the Jardin des Plantes as if they had nowhere to go, sitting on the winter days in the galleries of the Louvre, so splendidly ironical to the homeless, as if for the advantage of the *calorifère*. They joked about it sometimes: it was the sort of joke that was perfectly within the boy's compass. They figured themselves as part of the vast vague hand-to-mouth multitude of the enormous city and pretended they were proud of their position in it – it showed them 'such a lot of life' and made them conscious of a democratic brotherhood. If Pemberton couldn't feel a sympathy in destitution with his small companion – for after all Morgan's fond parents would never have let him really suffer – the boy would at least feel it with him, so it came to the same thing. He used sometimes to wonder what people would think they were – to fancy they were looked askance at, as if it might be a suspected case of kidnapping. Morgan wouldn't be taken for a young patrician with a preceptor – he wasn't smart enough; though he might pass for his companion's sickly little brother. Now and then he had a five-franc piece, and except once, when they bought a couple of lovely neckties, one of which he made Pemberton accept, they laid it out scientifically in old books. This was sure to be a great day, always spent on the quays, in a rummage of the dusty boxes that garnish the parapets. Such occasions helped them to live, for their books ran low very soon after the beginning of their acquaintance. Pemberton had a good many in England, but he was obliged to write to a friend and ask him kindly to get some fellow to give him something for them.

If they had to relinquish that summer the advantage of the bracing climate the young man couldn't but suspect this failure of the cup when at their very lips to have been the effect of a rude jostle of his own. This had represented his first blow-out, as he called it, with his patrons; his first successful attempt – though there was little other success about it – to bring them to a consideration of his impossible position. As the ostensible eve of a costly journey the moment had struck him as favourable to an earnest protest, the presentation of an ultimatum. Ridiculous as it sounded, he had never yet been able to compass an uninterrupted private interview with the elder pair or with either of them singly. They were always flanked by their elder children, and poor Pemberton usually had his own little charge at his side. He, was conscious of its being a house in which the surface of one's delicacy got rather smudged; nevertheless he had preserved the bloom of his scruple against announcing to Mr and Mrs Moreen with publicity that he shouldn't be able to go on longer without a little money. He was still simple enough to suppose Ulick and Paula and Amy might not know that since his arrival he had only had a hundred and forty

francs; and he was magnanimous enough to wish not to compromise their parents in their eyes. Mr Moreen now listened to
him, as he listened to every one and to every thing, like a man of
the world, and seemed to appeal to him – though not of course too
grossly – to try and be a little more of one himself. Pemberton
recognised in fact the importance of the character – from the
advantage it gave Mr Moreen. He was not even confused or
embarrassed, whereas the young man in his service was more so
than there was any reason for. Neither was he surprised – at least
any more than a gentleman had to be who freely confessed himself
a little shocked – though not perhaps strictly at Pemberton.

'We must go into this, mustn't we, dear?' he said to his wife. He
assured his young friend that the matter should have his very best
attention; and he melted into space as elusively as if, at the door, he
were taking an inevitable but deprecatory precedence. When, the
next moment, Pemberton found himself alone with Mrs Moreen it
was to hear her say 'I see, I see' – stroking the roundness of her chin
and looking as if she were only hesitating between a dozen easy
remedies. If they didn't make their push Mr Moreen could at least
disappear for several days. During his absence his wife took up the
subject again spontaneously, but her contribution to it was merely
that she had thought all the while they were getting on so beautifully.
Pemberton's reply to this revelation was that unless they immediately
put down something on account he would leave them on the spot
and for ever. He knew she would wonder how he would get away,
and for a moment expected her to enquire. She didn't, for which he
was almost grateful to her, so little was he in a position to tell.

'You won't, you *know* you won't – you're too interested,' she
said. 'You *are* interested, you know you are, you dear kind man!'
She laughed with almost condemnatory archness, as if it were a
reproach – though she wouldn't insist; and flirted a soiled pocket-
handkerchief at him.

Pemberton's mind was fully made up to take his step the
following week. This would give him time to get an answer to a

letter he had dispatched to England. If he did in the event nothing of the sort – that is if he stayed another year and then went away only for three months – it was not merely because before the answer to his letter came (most unsatisfactory when it did arrive) Mr Moreen generously counted out to him, and again with the sacrifice to 'form' of a marked man of the world, three hundred francs in elegant ringing gold. He was irritated to find that Mrs Moreen was right, that he couldn't at the pinch bear to leave the child. This stood out clearer for the very reason that, the night of his desperate appeal to his patrons, he had seen fully for the first time where he was. Wasn't it another proof of the success with which those patrons practised their arts that they had managed to avert for so long the illuminating flash? It descended on our friend with a breadth of effect which perhaps would have struck a spectator as comical, after he had returned to his little servile room, which looked into a close court where a bare dirty opposite wall took, with the sound of shrill clatter, the reflection of lighted back windows. He had simply given himself away to a band of adventurers. The idea, the word itself, wore a romantic horror for him – he had always lived on such safe lines. Later it assumed a more interesting, almost a soothing, sense: it pointed a moral, and Pemberton could enjoy a moral. The Moreens were adventurers not merely because they didn't pay their debts, because they lived on society, but because their whole view of life, dim and confused and instinctive, like that of clever colour-blind animals, was speculative and rapacious and mean. Oh they were 'respectable', and that only made them more *immondes*! The young man's analysis, while he brooded, put it at last very simply – they were adventurers because they were toadies and snobs. That was the completest account of them – it was the law of their being. Even when this truth became vivid to their ingenious inmate he remained unconscious of how much his mind had been prepared for it by the extraordinary little boy who had now become such a complication in his life. Much less could he then calculate on the information he was still to owe the extraordinary little boy.

V

BUT it was during the ensuing time that the real problem came up – the problem of how far it was excusable to discuss the turpitude of parents with a child of twelve, of thirteen, of fourteen. Absolutely inexcusable and quite impossible it of course at first appeared; and indeed the question didn't press for some time after Pemberton had received his three hundred francs. They produced a temporary lull, a relief from the sharpest pressure. The young man frugally amended his wardrobe and even had a few francs in his pocket. He thought the Moreens looked at him as if he were almost too smart, as if they ought to take care not to spoil him. If Mr Moreen hadn't been such a man of the world he would perhaps have spoken of the freedom of such neckties on the part of a subordinate. But Mr Moreen was always enough a man of the world to let things pass – he had certainly shown that. It was singular how Pemberton guessed that Morgan, though saying nothing about it, knew something had happened. But three hundred francs, especially when one owed money, couldn't last for ever; and when the treasure was gone – the boy knew when it had failed – Morgan did break ground. The party had returned to Nice at the beginning of the winter, but not to the charming villa. They went to an hotel, where they stayed three months, and then moved to another establishment, explaining that they had left the first because, after waiting and waiting, they couldn't get the rooms they wanted. These apartments, the rooms they wanted, were generally very splendid; but fortunately they never *could* get them – fortunately, I mean, for Pemberton, who reflected always that if they had got them there would have been a still scanter educational fund. What Morgan said at last was said suddenly, irrelevantly, when the moment came, in the middle of a lesson, and consisted of the apparently unfeeling words: 'You ought to *filer*, you know – you really ought.'

Pemberton stared. He had learnt enough French slang from Morgan to know that to *filer* meant to cut sticks. 'Ah my dear fellow, don't turn me off!'

Morgan pulled a Greek lexicon toward him – he used a Greek-German – to look out a word, instead of asking it of Pemberton. 'You can't go on like this, you know.'

'Like what, my boy?'

'You know they don't pay you up,' said Morgan, blushing and turning his leaves.

'Don't pay me?' Pemberton stared again and feigned amazement. 'What on earth put that into your head?'

'It has been there a long time,' the boy replied rummaging his book.

Pemberton was silent, then he went on: 'I say, what are you hunting for? They pay me beautifully.'

'I'm hunting for the Greek for awful whopper,' Morgan dropped.

'Find that rather for gross impertinence and disabuse your mind. What do I want of money?'

'Oh that's another question!'

Pemberton wavered – he was drawn in different ways. The severely correct thing would have been to tell the boy that such a matter was none of his business and bid him go on with his lines. But they were really too intimate for that; it was not the way he was in the habit of treating him; there had been no reason it should be. On the other hand Morgan had quite lighted on the truth – he really shouldn't be able to keep it up much longer; therefore why not let him know one's real motive for forsaking him? At the same time it wasn't decent to abuse to one's pupil the family of one's pupil; it was better to misrepresent than to do that. So in reply to his comrade's last exclamation he just declared, to dismiss the subject, that he had received several payments.

'I say – I say!' the boy ejaculated, laughing.

'That's all right,' Pemberton insisted. 'Give me your written rendering.'

Morgan pushed a copybook across the table, and he began to read the page, but with something running in his head that made it no sense. Looking up after a minute or two he found the child's eyes fixed on him and felt in them something strange. Then Morgan said: 'I'm not afraid of the stern reality.'

'I haven't yet seen the thing you *are* afraid of – I'll do you that justice!'

This came out with a jump – it was perfectly true – and evidently gave Morgan pleasure. 'I've thought of it a long time,' he presently resumed.

'Well, don't think of it any more.'

The boy appeared to comply, and they had a comfortable and even an amusing hour. They had a theory that they were very thorough, and yet they seemed always to be in the amusing part of lessons, the intervals between the dull dark tunnels, where there were waysides and jolly views. Yet the morning was brought to a violent end by Morgan's suddenly leaning his arms on the table, burying his head in them and bursting into tears: at which Pemberton was the more startled that, as it then came over him, it was the first time he had ever seen the boy cry and that the impression was consequently quite awful.

The next day, after much thought, he took a decision and, believing it to be just, immediately acted on it. He cornered Mr and Mrs Moreen again and let them know that if on the spot they didn't pay him all they owed him he wouldn't only leave their house but would tell Morgan exactly what had brought him to it.

'Oh you *haven't* told him?' cried Mrs Moreen with a pacifying hand on her well-dressed bosom.

'Without warning you? For what do you take me?' the young man returned.

Mr and Mrs Moreen looked at each other; he could see that they appreciated, as tending to their security, his superstition of delicacy, and yet that there was a certain alarm in their relief. 'My dear fellow,' Mr Moreen demanded, 'what use *can* you have, leading the quiet life we all do, for such a lot of money?' – a question to which Pemberton made no answer, occupied as he was in noting that what passed in the mind of his patrons was something like: 'Oh then, if we've felt that the child, dear little angel, has judged us and how he regards us, and we haven't been betrayed, he must have guessed – and in short it's *general*!' an inference that rather stirred up Mr and Mrs Moreen, as Pemberton had desired it should. At the same time, if he had supposed his threat would do something towards bringing them round, he was disappointed to find them taking for granted – how vulgar their perception *had* been! – that he had already given them away. There was a mystic uneasiness in their parental breasts, and that had been the inferior sense of it. None the less, however, his threat did touch them; for if they had escaped it was only to meet a new danger. Mr Moreen appealed to him, on every precedent, as a man of the world; but his wife had recourse, for the first time since his domestication with them, to a fine *hauteur*, reminding him that a devoted mother, with her child, had arts that protected her against gross misrepresentation.

'I should misrepresent you grossly if I accused you of common honesty!' our friend replied; but as he closed the door behind him sharply, thinking he had not done himself much good, while Mr Moreen lighted another cigarette, he heard his hostess shout after him more touchingly:

'Oh you do, you *do*, put the knife to one's throat!'

The next morning, very early, she came to his room. He recognised her knock, but had no hope she brought him money; as to which he was wrong, for she had fifty francs in her hand. She squeezed forward in her dressing-gown, and he received her in his own, between his bath-tub and his bed. He had been tolerably schooled by this time to the 'foreign ways' of his hosts. Mrs Moreen was ardent, and when she was ardent she didn't care what she did; so she now sat down on his bed, his clothes being on the chairs, and, in her preoccupation, forgot, as she glanced round, to be ashamed of giving him such a horrid room. What Mrs Moreen's ardour now bore upon was the design of persuading him that in the first place she was very good-natured to bring him fifty francs, and that in the second, if he would only see it, he was really too absurd to expect to be *paid*. Wasn't he paid enough without perpetual money – wasn't he paid by the comfortable luxurious home he enjoyed with them all, without a care, an anxiety, a solitary want? Wasn't he sure of his position, and wasn't that everything to a young man like him, quite unknown, with singularly little to show, the ground of whose exorbitant pretensions it had never been easy to discover? Wasn't he paid above all by the sweet relation he had established with Morgan – quite ideal as from master to pupil – and by the simple privilege of knowing and living with so amazingly gifted a child; than whom really (and she meant literally what she said) there was no better company in Europe? Mrs Moreen herself took to appealing to him as a man of the world; she said 'Voyons, mon cher,' and 'My dear man, look here now'; and urged him to be reasonable, putting it before him that it was truly a chance for him. She spoke as if, according as he *should* be reasonable, he would prove himself worthy to be her son's tutor and of the extraordinary confidence they had placed in him.

After all, Pemberton reflected, it was only a difference of theory and the theory didn't matter much. They had hitherto gone on that of remunerated, as now they would go on that of gratuitous, service; but why should they have so many words about it? Mrs Moreen at all events continued to be convincing; sitting there with her fifty francs she talked and reiterated, as women reiterate, and bored and irritated him, while he leaned against the wall with his hands in the pockets of his wrapper, drawing it together round his legs and looking over the head of his visitor at the grey negations of his window. She wound up with saying: 'You see I bring you a definite proposal.'

'A definite proposal?'

'To make our relations regular, as it were – to put them on a comfortable footing.'

'I see – it's a system,' said Pemberton. 'A kind of organised blackmail.'

Mrs Moreen bounded up, which was exactly what he wanted. 'What do you mean by that?'

'You practise on one's fears – one's fears about the child if one should go away.'

'And pray what would happen to him in that event?' she demanded with majesty.

'Why he'd be alone with *you*.'

'And pray with whom *should* a child be but with those whom he loves most?'

'If you think that, why don't you dismiss me?'

'Do you pretend he loves you more than he loves *us*?' cried Mrs Moreen.

'I think he ought to. I make sacrifices for him. Though I've heard of those *you* make I don't see them.'

Mrs Moreen stared a moment; then with emotion she grasped her inmate's hand. '*Will* you make it – the sacrifice?'

He burst out laughing. 'I'll see. I'll do what I can. I'll stay a little longer. Your calculation's just – *I do* hate intensely to give him up; I'm fond of him and he thoroughly interests me, in spite of the inconvenience I suffer. You know my situation perfectly. I haven't a penny in the world and, occupied as you see me with Morgan, am unable to earn money.'

Mrs Moreen tapped her undressed arm with her folded bank-note. 'Can't you write articles? Can't you translate as *I* do?'

'I don't know about translating; it's wretchedly paid.'

'I'm glad to earn what I can,' said Mrs Moreen with prodigious virtue.

'You ought to tell me who you do it for.' Pemberton paused a moment, and she said nothing; so he added: 'I've tried to turn off some little sketches, but the magazines won't have them – they're declined with thanks.'

'You see then you're not such a phoenix,' his visitor pointedly smiled – 'to pretend to abilities you're sacrificing for our sake.'

'I haven't time to do things properly,' he ruefully went on. Then as it came over him that he was almost abjectly good-natured to give these explanations he added: 'If I stay on longer it must be on one condition – that Morgan shall know distinctly on what footing I am.'

Mrs Moreen demurred. 'Surely you don't want to show off to a child?'

'To show *you* off, do you mean?'

Again she cast about, but this time it was to produce a still finer flower. 'And *you* talk of blackmail!'

'You can easily prevent it,' said Pemberton.

'And *you* talk of practising on fears!' she bravely pushed on.

'Yes, there's no doubt I'm a great scoundrel.'

His patroness met his eyes – it was clear she was in straits. Then she thrust out her money at him. 'Mr Moreen desired me to give you this on account.'

'I'm much obliged to Mr Moreen, but we *have* no account.'

'You won't take it?'

'That leaves me more free,' said Pemberton.

'To poison my darling's mind?' groaned Mrs Moreen.

'Oh your darling's mind –!' the young man laughed.

She fixed him a moment, and he thought she was going to break out tormentedly, pleadingly: 'For God's sake, tell me what *is* in it!' But she checked this impulse – another was stronger. She pocketed the money – the crudity of the alternative was comical – and swept out of the room with the desperate concession: 'You may tell him any horror you like!'

VI

A COUPLE of days after this, during which he had failed to profit by so free a permission, he had been for a quarter of an hour walking with his charge in silence when the boy became sociable again with the remark: 'I'll tell you how I know it; I know it through Zénobie.'

'Zénobie? Who in the world is *she*?'

'A nurse I used to have − ever so many years ago. A charming woman. I liked her awfully, and she liked me.'

'There's no accounting for tastes. What is it you know through her?'

'Why what their idea is. She went away because they didn't fork out. She did like me awfully, and she stayed two years. She told me all about it − that at last she could never get her wages. As soon as they saw how much she liked me they stopped giving her anything. They thought she'd stay for nothing − just *because*, don't you know?' And Morgan had a queer little conscious lucid look. 'She did stay ever so long − as long as she could. She was only a poor girl. She used to send money to her mother. At last she couldn't afford it any longer, and went away in a fearful rage one night − I mean of course in a rage against *them*. She cried over me tremendously, she hugged me nearly to death. She told me all about it,' the boy repeated. 'She told me it was their idea. So I guessed, ever so long ago, that they have had the same idea with you.'

'Zénobie was very sharp,' said Pemberton. 'And she made you so.'

'Oh that wasn't Zénobie; that was nature. And experience!' Morgan laughed.

'Well, Zénobie was a part of your experience.'

'Certainly I was a part of hers, poor dear!' the boy wisely sighed. 'And I'm part of yours.'

'A very important part. But I don't see how you know I've been treated like Zénobie.'

'Do you take me for the biggest dunce you've known?' Morgan asked. 'Haven't I been conscious of what we've been through together?'

'What we've been through?'

'Our privations – our dark days.'

'Oh our days have been bright enough.'

Morgan went on in silence for a moment. Then he said: 'My dear chap, you're a hero!'

'Well, you're another!' Pemberton retorted.

'No I'm not, but I ain't a baby. I won't stand it any longer. You must get some occupation that pays. I'm ashamed, I'm ashamed!' quavered the boy with a ring of passion, like some high silver note from a small cathedral chorister, that deeply touched his friend.

'We ought to go off and live somewhere together,' the young man said.

'I'll go like a shot if you'll take me.'

'I'd get some work that would keep us both afloat,' Pemberton continued.

'So would I. Why shouldn't *I* work? I ain't such a beastly little muff as *that* comes to.'

'The difficulty is that your parents wouldn't hear of it. They'd never part with you; they worship the ground you tread on. Don't you see the proof of it?' Pemberton developed. 'They don't dislike me; they wish me no harm; they're very amiable people; but they're perfectly ready to expose me to any awkwardness in life for your sake.'

The silence in which Morgan received his fond sophistry struck Pemberton somehow as expressive. After a moment the child repeated: 'You *are* a hero!' Then he added: 'They leave me with you altogether. You've all the responsibility. They put me off on you from morning till night. Why then should they object to my taking up with you completely? I'd help you.'

'They're not particularly keen about my being helped, and they delight in thinking of you as *theirs*. They're tremendously proud of you.'

'I'm not proud of *them*. But you know that,' Morgan returned.

'Except for the little matter we speak of they're charming people,' said Pemberton, not taking up the point made for his intelligence, but wondering greatly at the boy's own, and especially at this fresh reminder of something he had been conscious of from the first – the strangest thing in his friend's large little composition, a temper, a sensibility, even a private ideal, which made him as privately disown the stuff his people were made of. Morgan had in secret a small loftiness which made him acute about betrayed meanness; as well as a critical sense for the manners immediately surrounding him that was quite without precedent in a juvenile nature, especially when one noted that it had not made this nature 'old-fashioned', as the word is of children – quaint or wizened or offensive. It was as if he had been a little gentleman and had paid the penalty by discovering that he was the only such person in his family. This comparison didn't make him vain, but it could make him melancholy and a trifle austere. While Pemberton guessed at these dim young things, shadows of shadows, he was partly drawn on and partly checked, as for a scruple, by the charm of attempting to sound the little cool shallows that were so quickly growing deeper. When he tried to figure to himself the morning twilight of childhood, so as to deal with it safely, he saw it was never fixed, never arrested, that ignorance, at the instant he touched it, was already flushing faintly into knowledge, that there was nothing that at a given moment you could say an intelligent child didn't know. It seemed to him that he himself knew too much to imagine Morgan's simplicity and too little to disembroil his tangle.

The boy paid no heed to his last remark; he only went on: 'I'd have spoken to them about their idea, as I call it, long ago, if I hadn't been sure what they'd say.'

'And what would they say?'

'Just what they said about what poor Zénobie told me – that it was a horrid dreadful story, that they had paid her every penny they owed her.'

'Well, perhaps they had,' said Pemberton.

'Perhaps they've paid you!'

'Let us pretend they have, and *n'en parlons plus*.'

'They accused her of lying and cheating' – Morgan stuck to historic truth. 'That's why I don't want to speak to them.'

'Lest they should accuse me too?' To this Morgan made no answer, and his companion, looking down at him – the boy turned away his eyes, which had filled – saw that he couldn't have trusted himself to utter. 'You're right. Don't worry them,' Pemberton pursued. 'Except for that, they *are* charming people.'

'Except for *their* lying and *their* cheating?'

'I say – I say!' cried Pemberton, imitating a little tone of the lad's which was itself an imitation.

'We must be frank, at the last; we *must* come to an understanding,' said Morgan with the importance of the small boy who lets himself think he is arranging great affairs – almost playing at shipwreck or at Indians. 'I know all about everything.'

'I dare say your father has his reasons,' Pemberton replied, but too vaguely, as he was aware.

'For lying and cheating?'

'For saving and managing and turning his means to the best account. He has plenty to do with his money. You're an expensive family.'

'Yes, I'm very expensive,' Morgan concurred in a manner that made his preceptor burst out laughing.

'He's saving for *you*,' said Pemberton. 'They think of you in everything they do.'

'He might, while he's about it, save a little –' The boy paused, and his friend waited to hear what. Then Morgan brought out oddly: 'A little reputation.'

'Oh there's plenty of that. That's all right!'

'Enough of it for the people they know, no doubt. The people they know are awful.'

'Do you mean the princes? We mustn't abuse the princes.'

'Why not? They haven't married Paula – they haven't married Amy. They only clean out Ulick.'

'You *do* know everything!' Pemberton declared.

'No I don't after all. I don't know what they live on, or how they live, or *why* they live! What have they got and how did they get it? Are they rich, are they poor, or have they a *modeste aisance*? Why are they always chiveying me about – living one year like ambassadors and the next like paupers? Who are they, anyway, and what are they? I've thought of all that – I've thought of a lot of things. They're so beastly worldly. That's what I hate most – oh I've *seen* it! All they care about is to make an appearance and to pass for something or other. What the dickens do they want to pass for? What *do* they, Mr Pemberton?'

'You pause for a reply,' said Pemberton, treating the question as a joke, yet wondering too and greatly struck with his mate's intense if imperfect vision. 'I haven't the least idea.'

'And what good does it do? Haven't I seen the way people treat them – the "nice" people, the ones they want to know? They'll take anything from them – they'll lie down and be trampled on. The nice ones hate that – they just sicken them. You're the only really nice person we know.'

'Are you sure? They don't lie down for me!'

'Well, you shan't lie down for them. You've got to go – that's what you've got to do,' said Morgan.

'And what will become of you?'

'Oh I'm growing up. I shall get off before long. I'll see you later.'

'You had better let me finish you,' Pemberton urged, lending himself to the child's strange superiority.

Morgan stopped in their walk, looking up at him. He had to look up much less than a couple of years before – he had grown, in his loose leanness, so long and high. 'Finish me?' he echoed.

'There are such a lot of jolly things we can do together yet. I want to turn you out – I want you to do me credit.'

Morgan continued to look at him. 'To give you credit – do you mean?'

'My dear fellow, you're too clever to live.'

'That's just what I'm afraid you think. No, no; it isn't fair – I can't endure it. We'll separate next week. The sooner it's over the sooner to sleep.'

'If I hear of anything – any other chance – I promise to go,' Pemberton said.

Morgan consented to consider this. 'But you'll be honest,' he demanded; 'you won't pretend you haven't heard?'

'I'm much more likely to pretend I have.'

'But what can you hear of, this way, stuck in a hole with us? You ought to be on the spot, to go to England – you ought to go to America.'

'One would think you were *my* tutor!' said Pemberton.

Morgan walked on and after a little had begun again: 'Well, now that you know I know and that we look at the facts and keep nothing back – it's much more comfortable, isn't it?'

'My dear boy, it's so amusing, so interesting, that it will surely be quite impossible for me to forego such hours as these.'

This made Morgan stop once more. 'You *do* keep something back. Oh you're not straight – *I* am!'

'How am I not straight?'

'Oh you've got your idea!'

'My idea?'

'Why that I probably shan't make old – make older – bones, and that you can stick it out till I'm removed.'

'You *are* too clever to live!' Pemberton repeated.

'I call it a mean idea,' Morgan pursued. 'But I shall punish you by the way I hang on.'

'Look out or I'll poison you!' Pemberton laughed.

'I'm stronger and better every year. Haven't you noticed that there hasn't been a doctor near me since you came?'

'*I'm* your doctor,' said the young man, taking his arm and drawing him tenderly on again.

Morgan proceeded and after a few steps gave a sigh of mingled weariness and relief. 'Ah now that we look at the facts it's all right!'

VII

THEY looked at the facts a good deal after this; and one of the first consequences of their doing so was that Pemberton stuck it out, in his friend's parlance, for the purpose. Morgan made the facts so vivid and so droll, and at the same time so bald and so ugly, that there was fascination in talking them over with him, just as there would have been heartlessness in leaving him alone with them. Now that the pair had such perceptions in common it was useless for them to pretend they didn't judge such people; but the very judgement and the exchange of perceptions created another tie. Morgan had never been so interesting as now that he himself was made plainer by the sidelight of these confidences. What came out in it most was the small fine passion of his pride. He had plenty of that, Pemberton felt – so much that one might perhaps wisely wish for it some early bruises. He would have liked his people to have a spirit and had waked up to the sense of their perpetually eating humble-pie. His mother would consume any amount, and his father would consume even more than his mother. He had a theory that Ulick had wriggled out of an 'affair' at Nice: there had once been a flurry at home, a regular panic, after which they all went to bed and took medicine, not to be accounted for on any other supposition. Morgan had a romantic imagination, fed by poetry and history, and he would have liked those who 'bore his name' – as he used to say to Pemberton with the humour that made his queer delicacies manly – to carry themselves with an air. But their one idea was to get in with people who didn't want them and to take snubs as if they were honourable scars. Why people didn't want them more he didn't know – that was people's own affair;

after all they weren't superficially repulsive, they were a hundred times cleverer than most of the dreary grandees, the 'poor swells' they rushed about Europe to catch up with. 'After all they *are* amusing – they are!' he used to pronounce with the wisdom of the ages. To which Pemberton always replied: 'Amusing – the great Moreen troupe? Why they're altogether delightful; and if it weren't for the hitch that you and I (feeble performers!) make in the *ensemble* they'd carry everything before them.'

What the boy couldn't get over was the fact that this particular blight seemed, in a tradition of self-respect, so undeserved and so arbitrary. No doubt people had a right to take the line they liked; but why should *his* people have liked the line of pushing and toadying and lying and cheating? What had their forefathers – all decent folk, so far as he knew – done to them, or what had *he* done to them? Who had poisoned their blood with the fifth-rate social ideal, the fixed idea of making smart acquaintances and getting into the *monde chic*, especially when it was foredoomed to failure and exposure? They showed so what they were after; that was what made the people they wanted not want *them*. And never a wince for dignity, never a throb of shame at looking each other in the face, never any independence or resentment or disgust. If his father or his brother would only knock some one down once or twice a year! Clever as they were they never guessed the impression they made. They were good-natured, yes – as good-natured as Jews at the doors of clothing-shops! But was that the model one wanted one's family to follow? Morgan had dim memories of an old grandfather, the maternal, in New York, whom he had been taken across the ocean at the age of five to see: a gentleman with a high neck-cloth and a good deal of pronunciation, who wore a dress-coat in the morning, which made one wonder what he wore in the evening, and had, or was supposed to have, 'property' and something to do with the Bible Society. It couldn't have been but that *he* was a good type. Pemberton himself remembered Mrs Clancy, a widowed sister of Mr Moreen's, who was as irritating as a moral tale and had paid a fortnight's visit to the family at Nice shortly after he came to live with them. She was 'pure and refined', as Amy said over the banjo, and had the air of not knowing what they meant when they talked, and of keeping something rather important back. Pemberton judged that what she kept back was an approval of many of their ways; therefore it was to be supposed that she too was of a good type, and that Mr and Mrs Moreen and Ulick and Paula and Amy might easily have been of a better one if they would.

But that they wouldn't was more and more perceptible from day to day. They continued to 'chivey', as Morgan called it, and in due time became aware of a variety of reasons for proceeding to Venice. They mentioned a great many of them – they were always strikingly frank and had the brightest friendly chatter, at the late foreign breakfast in especial, before the ladies had made up their faces, when they leaned their arms on the table, had something to follow the *demi-tasse*, and, in the heat of familiar discussion as to what they 'really ought' to do, fell inevitably into the languages in which they could *tutoyer*. Even Pemberton liked them then; he could endure even Ulick when he heard him give his little flat voice for the 'sweet sea-city'. That was what made him have a sneaking kindness for them – that they were so out of the workaday world and kept him so out of it. The summer had waned when, with cries of ecstasy, they all passed out on the balcony that overhung the Grand Canal. The sunsets then were splendid and the Dorringtons had arrived. The Dorringtons were the only reason they hadn't talked of at breakfast; but the reasons they didn't talk of at breakfast always came out in the end. The Dorringtons on the other hand came out very little; or else when they did they stayed – as was natural – for hours, during which periods Mrs Moreen and the girls sometimes called at their hotel (to see if they had returned) as many as three times running. The gondola was for the ladies, as in Venice too there were 'days', which Mrs Moreen knew in their order an hour after she arrived. She immediately took one herself, to which the Dorringtons never came, though on a certain occasion when Pemberton and his pupil were together at Saint Mark's – where, taking the best walks they had ever had and haunting a hundred churches, they spent a great deal of time – they saw the old lord turn up with Mr Moreen and Ulick, who showed him the dim basilica as if it belonged to them. Pemberton noted how much less, among its curiosities, Lord Dorrington carried himself as a man of the world; wondering too whether, for such services, his companions took a fee from him. The autumn at any rate waned, the Dorringtons departed, and Lord Verschoyle, the eldest son, had proposed neither for Amy nor for Paula.

One sad November day, while the wind roared round the old palace and the rain lashed the lagoon, Pemberton, for exercise and even somewhat for warmth – the Moreens were horribly frugal about fires; it was a cause of suffering to their inmate – walked up and down the big bare sala with his pupil. The scagliola floor was cold, the high battered casements shook in the storm, and the stately decay of the place was unrelieved by a particle of furniture. Pemberton's spirits were low, and it came over him that the fortune of the Moreens was now even lower. A blast of desolation, a portent of disgrace and disaster, seemed to draw through the comfortless hall. Mr Moreen and Ulick were in the Piazza, looking out for something, strolling drearily, in mackintoshes, under the arcades; but still, in spite of mackintoshes, unmistakeable men of the world. Paula and Amy were in bed – it might have been thought they were staying there to keep warm. Pemberton looked askance at the boy at his side, to see to what extent he was conscious of these dark omens. But Morgan, luckily for him, was now mainly conscious of growing taller and stronger and indeed of being in his fifteenth year. This fact was intensely interesting to him and the basis of a private theory – which, however, he had imparted to his tutor – that in a little while he should stand on his own feet. He considered that the situation would change – that in short he should be 'finished', grown up, producible in the world of affairs and ready to prove himself of sterling ability. Sharply as he was capable at times of analysing, as he called it, his life, there were happy hours when he remained, as he also called it – and as the name, really, of their right ideal – 'jolly' superficial; the proof of which was his fundamental assumption that he should presently go to Oxford, to Pemberton's college, and aided and abetted by Pemberton, do the most wonderful things. It depressed the young man to see how little in such a project he took account of ways and means: in other connections he mostly kept to the measure. Pemberton tried to imagine the Moreens at Oxford and fortunately failed; yet unless they were to adopt it as a residence there would be no *modus vivendi* for Morgan. How could he live without an allowance, and where was the allowance to come from? He, Pemberton, might live on Morgan; but how could Morgan live on *him*? What was to become of him anyhow? Somehow the fact that he was a big boy now, with better prospects of health, made the question of his future more difficult. So long as he was markedly frail the great consideration he inspired seemed enough of an answer to it. But at the bottom of Pemberton's heart was the recognition of his probably being strong enough to live and not yet strong enough to struggle or to thrive. Morgan himself at any rate was in the first flush of the rosiest consciousness of adolescence, so that the beating of the tempest seemed to him after all but the voice of life and the challenge of fate. He had on his shabby little over-coat, with the collar up, but was enjoying his walk.

It was interrupted at last by the appearance of his mother at the end of the sala. She beckoned him to come to her, and while Pemberton saw him, complaisant, pass down the long vista and over the damp false marble, he wondered what was in the air. Mrs Moreen said a word to the boy and made him go into the room she had quitted. Then, having closed the door after him, she directed her steps swiftly to Pemberton. There *was* something in the air, but his wildest flight of fancy wouldn't have suggested what it proved to be. She signified that she had made a pretext to get Morgan out of the way, and then she enquired – without hesitation – if the young man could favour her with the loan of three louis. While, before bursting into a laugh, he stared at her with surprise, she declared that she was awfully pressed for the money; she was desperate for it – it would save her life.

'Dear lady, *c'est trop fort!*' Pemberton laughed in the manner and with the borrowed grace of idiom that marked the best colloquial, the best anecdotic, moments of his friends themselves. 'Where in the world do you suppose I should get three louis, *du train dont vous allez?*'

'I thought you worked – wrote things. Don't they pay you?'

'Not a penny.'

'Are you such a fool as to work for nothing?'

'You ought surely to know that.'

Mrs Moreen stared, then she coloured a little. Pemberton saw she had quite forgotten the terms – if 'terms' they could be called – that he had ended by accepting from herself; they had burdened her memory as little as her conscience. 'Oh yes, I see what you mean – you've been very nice about that; but why drag it in so often?' She had been perfectly urbane with him ever since the rough scene of explanation in his room the morning he made her accept *his* 'terms' – the necessity of his making his case known to Morgan. She had felt no resentment after seeing there was no danger Morgan would take the matter up with her. Indeed, attributing this immunity to the good taste of his influence with the boy, she had once said to Pemberton 'My dear fellow, it's an immense comfort you're a gentleman.' She repeated this in substance now. 'Of course you're a gentleman – that's a bother the less!' Pemberton reminded her that he had not 'dragged in' anything that wasn't already in as much as his foot was in his shoe; and she also repeated her prayer that, somewhere and somehow, he would find her sixty francs. He took the liberty of hinting that if he could find them it wouldn't be to lend them to *her* – as to which he consciously did himself injustice, knowing that if he had them he would certainly put them at her disposal. He accused himself, at bottom and not unveraciously, of a fantastic, a demoralised sympathy with her. If misery made strange bedfellows it also made strange sympathies. It was moreover a part of the abasement of living with such people that one had to make vulgar retorts, quite out of one's own tradition of good manners. 'Morgan, Morgan, to what pass have I come for you?' he groaned while Mrs Moreen floated voluminously down the *sala* again to liberate the boy, wailing as she went that everything was too odious.

Before their young friend was liberated there came a thump at the door communicating with the staircase, followed by the apparition of a dripping youth who poked in his head. Pemberton recognised him as the bearer of a telegram and recognised the telegram as addressed to himself. Morgan came back as, after glancing at the signature – that of a relative in London – he was reading the words: 'Found jolly job for you, engagement to coach opulent youth on own terms. Come at once.' The answer happily was paid and the messenger waited. Morgan, who had drawn near, waited too and looked hard at Pemberton; and Pemberton, after a moment, having met his look, handed him the telegram. It was really by wise looks – they knew each other so well now – that, while the telegraph-boy, in his waterproof cape, made a great puddle on the floor, the thing was settled between them. Pemberton wrote the answer with a pencil against the frescoed wall, and the messenger departed. When he had gone the young man explained himself.

'I'll make a tremendous charge; I'll earn a lot of money in a short time, and we'll live on it.'

'Well, I hope the opulent youth will be a dismal dunce – he probably will,' Morgan parenthesised – 'and keep you a long time a-hammering of it in.'

'Of course the longer he keeps me the more we shall have for our old age.'

'But suppose *they* don't pay you!' Morgan awfully suggested.

'Oh there are not two such –!' But Pemberton pulled up; he had been on the point of using too invidious a term. Instead of this he said 'Two such fatalities.'

Morgan flushed – the tears came to his eyes. '*Dites toujours* two such rascally crews!' Then in a different tone he added: 'Happy opulent youth!'

'Not if he's a dismal dunce.'

'Oh they're happier then. But you can't have everything, can you?' the boy smiled.

Pemberton held him fast, hands on his shoulders – he had never loved him so. 'What will become of *you*, what will you do?' He thought of Mrs Moreen, desperate for sixty francs.

'I shall become an *homme fait*.' And then as if he recognised all the bearings of Pemberton's allusion: 'I shall get on with them better when you're not here.'

'Ah don't say that – it sounds as if I set you against them!'

'You do – the sight of you. It's all right; you know what I mean. I shall be beautiful. I'll take their affairs in hand; I'll marry my sisters.'

'You'll marry yourself!' joked Pemberton; as high, rather tense pleasantry would evidently be the right, or the safest, tone for their separation.

It was, however, not purely in this strain that Morgan suddenly asked: 'But I say – how will you get to your jolly job? You'll have to telegraph to the opulent youth for money to come on.'

Pemberton bethought himself. 'They won't like that, will they?'

'Oh look out for them!'

Then Pemberton brought out his remedy. 'I'll go to the American Consul; I'll borrow some money of him – just for the few days, on the strength of the telegram.'

Morgan was hilarious. 'Show him the telegram – then collar the money and stay!'

Pemberton entered into the joke sufficiently to reply that for Morgan he was really capable of that; but the boy, growing more

serious, and to prove he hadn't meant what he said, not only
hurried him off to the Consulate – since he was to start that
evening, as he had wired to his friend – but made sure of their affair
by going with him. They splashed through the tortuous per-
forations and over the humpbacked bridges, and they passed
through the Piazza, where they saw Mr Moreen and Ulick go into
a jeweller's shop. The Consul proved accommodating –
Pemberton said it wasn't the letter, but Morgan's grand air – and
on their way back they went into Saint Mark's for a hushed ten
minutes. Later they took up and kept up the fun of it to the very
end; and it seemed to Pemberton a part of that fun that Mrs
Moreen, who was very angry when he had announced her his
intention, should charge him, grotesquely and vulgarly and in
reference to the loan she had vainly endeavoured to effect, with
bolting lest they should 'get something out' of him. On the other
hand he had to do Mr Moreen and Ulick the justice to recognise
that when on coming in *they* heard the cruel news they took it like
perfect men of the world.

VIII

WHEN he got at work with the opulent youth, who was to be taken in hand for Balliol, he found himself unable to say if this aspirant had really such poor parts or if the appearance were only begotten of his own long association with an intensely living little mind. From Morgan he heard half a dozen times: the boy wrote charming young letters, a patchwork of tongues, with indulgent postscripts in the family Volapuk and, in little squares and rounds and crannies of the text, the drollest illustrations – letters that he was divided between the impulse to show his present charge as a vain, a wasted incentive, and the sense of something in them that publicity would profane. The opulent youth went up in due course and failed to pass; but it seemed to add to the presumption that brilliancy was not expected of him all at once that his parents, condoning the lapse, which they good-naturedly treated as little as possible as if it were Pemberton's, should have sounded the rally again, begged the young coach to renew the siege.

The young coach was now in a position to lend Mrs Moreen three louis, and he sent her a post-office order even for a larger amount. In return for this favour he received a frantic scribbled line from her: 'Implore you to come back instantly – Morgan dreadfully ill.' They were on the rebound, once more in Paris – often as Pemberton had seen them depressed he had never seen them crushed – and communication was therefore rapid. He wrote to the boy to ascertain the state of his health, but awaited the answer in vain. He accordingly, after three days, took an abrupt leave of the opulent youth and, crossing the Channel, alighted at the small hotel, in the quarter of the Champs Elysées, of which Mrs Moreen had given him the address. A deep if dumb dissatisfaction with this lady and her companions bore him company: they couldn't be vulgarly honest, but they could live at hotels, in velvety *entresols*, amid a smell of burnt pastilles, surrounded by the most expensive city in Europe. When he had left them in Venice it was with an irrepressible suspicion that something was going to happen; but the only thing that could have taken place was again their masterly retreat. 'How is he? where is he?' he asked of Mrs Moreen; but before she could speak these questions were answered by the pressure round his neck of a pair of arms, in shrunken sleeves, which still were perfectly capable of an effusive young foreign squeeze.

'Dreadfully ill – I don't see it!' the young man cried. And then to Morgan: 'Why on earth didn't you relieve me? Why didn't you answer my letter?'

Mrs Moreen declared that when she wrote he was very bad, and Pemberton learned at the same time from the boy that he had answered every letter he had received. This led to the clear inference that Pemberton's note had been kept from him so that the game to be practised should not be interfered with. Mrs Moreen was prepared to see the fact exposed, as Pemberton saw the moment he faced her that she was prepared for a good many other things. She was prepared above all to maintain that she had acted from a sense of duty, that she was enchanted she had got him over, whatever they might say, and that it was useless of him to pretend he didn't know in all his bones that his place at such a time was with Morgan. He had taken the boy away from them and now had no right to abandon him. He had created for himself the gravest responsibilities and must at least abide by what he had done.

'Taken him away from you?' Pemberton exclaimed indignantly.

'Do it – do it for pity's sake; that's just what I want. I can't stand *this* – and such scenes. They're awful frauds – poor dears!' These words broke from Morgan, who had intermitted his embrace, in a key which made Pemberton turn quickly to him and see that he had suddenly seated himself, was breathing in great pain and was very pale.

'*Now* do you say he's not in a state, my precious pet?' shouted his mother, dropping on her knees before him with clasped hands, but touching him no more than if he had been a gilded idol. 'It will pass – it's only for an instant; but don't say such dreadful things!'

'I'm all right – all right,' Morgan panted to Pemberton, whom he sat looking up at with a strange smile, his hands resting on either side on the sofa.

'Now do you pretend I've been dishonest, that I've deceived?' Mrs Moreen flashed at Pemberton as she got up.

'It isn't *he* says it, it's I!' the boy returned, apparently easier but sinking back against the wall; while his restored friend, who had sat down beside him, took his hand and bent over him.

'Darling child, one does what one can; there are so many things to consider,' urged Mrs Moreen. 'It's his *place* – his only place. You see *you* think it is now.'

'Take me away – take me away,' Morgan went on, smiling to Pemberton with his white face.

'Where shall I take you, and how – oh *how*, my boy?' the young man stammered, thinking of the rude way in which his friends in London held that, for his convenience, with no assurance of prompt return, he had thrown them over; of the just resentment with which they would already have called in a successor, and of the scant help to finding fresh employment that resided for him in the grossness of his having failed to pass his pupil.

'Oh we'll settle that. You used to talk about it,' said Morgan. 'If we can only go all the rest's a detail.'

'Talk about it as much as you like, but don't think you can attempt it. Mr Moreen would never consent – it would be so *very* hand-to-mouth,' Pemberton's hostess beautifully explained to him. Then to Morgan she made it clearer: 'It would destroy our peace, it would break our hearts. Now that he's back it will be all the same again. You'll have your life, your work and your freedom, and we'll all be happy as we used to be. You'll bloom and grow perfectly well, and we won't have any more silly experiments, will we? They're too absurd. It's Mr Pemberton's place – every one in his place. You in yours, your papa in his, me in mine – *n'est-ce pas, chéri*? We'll all forget how foolish we've been and have lovely times.'

She continued to talk and to surge vaguely about the little draped stuffy salon while Pemberton sat with the boy, whose colour gradually came back; and she mixed up her reasons, hinting that there were going to be changes, that the other children might scatter (who knew? – Paula had her ideas) and that then it might be fancied how much the poor old parent-birds would want the little nestling. Morgan looked at Pemberton, who wouldn't let him move; and Pemberton knew exactly how he felt at hearing himself called a little nestling. He admitted that he had had one or two bad days, but he protested afresh against the wrong of his mother's having made them the ground of an appeal to poor Pemberton. Poor Pemberton could laugh now, apart from the comicality of Mrs Moreen's mustering so much philosophy for her defence – she seemed to shake it out of her agitated petticoats, which knocked over the light gilt chairs – so little did their young companion, *marked*, unmistakeably marked at the best, strike him as qualified to repudiate any advantage.

He himself was in for it at any rate. He should have Morgan on his hands again indefinitely; though indeed he saw the lad had a private theory to produce which would be intended to smooth this down. He was obliged to him for it in advance; but the suggested amendment didn't keep his heart rather from sinking, any more than it prevented him from accepting the prospect on the spot, with some confidence moreover that he should do so even better if he could have a little supper. Mrs Moreen threw out more hints about the changes that were to be looked for, but she was such a mixture of smiles and shudders – she confessed she was very nervous – that he couldn't tell if she were in high feather or only in hysterics. If the family was really at last going to pieces why shouldn't she recognise the necessity of pitching Morgan into some sort of lifeboat? This presumption was fostered by the fact that they were established in luxurious quarters in the capital of pleasure; that was exactly where they naturally *would* be established in view of going to pieces. Moreover didn't she mention that Mr Moreen and the others were enjoying themselves at the opera with Mr Granger, and wasn't *that* also precisely where one would look for them on the eve of a smash? Pemberton gathered that Mr Granger was a rich vacant American – a big bill with a flourishy heading and no items; so that one of Paula's 'ideas' was probably that this time she hadn't missed fire – by which straight shot indeed she would have shattered the general cohesion. And if the cohesion was to crumble what would become of poor Pemberton? He felt quite enough bound up with them to figure to his alarm as a dislodged block in the edifice.

It was Morgan who eventually asked if no supper had been ordered for him; sitting with him below, later, at the dim delayed meal, in the presence of a great deal of corded green plush, a plate of ornamental biscuit and an aloofness marked on the part of the waiter. Mrs Moreen had explained that they had been obliged to secure a room for the visitor out of the house; and Morgan's consolation – he offered it while Pemberton reflected on the nastiness of lukewarm sauces – proved to be, largely, that this circumstance would facilitate their escape. He talked of their escape – recurring to it often afterwards – as if they were making up a 'boy's book' together. But he likewise expressed his sense that there was something in the air, that the Moreens couldn't keep it up much longer. In point of fact, as Pemberton was to see, they kept it up for five or six months. All the while, however, Morgan's contention was designed to cheer him. Mr Moreen and Ulick, whom he had met the day after his return, accepted that return like perfect men of the world. If Paula and Amy treated it even with less formality an allowance was to be made for them, inasmuch as Mr

Granger hadn't come to the opera after all. He had only placed his box at their service, with a bouquet for each of the party; there was even one apiece, embittering the thought of his profusion, for Mr Moreen and Ulick. 'They're all like that,' was Morgan's comment; 'at the very last, just when we think we've landed them they're back in the deep sea!'

Morgan's comments in these days were more and more free; they even included a large recognition of the extraordinary tenderness with which he had been treated while Pemberton was away. Oh yes, they couldn't do enough to be nice to him, to show him they had him on their mind and make up for his loss. That was just what made the whole thing so sad and caused him to rejoice after all in Pernberton's return – he had to keep thinking of their affection less, had less sense of obligation. Pemberton laughed out at this last reason, and Morgan blushed and said 'Well, dash it, you know what I mean.' Pemberton knew perfectly what he meant; but there were a good many things that – dash it too! – it didn't make any clearer. This episode of his second sojourn in Paris stretched itself out wearily, with their resumed readings and wanderings and maunderings, their potterings on the quays, their hauntings of the museums, their occasional lingerings in the Palais Royal when the first sharp weather came on and there was a comfort in warm emanations, before Chevet's wonderful succulent window. Morgan wanted to hear all about the opulent youth – he took an immense interest in him. Some of the details of his opulence – Pemberton could spare him none of them – evidently fed the boy's appreciation of all his friend had given up to come back to him; but in addition to the greater reciprocity established by that heroism he had always his little brooding theory, in which there was a frivolous gaiety too, that their long probation was drawing to a close. Morgan's conviction that the Moreens couldn't go on much longer kept pace with the unexpended impetus with which, from month to month, they did go on. Three weeks after Pemberton had rejoined them they went on to another hotel, a dingier one than the first; but Morgan rejoiced that his tutor had at least still not sacrificed the advantage of a room outside. He clung to the romantic utility of this when the day, or rather the night, should arrive for their escape.

For the first time, in this complicated connection, our friend felt his collar gall him. It was, as he had said to Mrs Moreen in Venice, *trop fort* – everything was *trop fort*. He could neither really throw off his blighting burden nor find in it the benefit of a pacified conscience or of a rewarded affection. He had spent all the money accruing to him in England, and he saw his youth going and that he was getting nothing back for it. It was all very well of Morgan to count it for reparation that he should now settle on him permanently – there was an irritating flaw in such a view. He saw what the boy had in his mind; the conception that as his friend had had the generosity to come back he must show his gratitude by giving him his life. But the poor friend didn't desire the gift – what could he do with Morgan's dreadful little life? Of course at the same time that Pemberton was irritated he remembered the reason, which was very honourable to Morgan and which dwelt simply in his making one so forget that he was no more than a patched urchin. If one dealt with him on a different basis one's mis-adventures were one's own fault. So Pemberton waited in a queer confusion of yearning and alarm for the catastrophe which was held to hang over the house of Moreen, of which he certainly at moments felt the symptoms brush his cheek and as to which he wondered much in what form it would find its liveliest effect.

Perhaps it would take the form of sudden dispersal – a frightened *sauve qui peut*, a scuttling into selfish corners. Certainly they were less elastic than of yore; they were evidently looking for something they didn't find. The Dorringtons hadn't re-appeared, the princes had scattered; wasn't that the beginning of the end? Mrs Moreen had lost her reckoning of the famous 'days'; her social calendar was blurred – it had turned its face to the wall. Pemberton suspected that the great, the cruel discomfiture had been the unspeakable behaviour of Mr Granger, who seemed not to know what he wanted, or, what was much worse, what *they* wanted. He kept sending flowers, as if to bestrew the path of his retreat, which was never the path of a return. Flowers were all very well, but – Pemberton could complete the proposition. It was now positively conspicuous that in the long run the Moreens were a social failure; so that the young man was almost grateful the run had not been short. Mr Moreen indeed was still occasionally able to get away on business and, what was more surprising, was likewise able to get back. Ulick had no club, but you couldn't have discovered it from his appearance, which was as much as ever that of a person looking at life from the window of such an institution; therefore Pemberton was doubly surprised at an answer he once heard him make his mother in the desperate tone of a man familiar with the worst privations. Her question Pemberton had not quite caught; it appeared to be an appeal for a suggestion as to whom they might get to take Amy. 'Let the Devil take her!' Ulick snapped; so that Pemberton could see that they had not only lost their amiability but had ceased to believe in themselves. He could also see that if Mrs Moreen was trying to get people to take her children she might be regarded as closing the hatches for the storm. But Morgan would be the last she would part with.

One winter afternoon – it was a Sunday – he and the boy walked far together in the Bois de Boulogne. The evening was so splendid, the cold lemon-coloured sunset so clear, the stream of carriages and pedestrians so amusing and the fascination of Paris so great, that they stayed out later than usual and became aware that they should have to hurry home to arrive in time for dinner. They hurried accordingly, arm-in-arm, good-humoured and hungry, agreeing that there was nothing like Paris after all and that after everything too that had come and gone they were not yet sated with innocent pleasures. When they reached the hotel they found that, though scandalously late, they were in time for all the dinner they were likely to sit down to. Confusion reigned in the apartments of the

Moreens – very shabby ones this time, but the best in the house –
and before the interrupted service of the table, with objects
displaced almost as if there had been a scuffle and a great wine-stain
from an overturned bottle, Pemberton couldn't blink the fact that
there had been a scene of the last proprietary firmness. The storm
had come – they were all seeking refuge. The hatches were down,
Paula and Amy were invisible – they had never tried the most
casual art upon Pemberton, but he felt they had enough of an eye
to him not to wish to meet him as young ladies whose frocks had
been confiscated – and Ulick appeared to have jumped overboard.
The host and his staff, in a word, had ceased to 'go on' at the pace
of their guests, and the air of embarrassed detention, thanks to a pile
of gaping trunks in the passage, was strangely commingled with the
air of indignant withdrawal.

When Morgan took all this in – and he took it in very quickly –
he coloured to the roots of his hair. He had walked from his infancy
among difficulties and dangers, but he had never seen a public
exposure. Pemberton noticed in a second glance at him that the
tears had rushed into his eyes and that they were tears of a new and
untasted bitterness. He wondered an instant, for the boy's sake,
whether he might successfully pretend not to understand. Not
successfully, he felt, as Mr and Mrs Moreen, dinnerless by their
extinguished hearth, rose before him in their little dishonoured
salon, casting about with glassy eyes for the nearest port in such a
storm. They were not prostrate but were horribly white, and Mrs
Moreen had evidently been crying. Pemberton quickly learned
however that her grief was not for the loss of her dinner, much as
she usually enjoyed it, but the fruit of a blow that struck even
deeper, as she made all haste to explain. He would see for himself,
so far as that went, how the great change had come, the dreadful
bolt had fallen, and how they would now all have to turn
themselves about. Therefore cruel as it was to them to part with
their darling she must look to him to carry a little further the
influence he had so fortunately acquired with the boy – to induce

his young charge to follow him into some modest retreat. They depended on him – that was the fact – to take their delightful child temporarily under his protection: it would leave Mr Moreen and herself so much more free to give the proper attention (too little, alas! had been given) to the readjustment of their affairs.

'We trust you – we feel we *can*,' said Mrs Moreen, slowly rubbing her plump white hands and looking with compunction hard at Morgan, whose chin, not to take liberties, her husband stroked with a tentative paternal forefinger.

'Oh yes – we feel that we *can*. We trust Mr Pemberton fully, Morgan,' Mr Moreen pursued.

Pemberton wondered again if he might pretend not to understand; but everything good gave way to the intensity of Morgan's understanding. 'Do you mean he may take me to live with him for ever and ever?' cried the boy. 'May take me away, away, anywhere he likes?'

'For ever and ever? *Comme vous-y-allez!*' Mr Moreen laughed indulgently. 'For as long as Mr Pemberton may be so good.'

'We've struggled, we've suffered,' his wife went on; 'but you've made him so your own that we've already been through the worst of the sacrifice.'

Morgan had turned away from his father – he stood looking at Pemberton with a light in his face. His sense of shame for their common humiliated state had dropped; the case had another side – the thing was to clutch at *that*. He had a moment of boyish joy, scarcely mitigated by the reflection that with this unexpected consecration of his hope – too sudden and too violent; the turn taken was away from a *good* boy's book – the 'escape' was left on their hands. The boyish joy was there an instant, and Pemberton was almost scared at the rush of gratitude and affection that broke through his first abasement. When he stammered 'My dear fellow, what do you say to *that*?' how could one not say something enthusiastic? But there was more need for courage at something else that immediately followed and that made the lad sit down quickly on the nearest chair. He had turned quite livid and had raised his hand to his left side. They were all three looking at him, but Mrs Moreen suddenly bounded forward. 'Ah his darling little heart!' she broke out; and this time, on her knees before him and without respect for the idol, she caught him ardently in her arms. 'You walked him too far, you hurried him too fast!' she hurled over her shoulder at Pemberton. Her son made no protest, and the next instant, still holding him, she sprang up with her face convulsed and with the terrified cry 'Help, help! he's going, he's gone!' Pemberton saw with equal horror, by Morgan's own stricken face, that he was beyond their wildest recall. He pulled him half out of his mother's hands, and for a moment, while they held him together, they looked all their dismay into each other's eyes. 'He couldn't stand it with his weak organ,' said Pemberton – 'the shock, the whole scene, the violent emotion.'

'But I thought he *wanted* to go to you!' wailed Mrs Moreen.

'I *told* you he didn't, my dear,' her husband made answer. Mr Moreen was trembling all over and was in his way as deeply affected as his wife. But after the very first he took his bereavement as a man of the world.

www.vintage-classics.info